PAMELA JEKEL

The Last of the California Girls

GRAFTON BOOKS
A Division of the Collins Publishing Group

LONDON GLASGOW
TORONTO SYDNEY AUCKLAND

Grafton Books
A Division of the Collins Publishing Group
8 Grafton Street, London W1X 3LA

A Grafton UK Paperback Original 1989

ISBN 0-586-20709-0

Printed and bound in Great Britain by
Collins, Glasgow

Set in Bodoni

By the same author

Sea Star
Columbia

for my resilient, audacious sister, the last of an endangered species, who has given me a lifetime of fierce support, secret-sharing, and stories in the night . . .

Acknowledgments

8

Part One

Hell is made up of yearnings. The wicked don't roast on beds of nails, they sit on comfortable chairs and are tortured with yearnings.

– Isaac Bashevis Singer

They say you know your music when you hear it. One day, that old black magic insinuates itself into a private Walkman you've got inside your head, and you fall in line and dance until you pay the piper.

They say you know your dream girl too. One day, while you're listening to your song, you'll see the other half of your soul walking down the street, and she'll know all your steps without having to watch your feet.

That's what they say. And I believed them when I was seventeen. But the simple moral tale I'm about to relate will prove, I think, not only that both those illusions are false, but that God turns a cold and baleful shoulder to those fools who buy into them. But you couldn't tell me that at seventeen. After all, I knew what was righteous, and I knew what was wrong. I knew what was bright, and I knew what was dark. And then I moved to California in my senior year, and I forgot everything I thought I knew.

David Levine at seventeen. So harmonious, it sounds almost ordained. I can remember who I was then, almost twenty-five years ago, more clearly than I can conjure up the man who stared back at me in the steamed shower mirror last month. I can summon seventeen-year-old feelings more readily than I can face forty, some mornings.

I'm getting older, but that's not the problem. Yes, I can smell loss moving toward me on the wind some nights, and when I waken, I can taste my own death in my mouth, but I know I'm not near through yet. I can still play full court basketball for an hour. I've still got my hair and a

13

thirty-four waist; hell, I've got several lifetimes ahead of me.

But a past lifetime tugs, and David Levine at seventeen haunts me. Or, rather, David Levine is haunted, by the ghost of a California girl, by the memories of a place where the sun was so seductive it could melt down all you've ever known or believed.

It was my summer of 1965, and the upper reaches of the Bronx seemed light-years away. As stellar distances went, I could imagine no more opposite eco-niches than Horace Mann School of Riverdale, New York, and Taft High School of the San Fernando Valley.

As I remember, I considered myself triply cursed. To have to move right before my senior year – that was bad enough. Then to have to move to Lotus Land personified, to Southern California, a place I'd lampooned publicly whenever one of those mindless surf songs came wafting east on the airwaves, and finally, to be set down amid what surely had to have been WASP heaven: Woodland Hills.

The very name offended me. The aforementioned hills were sere and brown (the natives called it 'gold') for ten months out of every year, and whatever woodlands might have existed were long since paved over to freeways and Bullock's and Bob's Big Boys.

Not that we didn't have plenty of concrete and congestion in the old neighborhood. In Riverdale we lived in a four-story apartment building with a nice enough view of the Hudson, but we didn't have the elbow room of the estates on the river. The rooms were high-ceilinged and spacious, white and alike as a row of teeth. We were the Bronx, but better. We didn't even say we were from the Bronx to those we knew would recognize the difference, but called ourselves Westchesterites, and wrote River-dale, not the Bronx, on our return addresses. One bridge, the Henry Hudson, made all the difference. Up above the effluvia of the Harlem River, buffered by the leafy sanctuaries of Van Cortlandt and Fort Tryon parks, we could look across to the Palisades of New Jersey and consider ourselves as suburban as Scarsdale.

We had all of Manhattan at our feet, yet at the same time, we were a neighborhood. Like so many distinct backwashes of the city, we knew who we were and we knew who didn't belong. Harlem with its horrors might nudge us from the rear, and the hick Bronx hordes loom perilously close, but *we* were private schools and almost-old money. We were Riverdale. And we were there first.

In Woodland Hills, on the other hand, no one seemed to know where they belonged, nor cared. And as far as who came first, the chief emphasis was on what was coming next.

So David Levine, seventeen, was ticked off. And when I came home from my first foray into enemy territory, itemizing the various things I resented about my recent transplanting, my parents had to suffer some of the most bitter indignation they had ever allowed from either of their two sons.

'Did anybody notice, they're all blond here?' I demanded of my father over dinner that night. 'Like a bunch of white-haired German giants, or something. And besides their follicules, the sun must have fried their brains, because they're barely up to solid planes in geometry – '

'Follicles,' my father said quietly. Rabbi Daniel Levine waited patiently for his eldest son to continue.

But I scarcely heard him. 'If you break this down to basics, it's a complete disaster on all sides. First, I'm going to stunt my intellectual growth, surrounded by these glazed-eyed sun freaks; second, I'm going to lose a good start in baseball, because these guys are all bigger and better than me, I guess from all the orange juice they drink or something, and they all think they were born to play catcher, *my* best position, so I might just as well kiss that off; and third, you can forget grandchildren, Mother, because I'll never get a date here for the rest of my life.' I met my parents' gazes and said intensely, 'I'm telling you, I fear for my soul.'

At that point, a certain invisible cat crept out from under the dining-room table and began to curl and curve itself around my legs. Nobody else could see the cat, of course, but it had followed me around since I was old enough to crawl up onto any available stage. Which was when it materialized most often. Whenever I felt I'd been particularly dramatic, flamboyant, or colorful, the cat slunk away, embarrassed by my evident excesses. That's how I knew what my audience reaction might be. When, on the other hand, I'd been effective, the cat purred and moved closer, shedding its usual disdain along with a few invisible hairs which I could never keep from brushing away.

I never told anyone of my private familiar, my feline clap-o-meter which could never be bought but could well be seduced. In my mind, it was a large white long-haired Persian with an especially aloof expression. The cat's tickling presence around my ankles signified to me that I must have made an impression.

My mother peered at me under her lashes as she helped Avrom to the Brussels sprouts. She clucked audibly and shook her head in mild reproof. To my little brother she said, as though he were actually capable of appreciating her wit, 'You see, son, this is what happens sometimes with firstborns. You love them and you listen to them and it makes them passionate and high-strung, not to mention convinced that they could part the seas with their tongue alone. Which' – she glanced up smiling at my father – 'if the Messiah ever does come, will be all to the better, but

16

in the meantime, it makes for some emotional meals.' She patted Avrom's shoulder. 'Be glad you were born second.'

To me she added calmly, 'David, you're upsetting yourself, and I made such a wonderful Shabbes supper for our new home.'

'Mom –'

'There's not a single thing you can find to like about this change? You, who complained always about the wet and the cold in New York? The sun is warm, right? So, here you can be out of doors all the time, and you'll find new sports to play if the old ones don't please you. Besides' – she smiled coyly at me now – 'I've seen a few of these California girls up close. These are horses of a different feather, I think. Possibly worth a little adjustment.'

I groaned. My mother had a gift for fracturing and rearranging aphorisms to her personal taste, managing to sound as if she just came off the boat. And with no justification whatsoever. She was well-educated and completely American – two generations the people of Myra Zobel Levine had been in New York – but when she wanted to make a point or give advice, she assumed this Jewish *bubeleh* pose, complete with a trace of an Old World accent, which made me wince and wish for Irish ancestors.

Avrom said in a completely serious tone, 'I don't know what you're complaining about. I've already been sent to the principal's office twice, and I think it's just because the teacher hates me. He can't even pronounce my name. The kids call me Avis, and the teacher says maybe I should try harder.'

My parents' attentions were swiftly diverted by this new and possible anti-Semitic attack, and even the Persian uncoiled itself and wandered away from my legs, moving closer to Avrom with an intrigued expression.

The whole scene reminded me of an essay in *The New Yorker* I'd read right before we left, where a man and his wife were awakened by the phone ringing at three o'clock in the morning. 'Get it, get it!' the wife screamed, certain that it must be an emergency. And when the man stumbled to the phone, smashing his toe in the process, a drunken woman's voice asked, 'Is Bud there?' A wrong number. The man angrily explained that he wasn't Bud, that Bud had never lived there, and furthermore, he didn't even *know* a Bud. He hung up. The woman called back. Again with the frenzy to answer the phone, his wife screamed that she'd kill the person on the other end, and this time the same drunken voice asked, 'Bud, what are you doing? Please talk to me, Bud.' The man simply dropped the phone on its back like a dead bug. At dawn (and he was never able to get back to sleep), he gingerly picked up the dangling receiver and put it to his ear silently.

The woman said happily, 'Oh, Bud, it's you.'

That's the way my life seemed to be going just then. At that moment, with all attention focused on Avrom's wrong number, I swore I knew exactly how the man in *The New Yorker* story felt. And worse, I knew how the drunken woman caller felt as well. *The New Yorker*. That was another thing I'd probably never see again for the rest of my natural life.

The next morning, as the school bus bore me away for another day of torture, I gazed balefully out at the California sunshine and made mental lists of insults, biting and sardonic stabs of wit to hurl at anyone who dared praise the state to me.

Food is fresher out here.

Yeah, and they'd eat kelp and sea-gull droppings if you served a nice white wine with it.

The sun is wonderful out here.

So is the smog. You could take a deep breath and chip a tooth.

The stars all live here.

Like Liberace of the dumpling cheeks and Tiny Tim of the Miss Vicki.

Well, they're *friendlier* out here.

So is a Mexican bandit.

How long, O Lord, how long? I inwardly groaned as the bus made its jostling, rumbling way around neighborhood streets. If my parents wanted sun, why didn't they pick Florida? Or Charleston? At least in the South they've achieved a sort of fond tolerance for minority groups in their midst. At least a Jew's not so damned obvious in a crowd, since they've got another, darker outcast which focuses their attention. I fondly imagined myself sipping juleps on a magnolia-entwined porch with some raven-ringleted nymph named Dahlia, a sweet, demure lady who begged me to tell her of my adventures up North.

And then the second half of that favored daydream floated up, a slim and lissome colored girl who had what they called back then 'sloe-eyes', who wore bright cotton swathed at her hips, and was well versed in the more exotic skills of fellatio. Black is Beautiful, Stokely Carmichael said, and Black is Powerful, said LeRoi Jones, and oh, I agreed, I agreed, but I wondered if anybody west of Las Vegas had heard them at all.

Clearly, I was in exile.

Other places, kids were burning draft cards, Dr Spock was being arrested, and the Russians were walking in space. Malcolm X was assassinated in Harlem, the SDSers were marching, and the number of American boys in Vietnam was up to 180,000, the East Coast papers said.

But here in the land of Mu by the sea, life was just a balmy progression of Beach Boys harmonies. Nothing but soft ice cream just waiting for us to spoon it up. I'd been

19

plopped down into *Gidget*, where the surf report was read right along with the morning news, where they sprayed their Christmas trees orange, and they actually thought it was normal to eat at a restaurant in the shape of a hot dog.

The bus gradually filled with kids as it made its way over winding residential streets. There was something about my fellow passengers that made me feel crumpled. They seemed taller, somehow, neater, more casually but naturally groomed, as though they didn't give a damn because they had it all anyway.

Not a tie among them. The guys wore sneakers, deck shoes, or hueraches. I slid my saddle shoes deeper under my seat. Short shirt-sleeves, madras, tight chinos, no jackets, long hair falling down close to their eyes, like a tribe of conquering heroes they moved to their seats, laughing and exchanging quips with an easy grace.

Nobody slouched, nobody had the roseate bloom of acne, and damned few even wore glasses. I felt the difference between myself and these healthy specimens was more than sartorial; it came almost from the flesh itself.

And the girls. Even the ugly ones weren't. No braces. They must have these kids in the orthodontist chair as soon as they're on solids, I thought. All long-haired, smooth, and gleaming, with short skirts, sleek legs in nylons. They wore little heels or flats, colored to match their purses, and there wasn't a bobby sock or a scuffed Weejun in the whole covey.

At the last stop a guy slid into the seat next to me, punching the kid in front of us on the shoulder.

'Hey, Walker, you get that one on dihedral angles? That one busted my ass last night. Whadja get?'

Walker stretched and yawned a mighty white flash of

teeth. 'I passed, man. I figure some dipshit'll ask him before we have to turn it in.'

Suddenly my seatmate focused on me, grinning. 'Hey. Aren't you in our class? The new guy, right?'

I mustered my wryest, most laconic smile. 'Yeah. Levine.'

'Jim Foote,' he said, 'this guy is Mike Walker, didja get the one on dihedrals?'

'Sure.'

'Hey, you know this shit?' Jim asked eagerly.

'When I step in it.' The Persian came out from under the bus seat and crawled up in my lap, purring loudly.

Foote laughed amiably and punched his pal again. 'Hear that, Walker? The man knows dihedrals!'

With a twinge of self-hatred I opened my notebook and started to explain the thorny problem on page thirty-eight.

'So whadja get?' Walker asked impatiently. 'We don't need the whole fuckin' lecture over again.'

I pushed my glasses back up my nose and gave the guy a level stare. 'This stuff is going to be on the midterm, you know.'

'So I'll learn it by then. Just get to the meat, man.'

'Hey, Mike, give the guy a break.' Foote laughed. 'Some of us need all the help we can get.'

I finished explaining how I got the answer, but Walker snorted with disgust and was quickly diverted by the girl across the aisle from him.

Jim Foote said casually, 'Hey, don't let him bug you, Levine. He's got the brains of a pothole.'

He was tanned, just like all the rest of them, with a swatch of straw hair and a permanently sunburned nose. 'No sweat,' I managed to say.

'Where you from?'

'New York. By way of the Bronx.'

21

'Yeah? I'm from Arizona myself. By way of Tucson.'

I relaxed. 'You're not a native?'

'*Es verdad, gringo*. Neither is ninety percent of the state. Nobody's really *from* California, man. At least damn few.'

'Well, you sure look the part.'

'So will you, in a while. The sun bleaches everything out, I guess, down to the same colors.'

The bus was laboring up the hill into the parking lot; kids milled around, calling out to one another, and the light was dazzling.

'So I guess I'll see you in class,' I said, lurching up as everybody else did before the bus was fully parked.

'Yeah – oh, hey, look for me in the quad at lunch, Levine.'

The bewildered pleasure must have shown on my face.

'We can always use a man who knows the angles.'

The Persian glanced back once, gave me a quick look of disdain, and trotted off after Jim Foote.

In the parking lot I could see that there was another group even more elite than the bus bunch. The kids with the cars were jockeying for a position now, creating an amiable jostling chaos, a blur of speed and beauty and wealth.

Camaros and little Spitfires, Thunderbirds and Mustangs, Volkswagens, converted surf buggies, and motorcycles spilled past the gates, narrowly missing one another, filled with arms waving out the windows, sunglasses flashing, and rock and roll blaring from a hundred radios.

> If everybody had an ocean, across the U-S-Aaaa,
> Then everybody'd be surfin', like Cal-i-for-ni-aaa!

A bunch of blondes in a red Malibu swerved past me, giggling and singing at the top of their lungs, all taut breasts and tanned arms.

I suddenly felt exhausted by so much energy and noise and movement. And the day's barely started, I thought with quiet horror. I'll never make it. I followed the herd of laughing lemmings into the high white corridors of education, and the palm trees over my head rattled in the warm breeze like snakes.

English, European history, then 'nutrition', that fifteen-minute stretch when everybody raced out to the quad to gulp down sticky cinnamon buns or flattened, crusty grilled-cheese sandwiches, then calculus, and French and the day was half gone.

It was eleven-thirty before I could breathe. The lunch bell rang, and I followed a thousand kids down the corridors, through the maze of open lockers, past solid knots of gossiping girls, lines of sauntering boys leaning against the walls and calling to one another, their eyes trailing the tight short skirts. I threaded my way past couples embracing as though they hadn't seen each other in months, and was finally out again into the blinding sunlight.

Now I didn't feel so alone. There were a few guys who looked as if they just washed up on these shores, too, a few more pale and blinking outcasts like myself. I'd seen some of them in French class. The popular kids filled the Spanish classes because they were known to be Mickey Mouse. I smiled when I first heard that. Back in New York it meant something so easy as to earn disdain. Here it was easy and, so, desirable. It figured. I'd been college prep since my freshman year, already collected apps for Columbia and NYU, and was gearing up for the SATs. So far as I could see, my fellow students at Taft seemed to expect to stay in high school forever.

The quad was thronged with kids, but each gravitated by instinct to his place. I'd heard so much about the democracy of the West, how tradition and social status just weren't as important as back east. How they scorned china patterns and silver. But here at Taft there were definite tiers of privilege. The more beautiful clans flocked together, the right crowds and the less-right had their separate tables, and the most elite, the 'soche' crowd – the football players, the student body officers, the cheer-leaders – held court on a table high above the other tribes, closest to the vending machines.

'Hey, man!'

I turned at the familiar voice. Jim Foote was hailing me over. He sat at a table littered with the sprawl and refuse of eight guys, and not a woman in sight. Introductions all around, and I sat down next to Eric Arne. He was obviously a jock of some kind, judging by the size of his shoulders.

'You go out for any sports?' no-neck asked around a bite of tuna fish.

'Baseball,' I said quickly. 'Catcher, mostly.'

No-neck eyed me briskly. 'You got no upperbody, man. But if your legs can take it, track'd be good.' He began to fill me in on the intricacies of athletics Taft had to offer, when a sudden hush came over the rest of the table. My eyes were drawn irresistibly upward, and I found myself staring into the face of the most beautiful girl I had ever seen.

She glanced at me briefly, but the full brilliance of her smile skidded past Jim Foote and the others and landed directly on the now silent Eric Arne, who began to rummage in his lunch sack as though it contained some long-lost and vital treasure.

'Hi, Eric,' the girl said, her voice soft and warm. She waited, supremely confident that she would not be ignored.

'Uh, hi, Sherry,' Eric mumbled.

I felt the heat pour off the man as off a hard-ridden

horse. Out of courtesy I didn't look at his face. Besides, it seemed spectacularly rude not to give this girl my undivided attention, even if her eyes never met mine again.

It was clear that this was a two-person drama, and all the rest of us at the table were only supernumeraries to add texture to the scene. The guys sat like a bunch of board members, clearing their throats to see who had accumulated the most phlegm. But their eyes never left her.

Sherry was small and slender, with that long-waisted curve that made her breasts and rear seem incredibly high, almost Negroid in their roundness. Her face was small-featured, perfect, and her hair a long float of silken light to her waist.

'Good luck in the game,' she said.

Posters were up all over school announcing the first football scrimmage of the year with Reseda.

'Thanks,' Arne said quietly. 'You going?'

'I might.'

Arne nodded, seemingly at a loss.

She waited an instant, flipping an errant tendril back from her shoulders. Her fingers were facile and tan, the nails pearly white with some sort of strange luminescence. She herself finally broke the spell by moving her smile around the table. As she did so, each guy before her brightened and smiled back involuntarily. 'Bye,' she said, and walked away.

'Jesus,' I murmured, scarcely aware I'd spoken.

Eric turned suddenly kindled eyes upon me. 'You like that?' His face was flushed and glowering.

I shrugged, instantly casual. 'What's not to like?'

An ugly, bitter growl. 'Believe me, asswipe, you couldn't handle it.'

Jim Foote broke in, a peace-making laugh from down

the table. 'I don't think there's a man here who could, Arne. Not and get out alive.'

'Who'd want to get out?' I asked quietly.

A whoosh of relieved guffaws rippled down the lines, and the Persian left its post by Jim's side and sauntered regally, with just the touch of a smirk, over toward me. That was the second time Jim'd come between me and hassle. I caught his eye and smiled my thanks, and he had the grace to ignore my gratitude.

While the conversations rose around me, I tried to think what I would have done if Arne had actually wanted to fight. I had this vague sense that the rules were different out here. Back in the Bronx there were two forms of fighting: you either got swarmed, or you insulted some guy's mother.

A swarm was a Force of God, like tornadoes and hurricanes. You'd be walking along, maybe through a tunnel in Inwood Hill Park or in the backstreets of Washington Heights, when all of a sudden a mob of mutants from some other block would descend on your shoulders, pound you senseless, and then take off. Nothing much to do about it. Not your guys, man. Like the wind The Intruders came, you got up and brushed off your pants, and waited for your turn.

But mothers had nothing whatsoever to do with God. This was strictly personal. In fact, the more personal, the better. Some guy trashed your mother or you trashed his, and you each attempted to rip the other's esophagus to shreds. It started with, 'Hey, man, your mother's a carpenter's dream. Flat as a board and easy to screw,' and you circled each other, crooning a litany of horror of what you'd do if the other one would just stand still, and then fire back, 'Oh yeah? Well, *your* mother's like the Senate. She's got two guys from every state.' Then somebody got beaten into the concrete.

26

There were rules, and everybody knew them, so long as you stayed in your neighborhood. But out here? For all I knew, maybe they creamed one another with Pogo sticks or bongo drums. I could stand my own on familiar turf, but in California it was obvious that anything could happen.

After lunch Jim said, 'Don't let Arne rag you, man. He's had a hard-on for that girl so long, if a fucking celibate priest said her name, he'd punch him out.'

I was barely listening, so focused was I on one singular fact: I was walking to class, down these crowded corridors, with Jim Foote by my side. My embarrassed pride was somewhat mitigated by guilt. Okay, I was susceptible to peer pressure, but it wasn't total abdication. With my first friend I began to feel less like Gulliver among the Yahoos, and I tried to relax.

'So who is she?' I asked, keeping my voice nonchalant.

'Her name's Sherry Gentry. She's head cheerleader, probably going to be May Queen this year, and one of the foxiest women in the Valley. She got Class Flirt and Best Ass last year – '

At my startled glance he added, 'Underground poll, man. You won't see those last two in the yearbook.'

'What year is she in?'

'Same as us, believe it or not.' Jim grinned and waved at two girls passing, who caroled back, 'Hi, Jim!' all giggles and swishing skirts. 'Imagine what she's going to be like when she's twenty-one!' He rolled his eyes lubriciously.

I was humbled. That girl who had stood before me, that vision of poise and control, was actually my age, despite the fact that she was dangerously bright-looking and adult. 'So what was the deal with Arne? They used to date or something?'

We rounded the corner to biology and began to edge

through the kids milling outside the class, couples once more saying their farewells as though they wouldn't see each other again for an entire summer.

'Or something,' Jim snorted. He turned to me, suddenly serious. 'You know, it's really pretty pitiful. That guy had it together last year. Going to make varsity way before his time, probably a scholarship to some pack-ten biggie. Then Sherry moved him down and left him for dead. They only dated about two months, I think, but the guy'll never be the same. Come on, the bell's about to ring – '

And we slipped into class just ahead of Mr Casey, the bio teacher.

Normally, biology was one of my favorite subjects, and I rarely watched the clock as I did in English, which was basically a five-minute lecture crammed into an hour. The science classroom pleased me, with its Bunsen burners and multicolored charts and the air redolently acrid from chemicals and formaldehyde. Biology seemed to me to be one really relevant field of study for man – the study of his place in the world of other animals. But today Mr Casey's voice droned on forever about worlds that seemed to have no touch with reality.

I kept replaying Jim's words over and over, picturing her blond loveliness as she stood before me, over me somehow, though she certainly wasn't that tall. I had felt strangely foreshortened in Sherry Gentry's presence. As if I had spent a lifetime slumping and bowing, and she had never faced life in any other posture than straight on, with her chin held high.

Later in the week, I got to see that chin in a different position. The bus dropped me about five blocks from my house, and I got off in a small knot of kids who strode away in twos and threes as though they'd been born on these streets and could walk them blindfolded.

I glanced up at the sun and winced, jerking my head down. So huge. At home I always seemed to see the sun at the end of a long tunnel of tall buildings, glowing like a large caution light. Here it covered half the sky.

Today was as good as any, I decided, to see if there might be a more efficient route home. There was one street in particular, if it went through, that could cut a block off the trip.

I had to slice a corner off a large unfenced swath of lawn to do it, but I found myself on a street I hadn't explored before, even farther afield than if I had taken the familiar route. The houses here were larger than ours and newer.

These were what they called ranch-style in California, sprawling stucco haciendas with red-tiled roofs and phony Mexican touches like black wrought iron and elaborate lanterns in the entryways. The air here was strong and peppery with eucalyptus, which smelled like wet asphalt, and there were more patterns of gravel and stone than grass. Even the sun seemed brighter, reflected off the wide expanses of stucco. I might have been on another side of town altogether.

And then I stopped walking and froze in silent wonder.

Across the street sat a pale blue MG convertible. The woman in the driver's seat had her back to me; indeed, she was bent forward as though she were fiddling with the radio, but that long flow of white-blond hair was unmistakable. It had to be Sherry Gentry parked in the wrong direction, on this of all streets.

I looked around me for a clue. Not another person walked this road, and the houses themselves seemed empty and lifeless. Not another car parked anywhere.

I have three choices, I thought, quickly listing my

options as I always did when faced with a sense of vertigo. I can walk on by and pretend I don't even see her. That's certainly the easiest. Or better yet, turn back, so she doesn't see me. Avoid the whole damn thing. Or I can walk by and casually wave, speaking only if she says hi first, which she won't. That's really the safest option, because I won't look like a puerile adolescent in case she sees me turning away and running. Or I can walk right over and say hello like an adult.

I quickly discarded that last option as impossible, for she surely wouldn't recognize me. She scarcely glanced at me that day at the lunch table. But the sun was hot, I needed a bathroom and a Coke in the worst way, so I continued up the sidewalk, past the blue MG. She won't speak, I thought, even as I lifted my hand in a casual manner, but she might wave back.

However, as I drew closer I could see that she wasn't fiddling with the radio at all. In fact, I could hear now that the sounds I'd noticed from a distance were not music. Sherry Gentry was weeping – and not gently either. She was bent over, one hand to her lovely face, and her sobs were quite audible from clear across the street.

I was quickly and utterly shorn of any resolve to just walk on by. But it seemed equally impossible to speak and intrude on her despair. At that moment she lifted her head and gazed at me, and her face was such an amalgam of beauty, helplessness, pride, and complete woe, I felt totally inadequate.

I had dealt with grief before, you understand, and had there-there'd and patted various female relations at funerals and sickbeds, for a Jewish male is expected to take on the yoke of such responsibilities at an early age. But I had never felt so disarmed, so swept up in another person's obvious tragedy, so drawn to *do* something to console, succor, and support. And I had the vague sense that whatever I did would not be enough, could never be sufficient to make up for whatever terrible wrong had been done by the world to make such a girl cry.

Yet I stepped blindly forward and asked, 'Sherry? Is something wrong?' One part of my mind screamed *Fool*! in outrage at my banality, but she didn't seem to notice my idiot question.

She pressed the heels of her hands to her eyes and gasped softly, trying to regain control.

I moved closer to the car. 'Can I do anything for you?'

She looked at me now, as though seeing me for the first time. 'Who are you?' she moaned. 'Do I know you?'

I cleared my throat. 'David Levine. You don't really know me.' For some reason I thought that might make it easier for her.

'Please go away,' she sighed, breathing a despair past telling.

Go, my mind said. And at any other time, in any other place, with any other person in the world, I might have retreated quietly and left them to their sorrow. But for some reason I couldn't abandon her. It just seemed impossible that she had appeared right before me, on this street, so vulnerable and lovely. And walking away from her then would have been like finding a baby bird cheeping in a half-broken shell on that hot sidewalk and not even moving it to a patch of shade. I couldn't do it.

Her sobs were beginning to calm. She made no effort to hide her face, to turn away, or to rummage in her purse for tissues. She just sat there and let the tears dry on her cheeks as though she knew she could never be anything but naturally beautiful, no matter what she did.

Finally I asked, 'Do you live nearby?'

She nodded.

'So do I, or anyway, just a few blocks. Listen, I met you a few days ago, you probably don't remember, but I

31

was sitting next to Eric Arne when you stopped to say hi at lunch, and if you're okay, I'll get out of your life. I mean, I don't want to intrude. If you're okay now.' Just shut *up*, I screamed internally. The Persian cat, completely in agreement, stalked away indignantly, its tail high and stiff.

Sherry peered up at me, and a glint of a smile tucked up one corner of her mouth.

Nothing like a guy making a babbling ass out of himself before her to improve the view, I thought weakly.

'You're a friend of Eric's?' She was composed now, and she glanced in the rearview mirror, tossed her hair back over her shoulder, and took two quick fingers to the slight smudges under her eyes.

'I'm new,' I said. 'David Levine. I'm in your class.'

She smiled brightly at me, a hard, sparkling flash of white teeth. 'Well, what do you think, David Levine? Will I pass?'

The shadows of despair still lingered on the sides of her face and in the corners of her mouth; small, dark, and premonitory of a fragile shoring-up, an irresistible pull toward destruction. But I couldn't see that then. Only that she was incredibly perfect in her pride, not a trace of shyness or humbleness or shame about her, all sun and open air.

I summoned the strength to say, 'You look fine. Most girls I know look like hell when they cry.'

She appraised me, not unkindly. 'I'm not like any other girl you've known before, David Levine.'

Before I could recover with some clever witticism or even another try at hapless flattery, she wheeled the MG away from the curb and was gone. I could have sworn the Persian sat at her side.

I turned on my heel and went back down the street, the details of our encounter a vertiginous blur in my mind.

She must live nearby. She must have parked there so she could have her cry before her mother saw her, or the servant or something. But what could have caused her such sorrow? Surely not that tiny incident with Eric Arne; she must have another boyfriend who's giving her trouble. But probably not some high school kid.

I suddenly recalled a saying my mother had, an old Jewish proverb she liked to repeat when the aunts asked did she never wish for a daughter?

'A pretty face costs,' she would say, shaking her head. 'Costs in money, costs in time, costs in heartache. My boys are enough for me.'

'But a daughter! A daughter is always your child.'

'And who needs such a thing? And beautiful besides? That's like trying to guard a sackful of fleas. Or like raising chickens is like raising a pretty girl. Both,' she added with a knowing smile, 'will make you old before your time.'

A pretty face costs. It was not all tanned sleek skin, white smiles, and halcyon days. Even for the most beautiful shiksa I had ever seen.

I walked purposefully now, my bladder having reasserted itself. And I realized with a start that there was a definite tumescence lingering as well. Just talking to her, standing next to her car, I had an erection hard enough to make me forget my need to piss.

Well, I grinned ruefully, maybe at least she'll remember my name. She said it twice.

I remember so clearly what California was like then. I'd heard plenty about it, specifically the southern part, before I'd even placed a wary and skeptical foot in the Valley. So many Jews had migrated here for their health that tales of its undisciplined luxuriance and promise of

33

invigoration wafted back east as regularly as matzo on Monday.

The very idea of California, with its unbridled decadence, its people too rich, its grass too green, its breezes too warm, encouraged a strange lure, half envy, half contempt. The stores were, if you could believe it, open seven days a week in a riot of irreverence, and you could buy liquor anywhere. Anytime! Half of Washington Heights had heard the tale of the woman who put her house up for sale on Easter Sunday and sold it within forty-five minutes at her asking price. And even for those of us who didn't celebrate Easter, that was somehow a slap in the face of all decorum. The other half had heard of the man who came out for business, got a job – boom! – just like that, as an upholsterer for Barker Brothers, rented a room in a shell-pink stucco bungalow, and wrote his wife in the Bronx, 'Sell everything and come to California!'

But to me, young as I was, the place was a paradox even then. I kept thinking of Uncle Saul, who came out to Burbank, sick with Parkinson's, because he thought the sun would cure him. He came all the way to the coast only to find death all alone, with no familiar faces around to offer comfort. And why not? the aunts asked. How could one expect to escape fate? So it was clear to me that Death could still get you in California, could follow you onto the broad and gaping daylight of a white beach and sneak up on you, strange and sinister, like a brilliant bloom rotting from too much sun. No one got out of California untanned or unchanged, so went the legend. Like Jerusalem or Lourdes.

And then there was the myth of Hollywood, a word which caused my eldest aunt to make the sign of the evil eye and spit once over her shoulder. A garden of earthly delights, they called it, a land of sensuous fullness, a pastel set of stages that was somehow exempt from the bourgeois morality of the Bronx. Hollywood was more than a town, they said, it was a state of mind. A tabula rasa upon which a nation could etch its every longing and fantasy: Sunset Boulevard, Benedict Canyon, Beverly Hills – words round and full in the mouth like fruit.

In fact, when I was ten I distinctly recall my mother saying some woman she knew had 'a voice like a Beverly Hills doorbell', and I had been consumed by curiosity to know what that meant. Now I knew: beautiful, emphatic, and rich.

Also, according to the aunts: divorced, probably a drug addict, and certainly experienced in orgies. People who burn their candles at both ends for a living, Aunt Lila said, deserve to get their fingers scorched.

When I told my friends, Joey and Irv and Beanie, I was being shipped off to Lotus Land, I felt their sorrow, contempt, and envy in full measure. Not a single one of the old gang had a good thing to say for California except Ruth. Ruth of the blackly curled hair, Ruth of the vaguely disconsolate smile, the white skin, the dark-eyed mystery of small dispassionate kisses in a musty parlor. On every Sunday that ornately over-stuffed room was ungraciously vacated by Ruth's frowning father and giggling small sisters so that she might 'entertain' her sole admirer. Ruth, the only Jewish girl I had ever embraced.

Not that I hadn't had plenty of other girls. I sometimes pulled out my mental list, in fact, to warm my hands with when I felt the insinuating chill of self-pity. That Polish girl, Ida, liked me well enough, especially when I touched her breasts. As though she had heat sensors in her blouse, her temperature rose alarmingly when I so much as brushed her front buttons. I fondled Ida in doorways, in movie theaters, on park benches, whenever I could get her coat open and her mouth shut long enough, and I know I'll hear in my memory until the day I die the way she used to moan, 'Yes, Davy, I can feel it, I can feel it, do you feel it?' over and over in a litany of lust.

I wonder what she would have done if I had reared back and screamed, 'Of *course* I can feel it, you bovine nymph, these are *my* hands doing this, in case you haven't noticed!'

I'd never touched Ida anyplace except on her large white tits. If I tried to touch her anyplace else, even a single foray down below her waist, she jerked back as if she were goosed, sometimes sailing half out of her seat, and all further fondlings were over.

And then there was that little red-haired, wide-mouthed vixen who wouldn't keep her hands off me when I couldn't do anything about it and then slapped me away when we were alone. Margaret, her name was. A true Irish wanton who convinced me once and for all that communion wafers could rot the brain.

Anna, a beautiful and intelligent Puerto Rican girl, spoke to me of Yeats and Faulkner, offering gentle probing kisses that actually made my heart flutter. I'd heard of such a thing, but before Anna I'd never known such tremulous passion.

Anyway, David Levine at seventeen wasn't exactly new-blown snow. I'd read D. H. Lawrence compulsively, and if I hadn't actually gone to the 'solstice and the equinox', as he called it, I'd certainly been close enough to feel the heat.

There was a lot of talk in 1965 about the sexual revolution. But at seventeen it was only talk. I knew it was actually possible to get the Pill, and I considered it an amazing stroke of God-ordained license that this new birth control device had occurred simultaneously with my own puberty. But the girls I knew had no idea how to get It, nor did they want to be the first in their group of

36

friends to try It. And somehow the idea of It seemed so *serious*, so incredibly brazen, to plan every day that you were actually going to be having carnal knowledge of somebody sometime later. It was a little hard to absorb.

With Ruth, for example, it was serious. She was the one girl of all my early sexual explorations whom I could have actually taken to my parents as marriage material. That is, if you could call careful parlor kissing sexual exploration. It was strange, now that I think of it. I never even wanted to do anything with Ruth but kiss and talk. She seemed to understand me before I spoke.

So when it came time to say farewell, it was only to Ruth that I went.

'Why does your father have to go all the way to California?' she asked mournfully, as though Rabbi Levine had chartered one of Columbus's ships to the edge of the world.

'He's had an offer from a big Reform congregation,' I said sadly, catching her tone. It was imperative that I sound at least as bereft as she did. 'He says it's a wonderful opportunity to bring the word of God to an arid land.'

At that, gentle Ruth almost snorted. 'I'm sure even in California they can hear Him if they want to. My father says, if God willed it, brooms would shoot, and your father is only chasing money out there.'

I was shocked at her censure, she, who scarcely seemed to prefer one ice cream flavor over another. I said, rather brusquely, 'Well, anyway, we're going.'

Ruth took my hand. 'Not forever, I hope,' she said softly. 'I hear it's very beautiful.'

I smiled. 'Maybe I'll find gold. There's got to be some of it left. Then I'll come back, buy up the Cloisters, and you can be my queen.'

At that, the Persian turned its back, hoisted one white leg, and began to lick its private parts.

Ruth said, 'Just come back.'

Of course I didn't, except a thousand times over in my memory. I can close my eyes today and feel the rush of the express elevator, up to the Empire State Building's 102nd, to see the gleaming pinnacles of steel and glass, aluminum and bronze, layered with haze from the shining river. I can taste the small bit of Manchego cheese from Spain that Manny the cheese man put on my tongue. 'Nice and nutty. No charge.' Cheese of All Nations, my mother's second stop on Thursdays, after the Fulton Fish Market. The headlights of cars on the George Washington Bridge, endless strips of pearls in the night. The beards and the guitar players and beatniks down in Washington Square on Sundays, the cross-eyed Bullwinkle blimp, floating down Central Park West, and Donald Duck bobbing behind, in the Macy's Thanksgiving Day parade. Taking a rainy Saturday bus to the Met, the Guggenheim and MOMA, ending up in the hush of the reading room of the New York Public Library, my eyes strained and my soul too full to speak. Streets always in an orgy of destructive construction, or constructive destruction, iron wrecking balls and piles of rubble, bulldozers and holes in the ground three stories deep. SELF-DEFENSE IS COMMON SENSE signs in the subway advertising a karate school, violent arts studios dotting the neighborhood where once tap-dancing schools flourished. The visiting Hasidim from Williamsburg dancing in the synagogue on holy days, a rabbi, in his eighties, the zaddik of the faithful, dancing alone, dressed in white and silver, with the Torah in his arms. The dirt, the rush, the blur of faces, a Black kid hollers, 'Want a taxi, want a taxi!' The taxi's standing right there, so you don't tip him, and he screams through the window, 'Cheap! Cheap!' An August night at the open-air Delacorte Theater in Central Park, where the magic of Shakespeare floated out on the floodlights, along with a thousand moths, spiraling up to the skyscrapers and their firefly lights. Times Square on New Year's, standing under the neon rainbows, a flashing '1964!' next to the hugely blinking BOAC sign: 52 COUNTRIES! 6 CONTINENTS!, and all of that seemed small next to the surging nation around me.

The Bronx. Manhattan. A million memories. And thoughts of Ruth always trigger them for me, bring them alive.

When I think of Ruth now, I picture her as I saw her last, standing at the top of the stairs in her father's house. She didn't lean against the curved banister but stood straight and tall, her dark hair down her back, her arm raised in a motionless farewell. Like brass or stone. Her character, her very spine, was firm as iron.

God, what a time of upheaval that was, and not just because of the move. And certainly not only for David Levine. It was bad enough to move on the edge of my senior year, but somehow my sense of bewilderment paled as I looked around me. No one knew the score anymore.

It seemed that we just got over the assassination of President Kennedy, when the Vietnam War began. I no more than got used to the idea of Lenny Bruce, when the Beatles arrived. Just about the time I began to think seriously about college and my future, I could hear nothing but the growing rumble of unrest from kids just a few years older than I, who could have been my older siblings, who might have come from dinner tables across America like my own.

And when, at that table, the idea of California was initially proposed, my parents, as always, presented a united front and brooked no rebellion.

'There's no real winter there,' my father said. 'It will

39

be good to live where you don't have to own three overcoats.'

'The possibilities, just imagine,' my mother added. 'The adventure.'

'But I'm going to be president of the science club next year!' I sputtered, at first too amazed to rally my forces with any sort of rational defense. 'I'm going to college!'

'I'm sure they've got science clubs at Taft. That's the name of the high school you'll go to, David. And of course you're going to college. I understand Taft's a fine school with an excellent college prep program.' Rabbi Levine smiled at Myra Levine.

They have this choreographed like a Fred and Ginger movie, I thought helplessly as my mother chimed in, 'And it's such a *big* school. They offer so many subjects you don't have here, with so many students! A thousand in his class, you said, Daniel, right?' She nodded brightly at my father. She would, I knew, have followed him even to the hostile wilderness of Utah if he'd asked.

A thousand! I felt my feet and fingers tingle with dread. 'That's a factory, not a school,' I finally managed to get out.

'Oh, David, you're grasping at straws,' my mother said cheerily.

'What about where I go?' Avrom piped up. 'They got hockey out there?' Avrom had been itching to play since he saw the Canadian exhibition games at the Garden.

My father frowned thoughtfully. 'Now, that I don't know, but they play every other sport known to man and boy, I'm sure. Your school is called Parkman. Parkman Junior High, after Francis Parkman, the famous historian.' His eyes suddenly twinkled with private wit. 'I am told they have a singularly fine band at Parkman. Since in California we'll have a big enough house for you to have

40

your own room, I see no reason why you shouldn't take up the drums, as you've been wanting.'

'Wow!'

My mother glanced at me. 'And perhaps a swimming pool? For after-school parties?'

Well, it was all over. I slumped lower in my chair, refusing the bribe. My little brother had been completely converted, I noted with disgust. It's a good thing Avrom didn't have a firstborn to offer up to the Parkman God, or there'd have been sacrificial blood on my mother's second-best tablecloth.

There was a long night of melancholy when I seriously considered offering myself up for adoption to any of several commiserating friends. I could have stayed with Beanie, for a few months at least, if I could stand Beanie's sister. Or maybe Irv Soroky or Georgie Rabkin. Their houses were like mine, their rooms held the same books, Maris and Mantle buttons, and Yankees pennants. I might not even know the difference when I woke up each morning, until I got to the breakfast table. But who was I kidding? The bottom line was brutally evident.

I was going to California. Even if I could have found an alternate harbor, my parents would never leave me. I was going to California because my parents wanted to go, I was seventeen, and I'd never seriously rebelled against their wishes in my entire life.

Once I got there, of course, I realized that there was actually no rational reason to hate an entire state. And, in time, I discovered that for every insult I heard about California, there was an opposite reason for admiration.

For example, it was true that the East Coast had all the adults. As though at its conception somebody tipped the nation to the right and all the stabilizers, the club members, and the money changers had clustered in the East.

But the West coast had all the kids. On the left side sat

all the experimenters, the adventurers, and the nonbelievers – or the believers in just about anything. It made for a heady mix, and if California seemed vulgar and immature, well, at least it wasn't fossilized in the traditions of the eastern caste system. If it glorified hedonistic escape, then it also allowed its children a second chance, a renewal. If it was hopelessly decadent and debauched, it was also one of the most utterly glamorous places I had ever seen.

And incredibly, for all the badmouthing California took from everybody back home, the place seemed to be simmering with Jews. Not specifically in Woodland Hills, perhaps, but in Burbank, in Santa Monica, in Hollywood, it was no trouble to find a myriad of kosher delis to choose from, and it took small search to hear Yiddish spoken with a Bronx inflection.

Of course, they didn't look like the Jews back home. Neither did Irish Catholics look like themselves. Everyone looked like one another, as though there were something in the water that diluted ethnic traits down to a blur of bland, benign, homogenized culture. It occurred to me that one of the reasons New York Jews hated the Golden State was because it had, neatly and without apology, seduced some of the Big Apple's best.

I thought often of one of the first things Jim Foote told me, something about the California sun bleaching everything down to the same colors.

I began to check myself in passing mirrors to see if I looked any more like a native. My dark, tightly curled hair was no straighter. I was maybe a little taller, a little broader in the shoulders, but that was more the daily laps I did in the pool than anything in the water. I was tanner, of course, so my complexion looked better, but my glasses were wedged just as deeply on my nose. Nice-looking, but obviously ethnic. I was learning to say 'hot shit, dude' with the rest of them, but there was still a subtle formality to my speech patterns, a trace of stiffness that branded me alien. I just couldn't learn to say 'fuck' with the saucy, languid ease that these guys managed.

But for two months, I wasn't doing too bad. I had a friend and I found a sport, rediscovered one, actually, that I used to enjoy back home: wrestling. I joined the JV team, learned some moves and new holds, got soundly slammed by the varsity guys in my weight class, but I began to look forward to practice. I liked the individuality of the combat, the tight confines of the rules and the circle, and the knowledge that it was just me out there, one body against another. Before wrestling I used to chew down three books a week, priding myself on accumulating new words and an edged glibness. But somehow, in California, it seemed almost unnatural to read so much, and I cut back. In no time I barely missed the museums at all.

I'd found a niche, of sorts. Even the music was beginning to grow on me.

One day, when it had to be about ninety degrees and I was getting a sun headache walking from the bus stop, a loud horn blatted behind me. I jumped and turned, about to flip off some smartass, when a familiar blur made me instantly yank my hand down from my vulgar salute.

It was a blue MG. Sherry Gentry waved me over as she idled in the middle of the street.

'Want a ride?' One hand lay nonchalantly on the wheel, a slender, tanned arm encircled by colorful, clanking bracelets. Her face was framed by oversize sunglasses and that long wave of hair.

I grinned sheepishly and walked closer. I had to fight down the urge to look over my shoulder to see if she was really talking to me.

'You're David, right?' she asked.

I nodded happily and hurried around to the passenger side, thinking, of *course* the upholstery had to be white, what else with that hair, probably real leather, and gasped as I sat down on the blistering seat. Seared me right through my pants, but I didn't care. I eased myself up an inch off the leather, slammed the door, and she punched the radio and the car into motion all at once.

'Too hot to walk today!' she hollered gaily over the music. 'Show me where to turn – '

How to prolong this! 'Right at the next corner!' I hollered back, wondering if I dared take her the long way around.

The radio was blaring out a Beach Boys' song I'd heard at least twice a day for the last week:

> And we'll have FUN, FUN, FUN, now that daddy took
> The T-bird a-waay-aay!

Sherry hummed along, patting her free hand on the car door, wheeling down the street. 'How're you doing these days? Making friends?'

'Oh yeah,' I said. Think of something to say!

'Isn't California far out?'

'Absolutely.' I grinned happily. And at that instant I truly thought so: the sun, the wind in my face, the girl next to me, the joyous pulsing rhythm of the drums. 'This your car? It's really fantastic.'

'My folks got it for me for Christmas last year.' She tossed me a teasing smile. 'To match my eyes.'

I didn't hesitate. 'You must have been good.'

'I always am,' she said. 'I thought that was you from the back. I figured I owed you one. You were really nice to stop that day.'

I wondered if she would speak of it. Now that she had, my confidence expanded. 'I doubt there's a male between ten and ninety who wouldn't have.'

44

'You'd be surprised,' she said lightly.

The music ended, another song segued right into the last, and I said, 'It's down at the end of this block on the right. That green house.'

'Where are you from?' she asked as she pulled up and parked.

Please don't let Avrom be coming home. 'New York City, originally. You must live in this neighborhood, then?'

'About six blocks over.' She sat relaxed, waiting for me to get out of the car.

It was now or never. 'Listen,' I said, turning slightly toward her, 'I hope whatever got you crying last time' – her eyes swiveled away quickly and I sensed my misstep and added – 'well, I just hope it's better for you now. You're too pretty to ever have to be sad.' I was almost out of breath with my audacity.

She said, 'Nobody's ever that pretty, David Levine.' She started up the car, and I slid out of the seat and closed the door, turning back to lean on it.

'Do you know anything much about me?' she asked, almost as an afterthought.

I rattled off, 'Sherry Gentry, Queen of Taft High, Class Flirt, most likely to be worshipped.' I took a deep breath and thought quickly. Here, you either make it memorable or make it mud. 'Best *tochis* in the Valley. Or so they say.'

'Best – what?'

'Rump, dorsum, posterior.' In for a penny, in for a pyre. 'Ass.'

The Persian closed slitted amber eyes and heaved a scornful sigh. Sherry's eyes also narrowed, the blue turned colder, and a cloud suddenly blocked the sun.

'I'd heard that,' she said softly, 'but nobody ever said it to my face.'

45

I was genuinely shocked. 'No kidding? Not even one of your boyfriends?' God, even when she was hostile, she was beautiful. 'Where I come from, lots of girls would consider it a compliment.'

She softened somewhat. 'Well, the men I date don't mention it.'

'Who's that?'

'College men, mostly.' She rustled impatiently in her seat. 'Well, see you later – '

Before she could move away, I quickly said, 'Listen, I'm sorry I forgot my manners. Want to come in for a Coke or something? Maybe sit out by the pool? I promise not to sound like some subanthropoidal horse's *tochis*.'

A small smile.

Show her what a fool you're not. 'You're a real headspinner, you know that? I'm afraid I lost mine.'

The smile grew to one of wry amusement at my fumbles. 'No, it's still there. For what it's worth.'

'Well, come on in, and not a single other bodily part or function will be mentioned. Please?'

'Don't beg.'

'Beg? Who's begging? This isn't begging, it's beseeching. And if you can't tell the difference, you'll never win my heart.'

Now she laughed aloud. As the car pulled away, she called back over her shoulder, 'Maybe next time, David Levine.'

I stood and watched her until she rounded the corner. Shit. Another dazzling repartee executed by everyone's favorite Casanova, the delightfully cunning David Levine. She undoubtedly had *two* pools of her own, not to mention a dozen to choose from if she wanted to do something so boring as to go sit by one, moron. And was it absolutely necessary to mention her ass?

I was aware, from the instant I almost fried it on her

upholstery, that my cock was tense just being around her. She seemed everything female, Amazonian almost in her sense of poise and control, something almost *virile* about her power, and yet she made me feel completely male.

She could probably see your adolescent lust oozing out of every pore, dorkus, along with your sweat. Three minutes in a car with Sherry Gentry had accomplished what a hot bus ride and half a walk home in ninety degrees had not: my armpits were darkened in deep crescents of nervous perspiration.

To my amazement, however, the Persian was still following along, although it pretended not to know me. I ignored it. I knew that the more acknowledgment I gave it, the more I catered to its approval, the bigger it would get. With every glance in its direction, it fluffed and swelled itself and soon, if I wasn't careful, I'd be trailed all over the Valley by an invisible white cat the size of a sheep. I slammed in the house and headed for the refrigerator.

'Hi, Davy!' my mother caroled from some far part of the house. Steps coming down the hall, her welcoming smile around the corner of the cold Coke bottle I lifted gratefully to my mouth. I closed my eyes in almost physical pain at the bite of the peppery liquid and her eager eyes.

'So how was it today?'

Just keen. Until I grossed out myself and the best girl in the world, all in the space of a three-minute conversation. Doing swell until I ruined myself socially for life. If she were queen, I'd probably be in the Tower. People have been jellied in aspic for less.

'Okay,' I said wearily, and headed for the pool. Thinking better of it, I stopped and turned, kissed my mother on the cheek, and added, 'Pretty good, actually.' After all, she was a woman too.

47

I took my Coke out to the pool to a patch of shade I had privately christened my spiritual center. Like the Indians on a spirit quest used to do, I'd found a piece of ground and was waiting for it to speak to me. So far, this place of moving shadows under the single walnut tree in the yard had remained mute, but it eased me nonetheless to imagine it my own.

I tried to picture Sherry Gentry lying by my pool, just out of arm's reach, her body stretched out on the lounge chair. What sort of movies did she like? What sort of books did she read? Who were her heroes? Was she into sports? The arts? Did she think Eric Arne had a nice ass?

Well, I got her ticked off, but at least I didn't cave. That's something to face Mecca for, anyway.

I want to know all about this girl, I thought. She seems a little superficial, that's probably the way everyone thinks of her, but I know there's something more there, some mystery and sadness and need that others have missed.

I didn't realize it at the time, but in my mind Sherry Gentry began to emerge as a symbol of all things Californian, like the palms and the sun itself, of a life and a place that seemed all shine and iridescence, as the world must have been – as women must have been – at the beginning of time.

'Really, David, your mother and I are rather disappointed in this,' Rabbi Levine said gently.

I looked up in surprise. My father and I had been out by the pool, just talking and sharing a quart of orange juice, when all of a sudden and with no warning change of tone he took my report card out of his bermuda shorts pocket.

I felt a small hollow qualm open in my stomach.

'This is rather, a fraud, I think,' he added.

'What do you mean?'

'I mean that while this might do – might do quite well, actually – for any of a dozen of your classmates, it's certainly not up to your usual standards.' He tapped one clean and close-cut fingernail on the paper's edge. 'I think you're defrauding yourself, David, and in the process, your mother and myself.'

I took the report card from my father's hand and looked at it carefully, as though I had never seen it before. Two As in calculus and science. Three Bs in history, French, and PE, and a C in English. Of course, that C had been a shock, my first in high school, and usually I got As in English, but the lame yo-yo who taught the class thought haikus about the wind were the be-all and end-all of literature and nobody in the whole school seemed to give a shit for Shakespeare, after I'd read almost all the tragedies last year. Naturally, I didn't expect my father to pass out merit badges for this one, but neither had I anticipated any real concern. After all, I had outstanding grades overall, and I was going through a period of adjustment here –

'What do you think is the problem?' my father asked.

'Oh, Dad, it's just the midterm. I'll pull them up, don't worry.'

But Rabbi Levine wasn't having any. 'I do worry, son, and so does your mother. If you don't improve on these, none of your first choices will accept you. Any decent university's going to take maybe the top ten percent, no more. You did an excellent job on your SATs, as we knew you would, and that's fine. But your grades can't show a deviation right now. Your applications are due in a few weeks. So what's the problem?' He never took his eyes from my face.

I felt a cold sullenness steal over me. I fought it down, for I knew my father would sense any defiance and chip, chip, chip away at it.

'So?'

'I guess it's just the move,' I said quietly, keeping my voice even with an effort. It wouldn't do any good to holler what the hell's wrong with two As and three Bs? So what, a little C in a dipshit course anybody could sail through with his eyes closed, what difference could it possibly make in a whole lifetime of always pulling in the good grades, *always* being the good son, constantly doing what's expected? I knew he'd just think I was slipping worse than he suspected and tighten the snaffle even more.

'I guess it's taken a little punch out of me, but I'll be better now.' I took a swig of juice, averting my eyes. 'I've been a little distracted.'

My father visibly relaxed. 'We thought it might be something like that. I know it hasn't been easy for you.'

He looked away now, over the shimmering surface of the pool, and I felt my breath come easier.

'You know,' he continued, 'I understand more than you think, David.'

Yes, Papa.

'I know what it's like to leave a world behind.'

I love you too, Papa.

'If you think your friends were incredulous about your move out here, imagine what my colleagues had to say on the subject.' He smiled wistfully. 'Kooksville, they called it. Where all the fruits and nuts roll to the sea. This isn't a place, they said, it's a tumor. Lots of them questioned my sincerity.'

'Ruth's father said you were just after the money,' I said gently, hating myself.

He nodded sadly.

I felt a rising sense of injury and said with some contempt, 'Most of them have never been west of Newark.'

50

'Still, they're full of opinions.'

'So why did you decide to come?'

My father suddenly turned and gazed at me. 'I guess I felt the need to start over somehow. Back in New York it seemed I had traded my youth for discipline. Done the sensible thing. But I never felt completely right about it, you know? And California always seemed to me to be on the cutting edge of everything. The final frontier, sort of. A place that wasn't used up, but was full of fertility and promise and second chances. Do you understand?'

I could never recall my father speaking to me in this manner, as though I were his equal. A friend. His confidential tone rather than the words themselves moved me. I could scarcely do more than nod.

'I remember reading about some early Indian tribes out here, the Castonoans I think they were called. Anyway, they used to come from everywhere to dance on the California beaches. To dance on the brink of the world, they said. I think the West Coast still has that appeal. Which is probably why so many New Yorkers wish it would just sink into the sea,' he finished with a wry chuckle.

I gave a hollow laugh.

'But that's why I'm so concerned, David, about this trend toward mediocrity.' He took the report card from my hands and put it back into his pocket solemnly. 'You don't want to screw it up *here*. There's no place else to go for a second chance. This is it. Don't use this move as an excuse to allow yourself to fall behind. You're so close to everything you want now.'

I cleared my throat, found it workable, and said, 'Okay, Dad. I'll pull my grades up before they're on my record.'

'Good boy. Now, tell me, have you met some new friends? Any girls caught your eye?'

Back on level ground. I smiled shyly. 'A few.'

'A few. Listen to him. With a face and a brain like that, I would bet it's more than a few, eh?' He punched my arm softly. 'Am I right? Has my son got the moves?'

'Faster than the speed of heat.'

We grinned at each other, a shared conspiracy. David Levine was handsome and stunned the ladies right and left; his father couldn't be more proud and pleased, and both of us were vastly comfortable discussing the topic of my sex life in general. These were the lies we had wordlessly agreed to somewhere just after bar mitzvah, and I never had the heart to smash the code.

'So have you decided what you want to study in college? Last time we discussed it, you were narrowing it down.'

'Well, not really. I've still got time – '

'No,' my father said suddenly, his mouth stern. 'That's just what I've been trying to get you to see. You don't have as much time as you think. This all counts. Now, your mother and I have been talking about it, and we both agree in our assessment of your capabilities. There's no doubt you can do anything you want, David, anything at all if you give it your best. Even something in the didactic line, maybe teaching or something with a more spiritual bent.'

It was so smooth, I almost missed the transition.

'Perhaps the rabbinical life might be considered.' My father took off his glasses and wiped them carefully. 'After all, you like to give advice and you tend to be rather – sure – about your opinions for one so young. Have you considered this as a possibility?'

I was appalled. Not just because it seemed I was being asked to make a decision about my entire future right here and now by the pool, not only because the picture my parents seemed to have of me made me look like a pretentious and pompous bore, but most of all because I suddenly had a stark suspicion of what my father wanted

52

more than anything else: that his eldest son follow in his footsteps and become a rabbi.

'At the risk of sounding ridiculous,' my father added with an affectionate chuckle, 'I'd say you have a messianic way about you, son. Your mother and I have both noticed it.'

The vision of myself as a rabbi, of muttering through my years over a potage of dusty talmudic tomes, of getting humped shoulders from wearing always the woolen tallis, musty with the sweat of ancient righteousness, of conferring with the bearded elders, of consoling lines of bewigged widows and leading along eager bar mitzvah students by the hand, of layering myself slowly with credibility to reassure the less faithful, the least pious, achieving after so many years the cool granite mantle of a tribal leader. Of trying always to seem older and wiser than my years. I wanted to be young! I wanted women who were not, O God, like my mother.

In my desperation I bleated out quickly, 'A scientist. I want to be a scientist, Dad. I've already decided.'

Rabbi Levine said nothing.

I grew more voluble the longer I looked at my father's lengthening face. 'You remember how hard I worked on that science project last year, Dad? Lots of people said I had real talent, a *gift* some of them said, remember Mr Goldblume, the biology teacher said that I moved him with that display of horse evolution? *Moved* him, Dad, with eohippus! I've been giving it a lot of thought actually, and I think that's really what I want to do. Be a scientist. I think I could discover something, Dad. Really.'

'A scientist? Of what, exactly?'

'Well, I haven't decided that yet, maybe a biologist, I don't know. Maybe an entomologist.' That sounded impressive.

'You want to study bugs?' My father said it with the

same resigned sadness he might have reserved had his son told him he wanted to sell shoes for a living.

'Life. I want to study life.'

'Well. Life.' He stood up slowly and gazed down at me. 'There are worse things to study, I suppose. Though I have always thought that man himself was the most worthy subject of scrutiny. The humanities. But, of course, there's no real hurry. You have time to decide. To consider carefully your choices.' He touched my shoulder. 'And I will tell your mother that your next report will be substantially improved.'

'Okay, Dad.'

Having disappointed my father once, I was unable to do or say anything against his wishes for quite a while. And one day when I came home from school I realized that some parents sense this sort of advantage and are not above capitalizing on it.

My mother was bustling about the dining room, setting the table for what appeared to be an ornate and elaborate feast. Indeed, the linen could not have been more crisp, the sterling more shining if Ben-Gurion himself had been coming to dinner.

'What's going on?'

My mother beamed eagerly. 'We're having company tonight, David. Our first dinner party in our new home. Your father is bringing a very important man in the community, our new councilman! He and his lovely family' – she carefully smoothed an invisible wrinkle from the tablecloth – 'so I shouldn't use our very best dishes?' She recentered the flowers, stepped back, and I counted seven chairs.

'We aren't going to eat with you?'

'Of course you are, foolish, and Avrom also.'

'This guy has only one kid? A son?'

She moved quickly into the kitchen, throwing back over her shoulder, 'A mind like a trapdoor! He has one daughter just about your age, Mr Have-to-Know-It-All, but I doubt she'd be interested in such a *meshugge* boy as you, so don't worry your head for nothing.'

I rolled my eyes and leaned wearily against the wall. It had been a bad day. The Persian stuck its nose out from under the table and watched me with small interest. 'Ah, Ma, I'm not up for this tonight.'

She whirled back into the room, her hands on her hips. 'Not up for a fine meal and simple conversation? Not up, maybe, for extending yourself just a little for someone else for a change? I should maybe tell your father his temperamental son has decided to take a tray in his room?'

Lord. I slumped, my hands over my face, a beaten man.

'Ai-ai-ai, such drama, a person could bust.' She pulled me up and toward the door with an arm wrapped tightly around my neck. 'Now, go up and put on that nice shirt I ironed for you on your bed. And those new navy corduroys and your jacket. She will probably not even be able to eat a bite of my good brisket, she'll be so knocked dead by you.'

'No doubt,' I said morosely.

She squeezed me harder. 'So it would come as a surprise if I said that you are getting more and more handsome every day?'

'Yes.' I was trying to squirm loose.

'Surprise. Now, go get dressed, they'll be here in – oh, no, in thirty minutes!'

I was bested. Even the Persian knew it, following my mother into the kitchen, just the tip of its tail swishing back and forth with satisfaction.

As I was almost out of earshot, she called out, 'What

do you want, David, egg in your beard? She's a *lovely* girl!'

And in fact, she was. Miriam Weld, the councilman's daughter, was far past decent and well into pretty. She was seated across from me, even though that meant her mother had to sit across from Avrom. Clearly, the purpose of this evening was not just so that my parents and her parents could discuss civic affairs.

Miriam Weld had what appeared to be nicely adequate breasts. Not Winnebagos by any means, though it was hard to tell under the pink blouse and sweater vest that she wore. Her hair was dark and curled so violently that it fell almost horizontally out from her center part in a pyramid cascade down to her shoulders. Her face was pale, fragile and luminous, and her eyes were gray, almost flinty with intelligence.

I knew I was going to like her when I heard her response to my father's question, did she like California? Councilman Weld had already volunteered the information that they'd moved here three years before from Massachusetts (nobody's a native, I duly noted), and when Rabbi Levine asked her opinion of her adopted state, Miriam replied, 'It's a good place for condors.'

There was rather a startled hush around the table, and Mrs Weld hastened to add, 'Miriam is quite interested in animals, you understand. She's considering a major in biology in college.'

It was all I could do not to beam at my father.

'Actually,' Miriam said, 'it's a good region for all the raptors. Because we really don't have any seasons here, and the spring foliage lasts only a month or so, and then you have the only real California season – summer – which lasts most of the year, with the yellow hills and the dry brush, so the rodent population breeds almost all year round. A very good home for birds of prey.'

56

I almost laughed aloud, I was so charmed. I gave her a conspiratorial grin. 'Great for bugs too.'

Avrom got into the act. 'And snakes.'

And then the mood was broken. With relieved laughter the adults steered us back to news of the synagogue, where the Welds were also members, the problems with the freeways, and the expansion of Ventura Boulevard.

The evening went more swiftly than I'd expected, and when we somehow found ourselves out by the pool alone, miraculously without parental eyes on us, I said, 'I'd like to see you again. This time without an audience.'

'I'd like that too,' she said.

With a bravado born of a sense that everyone expected it sooner or later, I leaned forward into the shadows where she stood and kissed her gently. A chaste kiss, one she didn't seem to mind. I moved closer and slipped one hand to her waist. 'Are you dating anyone special?'

'Not now,' she said.

'Used to?'

She leaned into me slightly. 'Back home.'

I thought of Ruth, and some of the sparkle went out of the evening. Even after three years here, Miriam still thought of someplace else as 'back home'. Almost for lack of anything else to do or say, I went to kiss her again. But this time she pulled slightly away.

'I don't want you to get the wrong impression,' she said lightly. Her voice sounded now as though she'd just put on her glasses. 'I'm not a California girl, after all.'

I made a weak smile. 'That mean you don't like to kiss?'

'That means I've got my limits.'

I slid my arm from around her as our parents drifted out now onto the decking, drinks in hand. High, light laughter came to us across the yard.

'I just don't want you to be disappointed,' she added.

'Hey, I've got my limits too.' I held up my hands in mock defense.

She smiled wryly. 'How wonderful we have so much in common.'

A worthy adversary. A sudden thought came to me then, and I remember it so well. I realized that one day, many years hence, I would wish to be seventeen again. I'd heard adults say they wished for their youth recaptured, and even then I knew I was no different. Someday I would yearn to have all this back again, I thought, and I just hope I remember that it wasn't all that great.

Even if I'd wanted to, I could scarcely avoid asking Miriam out. First, both sets of parents grinned over us as if they'd just invented us. Second, after griping for months that no girl in the Valley'd go out with me, it was pretty tough to turn down a willing woman.

'I really think,' she said to me on our third date, 'that I could tell my parents you ran a drug ring in school, and they'd smile and say, "Isn't it marvelous that he's so business-oriented. A fine head on those shoulders."'

We were sitting in the back booth of Denny's, the only coffee shop in the Valley open past ten. You had to talk over the shouts and rumbling crashes from the bowling alley next door. 'I could tell my mother that you were well acquainted with the backseat of every Chevy in the senior class, and she'd say, "That girl is so warm and friendly!"'

She laughed lightly. 'So, did you promise to see me twice a month just to keep them off your back?'

'Actually,' I said solemnly, 'the specifics of the contract called for our firstborn. Your father plans to stack the council with our issue.'

She took my hand. Her fingers were pale and strong-looking as though they could plow fields, birth babies, and knock together a solid barn if they had to. I couldn't help comparing her hand to Sherry's – I could see her hands as clearly as though she sat beside me, even though it had been more than a month since she had – Sherry Gentry's hands were always moving, never still, full of nervous energy. Miriam's felt as soothing as a cool cloth on a hot day.

She was saying, 'So if you can get the car, there's an open party at a friend of mine's next Saturday.'

This was another door that dating Miriam had opened. Like an open sesame, I had but to say her name and my father's car was miraculously available. My license was still so new that the picture looked just like me, and my parents came to the door to wave good-bye each time I backed down the driveway, but Miriam on my arm gave me instant credibility. 'An open party?'

'Didn't you hear about the one up on Mulholland last month? A hundred kids showed up, and somebody floated beer kegs in the pool.'

I raised my eyebrows in mock alarm. 'You went to this debauch?'

She grinned. 'No, I missed out. But this one won't be anything like that. There'll be a lot of people, but Janet's folks will be there, so it won't get out of hand. They're hiring a band and everything. I think we should go.'

'No mayhem?'

'Mild.'

'No crazed mutants running amok?'

She laughed fondly.

With a disappointed sigh, I said, 'I'll pick you up at eight.'

There were cars parked all the way down the hill, and it looked as if half the party was on the street. Kids tossed beer cans back and forth, leaned against the cars, fondling each other under the streetlamps, and the warm night breeze softened all the edges. By some silent signal all the radios seemed tuned to the same station, and the Mamas and Papas' lilting harmonies wafted out to us from open convertibles.

> I'd be safe and warm, if I was in LA,
> California dreamin' . . . on such a winter's day –

Inside the house, kids were packed in like a plate of hors d'oeuvres, shoulder to shoulder. Except for in one room. In the den, just off the entry, Miriam's friend sat with her parents, making small talk with an amorphous group with a rapid turnover. There would have been room to dance in that room, but nobody did.

'Let's go say our hellos,' Miriam said, leading me into the audience room. 'Hi, Janet!' she called to a small, dark waif perched on the plaid sofa.

Janet waved back over the din. 'You made it!' she hollered. 'These are my folks!'

As if we couldn't tell. A paunchy man with a tie leaned over two couples at his feet and shook my hand vigorously. 'There's sodas in the kitchen!' he screamed. 'Snacks in the living room!'

'Thank you!' I hollered back, waving and smiling at Janet and her mother, who looked like an older Mrs Cleaver. The conversation around her began again earnestly, and she patted Janet's hand in obvious pleasure.

The band, four guys in ill-fitting red sports jackets, labored through a cleaned-up version of 'Louie, Louie'. Some couples were dancing, but the real action was happening right outside the door, where the car radios created a raucous thudding through the night – where the soche crowd gathered.

I glanced back at Janet and felt a familiar desperate

smile freeze my face, the same smile that appeared when a comedian on TV was trying too hard, a painful rictus of embarrassment and pity, and I turned away. Basically, it looked as if Janet had talked her folks into this thing, hoping to attract some attention. Well, the beautiful, popular kids came, but I doubted that any of them would know on Monday morning who she was.

We fished a couple of cold Cokes out of the ice cubes in the laundry tubs in the kitchen and salvaged the last few pretzels from a Tupperware bowl in the dining room. Somebody had brazenly tossed an empty Bacardi bottle in the kitchen sink, and I could feel the potato chips crunching under my shoes in the shag carpet.

'You want to dance?' I screamed at Miriam over the music.

She shook her head, spied a girl she knew across the room, and dashed over to say hello. I wandered away from the screeching saxophone and outside onto the porch.

I heard her coming way before I ever saw her. High calls of 'Hey, Sherry!' and 'Look who's here!' rose over the radios, and Sherry Gentry pulled up outside, blocking the driveway. She sat in a white T-bird convertible, some guy's free arm draped casually over her shoulder.

'How's the party?' she called out gaily.

'Great!' a dozen voices eagerly responded.

I could hear her light, clear laugh over the crowd, and then she was coming up the walk, her date behind her. She was dressed all in yellow, some sort of strapless sarong-type outfit with a yellow flower at her ear, her pale hair falling down her back, and a white sweater on her shoulders that looked as if it had been woven from the eyelashes of a million lambs.

Amazingly, she went right in to where Janet and her folks held court. She made her courtesies to the parents, gave Janet such a dazzling hello and smile that the girl ducked her head in dumbfounded pleasure, and then she swept back out of the room. Instantly, about a dozen other couples hurried in to follow her example, and the parents were suddenly swamped with attention.

Her date came to her side with two Cokes and she was back out on the porch in the darkness. Less than five minutes had passed since she'd arrived. I slipped outside again, leaned in the shadows, and watched her quietly.

'Try some of this,' her date said, pulling a small flask from his pocket to add to her Coke.

But Sherry didn't seem in any hurry to do his bidding. She gazed out over the porch, down to the parked cars. I was close enough to see the slight, even rocking of her hips to the music. She was dressed as though she had come from or was going to someplace else more important than where she was now. Her date wore a jacket. I didn't recognize him.

'Let's dance,' she said suddenly, pulling the guy away from the porch railing. With one hand on her Coke and the other around his neck, she swayed to the music, humming softly to herself. 'Ain't no use to sit and wonder why, babe, if you don't know by now.' Dylan's song of lost love.

Several other girls glanced at her and then dragged their own dates into their arms. In moments the whole porch was vibrating with moving bodies.

I felt a surge of pride for her that so many found her intriguing. Even the girls watched her with admiration. At that moment the public premium on her was high, and she was completely desirable. As she moved around the porch it was as if she were a magnet and the rest of the bodies so many iron filings to be pulled and drawn.

'There you are,' a light voice said at my elbow. Miriam's

pale face loomed out of the shadows. 'Having a good time?'

'Let's dance,' I said, and took her in my arms, moving closer to where Sherry stood and swayed.

'I just had the most interesting conversation with Janet's dad,' Miriam said.

I could hear Sherry still humming, her voice low.

'They came from Georgia, you know, some little town outside Atlanta where he worked for the university? He was making this really neat comparison between the South and the West – '

Sherry was saying something now to her date, and I strained to hear, keeping Miriam's back to them both.

' – about how the South was born out of poverty and defeat, and how it's still part of their mindset down there, but how California was born out of this incredible sense of good fortune. So he made the point, and I think it's a good one, that California has no sense of responsibility. No tragic awareness. It's all just sort of forgotten in the sunshine. Where in the South, they take responsibility for *everything* and everybody feels guilty, here they don't even know the meaning of the word.'

'Californians have seen the future, and it plays,' I murmured.

'What?'

'Just something I heard on the radio.'

Sherry was saying, 'I don't feel like leaving yet, Rod. If you want to go, go on.' She leaned way back in his arms, her hair falling over his wrists. 'I can get a ride home.'

The Righteous Brothers were bellowing out, 'You've lost that lovin' feeling!' and Rod was singing in Sherry's ear, pulling her inexorably toward the edge of the porch, out to the waiting car.

'Don't you think that's interesting?' Miriam asked, leaning back and peering at me in the darkness.

63

Suddenly, Rod fell to his knees, his hands clasped in supplication. 'Baby, baby! I'd get down on my knees for you!' he sang along with the music at the top of his voice.

Two couples nearby broke up with half-embarrassed laughter.

'If you would only *love* me, like you used to do!' he went on, the Righteous Brothers providing background harmony.

Now the whole porch was watching, some shrieks and nervous applause, and I only vaguely heard Miriam mutter 'that poor idiot' under her breath, because I was completely focused on Sherry's response.

As an actress, even in the intensity of her opening night, gets a deep impression of the people in the front row, she sized up her audience. She saw people gathering, took a reading, and gave Rod one slender hand. Her head was bowed demurely. As he sang the last verse to her, with all eyes on them both, she danced in a circle around him, pivoting gracefully, her fingers touching his in what seemed almost a rehearsed ballet movement. By doing so, she took his clumsy gesture and made it her own, made it drama, and also made it a parody of itself. Now it was acceptable to laugh, and everybody did.

The song ended, Rod stood up, and I could see in his face the passion ebbing, the awareness of how he had exposed himself as though he woke from a dream. He joined in the general laughter now, accepting everyone's congratulations for a good show, dusting off his knees, taking a bow, and I wondered if anyone else realized that the guy had meant his gesture sincerely. He had, at that moment, been so dazzled by this girl and his need for her that he had committed the ultimate embarrassment: He had been uncool.

She had saved him. Saved them both. But she would likely never forgive him his failing, and I doubted that

Sherry Gentry would ride in that particular T-bird much longer.

Now, as part of the show, she led him away from the porch to the car, supposedly to get his reward, and a few of his buddies called out encouragement.

'That poor guy,' Miriam said softly.

I glanced at her quickly, surprised.

'He's in way over his head.'

I took her in my arms again and turned my face away. 'What do you think of her?' I asked lightly.

She thought for a moment. 'I don't really know her. I just know what the other girls say about her.'

'Which is?'

Yesterday, all my troubles seemed so far away, McCartney was singing –

'Well, she doesn't really have a lot of girlfriends, I guess. She runs with a few of the cheerleaders. The beautiful ones.'

'So she doesn't suffer from a lack of confidence.'

She snorted delicately. 'I think you could get general agreement on that one.'

'So what else do they say about her?'

'Mostly just that she's not what she seems.'

I thought about that an instant, turning her around. 'Well, I guess hardly anybody is.'

'Oh, I don't believe that,' she said. 'I think most everybody reveals who they really are sooner or later. Especially at our age. But a pretty girl has got an extra mask to hide behind. People don't usually ask her to be real; it's enough that she's pretty. Soon she doesn't ask herself to be real, either.'

'So you think she's a phony?'

'I didn't say that. I told you, I barely know her. I just think she's a girl who believes in a good mirror when she sees one.'

I laughed. 'But she wouldn't eat her young?'

She smirked. 'I think she likes them a little older. I'm sure you must have noticed, she doesn't hang out with the girls much. Like tonight, she'll either be with her date or over talking to the boys.'

'Maybe she likes what they talk about better.'

Miriam's mouth stiffened. 'They talk about her.'

'I can understand that,' I said casually.

She pulled back and appraised me. 'Can you? Well, so can I. But I can't understand planning my life around it like she does. Now, can we possibly talk about something else besides the rare and talented Miss Gentry?'

A tenderness came over me, and I held Miriam close. She was jealous, of course, and who could blame her? I had been clumsily insensitive. How fragile were women in some ways and how strong in others. Yet if they only realized, I thought, they hold the reins completely. They create the desire and they control it. They say when and if anything'll come of it, and they can fire it up or shut it down at will. We're just leaves on their winds.

'So what else did Janet's dad have to say?' I asked as McCartney sang, *Oh, I believe in yesterday*.

'He said that Californians are doomed to repeat history because they are ignorant of it,' she said shortly.

'The man's a veritable fountain of truth.'

She didn't bother to laugh.

The next time I saw Sherry, she was telescoped several hundred feet away, but from a seat midway up the bleachers I could still see the flash of teeth when she smiled.

It was Taft's first B-team game, and the head cheerleader normally didn't show up for such unimportant contests. They saved Sherry for the A team's Friday night battles, when all the lights were on, the field blazed with color and glory, and the band pounded out the fight song.

The B team played after school in the middle of the week, and it was commonly acknowledged that they were so lousy, the JV song girls had to learn only two cheers: 'Push 'em back, push 'em back, wa-a-ay back!' and 'Block that kick, *hey*!'

I leaned back on my elbows and looked up at the hills beyond the field. Fall was different here. Everything was still blond, even the grass. Nothing brisk in the air, no falling red leaves, just this Utopian perfection of weather which didn't change, like a vacuum, somehow apart from the rest of the world. So different from autumn in New York, with the copper maples against the dark pines in Fort Tryon Park. The glittering aspens and rolling fire of the changing trees on the Columbia campus. My applications were off to four schools: Columbia, NYU, Cornell and Harvard. For me, as for the year, it was a time of waiting. But here in California, it seemed as though the wait was under amber glass, time stopped, the future held off forever. Even my old heroes, Maris and the Yankees, Namath and the Jets, seemed far away and somehow less important than they had before.

But Sherry out there, spangled in red and gold, gave the dusty track a whole new dimension of glamour. She was discreetly coaching two of the junior song girls at the same time she was leading the cheers, and the spectators obviously found the show before them on the track infinitely more interesting than the one on the field.

'Yay, Sherry!' some guy yelled from the upper rows, 'show 'em how to shake that thing!'

The crowd good-naturedly took up the chant, and for all the attention paid to the players, they might as well have been reading plays instead of running them. I was glad, for the tenth time, that I hadn't been seduced into trying out for the team. If I couldn't play with the best, then I really wasn't interested.

The next week it was the real thing. Taft played Canoga, an arch crosstown rival, and it was first team all the way. The cheerleaders were out in full regalia, the varsity took the field, and the band split the night with raucous music. The drill team carried a huge hoop covered with gold paper, splashed with 'Whomp-em!' in red letters, and a dumb-looking bull's head in the center, for Taft High Toreadors. One by one, as the crowd roared, the players crashed through the hoop and the cheerleaders jumped and twirled and screamed in ecstasy as though victory were already theirs.

Now Sherry ran onto the dirt track right in front of the stadium, followed by a train of squealing song girls. The band struck up a samba rhythm, and she began to undulate her hips to one of the crowd's favorites, 'T-Fat, T-Fat Srodaerot!' which was Taft Toreadors spelled backward. Her hair flew, her white-gloved hands pumped out the beat, and her skirt swished and twisted around her hips like a Hula Hoop, her legs kicking high.

'She's something else!' a guy next to me said, his face a blaze of eagerness.

'You got that right,' I replied, scarcely hating him at all. No doubt about it, you could feel her electricity way up in the bleacher seats. And the crowd loved her. Even if she made a mistake, started the wrong cheer, or led the girls too fast for the music, they screamed their approval.

So the game rolled on, point by point, and in between plays I was diverted by a different game going on beneath me. Under the bleacher rows, five or six kids stood and smoked. They were obviously of the greaser crowd, the ones who wore leather jackets, with or without motorcycles under them, the ones who dated girls with a lot of black mascara and teased beehive hair, those Toreadors who had little investment in who the hell won the football game.

I could occasionally catch a sentence or two floating up to me over the noise of the crowd.

'Did you see Jensen's new wheels?'

'Hot?'

'Fuckin' A.'

One of the thugs talking was casually fondling his date, running his hand down her back, cupping her hip, squeezing her waist. She stood with an arm wrapped around his neck, holding a glowing cigarette.

'That ain't gonna help him where it counts,' another girl giggled.

'Yeah? Where's that, baby?' her date asked, pushing her gently back against the stadium post. One hand went to her breast, another to her rear, and her giggles were smothered now by his mouth. Those standing around the couple merely grinned and looked away. It was strange to look through my legs down at them, as though they were unaware ant tribes.

Another subculture, I thought. A whole other clan like the Morlocks in H. G. Wells's *Time Machine*, but they're not in power and probably never will be. They don't even look like the same species of kids as the ones who hold their space in the sun. They'll grow up to be the gas station jockeys and mechanics and hairdressers of the eighties, their fates already decided now, in the darkness below the bleachers. It wasn't fair, but even then I knew it was fact.

We beat Canoga, and the dance later that week was transformed into an impromptu victory celebration. I took Miriam to a gym scarcely recognizable under festooned crepe paper, colored lights, and garish banners. She was wearing a sweater and skirt, and I was incredibly aware of her body that night.

We stood at the punch bowl appraising the dangling streamers and fake goal posts which had been erected in the corner. Stuffed football uniforms, bloodied and crumpled and made to look like the corpses of defeated rivals, had been strewn about in mock battle.

'Homey touch,' I said, grinning.

The band blared out the opening number, and Miriam shouted over the music, 'Just be glad you weren't on the decorating committee! We fought for an hour over how to kill a Cavalier!'

I led her to the floor to get in line for the stroll. 'Stro-o-ollin',' the bass singer moaned lugubriously, 'let's go stro-o-ollin' down won-der land!'

Down at the end of the line of dancers I saw Sherry come onto the dance floor with a partner. She looked like some Hollywood writer's idea of what a schoolgirl should be. She had a high gloss to her, as though she were backlit, and her tight skirt and loose sweater set, her single strand of pearls, looked more costume than clothing. Normally, school dances would have been beneath her, but since it was a victory celebration, all the cheerleaders were expected to be there.

I waited until Miriam drifted off to the rest room and then moved to the wall closest to where Sherry was dancing. Of course, I knew nobody ever cut in. It just wasn't done. In fact, there was a real chance that Sherry's date, some big jock from the defensive line, might not even understand what I wanted and decide to neuter me. But I didn't give myself time to think about it, I just wove through the dancers and tapped the guy on the shoulder.

Sherry's date turned around, blinked, and stopped moving abruptly. 'Yeah?'

Adjusting my glasses, I gave him an ingratiating grin. 'Mind if I cut in?'

'What?'

Sherry laughed then and moved quickly into my arms, useless limbs which suddenly felt completely ill-prepared to actually hold her. 'He wants to *dance* with me, Lance. Go get us some punch, okay? I'll see you in a minute.'

Lance's eyes widened in confusion and, with a deepening frown, he picked his way through the moving bodies.

'He's going to be mad,' Sherry said lightly.

'Naturally, I'll challenge him to a duel,' I said.

She giggled, a delicious warm sound amazingly close to my ear. 'So how've you been, David Levine?'

She remembered my name. I felt a surge of powerful confidence. 'Festering,' I said.

'Well, don't pick it,' she replied.

'I've been watching you,' I said.

'Why?'

'Hoping for a chance to impress you again.' I turned her around a few twirls. 'That guy anything monumental in your life?'

'Lance?' She rolled her eyes. 'Be serious.'

'So you're not going steady with anyone?'

'I don't do that.'

I saw Miriam coming out to the edge of the dance floor, looking around for me. Lance, meanwhile, had managed to fill two cups of punch and was elbowing his way back to the fray. The song would be over soon –

I stepped her through a few fancy moves, inwardly breathed a prayer of gratitude to my mother for having insisted on Mrs Meltzer's Tap and Ballroom Salon, and then said nonchalantly, 'Well, why don't we go out sometime then?'

To my great relief, she didn't collapse in mocking laughter. She only cocked her head and appraised me with a small smile. 'You and I?'

'Unless Lance would like to come along.'

71

She shook her head, laughing now. 'I don't think so, David. Do your friends call you that? Dave? Davy?'

'Dave is fine. Why not? We'll have a good time, a few laughs, where would you like to go?' My heart was thudding and my mouth was cotton, but I kept my face bland, my voice light. Can't appear to care too much.

'I'd like us to be friends,' she said firmly.

That time-honored, hackneyed demurral was about all it took to set my frenzied nerves into rebellion. I swirled her around swiftly to the closing bars of the song and, as the chorus faded, dipped her extravagantly back over my arm, her hair trailing nearly to the floor.

'This, my dear,' I said, scarcely panting, 'is how Dorothy got to Oz.'

A heavy cuff on my shoulder. I righted her and said to the glowering Lance, 'Okay, bud. She shouldn't give you any more trouble.'

A moment later I was on the dance floor with Miriam, and she said, 'You did that quite well.'

'Which?'

'That step. I could tell you've done it before.'

'They called me the Dip King in my youth.'

Go away, little girl, Steve Lawrence sang. *Go away, little girl. I'm not supposed to be alone with you –*

'I guess you're afraid you'll drop me.'

'What?'

'Well, I noticed it's the slender ones who always get dipped.'

'You're hardly a tub.'

She didn't say anything for a long while, but neither did she rest her chin on my shoulder. Finally, she said, 'I'm not going to play this game, David.'

I pulled back and looked at her quizzically. I sensed what this was leading up to, and I hoped if I forced her to spell it out, she'd retreat. But Miriam was not built for retreat.

'I know she's pretty – '

'So are you.'

'No, I'm not,' she smiled. 'I'm attractive. There's beautiful, which is fairly impossible in high school; there's pretty, which is what Sherry Gentry is; there's cute, which is useful for about twenty years at most, and then there's attractive, which is what I am. Attractive means you might get lucky and graduate to striking when you're thirty.'

'Should I be writing this down?'

'No, but you better listen, because it's going to take all my courage to say this even once.' She took a breath and went on in a rush. 'Look, I know I'm not in her league in the looks department, but I'm smarter and kinder and better for you in about a hundred ways. And I know I'm supposed to not notice you noticing her, and I'm supposed to act like I don't care so that you'll worry about losing me. I'm supposed to pretend to be busy when you call just so you don't start thinking you can take me for granted. I'm supposed to flirt with other guys to make you jealous, and if I do any crying, I'm supposed to accomplish it in private, in my lonely pillow at night.'

When you are near me like this, you're much too hard to resist, the music soared upward –

'But I'm not going to play that with you, David. I have too much respect for us both.'

I didn't have the slightest idea what I should say after such a speech.

'And I'm not going to tell you that you haven't got a chance on God's green earth of getting near her.'

'I thank you for that vote of confidence.'

'I'm sure if you're willing to worship the ground she walks on and be available for the doormat shift, she'll be happy to add you to her stringers and, no doubt, of all of them, you'll be the one she calls late at night to tell you about the troubles she's having with her college men.'

Now I felt my back begin to stiffen. 'Sounds like a great deal. A rewarding relationship,' I said, 'rich with give and take.'

'Yes. And you'd probably put up with it just long enough to ruin what we might have together, if I let you.'

The music stopped. I dropped my hands and stared at them.

She peered at my hands also. 'What?'

I looked up, bewildered. 'I'm looking for the wedding ring. It must be here somewhere. Or maybe handcuffs.'

She laughed amiably, some of the tension gone from her face. 'Don't flatter yourself, Mr Levine. You're not ready for me yet, and you never will be if you waste your whole senior year chasing some beautiful butterfly who's going to have a very short season.' She patted my cheek softly, a gesture that both charmed and chafed me. 'I do think you've got potential, though. I'd hate to see you blow it.'

'I know what I'm doing, my dear, believe me.'

'That's what Custer said.'

Bobby Vinton started up on 'There, I've Said It Again', and I put one hand over her mouth and the other around her waist. 'I've found that if I can hear the music, I can usually keep to the beat a little better. Want to try it with me? One-two-three, one-two-three – '

When I took my hand down and smiled at her, she said softly, 'Okay, but don't think I'm going to give up on you that easily. I think you should choose me.'

'You're so modest and shy, how could I not?'

But, of course, I didn't. I took Miriam out into the night, and on the way to the car she stopped and looked up at the dark sky.

'Orion is particularly clear tonight. Can you see the club there, just above Betelgeuse?'

I looked up, and she moved into my arms.

'They call him the Giant Hunter,' she whispered.

I kissed her gently, folding her closer. There was something incredibly soft and vulnerable about Miriam's lips, as though they went deeper into her mouth than some girls'. With a feeling that I could just keep applying pressure and she would continue to yield, I finally pulled myself out of that dark fragrant warmth and opened my eyes.

I had the uneasy sense that hers had never been closed. I closed my eyes again, moved my mouth to her neck and one hand to the bottom of her breast. I could feel the line of her bra band and the rise and fall of her rib cage under her blouse and, though I knew it was a mistake, my hand moved up of its own volition and cupped her breast gently. A low moan, almost a hum, came from her throat.

A snarling crunch of gravel behind us, a slash of headlights, and a car pulled into the parking lot. We wrenched away, and she moved quickly to her door. Over the top of the car she said, 'David, you're a lucky guy, you know that?'

For the second time that evening I didn't know what to say.

'Things have always come so easy for you.'

'Why do you say that?' I asked, suddenly irritated. 'What makes you think any of this is easy?'

'Isn't it?'

'Hell, no.' I was being short with her, I knew, but, dammit, this whole thing was getting out of hand. Somewhere I'd lost control, and where did she get off talking to me like some kind of older and wiser Dear Abby?

'Well, at least you get to do the choosing.'

'Is that so? You could have fooled me.'

She smiled brightly. 'If you think it's tough now, wait a few years. When it counts.' Despite the upturned mouth, her eyes, in the streetlamp, were hooded and shadowed, somehow sad. She opened her door, got in, and immediately directed the conversation to three topics at once, all of them safe, nondirectional, and entertaining.

Even as she spoke, my mind wandered.

Within a week I had devised my plan. More than a plan, a masterstroke stratagem, a systematic machination to accomplish one simple goal: the capture of Sherry Gentry. The way I pictured it, the campaign began, naturally, with the diffident approach, moved into fawning compliments, and developed further when I asked her to dance and then took a giant step forward when I asked her to go out with me.

Of course she'd say no the first time, I thought triumphantly, as she had. And she will no doubt turn me down the second time, maybe even the third time as well. But each time I ask and she refuses, I get a little closer. She gets a little more obligated, a bit nearer to capitulation. If nothing else, she's got to admire my determination and endurance, and as Mother says, it takes two to tangle.

I didn't think much past her acceptance. Since I couldn't quite picture myself actually out on a date with Sherry Gentry, I didn't imagine the scenario past the yes. The getting of the yes was all that mattered to me.

And to that end I began the second campaign to get what I also would need should I succeed in the yes: a car. Not just the family car, mind you, not a car I'd have to stand in line for, but a real honest-to-God set of wheels of my own, preferably with a little pizzazz to them.

Fill 'er up, I thought, and then pictured myself turning down the radio a tad, sneaking a quick glance in the

76

rearview mirror, and turning to Sherry in the passenger seat with a knowing smile . . .

Check under that hood for you tonight, sir? The Man with the Star would say, Want me to check the tires too?

Ah, yes. A Corvette Stingray would be nice. A 327-cubic-inch fuel-injected V-8, four on the floor, with shark gills on the side and lines that slay at a glance. Only about four grand. And about as much chance of that as St Peter asking Lenny Bruce to entertain for the new recruits.

Or maybe a Camaro convertible. With triple-deuce carbs, Positraction, glass packs, and street slicks. Uh-huh. And then I could get a black leather jacket, rumble through Bob's Big Boy, staring at women through a pair of shades. Once again, not even in the realm of died-and-gone-to-heaven possibilities.

Frankly, I'd have settled for a used Rambler with a weeny four-cylinder in a color only the aunts would pick. Anything, so long as it was mine.

And so I began to drop hints, meaning to work from subtle up to extravagant, that what every boy needed was not a dog, but a car. Or a loan for a car. But what I never expected, had never guessed, was the prospect of what actually was offered.

On 3 December, a glorious Saturday (I will remember the date for the rest of my natural life), my father came to me with negligible ceremony and said, 'Your mother and I have been talking. It's pretty hard to live in California without transportation, we know. And you've always been a responsible individual, David. Soon you'll be off to college and on your own.'

I held my breath, wondering if seventeen-year-old heart attacks were within the range of statistical possibilities.

'It's not much, of course, in the way of style, but it's dependable,' he was saying. 'And, of course, insurance should be reasonable. You'd have to pay for that yourself.'

'I would?' I was opening and closing my mouth like an excited carp.

'Sure,' my father continued. 'You couldn't expect us to both hand the wagon over to you and also maintain its upkeep, could you?'

'You're *giving* me the car?'

My father slowly smiled. 'On the condition that you take good care of it. And yourself.'

Incredible. The family station wagon. Used only by my mother for shopping forays, a car with a decent radio, hardly any dings, gulped gas like a swine, of course, but at least the tires were good and omichrist, the back folded down into almost a bed. With mattresses already there from camping trips, no less! I could scarcely contain myself.

I tried for a mellow stance. 'Dad, that's great. Really.' And then I couldn't suppress it. 'Wow!'

'We thought you'd be pleased.' My father grinned. 'Your mother has been wanting a new car, and I thought I'd surprise her for the holidays with a new Thunderbird.'

Doubly incredible. Not only was I to have the mobile bed, but there was also going to be a new T-bird somewhat within reach.

'That's terrific,' I said dazedly. 'Can I have it painted?'

'The wagon?' My father frowned. 'You don't like the color?'

I felt like a piker complaining, and I wouldn't have, not for the world, but the wagon was about the color of the mold around the inside of the locker room shower. 'Well, it's not too bad, I guess, but something in a dark blue would be great.' Like just a little darker than a certain well-known MG.

'I suppose that would be all right,' Rabbi Levine said judiciously. 'So long as you pay for it yourself.'

As I leapt to my feet to go inspect my new property, my father called out, 'For a while, son, I want you to tell your mother or me whenever you want to use it. You may consider it yours, but the privilege to drive it is ours to give.'

'Okay!' I threw over my shoulder, scarcely noticing the small fence which just went up around what seemed to be a limitless horizon.

It sat out in the driveway, waiting. My mother had taken it to be washed and waxed, and the wagon looked quite presentable, even in its current disguise as a family car.

Now all those hours each summer sweating away at jobs like grocery bagger and dry cleaner counterman seemed worthwhile. In fact, I knew that they would glow in my memory forever, ignominious degradations though they were, because of what they had harvested: money to fix up the wagon.

I walked around it in a careful inspection. New paint, some new wire wheels, a leather band around the steering wheel, would really spiff it up. A cassette player, seat cushions, new rugs, and maybe even pinstripes.

And then I contemplated the best of all – the backseat. The seats were folded down, layered with denim-covered mattresses which we'd used on the last family camping trip to the Tetons, leaving almost ten feet of cushioned space.

I closed my eyes in reverie. There were a few things you couldn't do on such a backseat, I thought, even on acreage like this. Couldn't play tennis. Couldn't keep cattle. Probably couldn't swim laps, either. But just about every other possibility was within the realm. I thought of Joe Spilling and Bonnie Finkle and what happened to them in a backseat. They had been making out on the only makeout road in all of Riverdale, the hill known as High Hill, humping away like two hamsters, when all of a sudden something snapped, and he was stuck inside her like a dog. The ambulance crew had to load them on the same stretcher.

I'd never met Joe and Bonnie, of course, nor did I know anyone else who had, but they were like Davy Crockett and Sacajawea, trailblazers who went where no teenagers had gone before.

I remembered, too, the last and only time I'd been to the drive-in, double-dating with a friend in a Volkswagen. Janie Rasmussen brushed the back of her wrist against my jeans zipper in a way that I will never believe was inadvertent, and there wasn't a damn thing I could do about it, what with the other two up front and all of three feet to maneuver in on sticky vinyl seats.

But this! Add a small shelf for drinks along one wall, maybe a new speaker back there, curtains on the side windows. A guy could live in it – and certainly love in it. Assuming I could slip these home improvements past my parents.

But wasn't that what a car was for, after all? Freedom. The freedom to create an entirely new personality, fast-moving and forever changing both direction and view, freedom to run the highways over and over until you knew them so well, you could drive with a few fingers, never braking around curves. Like a riverman runs a river, you could drive these flawless hot concrete rapids, every day making speed more a part of you.

I wanted to sleep out in the wagon. I wanted to take every meal behind the wheel, wanted to give it a private, secret name, wanted to be so much within its cradling armrests that it would begin to *smell* like me. And when Sherry Gentry rode beside me, she would know, instinc-

80

tively, and with no other evidence necessary, that I was a man with boundless horizons.

A man on the move.

I wasn't the only one moving that year. All around me things were changing faster than I could keep score. California itself was a moving panorama of everything that was overlarge, overloud, and overdone. Now that I'm older, I can sort it out, but at seventeen I had never felt so small and pale in my life.

California was busy inventing the tract house, the barbecue, the drive-in, the supermarket, house trailers, the suntan, blondes, and the bare midriff. We were making more money and leading the nation in suicides, divorces, and crime. We bought more clothes, more frozen foods, foreign cars, and made fewer babies, but we had more sex, drank more wine, paid more taxes, and took more vacations. In short, Californians were treating life like one big Mexican *piñata*: we took a stick to it and beat it till the last goodies fell out.

Californians liked to say that California *was* America – only more so. Even the state motto trumpeted arrogance: 'Eureka – I have found it!' We called Los Angeles Smogville, Off-Ramp City, the First City to Say the Hell with It, a place where the automobile was treated like the cow in India. 'You may be too much for Newark, baby, but you ain't enough for LA.' And this is tomorrow already in California, so keep movin', kid, your seat is up front.

There was one thing you could say about California back then, though, and that was it had a sense of humor. It took a certain rollicking glee to produce men like Sam Yorty and Ronald Reagan. To plant seventy-six thousand dollars worth of plastic trees and flowers along a major street to save water bills. To come up with the idea that the way to ease freeway gridlock was to shut down one lane during the rush hour. After all, the California Civil Code, Section 1597, put it down in black and white: 'Everything is decreed possible except that which is impossible in the nature of things.'

We were mad and many times mad back then, but we knew how to have a good laugh. And at no other time did I see more evidence of it than on the morning when the California earth began to jiggle like Santa Claus's Jell-O belly.

It was just dawn, and I was sound asleep, not conscious of dreaming. There wasn't even a warning noise or rumble of thunder or anything else that usually preceded disasters. I was simply and precisely thrown out of bed right onto one elbow.

While I lay there for an instant, stunned and wondering who shoved me, the lamp on the table next to my bed fell on my shoulder. I groped for my glasses, now aware that the floor itself was pitching and heaving like the bouncing bed I had just vacated.

Noise down the hall, shouts from my brother, I could hear my mother's call, high and hysterical. I stood up and staggered to the bedroom door, wrenching it open, one part of my mind still wondering in bewilderment who had moved my glasses which I always left right by the bed on my dresser, the better to see when anything disastrous might happen, and now it had, and where were they? The carpet seemed to crawl under my bare feet like a hundred soft bristling beetles, and I looked back once, over my aching shoulder, to see the actual walls of my room rippling and bulging gently inward toward me.

Now I felt sharp panic, and I began to hurry down the hall, my mother and father calling me, both of them in their nightclothes, their hair standing up every which way, but the floor under my feet was shifting, and I was thrown back and forth, my hands out to stop myself, hitting first one side of the hallway and then the other as in a crazy funhouse game. Now the noise was deafening, a growing roaring rattling groan that seemed to come from the air rather than from the earth. My brother was somehow behind me, he fell against my legs once, scrambled to his feet, and almost took us both down. My father reached out and grabbed my shoulder, shouting, 'Get out! Get out!' and the four of us stumbled to the front door. A loud hissing smash made us stop momentarily and turn. The water from the pool, sloshed back and forth violently, had suddenly escaped its concrete lips, crashed through the sliding glass doors, and was washing through the living room toward us.

My father yanked open the front door and pushed us through, out into the yard. 'Lie flat!' my mother cried, falling facedown on the driveway. 'Avrom, get down!'

Avrom was standing gape-mouthed and pale, shivering as violently as the trees to the right of the house. My father clapped him hard on the back, shoved him down, and the whole family lay almost on top of each other, bellies down on the concrete, hands over our heads and screeching blindly.

In seconds, the earth slowed its jolts, its rhythmic waves and shivers, and there was a long moment of silence. I became aware of the soothing warmth of the asphalt under my stomach. I lifted my head. Pool water had darkened most of the driveway, a steady trickle now coursed down to the street, rapidly diminishing.

'Do you know where my glasses are?' I asked my mother, my voice bewildered.

My mother raised her head, and I could see streaks of tears, small gravel from the driveway embedded in one cheek. 'In the middle of an earthquake, you ask me this?'

'Not in the middle – ' I started to say, but my little brother cut me off.

'An earthquake!' Avrom shouted. 'We had an earthquake!'

Now I felt some of the adrenaline, too, an almost guilty excitement. An earthquake. We'd heard about them for so long, and finally, here it was.

'Everyone is okay?' my father asked, peering at each of us closely, helping my mother to stand. 'I think we should go back inside, falling wires or something might be dangerous.'

'Better than falling walls,' my mother said firmly. 'You go in, Daniel, and bring out clothes, blankets for the boys. Look for David's glasses, they're probably by the bed someplace. We are staying out here, where we can at least see what is coming.'

My father shrugged, still half in shock himself, and started toward the house, now incredibly still and solid-looking as ever.

I stood and looked around. All up and down the street, neighbors were out of their houses, in various stages of undress, standing and clasping their hands, hollering across to one another, rushing about in aimless fear. From a great distance I heard screaming which suddenly stopped, as though a hysterical woman was slapped or clasped or otherwise restrained. A violent wave of nausea clutched me without warning, and I staggered to a small grassy patch by the lantana bushes and vomited up sour bile.

'Wow,' Avrom was saying over and over. 'Wow, that must have been a big one, how big do you think it was, Mama? Do you think the pool is cracked? Will the phones work? Will we have to go to school?'

'You are all right, David?' she called to me. 'Sit down here beside me and try to calm down.'

84

I stumbled weakly back to her and sat, leaning up against her knees. No wires down in the street that I could see, two trees down in yards, shattered glass in the Robsons' grass, and the Evans' driveway, the round one that curved off so their big trailer could park next to the electrical outlet, was cracked, the concrete jutting up at a crazy angle.

Mr Evans came from under the trailer at that moment, wriggling out on his back. He looked over at us and waved jocularly. 'No damage! She rode it out!'

My mother waved weakly. 'Your wife is okay?' she called out of courtesy.

'Oh yeah, oh yeah,' he laughed loudly. 'She's born and bred here, you know. Used to it! She calls herself the Queen of Rock and Roll!'

I shook my head, closed my eyes in exhaustion, and eased back down to the warm concrete again. No doubt about it, mad and many times mad.

The reports began to flood in over the radio, and we spent the day cleaning up the mess and feeling fortunate when we heard the damage others had survived. An entire freeway offramp had collapsed; a dam had cracked, sending thousands refugeeing in panic. A whole hospital out in Simi had fallen over, and live wires, toppled trees, and unsettled nerves were definitely the order of the day. It had been a 7.6 on the Richter scale, that crazy barometer of earth movement that Californians could quote as financiers quoted the stock market.

I was surprised that most people, deejays, callers-in, neighbors, almost everyone I spoke with or listened to, took the event with distinct poise and a rather gallant levity. Citizens went out and cleaned up one another's broken glass; restaurants stayed open, offering free coffee, cookies, and juice for shaky hands; lovers called in, leaving messages for long-lost friends, saying they didn't want another day to go by without making contact.

And by the end of the day the earthquake itself had been transformed into a source of entertainment. There were fewer deaths than everybody figured, so the relief grew into gaiety. I sensed that people actually *liked* to be reminded that despite all their scurryings, dealings, and finaglings, the Republican party wasn't running everything. Or the Democratic party, either.

What struck me most of all was the earthquake's total unpredictability. No signs at all, though every seer and prophet stepped forward to a microphone to claim the exact opposite. There were no sudden changes in the barometer, no rising winds, no threatening clouds – just a sudden and total slippage of reality. And incredibly enough, lots of people seemed to appreciate that aspect of the earthquake most of all.

People asked one another over and over, 'Were you afraid?'

The answers were always extreme. Either 'God, I thought I was having a heart attack!' or 'No, not really. I just hung on and rode it out.'

Of course, the present became history instantly. Over at CalTech, Kent Clark, Elliott Davis, and a bunch of science students put together a ditty that flooded the airwaves in tidal intervals, and Jack Smith put it in his *Los Angeles Times* column, verbatim.

Charley Richter made a scale for calibrating earthquakes
Gives a true and lucid reading every time the earth shakes
Increments are exponential, numbers 0 to nine
When the first shock hit the seismo, everything worked out
    fine
It measured
One two on the Richter scale, a shabby little shiver
One two on the Richter scale, a queasy little quiver

And the song went on to lead listeners right up the scale through some of the big ones of the past. The Long Beach quake:

Nineteen hundred thirty-three and Long Beach rocked and rumbled
Schoolhouse walls and crockery and oil derricks tumbled
Hollywood got hit but good, it even shook the stars
Shattered glass and spilled martinis on a hundred bars,
It measured six three on the Richter scale . . .

Then the Tehachapi quake:

Came the turn of County Kern, the mountains lurched and trembled,
Bakersfield, which jerked and reeled, was almost disassembled
It measured
Seven eight on the Richter scale, it fractured rails and melons
Seven eight on the Richter scale, it fractured female felons

The Alaska quake:

Eight five on the Richter scale, it loosened kelp and corals
Eight five on the Richter scale, it loosened faith and morals

Finally, the Big One in the near future:

Someday pretty soon we fear our many faults will fail us
Slide and slip and rip and dip and all at once assail us
Seismic jolts like lightning bolts will flatten us that day
When the concrete settles down, geologists will say
It measured eight nine on the Richter scale . . .

And people hummed it for weeks.

The next day I drove the wagon past Sherry's house to see if it was damaged. I didn't expect to see her; I just wanted to check to be sure she was okay. I figured, if there were no major cracks or gaping rifts in the earth, she probably didn't fall in.

I pulled the car up to the curb opposite her house and turned down the radio. I just sat for a long moment, staring.

Her address in the phone book hadn't prepared me for where she lived. Sherry Gentry's house seemed to be spun entirely out of fairy frosting. With no visible brick, stone, and barely any wood, the house looked as though it were held together with gossamer string, white and piled shining in the sun. Two high plaster turrets jutted up under tall skinny palms; black tracery of wrought iron wrapped around wide balconies and up the white steps. Two large windows fronted the street, and I could see a gleaming chandelier with candle bulbs lit in the entry, even in the daylight. Very few flowers, no lawn to speak of, the house was bordered by patterned pathways of colored gravel and spiny cacti. One huge barrel cactus sprawled on the edge of the driveway like a feisty guard dog. In wine barrels, trailing Technicolor ranunculus spilled over the edges, but since they never touched the ground, the effect was one of impermanence, as though the house could be picked up or floated off at the slightest whim.

Suddenly, to my alarm, the front door to this castle opened. I could almost imagine the cool, dark air spilling out into the heat, and I squinted to see who might be coming out, my hands on the keys, ready to drive off.

Sherry Gentry peered at me and then lifted her hand in a wave.

My hell, I thought frantically, now she thinks I've got nothing better to do than bird-dog her house.

She glanced back over her shoulder, hesitated an instant, and then closed the door. Before I could decide what to do or say, she was skipping down the steps toward me, her long legs almost bare in the shortest shorts I'd seen outside the pages of *Playboy*.

'Hi,' she said, coming over to the car.

Thank God I put the pinstripes on it and the backseats up, I thought. 'Hi!' Much too eager. I turned up the radio slightly and leaned down, the better to see her. 'I was just driving by. Thought I'd check to see if you slid off the face of the earth.' I looked past her to the house. 'I don't see any cracks.'

She leaned against the car door, her arms crossed under her breasts. 'The pool flooded the rec room, and some china fell, is all. Did you hear what happened to Debbie Highley's house? Fell right into the pool! It was on this hill, and the whole thing slid right away. She's okay, but her little sister's got a broken arm. Do you believe it?'

I offered the required 'Incredible.'

'Was your house okay?'

'One escaped pool, some broken glass, nothing too outrageous.'

'Nobody hurt?'

'Just my mother's feelings.'

She smiled. 'Oh, mine too. She took to her bed. That's the way my mother tells my aunt back east, "I took to my bed." Got a lot of mileage out of it. Want to come in?'

I felt a quick shot of adrenaline at the back of my knees. 'Sure,' I said, glancing at my watch. 'But just for a minute. I've got stuff to do.'

'Is this your car?' she asked, glancing smoothly over the dark blue paint job.

'Yeah, all mine. I took her home from the pound and saved her from certain death.'

She ran her finger over a pinstripe. 'She's cute.' She bent down lower and inspected the potentially vast expanse of mattressed backseat, complete with speaker,

89

drink shelf, and Kleenex holder. 'But you better get her spayed.' She grinned at her own joke. 'Come on in.'

I followed her up the steps into the fairy castle, feeling slightly overwhelmed at so much to take in so quickly. Massive oil paintings covered the high walls, thickly spread with bright colors. The furniture was brazenly impractical white, and the carpeting was thick and pale and seductive. The textures and the softness, the effect of light everywhere, made me want to be left alone in the room so that I could run my bare hands over everything, take off my shoes, and wade barefoot through the rugs. But before me Sherry strolled through the house grace-fully, and the movement of her hips was the most compel-ling diversion of all.

Through the dining room – 'that's where the china fell out of the cabinet' – the game room – 'the water came all the way up the door here' – passing through the gleaming kitchen – 'you want a Coke? I'll have Mags bring it out' – and through two sliding glass doors to a spreading blue sea of a pool.

The instant I sat down next to the pool I was filled with a sense of serenity the likes of which I could scarcely remember. Tall pines flanked one edge of the long sinuous sweep of blue water, shading the shallow end. Cedar decking wrapped around the deep end, with small clever steps leading to the rocks that held the diving board. It was as though we'd stumbled on this private lake in the woods, and no one was around for miles.

Sherry walked over to the far side and pointed under the diving board. 'See? It's a wonder the water didn't all drain out. My father says the pressure of the earth holds it in.'

Sure enough, there was a zigzagged black crack that ran halfway down the pool side, like a single wrinkle on a smooth face. A plump Mexican maid with an enormous white-aproned bosom came out of the sliding glass doors, bearing a large tray with Coke, ice, striped straws, and sliced lime. Even a bowl of chips and a portable phone which she plugged into a hidden receptacle in the table between us. She set down her burden, grinned at me, and silently bounced away.

The phone rang immediately. I expected Sherry to pick it up, but she just lay back on the chaise longue, reaching idly for the glass and the ice. It rang eight times and finally lapsed into silence.

'Must not be important,' she said.

'Why didn't you get it?'

'I think that's rude, when you have a guest.' She handed me a glass and poured. 'Would you like a lime?'

The glasses were frosted. And the ice wasn't just your typical cubes, but crushed. 'Sure,' I said, watching to see how she squeezed the lime and then let it float casually on the top of her drink. 'So I guess you've been in earthquakes before.'

'Well, I've lived through a seven. This one was fairly hairy, though. I think the epicenter was closer. You know what? You're a pretty good dancer.'

I was completely taken off guard, but there was something about the way her mind moved, skipping like a stone across water from one thing to another, sending out cross-lapped ripples, that I liked. It seemed so alive. 'Well,' I said in my best John Wayne, 'when I dip 'em, missy, they know they've been dipped.'

She put a corn chip in her mouth, but she didn't chew. Simply held it, sucking gently at the salt.

'We should do it again sometime,' I ventured casually. 'Maybe go into the City and be dancing fools.' Everybody called Hollywood the City, just as everything beyond was the Valley. Except for the Strip, which was never called anything else and was generally out of bounds unless you had fake ID.

Her eyes were lowered as she sipped her Coke, perfect lips pursed around the striped straw. 'Like a date?' she finally asked.

'More like a mission.' The Persian grinned amiably at that and jumped from my chair to the decking. Purring loudly, it batted at my leg which was nervously jittering despite my attempts to hold it still.

Sherry's eyes glimmered, but she kept her mouth firm.

'To find out who put the bop in the bop-she-bop-she-bop,' I finished, tapping my glass to the beat. 'Want to?'

'Well, I don't know – '

God, she's going to play this for all it's worth, I groaned inwardly. And I don't even care. The harder she makes it, the more it'll mean, the more I'll prove by hanging in there. This is only the second time I've asked her, and I can do this a dozen times. She can't hold out forever. But I'm not going to beg. David Levine doesn't need pity. 'Anyplace you want to go, anything you want to do.'

The expression on her face changed suddenly from soft dreamy consideration to alert animation as she watched something over my shoulder. I turned in time to see a man coming toward us, tall and blocking out the sun, almost as blond as Sherry.

'Hi, honey,' a voice said, distinctly parental. 'I didn't know you had company.'

'Daddy,' she said with easy affection, 'this is David, a new friend from school. His pool didn't crack.'

I got to my feet quickly and held out my hand. 'Mr Gentry. We moved in a few blocks over. Your daughter graciously extended me a moment in the shade and a cold Coke.' I glanced at Sherry, who watched her father's eyes – eyes laid like blue Easter eggs in a basket of squint lines. This is the one to win, I thought, and smiled as sincerely as I knew how.

Mr Gentry shook hands as though it were a karate maneuver. He was obviously amused at my poise. He took in my shirt, my pants, my shoes, and finally my curly hair. His own hair was as lankly youthful as any surfer's at Malibu.

'Have any major damage?' he asked politely. It was the standard conversation opening this week.

'Nothing that insurance didn't cover. Unless you count my mother's ten new gray hairs.' Yes, we have something in common, sir, we each have a woman in the house given to drama. Nothing to build a relationship on, of course, but it's a start –

'So you're in Sherry's class?'

'Not by a mile, sir.'

Now her father's smile was genuine. He nodded slightly, acknowledging the victory.

'But we're in the same year.'

To my surprise, he pulled up another chaise and sat down right next to us, reaching for the bowl of chips. 'So you're going to college soon? Or do you have a job?'

'Oh, I'm definitely going. I haven't made the decision about *where* yet, but the *whether* certainly is solid.' I grinned. 'That one was made when I was in the womb, I think.' And that will be the last reference you make, however subtle, to *any* part of the female anatomy, I swore internally.

'So what do you think of California, David? You're a newcomer, right?' He stretched expansively and patted Sherry absently on the thigh. 'Hollywood. Movie stars. Sun and sand and bullshit.'

I tensed, glancing at Sherry quickly for a cue. But she giggled, evidently used to the line.

'Bullshit capital of the world. And I should know, I'm

a major stockholder in bullshit production.' He paused and took a long swig of his drink. 'I have cornered the market on the world supply.'

I was unsure of the proper response. I finally attempted, 'Is that so?' Safe enough.

'Did my daughter tell you what I do? To keep all this' – he gestured to the pool, the pines, the house beyond – 'in Cokes and chips? I make false fronts. Backings. I've got a company that turns them out like flapjacks. You see a picture where the hero's riding across the range, right? Into the sunset. And behind him is a major mountain and trees and sage and a sky wide as God.' He smiled. 'That's me. I paint that stuff. Well, anyway, I used to. Now I've got crews that paint these things for me and I lease them to the studios.' He laughed suddenly. 'So I don't even sell bullshit, I rent it.'

'Obviously,' I murmured, glancing over the pool, the house, and the gardens, 'the gods are not angry with you.'

Sherry slapped her father lightly on the shoulder. 'Daddy, you're terrible. Don't tease him like this.'

I was distinctly disappointed. It wasn't that her remark was inadequate, not even that it was unsubtle. But that it wasn't *necessary*.

'Ah hell,' Mr Gentry said, 'I used to think of it as dreams. I painted mirages, backdrops for fantasies. But as the years go on, you get a little tired of faking reality, you know?'

I nodded solemnly. 'Still, it looks like fulfilling fantasies has its rewards.'

'Doesn't it always? But after a while you want more substance in your life. So I'm thinking of getting out of the business. Selling the whole thing and moving on to the next slide.'

I was flattered, of course, but I couldn't help wondering

why this father was unloading his soul to a seventeen-year-old stranger. Fathers – especially those of girls – were tough to fathom. My own hardly fit the stereotype of Ward Cleaver, Fred MacMurray, or Ozzie Nelson, but I doubt he'd have confided to Jim Foote, while out by our pool, his darkest dreams and fears and failings. Maybe this guy was just desperate for a male ear.

My favorite of all the paternal icons was Jim Anderson. He was a benevolent king who dispensed wisdom and authority to Princess, Kitten, and Bud with geniality and a genuine WASP ease. He truly *did* know best, a flawless fatherly fairy tale which I never saw mirrored in my own household or in any other.

But then, neither was Mr Gentry like most fathers I'd known. Now he was saying, 'So what does your father do?'

This was about the longest conversation I'd ever had with a girl's father, and this final question was the capper. The moment I began to formulate my answer, I knew that further progress with Sherry Gentry was probably doomed. No way this shiksa's keeper of the castle was going to let her loose into the arms of an alien marauder with black curly hair, a bigger-than-Californian nose and a rabbi for a father. But neither was I completely willing to sell my soul for a date.

'He's a rabbi,' I said calmly. 'Reform.' As though that might help somewhere in the tally-up process.

'Really?' Mr Gentry said politely. 'How interesting. You know, I have a lot of friends who are Jewish.'

Uh-huh.

'And as a matter of fact, if I could accept any institutionalized religion at all, it'd probably be Judaism.'

The sun seemed suddenly brighter.

'Maybe I'll give him a call sometime. Invite myself to your temple for a look-see.'

The birds were caroling merrily and the world was a wonderful place. 'I'm sure he'd welcome you with open arms,' I said. 'He's a great debater. Loves to seduce new converts.' I could scarcely contain my grin. I actually said 'seduce' to a girl's father.

'Well, I don't know if I can be seduced,' Mr Gentry said amiably, 'but I can certainly be had.'

On that amazing note, another shadow fell across my shoulder and a woman's voice said, 'Well, here you all are. I thought the place was deserted.'

I turned to see a lovely girl – woman, actually – older than Sherry by maybe five years, but obviously related.

'Hi, honey,' Mr Gentry said, patting the empty chair next to him, 'come and join us. This is Sherry's sister, Kim,' he said to me. 'Three years apart, but they could be twins, right?'

No, I wanted to say, not in the least. Kim didn't have nearly the freshness, the sense that all things were still possible, untried, and new about her that Sherry had. They were both blond, tan, pretty, slender, with small sharp noses and perfect lips, and that's all I could see alike.

'I'd have to take a longer look,' I said. 'Or at least, closer.'

To my relief, all of them laughed.

'Your mom's not in the house?' Mr Gentry asked his oldest daughter.

'Oh, yeah, but she's in her room reading, and the do not disturb sign's out.'

At my curious glance Sherry said, 'Mom agrees with Virginia Woolf that every woman should have a room of her own. So she puts out this little plaque on the door when we're not supposed to bother her.'

I tried to picture Myra Levine cloistered in a room of her own with a no trespassing sign barring the way, but it wouldn't focus. No way she could stand to be left out of what might be going on someplace else.

'Well, you could have knocked if it was important,' Mr Gentry said mildly. 'You know she's always available to you girls when you need her.'

'Right,' Kim said dryly. 'We know that, don't we, Sherry?'

Sherry shrugged and looked away. 'She'll come out when she's ready.'

'Or when *you* need her,' Kim said to her father.

Mr Gentry glanced at me, obviously uncomfortable with the turn the conversation had taken. I felt sorry for him. 'When *my* mom wants to be alone, she just starts cleaning house. It's miraculous how quickly my brother and I disappear,' I said.

Mr Gentry smiled. 'You've got just the one brother, then?'

'Sometimes it seems like more than one brother, but I have it on good authority that he's my only sibling.'

'That's a shame you don't have any sisters. Girls can be quite interesting.'

I opened my hands expansively. 'You won't get an argument from me on that one.' I glanced at Sherry and saw that she was watching me closely, as though she knew exactly what I was trying to do. Her eyes had a way of seeing into mine, without revealing her own, somehow, as though she wore a veil which she could drop at will.

We made idle conversation back and forth, and when Mr Gentry and Kim finally wandered off, I began to relax again. I noticed that Sherry seemed more receptive to me as well. 'So what do you think?' I asked as though the last twenty minutes of conversation were no more than a blip on the screen. 'Let's pick a Saturday night and shake it up. I promise not to step on your blue suede shoes.'

'I'm busy next Saturday.'

'Of course you are.'

'And the Saturday after that.'

'I knew that. How about February eighth?'

'That's over two months away,' she giggled. 'Why then?'

'Because it's Fred Astaire's birthday. Normally, we just exchange cards, he and I, but since he's going to be sixty-five, I think it calls for a rather grander gesture, and I can think of no one I'd rather gesture grandly with than you.'

'Okay,' she said, almost shyly. 'I guess that'll be all right.'

I leaned a little closer and whispered, 'Will you really make me wait that long?'

She drew back, suddenly brisk. 'Okay. I'm free four weeks from tomorrow, but you better call me the night before, just to make sure.'

I got up to go. 'I shall have my secretary make a note of it.' To my satisfaction, I noticed that the Persian had to trot to keep up.

On the way home I replayed the conversations, all of them, over and over again in my mind. Looking back, I couldn't believe my bravado. Where did that come from? From what magical spring of brazen wit did it all bubble? I could see respect on Gentry's face. The man obviously hadn't had a genuine conversation with anybody under the age of eighteen before. Or if he had attempted to talk with one of Sherry's no-necks, the guy must have had the brains of a Sen-Sen. Likely, she didn't pick them for their vocabulary.

Yet, she responded well to humor. Genuinely seemed to appreciate my efforts to make her smile. No doubt about it, I made a hit. I'll bet that if her dad hadn't come out there, if I hadn't had a chance to shine before his scrutiny, it would have been at least another three tries before she said yes.

And what a yes. Call me the night before. God knows, the girl's not lacking for gumption. And what was all that about her old man's business ventures, the cornering-the-crap fusillade he tossed in my lap. Wonder what he expected me to say? Wonder who he was really talking to?

Because the fact is, I just lucked into it, really. Got off a couple of quick ones, a few semi-droll replies, and snagged her promise before she could recover her balance. We had a date in one month. And I wasn't going to give her a chance to back out.

One of the quickest ways I knew to insure that Sherry Gentry would not be accompanying me across the street, much less anyplace else, was to spread the news around to my friends. Therefore, the next time I was in the locker room suiting up for PE, I had to all but stuff my jock in my mouth to keep from screaming my triumph.

Critter, the tall kid with acne who had the locker under me, happened to make it all the tougher by bringing up her name. Now, Critter rarely dated anybody but Marsha Swipe, because most women were repulsed by the angry pustules that cratered his face. Marsha had her own cross to bear, though: the less sensitive of Critter's teammates referred to her as 'Swipe the Slag' or 'Combine', because they said she had a face that looked like it had been plowed.

But Critter was not above worshipping from afar, and he happened to mention that day that he'd seen Sherry Gentry putting on her lipstick at her locker. 'Man, that woman could put a liplock on me any day,' he sighed.

'Right, Pizza Face, and catch leprosy,' somebody said.

It was all I could do not to say quite casually, 'Well, I'll tell her how you feel, Critter, when I take her out next month.' But I restrained myself. I remembered, after all, what happened the time Bradley came in and announced he had a new girlfriend. Bradley was the water boy, big enough to play but spazzy. A nice guy, but you got the impression he couldn't pound nails into a snowbank. Nevertheless, he was dating this semi-cute freshman, and he couldn't keep it to himself.

One of the linemen walked over, naked and scratching his groin. 'Oh yeah. Redhead,' he said. 'Decent hooters. I did her and so did my dog. Give her our best.'

And all Bradley could do was stand there grinning desperately like a dumb fuck and take a halfhearted swipe at the guy's bare ass with his towel.

What he should have said was 'Hey, man, what's that thing you've got there? Oh, yeah. For a minute it looked like a dick, only smaller. Guess that's why you had to ask your dog to give you a hand.'

He'd have been hit so hard, they'd have arrested him in Canoga for speeding, but he'd have been triumphant.

No, the last thing I wanted was for word to get out that Sherry Gentry had allowed she might actually date me. In fact, in that arena of sweaty socks and wet feet and jokes about women – not the whole woman, mind you, but just some of her more pertinent parts – I didn't even want her name mentioned at all.

Now, you might well ask, where was Miriam all this time? I'm not proud to admit this, but she was there all along. I still went out with her at least once a weekend; sometimes I'd see her on Sunday afternoon as well. But it's as though she were background music and Sherry Gentry was singing solo lead. I didn't want to give Miriam up, but I didn't want to get so close to her that I'd have to forsake the hope of what might be coming around the corner. And if she knew of my distraction, she never spoke it aloud. At least not then.

So for a month I made sure that Sherry didn't forget

her promise. But I didn't call her a lot or trail after her at school. I remembered this guy, some poor drool in tenth grade who was hot for a girl in his homeroom, and he called her up, talked to her for an hour each night or more, until she finally pulled me aside, one of his close friends, to beg, 'Please tell Stan not to call me so often. I mean, cripes, I can't even wash my hair in peace without the phone rings and my dad's getting really ticked. Can you sort of advise him nicely to lay off for a while?'

I had so advised, and I never forgot my own counsel. I told Stanley: 'Listen, did you ever see two dogs getting ready to do it? The bitch runs around like crazy, keeping just a length ahead of the male, see, and he's chasing her like mad and he's wheezing and panting and wiping the sweat out of his eyes, and always she keeps just ahead of him, looking back over her shoulder and laughing at him. Until finally he can't take another step. I mean, if the canine equivalent of Marilyn Monroe came over and licked his ear, he'd be too tired to get it up, right? But the bitch sees him slowing. Then she finally looks back and he's stopped. What does she do? She whirls around so fast it makes her ears flap, and runs back to his side, nosing him to get on with it. If he's got any strength left at all, he staggers to his feet then, and she stands there, taking it like she planned it that way all along.'

'Yeah?' Stanley said.

'Yeah. Don't call Marge so much, man. She told me to tell you.'

I swore this would never happen to me. So I didn't call Sherry more than once a week, and then I always had a good reason – like, did she do okay on that test she was worried about, or there was some function down at the temple, in case her father wanted to drop by. Nothing too obvious. Instead, what I did was write letters.

Now, I was perfectly aware that nobody did that

anymore, which is why this particular barrage appealed to me. Subtlety. Finesse. Just a little bit of self-effacing self-exposé which I sensed would be different from the men she'd known before. I went to a stationery store and picked out four of the most masculine patterns I could find: nothing with dots or pastels, just bold graphics and stuff that spelled 'literate'. I bought four pens, color-coded to each paper.

She couldn't get much mail, most kids don't, even Teen Queens. The arrival of letters on a regular basis, especially ones that smacked of substance and maturity, would certainly catch the eye of most everyone in the house, especially Kim. And Kim would, with luck, make enough asides and remarks that Sherry would get the point. Mail means Attention Is Being Paid. Letters are Serious Courtship.

But at no time could these letters get too personal. No pleadings for consideration, for future dates or other hearts-and-flowers stuff. Instead, my letters had to speak of Life, of the Nature of Man, of Science and Art and Poetry, so that they would be objects of respect. In this way she'd come to admire me before she got to know me too well.

Of course, in each letter I referenced our upcoming date in some slight way. Nothing heavy, no panting I-can't-waits, but strictly a small tug at her memory. For example, I might mention that I saw Stepin Fetchit making rhythm with Shirley Temple on some old movie, or that I liked the new Stones song – good beat to *dance* to. No letter went out without the reminder: We're going dancing. You and me. Not some stranger, some blind-date dorkus from Canoga, but me. The guy who's given you something to look forward to every day when you come home.

Every day. The letters took me an hour each night, but I didn't skip a mail pickup. I considered she was worth it.

So finally, the Friday before the Saturday arrived, and I called her that afternoon. It had been six days since we'd spoken, six days when I'd deliberately taken alternate routes to class so as not to pass her locker, six days of only quick waves in the hall or the quad, because I wanted her to get a chance to miss me.

When she answered her private line, I said, 'Hi. What time should I pick you up tomorrow night?'

'David? Just a minute.'

I heard her get off the bed and pad across to close her door. 'Listen,' she said when she came back, 'in your last letter you quoted somebody who said it's an iron universe.'

I said eagerly, 'Don Marquis, yes. From his *Almost Perfect State*.'

'Where he says, when the spears go into your belly you're supposed to be happy?'

'When the spears go into you, rejoice. Because the iron gets into your blood that way.'

'Did you have to read that for a class?'

'Nope, my parents weaned me on big books early. I keep up.'

'Well. Do you really believe that?'

Uh-oh. That line's about disappointment. Could she possibly be so canny as to hand my quotes back to me for solace because she intends to inflict some? 'Well, I guess I do believe that in every heartache there's growth.' I tried to laugh. 'Or something like that. Why?'

'Pretty cerebral.'

'Well, back east it rains a lot, you know? So we do a lot of reading.' This is going all wrong, I thought frantically. I'm sounding like a bow-tied pedant when I need to sound like Cary Grant. 'So, when should I pick you up tomorrow night? I've got my high-heeled sneakers polished.' Even to my ear it fell flat.

There was a small, ever-so-sullen silence.

'I figure about seven. It'll take forty minutes to get to the restaurant, maybe more – '

'David. I don't think I can make it.'

I took a deep breath. 'Oh? Why is that?'

'I don't think I want to.'

I hadn't expected honesty. I was prepared for flimsy excuses, headaches, colds, Grandmother-is-in-from-out-of-town but I hadn't considered that she might just say that she didn't *want* to go out with me. The sadness encircled my throat like hands. 'Why?'

'Look, I'm sorry. I should have gone with my original instincts. I just don't think we're ever going to be anything more than friends. I liked your letters and all, but we're so different.'

My brain leapt furtively from one high branch to another, trying to pull myself up so I could see over –

'I'm just not comfortable,' she said after a minute pause.

'With me? I thought the letters would make you more comfortable. Let you get to know me better.'

'I *do* feel like I know you better, but I also feel like you're trying to make me do something. Be something.' She tried a sad little laugh. 'It's a strain. I'm used to jocks, you know?'

'You're used to jerks.' I couldn't help it.

'Maybe so,' she said, her voice still gentle. 'I don't blame you for being mad.'

'I'm not mad. I'm disappointed. You're used to jerks, and you're used to always having the upper hand, being smarter than them, more desirable on the marketplace, not having to do anything at all to get your worship quota in for the evening. Is it because I didn't tell you that you're a goddess, and I'll throw myself on the freeway if you don't go out with me? It's true, of course, and I'd have said it if I thought I had to – '

For some insane reason the voice of Jimmy the Mouseketeer chanted softly in my head. 'Proverbs, proverbs, they're so true,' Jimmy sang, his eyes sincere, his Mouseguitar plunking gently, 'proverbs tell us what to do; proverbs help us all to be-ee – better – Mouse-ke-teers.' He set down his guitar carefully and asked, 'Now, what does this mean, boys and girls?' I realized that Sherry had been stone-cold silent, and I plunged back in desperately.

'I mean,' I continued struggling for the same careful gentleness of Jimmy's tone, 'you're worth so much more than that, Sherry. You're probably worth more than even *I* give you credit for. And if you don't try something new once in a while, you'll stunt your potential. I know I'm not the best-looking guy hanging around you, but I bet I'm the smartest. Hang out with morons, and you'll become one.'

A pause. 'Well, I guess you're not so different from the rest of them after all.'

'What do you mean?'

'You all want something. You all make me feel like I better deliver.'

I could scarcely speak. With what strength I could muster, I cursed myself violently, silently, for being such a goddamned smartass, for being condescending to her, for coming on too strong, for a hundred things I had said and should have said, and the sadness, the fierce sense of loss, welled up in my throat and stifled me completely. She was right. I just wanted to own her, like all the others. Even more insulting, I wanted to own her mind as well as her body.

'David?'

My silence had troubled her. Her voice was less querulous.

'I'm still here,' I said, clearing my throat. 'Look, I'm sorry. I didn't mean to play' – I was going to say Svengali, but I didn't want to sound like a show-off again – 'it this way. Like I was the teacher and you were the student. I just want to see you. I'm really disappointed.'

'Why me?'

'Because I like to think I see something in you that nobody else does. You're not just beautiful, you're unique. You've got depths to you that nobody's ever explored, I think.' I went on, blindly now. 'I believe you're a lot more complex than you show.'

Now it was her turn to be silent.

'Sherry?'

Almost wistful. 'I write poetry.'

'You do?'

'Not very good, but – '

'I'd love to hear it. Would you read some to me?'

'Now? I don't even know for sure where I put them – '

'I'll wait. Really. I'd like to hear some of your poems.'

Another silence, and then the phone was laid down on what I could only imagine was a soft silken coverlet, pink probably, or pale ivory, a rustle in drawers, steps across the rug, more silence, and then she was back. Her voice was softer now, very private. 'I wrote this last year.' It took on a faraway chanting quality, and I had to listen closely to catch each word.

'I drank at two love vines, the last was like the first,
But I could find no wine as urgent as my thirst.
I gnawed at every root; I sampled every plant,
But I could find no fruit as lovely as my want.
So use the grape for dye and use the flower for seed,
In short of both, I'll lie down
Lean with thirst and love my need.'

I instantly recognized an old poem I'd read several years back, but it was different somehow. What was it? Could I be mistaken? 'Will you read it again?'

She did, this time with more confidence. I quickly wrote down the first half as fast as I could. 'That's wonderful,' I said. 'How long ago did you write that?'

'About a year,' she said, almost shy.

There's something wrong here, I thought, but now's not the time to point it out. 'I was right about you. Have you read that to anybody else?'

'Just my father.'

Of course. 'Well, it's terrific. I tried to write some poetry once, but it wasn't any good. Didn't have the feeling to it that yours does. Someday, I'd really like to see some more of your work.'

Another pause.

'Sherry? Let's give it a try. I promise not to talk about Tolstoy or pentameter or grain futures. We'll just have a good time, dance till our ankles are nubs, but nothing heavy, and if you don't like the way I lead, I won't bother you again.'

'And you won't ask me to marry you?' Her voice was more flirtatious, back to familiar ground.

'Of course I'll ask, but you have my complete permission to say no.'

She laughed then, a silvery shiver of victory like wind in glass chimes. 'Well, okay, then. Seven. Just honk.'

When I hung up, I went instantly to my bookshelf to hunt for the genesis of her poem. Finally, after checking Sara Teasdale, Rossetti, Yeats, and several others I thought she might have been drawn to, I found 'Feast' by Edna St Vincent Millay.

I drank at every vine. The last was like the first.
I came upon no wine so wonderful as thirst.

I gnawed at every root. I ate of every plant.
I came upon no fruit so wonderful as want.
Feed the grape and bean to the vintner and the monger;
I will lie down lean with my thirst and my hunger.

If I were to be strictly pristine about it, of course, she had lied and plagiarized the poem. The question was, had she also lied to herself? Did she actually believe she had written it? Absorbed Millay's work as just so much fodder for a still-undeveloped but potentially poetic soul?

I read the two together again, writing out what I recalled of hers and comparing it line by line to Millay's. No matter how objective I tried to be, I couldn't get over the feeling that somehow hers was the better effort, even if it wasn't original. I felt I had just discovered she could make gold from straw.

I was dressed by four o'clock and in front of the mirror searching for spots. All clear. I usually wasn't troubled much by zits, but once in a while I'd get one of those subsurface behemoths, the kind that takes two days to come up and two weeks to go down. My personal favorite was a dead-center egg that liked to hatch between my eyes, joining my eyebrows together and making me look like an escaped con. But I was in luck. No big boys in town for the night I'd waited for all month. The car was immaculate, the radio buttons preset, and I was as presentable as I'd ever be.

So when I pulled up the wagon before the Gentry home, I went to the door with a flourish. Just honk, my ass. Would Dante have honked for Beatrice? I expected Maggie, but an older woman answered the bell.

'Hi, David, I'm Wendy Gentry,' she said, stepping back and gesturing me inside. 'Sherry'll be ready in a minute. Have a seat.'

I put out my hand and said formally, 'Mrs Gentry, I'm happy to meet you – '

But she laughed and drew me to the white expanse of sofa. 'Oh, we don't stand on ceremony around here. Just call me Wendy, like in Peter Pan. I feel like I'm hardly old enough to be Sherry's mother. So where are you two going tonight?'

She was almost as blond as Sherry, with her hair in a short flip like a lacquered helmet, as slender and quick as a girl. But her skin was stiff and orangeish from too much sun, the wrinkles around her eyes etched over the edge of her cheekbones.

'To the House of Kwong. Sherry says she likes Chinese.'

She laughed delightedly. 'She does. She takes after me.'

'You do look like sisters,' I said.

'I was a child bride. So you're going dancing after? I love to dance. Can't get my husband to do much anymore, but we used to hit the Strip every weekend. Sherry says you're good!'

'Well, my mother made me take lessons – '

She jumped up and took my hand. 'Show me one of the latest steps, Davy, I'll bet I can do it.' She dropped my hand and hurried over to the stereo. She was wearing tight white jeans, white Keds, a blouse that came down almost to her knees, and I had to admit that she looked almost as good as she wanted to. 'I'll just put on a record, and you can warm up with me, okay? It'll be fun!'

I looked desperately at the stairs, hoping Sherry was coming fast. Mrs Gentry had found a Chubby Checker record, slapped it on the turntable, and turned up the volume, right in the middle of the song.

Hey-ey-ey, now! Round an' around, an-around, an around we gooo agin! Baby, let me know, you love me sooo agin!

She skipped over in front of me and pulled me up off the couch, already twisting her hips. I followed her lead,

109

twisting back and forth, rather lamely at first, but then I got into the beat. What the hell, I thought, at least she's trying to be a good sport, it's just not what I'm used to from moms, but she's sure friendly.

'Let's twist again, like we did last summer!' she sang along with the record, 'Let's twist again, twistin' time is here!'

'Mom,' Sherry said, 'I think we better go now.'

I stopped abruptly, instantly guilty, as though I'd been caught kissing her sister. Sherry had come down the stairs and was standing there, her white sweater over her arm. A light blue dress, a matching blue headband, shoes and bag, her whole aura was blue, like a patch of sky with clouds. She was smiling, but she looked embarrassed.

Mrs Gentry stopped and went to her, linking her arm through Sherry's and turning to smile at me. 'I was just getting him warmed up for you, honey.'

Mercifully, the music stopped, the automatic arm dispensed with Chubby, and I said, 'You look great, Sherry. I can see where you got it,' I added, bowing slightly to Mrs Gentry.

She laughed delightedly. 'You two should stay and dance!'

Sherry untangled her arm, saying, 'We don't want to miss our reservation – '

Her mother let her go and turned to the stairs. 'Okay. Nice to see you, Davy. Come back soon, and I'll teach you the lindy.'

'We'll be back by midnight,' I said.

'Have a good time!' she caroled, disappearing up the stairs with a swish of jeans and a patter of Keds.

'Your mother's something else,' I said. That was about as noncommittal as I could manage.

'Everybody says that. They all think she's so young. Sometimes I think my dates don't know whether to take *her* to the car or me.' She smoothed her hair as we went out the door. 'She was the most popular girl in her class. She's still the life of every party.'

I opened the car door for her and she slid inside. 'It must be great to have a mother who's so much fun. More like a sister than a mom.'

I got in next to her and glanced over. She was arranging her purse and her sweater, finding small places to put her things as though she intended to stay for a while.

'Yes,' she said firmly. 'I'm really proud of her.'

She said it as if by rote, and I didn't feel I could probe any further. Besides, I wanted her to completely enjoy herself this evening, remember it all with not a single twinge of regret. As we went up the Ventura onramp, I turned up the radio and said, 'No sense in wasting time. I think we should drive right through to Las Vegas. We can be married by midnight.'

She looked down at her dress. 'I promised my mother.'

'What?'

'That I'd be married in white.'

'Oh. Well, next weekend, then.'

When I look back on that first date with Sherry, certain short but perfect moments stand out. The way she laughed when I attempted to speak to the waiter in fractured French, pronouncing the veal 'beaucoup far out'. The sideways smile she gave me when I took her hand and led her to the dance floor, at once eager and slightly defiant. The way her shoulder smelled just under my nose, the sweep of her long hair on my wrist as I held her, and other brief glittering snatches of triumph and giddy joy.

I remember feeling a great sense of certainty, something I was later to read described in a book by Thomas Wolfe: The certitude that the wellspring of youth would never run dry and that it was all *worth* it somehow.

111

David Levine at seventeen believed it was so. When did it cease being true?

We ate, we danced, the evening swept by before I could judge its success, and so when I finally took Sherry to her door, I still was unsure whether or not she had enjoyed it enough for an immediate encore.

A single light shone out of the fake wrought-iron lamp, and the strategically placed lawn strobes illuminated the giant cactus, exaggerating its spikes. I followed her up the steps, trying to think of one last quip to leave her with a smile. I had already decided that it would be a bad move to go for a kiss. Too obvious and expected. No sense in ending the evening on a downer. Let her wonder why I didn't try.

'I had a great time,' she said, glancing back at me as she pulled out her keys. 'You were even more clever than usual tonight.'

'Yeah, but clever is so exhausting. Tomorrow I'll go for trite, just to relax.' Stop it. Now. 'Next time,' I went on with scarcely a beat, 'I think we should try that place across from where we parked. It looked good, didn't it? Maybe more of a disco crowd.'

She had the door ajar now and the light from within haloed her hair. 'David, I enjoyed it, honestly, and I think you're one of the truly great guys. But I don't think we should go out again. Let's just be friends.'

'Well,' I said with a brave smile, 'of course we can be friends. But don't friends go out together too? I mean, we don't have to exchange vows of fidelity or anything, but I would like to see you again.'

'You will. At school. And you can come over once in a while like you did before. But let's not date.'

'It's because I broke my promise and asked you to marry me, isn't it?' I said, mock-morose. 'I knew that lacked in subtlety.'

She placed one cool palm on my cheek. Not patted; placed. 'You're going to make some lucky girl vastly happy, but I don't think it's going to be me, David.'

'After only one date?'

'That's all it takes to know.'

I felt as though she had just knocked me down flat and stood on my chest with her high heels. It was clear she was impervious to negotiation, and a swift black tidal sweep of despair filled my mouth with bile, made me feel altogether an outcast again, and almost forced out the words well-then-fuck-*you*-bitch! but I bit it down, leaned casually against the wall and said, 'Well, we don't have to decide now, I guess.'

'We just did,' she said softly, and went inside, the Persian trotting briskly at her heels.

I had the sudden and distinct sensation that I didn't exist for her any more than plankton existed for a whale. Just before the door closed, I asked, 'What about the letters? Should I still write?'

'Oh, yes,' she said with the ghost of a smile. 'I love your letters. If you want to, keep writing.' The door shut quietly, with the implacability of the tomb.

The image of Jimmy the Mouseketeer floated up again, this time singing, 'Proverbs, proverbs, they're so true, proverbs tell us what to do – here's another one, boys and girls. An oldie but a goldie. "Follow not truth too near the heels, lest it dash out thy teeth." Can you guess what this might mean?'

Part Two

She didn't need to make the slightest effort to make men fall in love with her. Dull men were afraid of her cleverness; intellectual men of her beauty, but all others were her natural prerogative.

– F. Scott Fitzgerald

Spring in California was enough to dissolve any disappointment, to heal all despair with a sun so strong that even the salt wouldn't sting. I wasn't dating Sherry, but Miriam and I seemed to have reached some sort of understanding. We never mentioned Sherry; neither did we talk of the future. It seemed so far away. I assumed Miriam dated only me. I could still feel Sherry in the back of my mind, but the heat on my skin diverted and led me, as all things in California inevitably did then, to the beach.

There was a road that started out in the Valley, seemed almost to begin in the Taft parking lot, and wound around the dusty mountains through chaparral and eucalyptus, past even a few pines at the highest elevations, through a tunnel, shivered around a precarious turn or two, and finally surfaced, shining and serene, at Malibu. In that spring of 1966, an endless caravan of Volkswagen buses, hot Mustangs, little imported sports cars, and old woodies streamed bumper to bumper to the sea like so many carapaced locusts.

'Let's hit the bitch!' the clarion call sounded, pronounced through grinning sunburned lips like 'bee-tch'. That's all it took to start a stampede from any of a dozen Bob's Big Boys or Thirty-one Flavors or Shakey's in the Valley. It didn't matter how you got there; it mattered only that you arrived.

> Let's go surfin' now, everybody's learnin' how,
> Come on, surf surfari with me!

The radios blatted out the hymnal, and a million kids genuflected to the Great Blue Pacific. It seemed irrelevant that elsewhere Americans were walking in space, President Johnson passed a bill that allowed the Treasury to make silver dimes and quarters out of alloys, thus halving the value of money, or that we were bombing Vietnam. Despite dire pronouncements on the six o'clock news, it was spring, a California spring, and the surf was up.

Surfing. Rincon, Laguna, Dana Point, La Jolla. Places that seemed to have religious significance. Icons of a secret fraternity. They wore a shark's tooth or a St Christopher's medal around their necks and plastered their cars with 'Pray for Surf' decals. They hitched up and down the coast, expecting that rides would stop and somehow accommodate their nine-foot boards. I remember feeling certain that a guy could get killed on one of those wooden tombstones. The damn boards were taller than even the basketball jocks, and you'd herniate yourself dragging one of them to the waves.

Furthermore, it was real obvious to me that those who spent a lot of time on their boards became drastically mutated: lank straw-blond hair, permanently red noses, huge knuckled calluses they called 'knobbies' on the tops of their feet and their knees which forbade all clothes but baggy shorts and any shoes at all, and sun-squint eyes, even on freshmen. And every one of those eyes blue, blue, blue.

On the other hand, I had to admit that there was no place else to be worth being, nothing else to do worth doing, and the beach was it. Tribes of kids spilled out onto Malibu and Zuma and Hueneme. Carillo Beach was rocky, but they managed; Trancas was elite, but they trespassed. And all the way down to Newport, Huntington, Laguna, Doheny, and San Onofre, there wasn't a parking space large enough to squeeze a dune buggy. So when they came to curbs painted red, they just white-washed them legal with a bucket of paint they kept in the trunk for the moment.

On the beach you saw the girls with major bodies in the minorest bikinis, or maybe orange bell-bottom hip-huggers with bare stomachs and tank tops. On the beach you crowded off the old crocks with their aluminum chairs and their orthopedic sandals and sent up a Frisbee set that spread across an acre of sand. On the beach the sun glared like a dentist's lamp, the smell of Sea & Ski was like Hawaiian flowers, and the biggest challenge of the afternoon was how late could you stay.

I was initiated properly the first April weekend when the temperature soared to eighty by nine A.M. The phone rang and a voice said, 'Hey, man, I've been waiting for an hour.'

I had just finished sweeping down the pool. An entire Saturday stretched out before me, endless and gleaming in my mind's eye. 'Foote? What do you mean?'

'I mean, fool, that the traffic'll be deadly by ten. Get your white ass over here in the Hog of Steel and let's do it.'

The Hog of Steel was what Foote had christened the station wagon, after I'd nudged it ungently into the gates at the Taft parking lot without even scraping the chrome. 'Do what? I got things to tend to, man.'

'Do them later. It's your first spring in California, so you can be excused, I guess, but I'd a thought you could *smell* it, if nothing else.'

I knew what was coming now – Foote's familiar litany. I just grinned silently.

'Flesh,' Jim whispered gently, teasingly. 'Tanned female bodies. Scarcely clothed. Bitchin' little bottoms already on their way over the mountain' – here his voice rose to a fevered pitch – 'sand and sun and saltwater.

119

Beer and hot dogs and Coppertone! And you sit there whining instead of wheelin'!'

'Well, I'm sorry,' I said, contrite. 'I'm new.'

'So is the day. Be here in ten.'

'What'll I bring?'

A huge despairing sigh. 'This is not a family picnic. You can leave the mayonnaise sandwiches and the umbrellas at home. You got a blanket? You got shades? You got ten minutes.' The phone went dead.

The view around the last few Malibu curves was infinite. A blue-green forever of shimmering sea that faded into the horizon and merged with the sky. One-handed, I took the roadbends like I was born to them, my other fist pounding the backbeat on the wagon's trusty side.

> Round, round, get-a-round, I get around, yeah
> Get around, whoo-oo-ooo!
> I'm gettin' bugged drivin' up an' down the same ol' strip,
> I got to find a new place, where the kids are hip!

We hit level asphalt again, and I could smell the hot sand. No parking place on the ocean side of Highway 1, of course, but we squeezed the car into a snatch of concrete next to the Minit-Mart across the street. Past a dozen no parking signs that threatened maiming if you left even a bicycle for longer than five minutes, I sidled alongside a yellow Spitfire, hopped out, and slammed the door for emphasis. If they were going to tow me, they'd have to tow a mile-long line of cars as well.

Foote was already leaning against the wagon, his towel over his shoulder, adjusting his shades to a new, cooler angle. With a practiced eye he scanned the cars lined end to end on the ocean side. 'Watts is here. That blue Chevy's his, I think. Nobody else yet.'

'I thought you said I was late.'

120

'You are. You got about one hour to get baked, brown, and broken in.'

As we hurried across traffic I said, 'You think I've never been to the beach before? We've got another whole ocean back east, you know, and they didn't exactly *invent* skin in California. Besides that, I've been a few times with my folks. I'm not a complete feeb.'

'It's not the same thing, man.'

Just then, three lithe, long-legged girls came skipping past us, giggling, and flouncing shining hair, with wide smiles, and nothing but tiny strips of gaily-colored cloth between them and the whole stark, staring world –

Both of us groaned audibly and quickened our pace over the sandy shoulder and onto the beach.

A whole new universe stretched beneath me. I could only stop and stare. Each car must have had a dozen bodies in it, because down the sandy rise it seemed like a thousand kids had taken over the entire coastline, as far as I could see.

What was interesting was that the acres of bright blankets and towels were not strewn haphazardly but were clumped together in tight enclaves, corner to corner, with wide expanses of sand between. Clearly, social lines held, even in the midst of a semi-nude debauch.

Foote scoped out the herd patterns quickly, raised one hand in a brazen wave, and hurried down the hill. 'There's Bevins over there. I knew he wouldn't miss opening day.'

Halfway to the water, Steve Bevins, one of the lunch crowd and a baseball jock with arms long enough to smoke a fast ball past probably even Mantle, was sprawling out on a chenille bedspread. Around him clustered Watts and a few of the guys, two beer coolers, and a disarray of magazines, Coke bottles, and Coppertone tubes. A portable radio blatted out some vintage rock and roll.

121

Bevins lifted up one end of his shades and said, 'Hey. Pull up some sand.'

Foote unrolled his towel, stripped off his T-shirt, and belly flopped down, all the while telling about some fantasy episode he and I had supposedly experienced in our wild ride across Malibu Canyon. I caught some hyperventilated detail about two crazed blondes in a red Jag, and then I turned my attention to the situation at hand.

Once I said hello to all present, unrolled my towel, smashed down the corners into the sand like everybody else, and adjusted my shades, it was time to prepare the flesh. I took off my shirt and oiled a few exposed surfaces, but after that there wasn't much else to explore.

It suddenly occurred to me that I'd never in my life been on a California beach in spring, driven here in my own car, minus a set of parents. Furthermore, I'd never given much thought to what I was supposed to do once I got here.

'Anybody bring a volleyball?' I asked.

Watts said, 'Nah. Somebody'll get up a game later.'

A few moments of silence while we all faced reverently to the sun. 'Got a deck of cards?' I finally ventured.

'Relax, man,' Foote said. 'Just let it happen.'

Silence again. So this was the big deal? The major beach migration I had to rush off for or miss the highlights – ?

And then I spied the dark moving dots out on the water. The surfers were in a ragged line, just beyond the wavebreak, a wonder I hadn't seen them from the highway. Nobody else seemed overawed, but I stretched myself a little higher to watch them.

The waves were like moving hills of water, and these guys were their masters, molding them, shaping their bodies to them, until they formed a private dance with the sea. Eight surfers sat on their boards, far out onto the waves. They clustered in twos and threes, riding mostly sideways to the surf. The waves were smooth now, and flat, rolling in clean and hissing with little thunder. Each head was a brilliant spot of blond light; each body a dark brown, looking competent, virile, and detached. It suddenly seemed to me that they must know something about all of this – the water, the sun, life itself – that I had missed learning.

'You guys ever surfed?' I asked casually, my eyes still on the water.

Bevins said, 'Sure. No big thing.'

Foote didn't even lift his head off the towel or open his eyes. 'Not when you tried it, Bevins, that's for sure. Never even made it past the surf line.'

'Hey, ratfink, the waves were gross that day!' Steve protested. 'I'd like to see *you* out there.'

'I've got no big yen to be part of the marine food chain.' Foote rolled over and said, 'Why, you want to give it a shot, Levine? They'd probably lend you a board for an hour.'

'Yeah. If nothing else, just for laughs,' Watts added.

I saw a whole line of surfers leaning against the concrete bulwarks of the highway. I hadn't noticed them before, over a dozen of them, with their boards stuck up in the sand like pale Stonehenge monoliths.

With a jaunty air I scarcely felt, I said, 'What the hell,' and got up to walk over there.

'Hey, man,' Bevins said, up on one elbow. 'Those guys don't hang with hodads.' A hodad was a fake, a phony, somebody who bragged about surfing and never made it in the water. It was a common taunt at Taft, in both surfer and greaser crowds.

Foote added mildly, 'It's a lot tougher than it looks.'

'So's your mama.' I grinned over my shoulder, and walked up the beach.

The guys leaning against the concrete pilings were all older, maybe even college jocks. They eyed me carelessly, eyeballs charred to little blue cinders from too much sun, squinting out from under straw hats. I went up to the smallest, a guy who sat a little apart from the others. Probably a fringer, I thought, not quite as elite as the rest.

'Hey, man,' I said with what I hoped was just the right amount of nonchalance. 'You going out anytime soon?'

The surfer glanced up at me with studied indifference. 'Maybe.'

'Would you mind if I took a board out for a spin?'

'A spin?' A wry glance at his fellows. 'It's not a fuckin' Cadillac, man.'

'Yeah,' I said patiently, 'I know. I mean, just to try it. Just for a half hour or so.'

'No action, man. It's flat.'

'So it's a good time to learn. Look,' I said genially, 'I won't fuck up too bad, and if I do, you can all get a good laugh over the noodle-dick dork out there, and it'll be worth it. Okay?'

One of the other surfers who looked like the head honcho said, 'Sure kid. What the hell. You can take this one.' He patted a board tilting crazily in the sand.

I smiled bravely. It was huge, evil yellow, and had a scag on it wider than my father's desk.

'Man, not Widow-Maker,' another guy laughed. 'Give the kid a break.'

Before they could change their minds, I said, 'Thanks. Thanks a lot, man,' and took ahold of the board to drag it away. I gave it a mighty heave, and it barely budged. Took another firmer grip and wrapped both arms around

124

it. It must have weighed a hundred pounds. Laughter broke out all around me.

The small guy who sat on the fringe came over and hoisted one end. 'You never ever got yours wet before, did you, kid?' Now that the scag was up and out of the sand, the two of us could carry it easily, one on each end. As we traipsed to the water I thought, that's the reason they hang out in tribes. It takes a full team just to get these suckers on and off the cars and down to the waves.

We plopped the huge yellow board into the foam, and the little guy was explaining, 'Just paddle out easy at first. Keep your feet off the sides for balance. Don't try to stand up, man, there's not enough action. Just practice belly-surfing with it until you catch on.'

I thanked him, lay down on the board, and propelled myself out into the moving water. Once, I glanced back over my shoulder to see Foote and the others up on their elbows watching me, and then I gave all my attention to the waves breaking far out in the distance.

The surfboard was incredibly light and buoyant in the water, and I felt a terrific sense of power as I realized that a single paddle by both arms could shoot it forward swiftly. I quickly reached the beginning of the surf, could no longer hear the sounds of the beach, and felt the rising swell of the green walls coming at me.

Now for the first time I felt the tantalizing danger of what I was doing, the seductive languidness of easy surging movement, of motion I scarcely controlled. The small edges of waves broke over my back, cold and startling in their reality. Before I had time to think, to prepare, the larger waves were on me and I couldn't turn, duck, or get away, could do nothing but be sucked into their churning, and I closed my eyes, felt myself and the board swept upward through buffeting lightness, even the

125

backs of my eyes were white, and then through it all to the calm on the other side.

I opened my eyes and saw that I gripped the board with white scraped knuckles. I had no idea what had drawn blood. I felt like a shell, with a roaring in my ears and sand in every crevice. Just a little farther ahead the surfers rested, dark torsos bobbing up and down in the water. The sun felt like a warm and heavy hand on my back, a blessing.

It seemed inappropriate to speak, but someone did. 'Hey, man, you sure did it the hard way.'

I looked to see that one of the surfers was talking to me. In the glare I could see no facial features, only a brown sheen. 'Yeah?'

'Yeah. You rolled in like a flipping turtle.'

Mild laughter all around. I sensed no rancor and little competition. 'My first time.'

'No shit. Next time, go at an angle, not straight on. You want to ride the board, not the other way around.'

Gulls floated next to me, as though I were one of their own. In that instant I could feel nothing but pride and pleasure. At least I was *out* there.

For long moments I only drifted, drying and warmed. I was just easing into a doze when I sensed movement around me. I opened my eyes to see the surfers lining up, facing the beach.

'First decent set all day,' one of them said quietly, and I looked beyond the boards to a rising swell of water moving on us, fast and green. Now we could hear the yells from the beach as the others saw the approaching waves and grabbed boards, racing for the water.

'You going to take it?' a voice asked, the original surfer who had spoken earlier. He had wheeled his board around closer to me.

'Yeah, I guess,' I said, sitting up tensely.

126

'Well, don't try to stand up, man. Not in this crowd; you'll kill somebody. Just belly in and keep out of the way.'

The waves were almost on us now, and I wheeled my board so that it pointed toward the shore. With my heart thudding hard, I began to paddle furiously, keeping in line with the others. The waves before me were erupting with boards, guys bursting through the line and struggling to get into position before the heavy set reached them.

Suddenly my board began to shoot forward, lifted by the wave swelling beneath me, faster than I could paddle, and I felt a rush of swift weightlessness, a soaring buoyancy, the hiss of the rushing water all around my head. Without thinking I pulled myself to my feet and, crouched on all fours, rode the wave most of the way to the shore.

When the scag crunched in the sand, Foote came running up and said, 'Man, that was a big one! A bunch of them wiped out.'

I looked back to see empty boards floating in the surf; one jackknifed suddenly in the air and flipped over behind the waveline, riderless. Many more, though, were still under control, being pushed out again into the new set.

Bevins strolled over. 'Did you get up?'

I was suddenly aware that I was grinning like an idiot. I scarcely noticed when the small surfer from the beach raced up to me, grabbed the board away, and slapped it back into the foam. 'Yeah!' I said gleefully. 'Did you see me?'

'*We* saw you,' a voice said, and I turned to see two girls walking by, smiling down at me. 'You looked bitchin'.' And they went on down the beach, their bottoms swishing rhythmically to and fro.

After the beach all day, the place to be at night was in the car, cruising in packs of three or four, with the speakers

127

throbbing out some hard-core rock and roll. Sunset Strip was the preferred cruise, of course, but parents get real nervous about what was basically a fifty-mile round trip just to slide slowly from traffic light to traffic light down a four-mile street.

Sunset wove over Mulholland pass, through Westwood and UCLA, skirting around Beverly Hills, and then finally down into Hollywood. Starting at Doheny, Sunset trickled into two lanes, one in each direction, hemmed in by the Playboy Club and assorted strip places. A right then a left, and you were on Hollywood Boulevard with Grauman's Chinese Theater on one side and Clifton's Cafeteria and the Brown Derby on the other at Vine. Christened the Strip, it was the siren call of the teenage capital of the world. On any Saturday night from April to September it took two hours to go ten blocks.

But, as Critter said to Foote in the backseat of the Hog of Steel that night, 'Life isn't a destination. It's a journey, man.'

I took one hand off the wheel, laid it on my heart, and said reverently, 'God, are you deep, Critter. I just never knew.'

'Yeah, deep in shit if Marsha gets wind he's here, carousing and baying at the moon,' Watts said, next to me. He was leaning way out the window and taking swipes at passing cars. When he missed, he howled and thumped and whistled as though all of life had just escaped his fingers. When he caught a door handle, he screamed at me to speed up or slow down so that he wouldn't have to turn loose. Fortunately, coming up on Doheny, no one could go faster than five miles an hour anyway.

'Marsha and me are *finito*,' Critter said quickly.

'Yeah? Since when?' Foote's attention was finally

diverted from the gorgeous strolling tide of women on both sides of the Strip.

'Since I found out she puts out for half of the senior class.'

I adjusted the rearview mirror so I could see Critter more plainly in the taillight glare. 'Man, you didn't take that seriously, did you? That moron was only blowing smoke; he hasn't touched her. Probably nobody else has either, if you haven't.'

'I didn't say I haven't,' Critter said.

The week before there had been another scene in the locker room, and this time Marsha Swipe's rep had been the one immortalized. Some jock said he bagged her; another one asked why'd he bother. 'Hell,' the guy had laughed, 'I wouldn't fuck her with *your* dick, man, much less my own.'

At the time Critter seemed to take it with his usual good humor, but evidently it finally got to him.

'Well, that doesn't mean anybody else has,' Foote said gently. 'Just because you did.'

'Yeah?' Critter's voice was tight. 'Man, if she'll let me touch it, she'll let anybody. And I didn't even have to tell her I loved her or ask her to go steady or anything.'

'Jeez,' Foote said, 'you two have been together almost all year. I guess she figured you were without you saying it.'

In the uncomfortable silence Critter laughed weakly. 'Hey, it's no big deal. I wasn't going to marry her or anything. No harm, no foul. Life sucks, but at least it's short.'

Another silence. Finally, Watts cleared his throat and said, 'So. You touched it, huh?'

A sheepish grin from Critter, you could hear it in his voice. 'Yeah. Sure.'

'Get outta here,' Watts said, playing along. I thought,

129

probably Watts got laid in the seventh grade, but he was just trying to make Critter feel tall.

'No lie,' Critter laughed ruefully. 'Saw it too.'

'Get *outta* here.'

'I swear.'

'So, what was it like?'

I smiled quietly to myself. Here's where the bullshit begins. What was Critter supposed to say? Well, actually, guys, it was rather a shock. I mean, nobody told me about all that *hair*.

Critter said, 'Great.'

'Yeah, but what did it *feel* like?'

Foote groaned audibly in the backseat, but Critter was in for the whole pound now. What – ? Was he going to admit it felt like a sticky muffin with bristles, and he'd probably never get the cramp out of his wrist?

'Like the gates to heaven, man.'

'Get *outta* here!' Foote and Watts chorused together.

'Help me, Rhonda!' came blasting over the radio, and the three of them were in an instantaneous shouted harmony, three hands banging on the sides of the wagon in beat.

I sang along, but I was thinking about Marsha Swipe and Critter and a swift collage of girls I'd known well enough to get close to touching. It was already happening. Kids were getting laid. And not just the greasers either; they didn't count. They were probably doing it back in the fourth grade. But the regular guys, guys like Critter, who had a curfew and watched *The Dick Van Dyke Show* with his folks and who got watery-eyed when the varsity creamed Canoga.

I remember so clearly the first time a friend told me he'd actually done it. Lord, I was only thirteen. This lucky bastard had gone to a summer camp with some girls' camp across the lake, and he got it in a canoe, floating on Lake

130

Neversink. I begged for two years to go to that camp, but the gods never blessed me.

Of course I had a girlfriend, even at thirteen. She was a sweet-faced kid who was even more nervous about anything physical than I was. It took us two months to get around to kissing. Kissing a girl then was a lot like taking a turn too fast in the gravel on your bike and almost missing it. Yet, some of my fondest memories were of anticipating it, angling for it, making my move, and finally getting that first touch of lips, however graceless it might have seemed at the time. The way her front door looked, washed in yellow light from the porch light; the way she'd glance back and smile at me as she slipped inside. Sometimes I'd walk by the next morning just to see if it looked as good in the daylight.

I felt sorry for Critter but sorrier for Marsha. It was that tired old joke about not wanting to join a club that was stupid enough to let you in. So it wasn't, I realized, much different here than in Dubuque.

Despite its luxurious facade, California cared just as much then about reputations as any small town in the American heartland. The tragic illusion was that it *seemed* to offer unbounded freedom. But California boys like Critter, just like his brothers in Iowa, were begging their Marshas to give them what they wanted, and then abandoning them when they did.

Help me, Rhonda, get her out of my hear-r-rt!

Spring unrolled before me that year, endless as a gift I could take forever to unwrap. Colleges announced in a month, so those of us who hooked our futures on that hope were in limbo. We could still figure every dream would come true. It was still a season of preludes, overtures, and dawns. That special time the whole year

131

had been working hard to produce when your days were new, your world seemed bronzed, and you were perfect. You could be an animal. You could be rank, take risks, and break rules. You might never again return to school or your own bed. A Senior Spring in California.

The big event of the season was the Beach Boys concert at the Valley civic center, a huge auditorium packed solid for this event. They didn't even try to put in chairs.

'Nobody would sit down anyway,' Miriam said as she maneuvered through the crowd ahead of me. 'Everybody will dance the whole two hours.'

I followed behind her, feeling vaguely guilty that I was managing to get so close to the front when so many had been there ahead of us. But Miriam seemed to have a way of getting shoulders to melt away for her with competence. 'Excuse me, excuse me,' I heard her saying brightly, and before long we were several yards away from the stage. At this range there was barely room to swivel, much less dance, and I had a sudden quiet panic that once the music actually started, the crowd would shove forward and press us all to jelly.

The stage was strewn with wires and cords and a hundred lights, mikes, and other acoustical paraphernalia. In both corners, four huge speakers were piled on top of one another like giant building blocks. Another realization. I would be jelly, and I would be deaf for life.

'Isn't this great?' Miriam asked, her voice raised over the noise of the crowd. 'I am completely psyched!'

I grinned and nodded enthusiastically, noticing how radiant she looked. She was just as crazed as the rest of these rockers, despite her usual cool poise. Just goes to show, I thought, that you don't have to be a native to be out of control, not when it comes to music. I had noticed, in fact, that Miriam had been rather an eager convert lately to all things Californian. As though she had decided not to fight it. Her hair was smoother, like she ironed it. Her dress was brighter, somehow more provocative, and her skin was tanned and gleaming. It wouldn't have surprised me to pick her up one night and notice that she'd somehow managed to grow blue eyes.

She bumped a little closer to me and squeezed my arm. There was something about the happy pulsing crowd all around us that was contagious and electric. Somebody onstage had turned up the voltage, and stereo music throbbed through the mass. It wasn't live and it wasn't loud, but it was enough to send a current through the bodies and make them move.

I'd been dating Miriam steadily, at least once a weekend. One night, I usually hung out with the guys; the next night, with her. She just sort of took it for granted that we'd be together. I guess I did too. But I didn't take as much comfort from the arrangement as I thought I would. I felt like I was always waiting for something else to happen, a sign, a watershed of a new beginning for my life. I was restless, restless, could hear that hiss in my blood, like a snake waiting to strike.

Suddenly the stage curtains closed, and the hum of the crowd instantly expanded into a higher-pitched cry, like that of a thousand birds taking wing all at once. There was nothing to see, even less than before the curtains closed but everyone knew the time was now. They were back *there*, and the wait before they would be out *here* was now measurable. A low thunder of heavy objects being moved onto the stage, scratches and crashes, distant voices, and with each noise the excitement of the crowd increased.

A disembodied voice came over a microphone, filling the hall and instantly silencing the ecstasy. 'Ladies and gentlemen,' the announcer said in hushed tones, 'the epoch makers. The band that has molded your music for

133

half a decade' – his voice was rising higher and higher –
'the guys who are California!' – until finally he paused –
then screamed – '*the Beach Boys!*'

An explosion of joy all around, screams that would
have surely drowned out the loudest rock, waves of sound
that rolled over and over the crowd until I felt I was
actually being held up by it, buoyed by it up above the
shoulders that pressed me in. Miriam was directly in front
of me, squeezed into my belly, her arms up in the air in a
hallelujah gesture. The curtain never moved. The screams
of the crowd slightly diminished, and then over the
speakers came:

> Ahhh, I love the colorful clothes she wears,
> And the way the sunlight plays upon her hair-airr.

The screaming jacked up to its original level, past it,
and into ranges no human ear could track. The curtain
slid slowly open, and there they were: five guys, looking
college age, surrounded by guitars, drums, and behind
them the mock-up of a huge sailboat, a sloop with
billowing colorful sails. Beach blankets and beach chairs
and sand littered the stage, all where there had been
nothing but bare wood before.

> I-I-I hear the sound of a cheerful word,
> On the wind that lifts her perfume through the airrr.

With that the audience picked up the beat, was swaying
with it like a single beast, singing along.

> I'm pickin' up good vibrations,
> She's givin' me ex-ci-ta-tions,
> Good (good, good) good vibrations!

I felt my mouth stretch to a wide grin, shouted the
words out loud with everyone else, and put my hands on

Miriam's shoulders with a feeling that I was somehow sharing her soul, sharing *everyone's* soul in the whole place.

Mike Love stood in front. Cool, narrow lips that barely moved when he sang. Dennis Wilson back on drums; Carl and Al and Brian on guitar. Brian Wilson's crystalline falsetto echoed above the roar of the crowd like a guiding light, singing about a world of leisure and freedom and fun in the promised land of California. Like pied pipers the band led the crowd from one song to another, and they sang together about surfing, girls, sunshine, and fast cars. Their harmonies were simultaneously frail and precise, extolling a dazzling paradise of escape.

> I never had a love of my own,
> Maybe that's why, when we're all alon-o-one,
> I can hear music, sweet sweet music

Sometimes they'd pause, and Mike Love or Dennis Wilson would come forward to chat, just to break up the tension. Brian Wilson never talked. In fact, he hardly smiled at all, but seemed almost uncomfortable onstage. Like a shy giant, he stood in the background, his eyes dreamy and vague.

'I can't believe how close we are!' Miriam screamed up at me once. 'This is incredible!'

Actually, I remember wishing, almost wistfully, that we were farther back in the crowd. Sort of like sitting too close at the ballet, I could have done without the noise of the clumping of the toeshoes and witnessing the sweat rivulets on the dancers' powdered faces. And I could have missed, gratefully, the almost painful discomfort in Brian Wilson's eyes.

The band wore identical short-sleeve, blue-striped shirts like awnings, tight white pegger pants, with tennis

135

shoes. As they sang the second set, a covey of long-legged girls in bikinis came onstage and danced the boogaloo behind them, their identical blond flips bouncing in rhythm. Mike Love rolled his eyes once but kept his cool stance.

I was reminded of a time I was walking with my father in Central Park. We noticed a white swan, a lovely, serene vision moving across the lake not far from us.

'Look how it glides,' I said.

'Yes, but underneath,' my father replied, 'the swan's legs are paddling like crazy. It takes a lot of work to look so natural and effortless.'

Somehow I was never able to see a swan after that without thinking of the strain to be beautiful, and it wasn't quite the same.

But it was a wonderful concert and on the way home Miriam snuggled close to me, her stockinged feet curled up on the seat. We went over every detail of the show and then finally there was a pause. 'Did you hear about Critter and Marsha?' she asked quietly.

'Yeah, he told us.'

'What did he say?'

I shrugged. I knew Miriam wouldn't tell Marsha, but still it seemed less than discreet to be repeating another man's confidence. 'Just that it was over.'

'Was he upset?'

I hesitated. 'Yeah, I guess. They've been going together for a long time.'

Miriam sat up slightly and pulled away, her face troubled. 'David, can I ask you something?'

I glanced at her and sensed that this canoe wasn't moving into easeful waters.

'I mean, as friend to friend, not as man to woman, you know? Would you just answer me like one human being to another?'

'I wasn't planning to be one of those tonight, but okay.'

136

She didn't smile. Sometimes I'd noticed that Miriam had a real thin-ice sense of humor that wouldn't support much of a joke. 'Seriously,' she said.

'Okay.'

'Why do guys hate girls who do what they want them to do?'

I was startled by her candor, by her perception, and most of all by the sudden despair in her voice. 'What do you mean?'

'You know. I mean, why does a guy beg and beg a girl to do stuff with him, to go further with him than with anybody else, to go all the way with him, even. And then if she does what he wants, he acts like he hates her. He leaves her.'

'Oh, come on, that doesn't happen all the time. Most guys aren't like that.'

'Maybe all guys aren't, but an awful lot are. Enough so that a girl can definitely begin to see a trend.'

I put my arm around her and drew her close. 'I've never begged you.'

I thought she'd smile, but she didn't. 'Like Yvette Mimieux in *Where the Boys Are*, did you see that movie? Her life was almost destroyed just because she went to bed with a boy. She was in a hospital with a nervous breakdown. And Dolores Hart, who held out and wouldn't hardly kiss George Hamilton, she gets a proposal and true love forever. And how about Natalie Wood in *Splendour in the Grass*? She went crazy, too, all because she did it with Warren Beatty. There's some sort of major message here.'

'Wait a minute, I saw that. I thought she went crazy because she *didn't* do it. And Yvette Mimieux didn't just go to bed with a guy, she got raped.'

'Yeah, by the guy's roommate, who thought because she had done it with his friend, she was fair game. Her

137

value on the marketplace was zilch because she did what he wanted her to do.'

'Look, it's just movies. They're not trying to make any heavy social commentary – '

She looked at me intently. 'You don't think so?'

'Absolutely not, guys don't think like that – '

She laughed lightly. 'I think that's probably what Critter said too. In fact, right now there's probably some version of this conversation going on in a million cars all over teenage America.'

'Somehow,' I said dryly, 'I doubt that there's as much *conversation* going on in nine hundred thousand of them.'

'You just want to *do* sex, not talk about it.'

'That's not it. I just don't see the point. I mean, it's no more fair of you to judge all guys by the action of one or two than it is when guys judge all women by a few bad apples.'

'Bad apples? Was Marsha a bad apple?'

'No, it's just that – '

'But he did break up with her because she went all the way with him.'

'I didn't say that!' I slumped heavily against the car door, holding my chest. 'God, I think you're giving me a spasm. How did we get into all this?'

'We got into all this because I asked you a simple question, one which you still haven't really answered. Why is it that guys want girls to go all the way with them and then reject them when they do?'

'They don't,' I said firmly. 'That's my answer. It's all in your mind.'

'Actually, we should all be grateful to her,' Miriam said softly, almost as though she hadn't heard that last. 'There's one in every class, I guess. The one who goes down for our sins. Who puts out so that the rest of us can live with clean reputations. The other girls in the class should give her a vote of thanks. But you watch, when the word gets around why Critter dumped her – and it will – the girls'll be just as hard on her as the guys. Oh, the guys'll flock around for a while, but not the ones she'd want. And the girls'll talk about her even worse. So they can all feel clean by comparison. Her life'll be ruined, at least what's left of it in high school. And all because she did what he wanted her to do.'

'For God's sake, Miriam, she's not pregnant, and she didn't even go all the way with him! You're making a big deal out of nothing.'

'It doesn't matter what she didn't do now. Do you think Critter's going to say he *didn't* do it?'

I had to turn away. She was right, guys would assume he had and Critter wouldn't deny it.

'It just seems to me that you don't like us if we won't and you end up not liking us if we do. I can remember walking down the street when I was younger, and the guys driving by real slow behind me, yelling out of the car, and if I didn't turn around and smile, they'd screech off hollering, "Bitch!" But then, if I did turn around and smile, they'd laugh and holler, "Cock-teaser!" Either way, you got hollered at, and all for wearing a short skirt and walking down a public road.'

For an instant I thought she was going to cry, and I stiffened in fear. If she wept, I was sunk. '*I* like you,' I said softly. 'Whatever you do or don't do, that won't change.'

She put one hand briefly over her eyes, took a deep breath, and then dropped her hand to her mouth, contemplating me. I saw with relief that her eyes were dry. Without another word she nuzzled over closer to me and kissed my neck passionately in the way she did when we'd parked infrequently. We were no place close to a convenient parking place with any sort of privacy, but I

139

pulled quickly into the back lot of a Von's market, where it was dark. Before I hardly got the car stopped, she was in my arms, her lips on mine, straining at me with an urgency, there between the dumpsters and the loading dock.

That was one of the first times I remember being absolutely certain that I would never understand the way women think. I knew that making out was all we'd do that night maybe all we'd *ever* do, but under the circumstances I considered myself lucky she hadn't set fire to my pants with the cigarette lighter.

Bob's Big Boy was the Valley's hottest drive-in. The place dominated Van Nuys Boulevard on Saturday nights, creating traffic almost as bad as that on the Strip. It was a hangout for kids from four high schools, and the waitresses usually had just graduated from one of them. They moved from car to car on roller skates, wearing short little stiff black skirts and frilly white blouses, silly black caps perched on their heads, carrying trays of cheeseburgers, fries, and lemon Cokes. Rock and roll blared from trumpet speakers on the top of the building, and every stall was filled, with lines waiting clear out to the street.

We were doubling with Foote and his date that night, a Chatty Cathy Doll from Miriam's gym class named Nancy. Except that she pronounced it 'Non-*see*', and made sure everybody knew it the minute she got in the car.

'It's French,' she said, climbing in the back of the Hog of Steel with a pert smile. 'My father wanted to call me Jolie which means "pretty", but he settled for Non-see, like the French town. You can call me Ci-ci for short, everybody does.'

'Really?' Miriam smiled politely. 'I didn't know Nancy was a French name. I always thought it was Jewish. Anyway, it's a Hebrew word.'

Nancy looked horrified. 'I never heard that. Anyway, not the way *I* pronounce it.'

I turned up the radio and said, 'Well, whatever, I'm starving. You guys starving? Hey, Foote, what's the good news?'

Jim had climbed in after Nancy and settled back with his arm around her for the duration. 'I'm Jumpin' Jack Flash, it's a gas, gas, gas!'

'Oh, don't you just *love* the Stones!' Nancy squealed, jumping up, her head nearly over the front seat. 'Have you ever seen them in concert? I did, in New York last year, and they're super marvelous! They're so sexy. Pure sex!'

'I can't stand the guy's lips,' Foote said. 'I like the music okay but his lips look like a fag.'

'Are you kidding?' Nancy asked in amazement, evidently shocked that she could have accepted a date with someone so dim. 'Mick Jagger is divine.' Now, with complete seriousness, 'I mean, the Beatles are sweet. Paul McCartney is good, but your *mom* probably likes them too. The Stones are incredible. They're all working class, you know, and they're leading the revolution in music. I think his lips are absolutely *demonic*.'

Foote struck a pose in the backseat and began to sing. I swiveled the rearview mirror to watch him as he turned his lips inside out, very gross and red. Transformed, Foote's lips seemed to hang off his face like a pair of giblets, and he crooned, 'Ah caaaaint GET noo . . .'

'Oh, stop!' she squealed again, giggling and shoving him away. 'Don't go *spaz* on me!'

Now Foote got into it, closed his eyes, and spread his lips into the most languid, wettest, lustiest grin imaginable. 'SAT-ISSS FACT-shhhun!'

'Stop it!' She laughed, pawing him and bouncing from one side of the car to the other.

Miriam glanced at me and smiled. 'Well, Jim's got himself another super-marvelous one,' she said softly.

'I think she's divine,' I murmured, still keeping one eye on Foote's progress in the back.

Miriam pinched me on the leg.

We made it through the maze at Bob's and corralled the Hog of Steel into one of the slots, honking at two familiar cars as we peeled in. A waitress slid over immediately, stopping her roller skates right at my door with an expert toe-brake action.

'Something quick,' I said, 'we're going to the Reseda right after.'

'You and every car in here,' she said amiably.

The Reseda was the Valley's largest drive-in, and tonight was a double feature of James Bond and some old Elvis flick. They'd be packed in like jujubes.

We ordered quick burgers, fries, and shakes while Nancy related to Miriam the sad tale of her induction into modern dance class in lieu of normal gym.

'I thought it would be outstanding,' she said, 'better than playing volleyball and running laps, for God's sake. But it's *so* embarrassing! First off, Miss Gwin makes us wear these leotards and tights, and you can see everything in that stuff – '

Foote interrupted his monologue about Sean Connery and the last Bond movie he'd seen long enough to ask, 'Yeah? What period's that?'

She cuffed him again and went on. 'And second, she's got these ideas about how we're supposed to pretend to be trees and the wind and the sea. Very bummeroso. So last time I just stood still for the whole period, getting smaller and smaller and smaller, like I sort of crouched down little by little until I was only about four feet tall. I told her I was "Aging Dancer".'

Miriam laughed, shaking her head. 'Did she kick you out?'

'She dug it!' Nancy smiled proudly. 'Thinks I'm super cerebral!'

Sure enough, the Reseda was bumper to bumper. We had to park way up front by the swing sets, and by the time we got the tinny metal speakers latched onto the windows, the cartoon was starting.

'Hey, man, let's go get the popcorn now. I don't want to miss the Bond intro. That's usually the best part,' Foote said, piling out.

Of course, the lines were long, but half of Taft seemed to be there, so it wasn't a strain to spend the time. When we got close to the cashier, Foote said, 'Get a big bucket,' eyeing the popcorn. 'The five-pounder.'

'Get serious. You should never eat more than you can lift, Foote.'

'No, really,' he said, all innocence. 'I might have to pee.'

I grinned. 'Well, then of course the five-pounder will barely hold that hog.'

'Hey, did Bevins tell you what he did to Watts a few weeks back?'

I was making a major decision between a Big Hunk and a Baby Ruth, and I just shook my head.

'Well, Bevins and Watts and Whalens – you remember Whalens, that guy from the bio lab? – big dude? – anyway, the three of them took about a dozen six-packs and went to see some double flick, and it started to rain like crazy. Really come down. Well, they'd been drinking beer all night and getting rowdy, and when Bevins needed to take a piss, it was too much effort to get out of the car, you know? Now you got to picture this: Watts behind the wheel in his dad's Buick, that big burgundy stretch job with the velour seats, Bevins in the middle, and this guy,

Whalens, in the passenger seat. So Bevins finishes off his popcorn and starts to piss in the bucket, see. Watts and Whalens give him just a rash for that, because they're drunk and it's gross, and Watts is sure he's going to dribble on his dad's carpet, and everything. Then Bevins finishes up, reaches across to toss the bucket out the side window, and – '

By this time Foote had my attention, along with that of half the line between the popcorn and the cashier.

'*Splat!* He didn't notice that Whalens had rolled up the window! Drunk on their asses, see, and it's raining, and now there's a bucket of piss all over Whalens and inside the whole right half of the car!' Foote started to laugh so hard, he could hardly continue.

'Jesus,' I said with a twisted smile, 'that's *so* bad.'

'No lie. And it gets worse. Whalens starts to puke when he sees what's all over him, Watts is screaming fit to kill, and Whalens barely gets the door open in time to lose it.'

Fortunately, there were mostly guys in line on both sides of us, but the cashier gave us the coldest look this side of Seattle. Foote didn't care, didn't even notice, just finished up with, 'And Bevins is laughing his ass off, he's so drunk!'

'What did Watts tell his dad?'

'Oh, Bevins had the answer for that too. He talked him into running the Buick through the car wash with the windows down. Watts said it was either that or set fire to it. I guess he figured his father would rather think he was just a dumb shit who forgot to roll them up than go on smelling Bevins's bodily waste in every corner for the rest of his life.'

The Bond intro was just starting when we finally made the long trek back to the car. *From Russia With Love* was the movie, and the titles came on, the steamy sound track with the undulating naked women in silhouette: the standard James Bond seduction of power, intrigue, and sex.

I had to wonder where they got girls who looked like that. It wasn't so much the bodies; you could see amazing constructions and arrangements on California beaches every day of the year. It wasn't just the beauty, the silky hair, the slanty cat's eyes. The women in the Bond movies all had something more: a quality of incredible accessibility.

Foote noticed it, too, and commented when we trudged back to the snack bar between shows. 'I mean, James comes back to his hotel room, and she's waiting for him! Under the covers already, like it's just a given.' He shook his head. 'He doesn't even have to ask them.'

'It's just a movie, man.'

'Yeah, but it's based on real life, I know it is. There's guys like Bond all over the world right now, getting it whenever they want, without even having to call a girl up.' He grinned as a thought struck him. 'Maybe it'll give Nancy some inspiration. You think?'

'Yeah. I think the day you look like Sean Connery, she'll be waiting in your hotel room for you.'

But during the Elvis movie Foote evidently decided to make his move, because the noises from the backseat began to change dramatically. It was the first time I'd ever doubled with somebody who then proceeded as though we weren't even there.

Nancy's voice got progressively softer and softer; her squeals and rapid-fire monologue diminished. There was a lot of rustling around and jockeying for position, and then a startling silence. I looked in the rearview mirror just once, but Miriam poked me and frowned.

She whispered, 'I can't believe this. I'm not doubling with them again, David.'

'Oh, relax,' I whispered back. I leaned over and kissed her, pulling her closer.

Then the silence in the backseat was punctuated by moist labial sounds; the long kiss was broken. Foote and his date were both breathing as though they'd run a race.

'Nancy?' Miriam called.

'Um-mmm,' a muffled voice answered.

'I'm going to the rest room, want to go?'

A long pause. 'Right now?'

'Yes. I'm thirsty too.'

A sigh. Finally, Nancy said reluctantly, 'Okay, I'll go.'

A despairing groan from Foote. More rustling, and then Nancy's head poked up between us, glancing from me to Miriam. 'Okay. Let's go, then. Hurry up, though.'

The two girls got out of the car, adjusting their skirts and patting their hair, and disappeared into the darkness down the rows of cars.

'Can't you control your woman?' Foote moaned from the backseat. He was stretched out, his feet up on the window. 'Man, I swear Miriam's got fuckin' antennae in the back of her head. Keep her occupied, will you?'

I laughed lightly. 'Sure, what do you suggest, Twenty Questions? Maybe a fast hand of gin?'

'Try just a fast hand, period.'

'You are such a rank individual, Foote. Most adults manage their mating rituals in private.'

'That's a good imitation of intelligent conversation, dildo, but you can't fool me. You're just jealous. And I'll be honest. I don't get it. Miriam's a cute girl and all, and she's got good tits from what I can tell, but she's hardly the most delectable truffle at Taft. I think you could do better. I *know* you could get more.'

'A major priority.'

Foote sat up suddenly and peered at me in the dark. 'Well, ain't it? I mean, tell me now if I'm just wasting my

146

breath, Levine, but I guess I figured, have gun will travel. I mean, you *do* drive around in a mobile motel here.' He indicated the cushions behind him. 'I don't know why you don't just back up to the screen.'

'Maybe I do,' I said patiently, 'when I don't have a peanut gallery watching.'

Foote grinned. 'Well, I sure fucking hope so.' He leaned forward and murmured conspiringly, 'And while we're on the subject, can I borrow it next weekend? I daresay Miss Non-see and myself could bring new meaning to the word "thermocouple".'

'You are a puking dog.'

The girls were soon back, tucking themselves into front and backseats cheerfully, as though they had no place they'd rather be. Miriam had a box of red licorice in her hand. She pulled out a length of candy and said spritely, 'Want a piece?'

And then both girls giggled hysterically.

Obviously, some sort of arrangement had been negotiated, probably that neither would gossip about the other, because Nancy snuggled right back into Foote's arms, and Miriam moved over and put her head on my shoulder. In no time Elvis was obscured by a thick humid fog that steamed the windows and made the Hog of Steel as private as a cocoon, and I didn't listen for any more sounds of kissing in the backseat. I was too diverted by my explorations in the front.

That spring, besides drive-ins and Beach Boy concerts, I went to my first night party on the beach. Looking back on it, that evening was pivotal in more ways than one.

We had a huge bonfire on one end of Zuma Beach, and couples clustered around it even though the night was warm. A few guitars strummed idly, and two or three groups took up one song after another. As they sang the

147

Beatles' 'When I Saw Her Standing There', and got to the chorus, everybody put back their heads and hollered 'whoo-oo-oo!' as loud as they could.

One kid, someone I didn't recognize in the dark, began to play a Bob Dylan song, imitating his harsh, croaking voice. 'The times, they are a-chaynnngin',' but nobody sang along and he soon quit.

Couples drifted in and out of the dark, some of them heading toward the dunes and privacy. From the sounds of the horns and the radios on the highway, there was almost as big a party up on the road as down on the sand. I was always amazed how so many kids found out about any party, like a silent tom-tom running underground through the jungle.

Miriam leaned against me as we sat at the bonfire. Her hair smelled of salt and fire smoke. 'I can't believe our senior year is going so fast,' she said. 'It's more than half over.'

'Yeah, I feel like it was supposed to be a bigger deal, somehow. Like I expected it to change me dramatically.'

'Maybe it has, and you just don't know it yet.'

'Have you heard yet from anyplace?'

'You know I'll tell you the minute I do. Is Harvard still your first choice?'

'I keep switching back and forth. Right now I think Columbia's it. But I could live with either one.'

She grinned. 'I guess.'

'Radcliffe still your first rave?'

She nodded. 'If I get in.' She slipped her arm through mine and leaned closer. 'You know, they're not so far apart, Columbia and Radcliffe.'

'Trains run all the time.'

I leaned over and kissed her softly. She put her head in the crook of my neck. She took my hand and spread the fingers gently, a game she liked to play. Running her finger up one finger and down between two more, up one finger and down between two more, until she ran out of digits, then back the other way. Actually, it tickled, but tonight I didn't draw my hand away.

'How did you get to be so sweet?' I murmured.

'How did you get to be so smart?'

'It's a full-time job, believe me.'

'I don't.' She smiled and took both of my hands in hers. 'You know, I'll never forget this year. The time we've had together.'

I nuzzled one white knuckle. 'What will you miss the most?'

'You.'

'Maybe you won't have to. But what would you miss most about me?'

'You're never boring,' she said, suddenly serious. 'And for me, that's saying a lot.'

I grinned. 'Bored often, are you?'

She giggled. 'Stupefied.' She began playing with my fingers again. 'Now I've got a question. Why haven't you ever taken me to temple?'

I looked up, surprised. 'We go every week.'

'Yes, but not together. I think it'd be great if *you* took me. We could sit together, not with our parents.'

There's something ominous here, I thought. A serious commitment is what she's talking about, me taking her to Shabbes in front of everybody. It's just one step shy of engagement. I said, very offhand, 'I don't know, Miriam, there're a lot of things I'll do for you. Fly you to Paris for dinner. Take your SATs for you, but take you to synagogue? That's a tall order.'

'I know,' she said softly. 'Forget it. It was just a whim. A whimette, even.'

The singing began again on one edge of the circle, the Beach Boys' 'Surfer Girl'.

Little surfer, little one,
Made my heart come all undone,
Do you love me, do you, surfer girl?

There was suddenly a rise in the noise level from the road, and I heard a girl's voice call out to a friend. Someone hurried down the sandy cliff, and I caught just a glimpse of blond hair in the firelight. The moving figure wore a rustling dress, a girl who lifted her head as she ran, and I instantly saw that Sherry had joined the party. She was carrying her shoes, white flats with tiny heels, and her face was flushed and glowing.

Half a dozen cries of welcome, people moving aside for her, making room for her to sit down, and the singers from the other side of the circle swelled their voices louder as though they were singing her personal anthem.

I have watched you on the shore,
Standing by the ocean's roar,
Do you love me, do you, surfer girl –

Some jerk began in a high falsetto, 'Sherrreee! Sherry, baby!' from that old song by the Four Seasons, but he was quickly hushed when those closest to her saw she wasn't smiling. In fact, now I could see that her eyes were glistening with tears.

At that instant she raised her head, flicked her hair back from her face, and saw me sitting four people away. I felt Miriam stiffen, her hand tighten on mine, but at that moment I was completely absorbed by the look of bewilderment and pain on Sherry's face. She looked directly at me and said, 'Oh, David – you're here too,' and then dropped her head and began to weep quietly.

Instant shocked silence around the circle. Without thinking I got to my feet, went to her, and pulled her away from the staring eyes, away from the light. She

150

followed me blindly, one hand over her face, now sobbing in smothered gasps. Away from the fire the night was incredibly black, and only a few yards away the ocean's hiss and murmur blocked out the noise of the party. I stopped, and she went into my arms.

'Oh, David – ' She wept, wiping at her eyes with the heel of her hand. 'You won't believe what just happened! I can't believe he did that – '

'Who?' I asked roughly. 'Who did what to you, Sherry?' I pulled back and looked at her face.

'That Don Swenson! He – he – ' And her mouth crumpled again into incoherence, and she just burrowed into my jacket like a small creature, sobbing loudly.

Well, she was either raped or she wasn't, I thought quickly, and nothing's going to change in the next five minutes, and I'm not going to get her to tell me until she's cried some of this out. Somewhere in the back of my mind I realized I'd just left Miriam sitting there without even explanation or apology and there'd be hell to pay, but I simply held on to Sherry while her sobs began to drain down into a less furious storm.

When I sensed she could speak, I said, 'Okay, Sherry. Easy, now.' She was rocking herself back and forth in my arms, moving me with her. I was incredibly aware of her softness, her fluidity. 'Okay, now,' I murmured, 'okay. Tell me what happened.'

'Don Swenson,' she gulped, 'Don Swenson took me out.'

'Okay.'

'And I thought we were having a good time!' she wailed.

'Okay – '

'And he drove up the coast by Trancas, you know, where everybody parks on that dirt road off 101? But God, I've gone out with him only once, and I told him I didn't want to stay there – ' Her voice began to rise again, and her body twisted angrily away. 'But he wouldn't stop! He just kept doing stuff, and he wouldn't listen, and I finally told him to quit it! Just stop!' Now she stood away from me, her hands clenched and her face contorted. 'And then the dumb jock crawled into the backseat and got under a blanket and wouldn't come out. Wouldn't even speak to me!'

I got this vivid mental picture of huge Don Swenson, Taft's best linebacker, huddled under a blanket, just a quivering mound of frustrated teen sex, and I could barely keep a straight face. 'So what happened?'

'I didn't know what to do! I mean, I didn't know if he was going to pull out a knife or his – his thing, or what – and he wouldn't come out. And he wouldn't answer me when I talked to him or anything.'

'Why didn't you just drive the car home?'

She was calmer now and wiping at her face; nothing but a mournful and regular hiccough marked the hysterical sobs of moments before. 'He had the keys in his pocket. All I could think of was, God, if I ever got out of there, I'd never park again in my whole life.'

Now I let my smile show. 'Well, I doubt you'll be held to that one, but what happened?'

She hugged herself, her head down. 'After about an hour he finally came out from under the blanket. Didn't say a word. Jammed the car into reverse and tore down the highway, never even looked at me. When we passed by the kids on the road up there, he pulled up, leaned across me, and opened the door.'

'Just dumped you off?' I felt my anger stir again.

She nodded sadly. 'Didn't even look at me. I got out of the car and he drove away.' She looked up at me in amazement. 'Do you believe it? That he'd do that to me? God, I was so – '

152

'You should have been pissed,' I said firmly. '*I* am.'

'I was so humiliated!'

'And frightened,' I said quietly.

'Yeah. You never know what a guy might do . . .' Her voice trailed off. 'I don't know why he thought he could do that to me. Why he thought I would do that with him. You know, I felt so – alone.'

I felt like taking her in my arms again, but I knew she wouldn't allow it. 'Hey, just forget it, Sherry. The guy's a jerk. Probably some guy you dated told him you – might do it, or something.'

'What guy? Have you heard stuff like that about me?' She was instantly alarmed.

'No, no, but guys make up shit all the time. Don Swenson is so queer for himself, he'd probably believe that the Singing Nun'd put out on the first date.'

A faint smile. 'Don't tell anybody, okay? Promise me, David. It would kill him if all his football buds found out.'

'He deserves it,' I said coldly. 'He ought to have his ass kicked.'

'Promise me.'

I nodded. 'You okay now?'

She was smoothing her hair with her hands. 'Yeah. Thanks for being there.' And then a startled look. 'You had a date, didn't you! Miriam what's-her-name?'

'Miriam Weld. Yeah.'

'Well, you better get back to her. She's going to hate me. I can get a ride home.'

We began to walk back to the fire. It seemed to me we had been gone for half an evening but it must have been only moments, because they were still singing the same song.

> So I say, from me to you,
> I will make your dreams come true,
> Do you love me, do you, surfer girl?

153

'You sure you're all right?'

She nodded. Her smile was now like half a dozen I'd seen her flash in the halls between classes. It was as though I'd never held her at all. 'You know,' she said, 'every time something bad happens lately, David Levine seems to show up.'

'Just your basic Knight in Shining Glasses.'

She laughed, low in her throat.

I said, 'Let's double sometime. You and anybody but that Swenson creep and whoever I'm dating after Miriam dumps me. Want to? Maybe go to a movie next week?'

'If I'm still alive.' She grinned, tripping away up the hill toward the cars.

'Well, if not, we'll go the week after!' I called. The White Persian, who hadn't been around much that spring, strode now out of the shadows, picking up one delicate paw and then the other, shaking off the sand with a vague expression of distaste. It looked after Sherry, then purred audibly and rubbed against my legs.

Miriam was still sitting in the fire circle, and when I took my place beside her again, she actually smiled a welcome. 'She okay?'

'Yeah, I think so. I mean, she was upset, but she's better now, I guess. Some guy was really rank to her, really incredible – ' Then I realized I was talking too much, too fast, and I stopped. 'Anyway, she'll get a ride home okay with somebody.'

'I'm surprised you didn't offer to take her home.'

'Hey.' I turned and looked at her sternly. '*You're* my date.'

'Goody.'

I peered quickly at her, looking for sarcasm. She was still smiling, though, tracing an idle pattern in the sand with a single finger.

'Actually, I don't know why I did it,' I said. 'Probably

she's got plenty of friends here who know her better than *I* do. But I didn't really think, when I saw her start to cry, I just thought, get her away from here – '

'I wonder why she came all the way down to the sand? There must have been a dozen cars up there with girls who could have helped her.'

I shrugged. 'Probably wasn't thinking straight.'

'There's a lot of that going around.' A pause. 'I was never very good at that.'

'What?'

'Crying.' She laughed lightly. 'I mean, when I cry, I could probably scare away any dragons hanging around, so I don't really need to attract guys to fight them for me.'

I began to glower. 'I don't think she was trying to attract guys, she was just upset.'

'And you were the first one to leap to her defense.'

'That's right. It was just a reflex.'

'So you'd have jumped up like that even if she were ugly?'

'I'd like to think so,' I said firmly.

Another pause, longer than the first one. 'So would I, David.'

Twice I brought up the subject of double-dating with Sherry, but Miriam never really took it seriously. The third time, I said, 'You know, I did say we'd do it sometime. She's going to think I'm avoiding her, or something.'

Miriam gave me The Look: the swivel of the eyes and the set of the lips, firm and thin and harboring the tiniest of sneers, that I'd come to associate with incredulity. She said, 'I'm sure she's tortured with anxiety.'

'Look, we're friends,' I said patiently, 'that's all. You're always telling me I don't understand women. I should think you'd be thrilled to death I have one as a friend.'

155

My soul scarcely writhed at all. 'If you had some guy as a friend, I wouldn't care if we doubled with his date and him.'

'I'm not always saying you don't understand women; I say you don't *listen* to them very well. Which makes my point.'

This was the sort of discussion we seemed to be having a lot of lately, the kind of words that went back and forth between us like battered shuttlecocks until neither of us knew whose fault it was or whose turn to serve. 'Well, anyway, I think it'd be fun. Why don't you call her and set up something?'

'Me? She's your friend, David. You call her.'

'Okay,' I said as casually as possible. 'I will. She's probably booked for the next six light-years, but what the hell. At least she'll know I'm not completely ignoring her.'

'And what a relief *that* will be.'

To my great surprise, Sherry actually remembered the conversation and said that the next weekend would be good.

'I've got a date with Rod, you know each other, right? He won't care. I'll just tell him we're old friends and we want to get caught up.'

'That's what I told Miriam.'

'Great. So do you want to drive or should I tell Rod to – '

'No, I'll drive. The Hog of Steel shall be the conveyance of choice for the evening.'

We talked for a moment about what to do, and then she said, 'Well, pick him up first, okay?'

But when I found out that Rod lived out of the way, I went by and picked up Sherry after I called for Miriam. In truth, the most efficient way would have been to get Sherry first, but I knew better than to push my luck. So, with one woman by my side and another stashed in the backseat, I drove as slowly as I dared across the Valley.

'You've been dating Rod a long time?' Miriam asked politely. She had greeted Sherry with a rather formal warmth, as though by welcoming her into the backseat, she had ushered her into her own home.

'A few months. Since he graduated. He goes to Pierce JC now, but he thinks he's getting into UCLA after two years.'

'Is it serious?'

Sherry laughed gaily, leaning forward to speak in the space between us. 'He wishes. No, it's no big thing. He's nice, but so are a lot of other guys. Do we have any classes together?' she asked Miriam. 'I know I've seen you around and all, but I can't remember.'

'Not this year,' Miriam said evenly. 'We had bio last year. I sat in the second row.'

'Oh, yeah, and I sat in the back. You ran around with Marcy and Sue and those guys, right? That was a *gross* class. The man was crazed for entrails. Every day it was either a frog or an earthworm or a rat or something. And right after lunch!'

I felt the rising heat of embarrassment. For some reason Sherry was sounding as twittery and trite as a half-dozen Nancys. None of the polish and poise and wit that she showed with me was coming through at all. She must be nervous I thought quickly. Miriam must be making her feel threatened in some way.

I jumped in quickly with both feet. 'So how are your parents doing? Your sister?' I grinned back in the rear-view mirror at her encouragingly. 'Have you written any more poetry lately?'

Miriam turned to gaze at me with cool calm.

'Not much,' Sherry said. 'My folks have been going

157

nuts with Kim. She's been a real pain. My mother says she's single-handedly turning her gray before her time.'

'This is your older sister?' Miriam asked.

'Yeah, three years. And she's pretty wild. I can remember when I was just a freshman the stuff she was doing then. Sneaking out at night, running off with some guy. My folks thought she had mono her whole senior year, because all she did was sleep all the time. But she was sneaking out her bedroom window at night and meeting her boyfriend. She'd come back home right before the alarm was set to go off. Naturally, when she got home from school, she'd have to go right to bed.'

'And your folks never caught her?' Now Miriam had turned around, her arm over the seat, completely engrossed.

'Finally. One night I woke up and my mom was sitting on my bed crying. She had come in to check on us for some reason or another and found Kim's bed empty. Of course, they had a fit. They were furious I hadn't told on her. I got grounded for a while, for being an "accomplice", my mom said, but then they dragged Kim off to a shrink, and he told them they had to ease up, so they let me off. The shrink told my mother that Kim had been trying to punish her for something. Also, that she had a lot of hostility about sex and men.' She giggled. 'Goes to show what *he* knew. Anyway, she's settled down a lot now.'

'Where they stricter with you because of her?' I asked.

'A little. I had a curfew, but that's okay. Everybody thought I'd be just like her, especially the teachers, and even a few of the guys. But I'm not.' She looked at Miriam and then away. 'I don't give them much to worry about.'

Miriam smiled politely. 'I guess every family's got someone like that. A kid who tests the waters first.'

158

'Well, Kim nearly *drowned* in them, but she's normal now. Anyway nearly.'

I was fascinated. I had this urge to ask Sherry how she felt when she woke up and found her mother weeping on her bed. Did she reach out and hold her? Console her as one would a heartbroken child? Did she, at that moment, hate her sister – or despise her parents for their blindness? What an interesting insight, also, into her mother's frantic friendliness, and maybe the whole compulsion about popularity that she expressed – but with Miriam there, I couldn't ask. Besides, we were pulling into Rod's driveway.

Sherry's date jumped into the car, and the Hog of Steel immediately seemed half as roomy. From the rearview mirror the guy looked to be all shoulders and neck, and he reached up and pumped my hand fiercely.

'Glad to see you, man,' he said, and then with a quick nod to Miriam, 'Hey. Nice to meet you.' He unabashedly enveloped Sherry in a gargantuan squeeze, forcing a squeal out of her. 'Hey, baby! How's my favorite kitten?'

Miriam smiled, perhaps her first show of genuine mirth in the evening, but Sherry pulled away and pouted. 'Don't call me that, Rod. You know I hate it.'

The two seemed incredibly mismatched. 'So!' I said, too loudly. 'Everybody hungry?'

'Hit it, kid. Make this baby fly!' Rod settled back with a jolt that made the Hog of Steel lurch on its axle, pulling Sherry back with him. 'And turn up that radio. My stomach feels like a freakin' alligator.'

'Bass!' I yelled, one hand on the wheel, the other on the volume. 'Decibels! Vibrato! We must have bass!' I caught Sherry's eye in the mirror, and she shook her head at us both with a rueful grin.

The Sportsman's Lodge was our destination, one of the few restaurants in the whole Valley that required a tie. Its

159

claim to fame was a dining room that faced a garden, a small waterfall, and a subtle array of invisible lights that made the whole outdoor night seem as though it were on the menu.

Miriam and I had discussed it thoroughly.

'Well, I'm not exactly keen to go to a drive-in with them,' she had said. 'I mean, I don't even know them.'

'That's cool,' I replied, 'you can't talk much at a drive-in anyway. You want to go dancing?' Miriam was a good dancer. Not inspired, but competent, as she was in most things.

'Let's just go to dinner and see how it works out. If we like them, then we can play it by ear.'

She was being cautious, and I couldn't pressure her without making the evening seem more important to me than she already suspected it was. In fact, I'd been looking forward to this night for weeks.

I knew that Sherry wouldn't go out with me, but I still wanted to be around her. I could never have explained my fascination to Miriam. Or to Sherry, either, for that matter.

Now I watched her across the dining table. She was so incredibly living. She danced too long and drove too fast and was always sunburned and smelling of open air. So many seemed to want Sherry, to respond to her brightness, and it was obvious that she would never wait for someone to catch up.

The first conflict was over bread sticks.

'I have a problem with this,' Rod said, picking one up and gesturing with it like a sword. 'You'd think at a restaurant like this, they could give you real bread, not this cheap Italian fake. Look' – and he stuck it in the butter, whereupon it broke in two, leaving crumbs all over – 'you can't even eat the thing right.'

'You're not supposed to put butter on it,' Sherry said,

'and if you do, you don't have to jab it in and make a mess.' She took a knife, slipped a small wad of butter on it, and delicately placed it on the end of a bread stick. A small crunch, and it was gone. 'Also, they don't expect you to be so starving that you'd want a loaf of bread before dinner is served.'

'They don't expect you to be hungry? Then why do they call it a restaurant?'

To my surprise, Miriam said mildly, gesturing rather ungracefully with a sesame-seed stick, 'These things aren't my favorite either, Rod. They're just one step up from crackers.'

Well, of course, in the pause that followed, I knew that an opinion from me was expected. And if I sided with Sherry against Miriam, it might well be the last opinion I'd have a chance to venture that night. 'What I really hate,' I confided, 'is that they put the salad on a plate instead of in a bowl. I always lose half of it over the side, and then when the waiter picks up my plate, there's this orbit of oily foliage exposing me as a slob.'

They all laughed politely, and I breathed a little easier. The battle of the bread sticks was momentarily forgotten. But the rest of the evening seemed to go like that, with sides being drawn, rounds being fired – but high and wide, over one another's heads – and you could hear the whistles of the missed shots only if you listened carefully. Unpleasantness à la carte.

We didn't go dancing. I knew better than to even suggest it. After we dropped Sherry off, then way across the Valley to Rod's, we crisscrossed back to Miriam's house in silence.

Finally, she said, 'Well, it was an okay evening, I guess. Slightly more fun than a bus ride over the Andes. She's no Einstein – '

'Neither is he.'

'At least he can maintain a conversation.'

'About what? Football and Pierce was all I heard him talk about all night. That and bread sticks.'

'If he'd have been William F. Buckley, I doubt he'd have been good enough for her as far as you're concerned. You've got a really unrealistic picture of that girl in your head, David.'

'Is that so?' I couldn't seem to stop my sarcasm.

Miriam ignored it. She leaned back on the passenger door and peered at me intently. 'Yes, that's so. But you can't take any criticism. Not about her and not about yourself.'

'I can take criticism when it's from an unbiased source.'

'That has yet to be proved in this lifetime, even if there were such a thing.'

'Go ahead,' I said lightly. 'Tell me the truth, the way you see it.'

'The truth you shall have,' she said softly, 'but it won't set you free. You, like most guys, have got us all divided up, neat and tidy, into princesses and sluts. And you've put her in the princess category. Which is incredibly funny, when you stop to think about it. She didn't get to be so popular by being an ice queen, you know.'

'Fasten your seat belt,' I said solemnly. 'We are about to ride that streetcar named Delusion.'

'I'm serious. It doesn't matter what she does or says, you've cemented her onto this pedestal. Without really even knowing her.'

'And I suppose you know her better?'

'Better than you do. Enough to know that she's got a lot of sadness ahead of her. I feel sorry for her and all the other girls you guys classify so easily. You feel more comfortable around them, I guess, once you've got them categorized. And those of us who can't be labeled get pushed aside until you're ready to get serious. She's just

162

a fantasy you worship at, David, and even if she *could* belong to any one guy, the minute you got close, you'd see there's not much there. I'll bet there's not a day in her life that Sherry Gentry doesn't fake something.'

I couldn't come up with a quick retort. Some truth was there, however overstated and emotional it might be. I ran swiftly over a few of Sherry's remarks that evening, trying to hear them again objectively. There was no doubt that she wasn't at her best tonight, but who was? A restless unhappiness seemed to come from her sometimes, an ominous sort of checking-over-her-shoulder as though she sensed something gaining on her.

On the other hand, she was undeniably lovely, as always. There was something about her, an electrical sense of motion, of changefulness, of an untapped and unique sexuality that made her slightest gesture appealing. Burned into the back of my eyes, when I closed them, was the way she had simply taken her seat at the restaurant. With one slender hand she swept her hair back from her shoulders, swung her hips around the chair, and tilted back her chin to smile at me. A continuum of grace. A vitality that drew me to her with a yearning so strong that it sometimes seemed almost a life-force.

It was like the women in the Bond movies, the sense of power and transient beauty. Sherry seemed to advertise her availability with every move, yet managed to persuade each of us who watched that it was for him alone that she arched her back, swept up her skirts, and grew her sunshine hair long. Her cheerful acquiescence to our worship, her taking it as her due, promised at once pleasure without shame and commitment without cost. It suddenly struck me. The magic of the California girl was not just being sexual or sensual, not just nymph and blue eyes and light. Being a California girl had to do with honey and champagne. And the champagne's *knowing* it was champagne . . .

'Why so pale and wan, fond lover?' Miriam asked suddenly. 'Did I strike a nerve?'

'Actually,' I said, 'I was thinking that the real issue isn't Sherry. The real issue is you and I.' I reached over and turned off the radio. 'Isn't that what this is really all about?'

She glanced out the window, her eyes shadowed. 'Maybe. But it doesn't make what I said any less true.'

'Just less relevant. You and I have been bickering a lot lately, Miriam. We're beginning to sound like two old marrieds. And I don't think the problem is Sherry. The problem is you're – '

'Say it and die.'

'Jealous. It's true.'

'I'm *not* jealous. Jealous implies I wish I were her, and I don't. I wish *you* didn't wish I were her.'

'I don't wish you were her.'

She sighed sadly. 'No, but you wish you could have us both, somehow. And you're so busy trying to catch hold of her skirt as she flits by, you're letting go with both hands of something that could make you happy.'

God, that rankled me. 'You sound like Dear Abby right now. If I wanted to date a *yenta*, I'd take out my mom.'

'You arrogant prick,' she said softly.

I couldn't have been more astounded if she had suddenly jumped out of the car. She instantly seemed a decade older and completely in control, this young woman whom I'd never heard mutter more than an occasional 'hell'. I felt a wild urge to giggle.

'You've been playing games with me,' she said with a cold fury. 'You haven't been honest about your feelings, not about me and not about Sherry. I've tried to tell you

164

the truth. But you don't want the truth from a girl; none of you do. You all want to take out striking beauties with IQs lower than a schefflera, and there just aren't enough of those to go around. You are *incredibly* arrogant, David, and worse, you're a coward.'

'What?'

'You're a chickenshit.'

'Why?'

'Because you take the easy way out. You prefer to be with some girl you only have to worship – and God knows, that's not tough to do with the women you want – but you never have to be real with them. You never have to get right down with her to human-being level. She doesn't ask anything from you but that you roll over. *I* ask that you stand up and be the best David Levine you can be.'

'Arrogant prick and chickenshit. Wonderful. Clearly, I'm talking to an English major.'

'That's what I mean,' she said tightly. 'You hide everything behind this witty demeanor. You're getting so incredibly California, I can't stand it. You glide, you coast, you never press. You just ain't that funny all the time, Levine. You think if you make me laugh, I'll just forget the fact that we hardly ever talk about anything serious. That I get the feeling that I'm just a handy girl to call up until Sherry decides to give you another chance.' She suddenly scooted across until her face was close to mine. 'You think,' she said, softly now, 'that I don't know that sometimes, when you kiss me, you pretend it's her?'

'I don't do that,' I said, genuinely alarmed. 'I never have!'

We pulled into her driveway and I cut off the engine. 'Listen, Miriam, whatever else you might think, I haven't been using you like that. I *like* you. I really do!'

'Well,' she said, calm now. 'I guess that's just not

enough for me anymore. And believe me, David, someday you're going to be even sorrier than I am now.' With
that, she got out of the car and walked away without even
a glance over her shoulder.

I waited, watching as she put her key in the lock and
went inside. I waited, certain that she would come back
out again, and say one more thing, change her mind, tell
me that I should call her in the morning, and we'd talk it
over. There was something about this whole scene that
reminded me of Ruth, and I felt incredibly sad. Finally,
the light over the porch went out, and she never appeared.

All the way home I weighed her words, sifting through
them for what she was really saying, trying to objectively
assess my own blame in all this.

Yes, I had taken her for granted. And maybe it wasn't
too cool to press this double-date scene. She wasn't blind,
and she wasn't a fool, and clearly, I had pushed my luck.

But on the other hand, I wasn't a chickenshit arrogant
prick. And each time I replayed her words in my mind, I
stiffened in righteous anger. I was really rotten to her all
right, I thought, really gave her a hard time. Took her
nice places, treated her with respect. And what I got back
was a lot of hard-core probing into my inner psyche. I
mean, does anybody mind if I just want to have a good
time? Did she ever hear about just cutting loose? God
forbid we should miss a single opportunity to open our
veins and analyze ourselves into stuttering depression.

Good riddance, I thought tightly. I was getting tired of
her, anyway. Finish up my senior year with somebody
who knows how to enjoy life a little. Somebody with a
decent sense of humor who can laugh without looking for
some goddamned Hidden Meaning in every word!

But I couldn't fight the feeling that I'd lost something
valuable – and that the way I'd lost it, with rancor and
anger, was far beneath both of us. I shouldn't have said I

liked her. I should have told the truth: I *cared* about her. When I thought of hearing from colleges and not having Miriam to tell it to, when I thought of her quick and cagey retorts, her softness and warmth, when I tried to picture the rest of the year – and beyond – without her, I felt bereft. And when I pictured my parents' faces when I told them I wouldn't be dating Miriam Weld anymore, I didn't feel proud of myself at all.

The one place I thought I'd never be troubled by sexual confusion was in my father's synagogue. I always thought of the Valley Reform Temple as Rabbi Levine's place, as though he had actually built it, pink stone by pink stone. When my father stood before the congregation, wreathed in his yarmulke and Shabbes robes, in my mind he took on the mantle of the village elder. I wouldn't have been surprised if, after the service, an occasional merchant had come forward and asked Rabbi Levine to arbitrate a quarrel over the price of cloth, or if one of the landowners had come to the podium, hat in hand, to request that Rabbi Levine tell his neighbor to keep his goats properly penned. When my father stood before me in temple, I felt there was no trouble this man of God could not turn aside.

Except for maybe one. Miriam still was sitting with her family near the aisle, as she had every week, about halfway back. Since our quarrel, she didn't look at me once. Before, she had always lingered after the service, linking her arm through mine proprietorily. Now she avoided my side of the aisle. And her parents merely nodded.

I never thought anything more could happen to make Shabbes less comfortable, until the day Sherry Gentry showed up at the Valley Reform Temple.

I saw her come in all alone, just as the service was

beginning. She walked in the door closest to the podium, saw that the cantor was about to begin, and hesitated, scanning the audience.

In the instant that I saw her, I was struck by her total poise and confidence. Here she was, in a strange synagogue, before an alien god, even, and she showed not the least timidity. I caught her eye and waved. She grinned, a gleam of instant recognition, and then – smiling at the cantor as she crossed in front of him – she sat down next to me, right in the middle of the first row, as though she had done it every Saturday of her life.

'What are you doing here?' I whispered with a quick glance at my mother. As usual, she had taken her seat down on the aisle. Normally, Myra Levine had eyes only for her husband through the Shabbes service, as though she expected to hear God's own thunder come out of his mouth at any moment. But now she was staring at Sherry with frank curiosity and a frown of faint disapproval.

'I decided to come and see what the Jewish religion is all about,' Sherry whispered back. 'I'm so glad you're here! I thought this was your temple, but I wasn't sure.'

Didn't come to see me, then. She wore no shoulder or head covering. In a more orthodox temple, she would never have been admitted, but she had coincidentally selected the one service where few would object to her California sheen. But they certainly would notice. I felt somehow responsible for her infidel intrusion. I glanced over my shoulder as though a hundred eyes burned into both our backs.

'I try to explore a new religion each month,' she was whispering earnestly. 'Last month I went with a girlfriend to mass over at St Mary's. The month before that I went to a Buddhist temple down on Sunset.' She beamed at me. 'I've done four so far this year.'

168

The cantor began to sing, and I could only smile, put a silencing finger to my lips, and turn my attention to God.

She sampled religions like other people tried new restaurants. What an incredible nerve!

But on the other hand, what an admirable exploration. She could have stayed home by the pool all weekend. Instead, she went from place to place sampling all the different forms of worship out of intellectual curiosity. I glanced at her sideways, keeping my face straight ahead. There was nothing irreverent about her posture, her clothing, or her expression. She didn't bow her head at the right times, but stared at my father, listening intently. I wondered how much she actually understood. Had she eaten the wafer at St Mary's just for the experience of it?

She turned, caught my eye, and smiled softly. I riveted my attention on the cantor and my father. The last thing I needed was to have the entire congregation see Rabbi Levine glare at his son for flirting with Sherry Gentry in God's house.

Somehow I got through the interminable service, and only when the last prayer was over and the people rose did I finally start to relax. Sherry began to ask questions, what did the cantor sing at the beginning, what was that book he held, why did the women answer and not the men, and why didn't anybody else sing along? I answered her in a daze, leading her out to the door where my father stood, saying his farewells as the people trickled out.

'Dad,' I said when there was a lull, 'I'd like you to meet Sherry Gentry, a friend of mine. She wanted to come and see what goes on in a reformed temple.'

'Miss Gentry,' my father said courteously. 'I am always happy to meet David's friends.'

'Rabbi Levine,' she said, completely correctly, 'I hope you don't mind my intruding on your lovely service today.

Had I known this was your temple, I certainly would have come before.'

'Then' – my father's brow rose – 'you are not David's guest?'

She laughed delightedly. 'No, I'm afraid I'm an interloper. Simply here to learn. I'm not Jewish. I guess,' she said with a dazzling smile, 'I'm not anything, really.'

'Ah. An inquiring mind.' Rabbi Levine turned a calm glance to me. 'We must see that Miss Gentry visits us again, David.'

'Thank you,' she said, inclining her head slightly. 'And now I have lots of questions which I hope David can answer for me.' She put her hand through my arm and led me away as gracefully as though she were my older aunt, rather than a girl I'd dipped at a school dance.

'You're really good at this,' I said under my breath.

'You seem to have a slight case of nerves.'

'More like a six-pack.'

'Why is that?' she asked – and then – 'Oh, there's Miriam! Hi!' She waved at Miriam, who stood a little apart from her parents. I instantly remembered that Miriam had once asked me to take her to temple, and I'd all but refused. I flushed vividly and felt the dampness spring to my armpits.

'Didn't mean to steal your guy,' Sherry said cheerfully, relinquishing my arm as she dragged me over.

Mercifully, Miriam matched her, cool for cool. 'Hello, Sherry,' she said gently, never glancing at me. 'Did you enjoy the service?'

'Oh, yes, it was really interesting. I liked it better than the Buddhist place I went to last month. But I didn't know you both went here too. It makes it nicer, to see familiar faces.'

'Oh? So, you're not a guest of anyone special?'

Sherry was beginning to sense something off-key. 'No,' she said, a little bewildered. 'Do I need to be?'

'No, no, not at all,' Miriam assured her. 'You're always welcome, of course. In fact, if you want to come again, call me sometime, and you can drive over with my family.' She looked around as though to find them. 'Oh, there they go now. Look, I'll see you in school, okay?' And she walked away quickly, her smile never altering.

A pause. Then Sherry asked, 'You two broke up?' She turned and faced me, touching my arm. 'You should have told me.'

'I didn't get a chance.'

She gazed at me quizzically. 'Your idea or hers?'

I gave her the expected courteous response. 'A mutual decision.' I was still irritated – at both of them – though I knew I had no good reason.

'I hope I didn't have anything to do with it.'

I was once again dazzled at her brilliant arrogance. 'No, not at all. Why would you think that?' I was suddenly determined that she not have the satisfaction.

'I don't know. I just felt her pushing me away the whole time we went out that night we doubled. Like she was saying in her mind, get off, he's mine, or something like that.'

I tried for a casual shrug. 'I would guess you get that sort of thing all the time. I mean, every time you double with somebody, the girl must wonder if her boyfriend would rather be with you.'

'Yes. It happens a lot. But I'd hate for our friendship to be a problem for you, David. I could talk to her if you like.'

Tell her you wouldn't consider me date material in a million light-years? 'No.' I looked around, suddenly aware of where we were, how many people were watching us. 'I told you, it's not a problem.' I saw my mother

171

disentangle herself from a group of women and come toward me. It was too late to steer Sherry away.

'David,' Myra Levine said brightly as she approached, 'you have not yet introduced me to your charming little friend.'

Well, that about said it all. She just told me how she wants this. Sherry is inconsequential, and I'm too young to have a relationship to worry about anyway. 'Mother,' I said, 'I'd like you to meet Sherry Gentry.'

'Mrs Levine,' Sherry said softly, 'it's my pleasure.'

'Oy, what blue eyes she has, David!' my mother crooned confidentially. 'And hair like flax in the fields.' She was really laying it on thick. 'Such a beauty! You know my David from the high school, yes?'

If I had closed my eyes and ignored the expensive modern dress, the elegant hair, the expert touch of judicious makeup, I could have sworn, from just listening, that my mother was a fat peasant with hay in her skirts, just off the boat.

But Sherry just smiled. 'We've had a few classes together. Actually, we're neighbors. I live just a few blocks from you, Mrs Levine.'

My mother swiveled her gaze to me now, a look full of questions.

'You recall me mentioning Sherry, Mother,' I said patiently. 'Her pool got a crack in it from the earthquake, remember?' Don't torture me. 'She just came by to see what temple was like. In fact, I'm about to walk her to her car.'

My mother visibly relaxed. 'Sure, sure, that's fine. I remember you now, dear. This is *that* Sherry!'

Vastly amusing. As though I had a dozen Sherrys in my life.

'Well, it was wonderful to meet you, and you should

172

come over and see us.' She waved to a group of women who were leaving and hurried over to make her good-byes.

'Come on,' I said. 'Before they *all* want to check you out.'

In the parking lot I felt like I was emerging from a long and exotic movie into reality. A little dazed, I steered us both to the familiar blue MG, half expecting it to dissolve in the shimmering heat.

'So,' I said, 'tell me about this religious pilgrimage you're on. Sort of smorgasbord of scriptures, or what?'

She laughed. 'Yeah, I like the cafeteria approach to life. Really, though, I'm a pagan through and through.'

'Have you found any one religion that you – like – more than any other?' I found the whole conversation disorienting.

'Not really. If I had to sum up my favorite philosophy, though, I could do it in two words. *Carpe diem*. And *laissez-faire* for everybody else.'

I grinned. God, she blew me away. 'Well,' I managed to say, 'you're way ahead of most of the unenlightened slugs I know.'

'I told you I was,' she said softly. 'The first time we met, I believe.'

'The second.'

'So who's counting. Want to come over later? We could swim or something. I've got a date tonight, but nothing's going on this afternoon.'

'Yeah,' I said quickly, wondering what it all meant, whether anything at all in my life had any order or purpose. 'Sure. I'll be over in an hour or so.'

And as I walked away, she called out, 'Hey, David Levine. I'm glad you're not spoken for anymore.' The MG whisked away with one slender hand waving out the top.

Spoken for. Strange way to put it, I thought as I walked

back into the temple. Almost old-fashioned. And then the realization hit me like a balloon inflating my chest. She likes me. She must, or she wouldn't have said that. Also, dorkus, in case you hadn't noticed in your complete stupor, she asked you over today.

In spite of the fact that I knew my mother was looking for it, despite all the solid reasons not to, I couldn't keep the grin from my mouth.

When I got to Sherry's, she was already in her bathing suit out by the pool, waiting. As before, Cokes and chips were brought to us, as though by wishing we could have anything we wanted.

Maybe it was the heat, maybe the dose of religion she'd had, but Sherry was in a meditative mood. We were sprawled on the lounge chairs, feeling only the sun, our hands within easy reaching distance of the chips and each other.

'You know,' she was saying, 'I always had this favorite fantasy. That somehow I had been adopted by my parents, that they really weren't my parents at all.'

'Who were your real parents?' I asked drowsily.

'A king and queen somewhere,' she said, completely serious. 'I used to think that while I was out driving around in the car with them, someone would see me and say, "There she is! Finally we've found her!" And I would be taken away and restored to my proper parents and rightful place as a princess.'

'You're kidding,' I said, not even opening my eyes. I couldn't believe she was telling me this. Did all beautiful girls have daydreams like this one?

'Nope. As I got older, the fantasy changed. I wasn't born a princess, but I just *become* one, like Grace Kelly or something. I get married to a prince and then everybody sees that all along this is what I was meant for.' She laughed aloud. 'Truly ludicrous, right?'

'Not so very.' I reached for my Coke. 'If you're ever in the mood to be adopted, just let me know. I'll sign up as guardian. I could take you out for ice cream, bounce you on my knee, tell you bedtime stories.'

'Would I have a room of my own?'

I opened my eyes and gave her my best James Bond leer.

'Talk about fantasies.'

'Kids these days,' I sighed, 'nothing but gimme, gimme, gimme.' The amazing thing was, I could picture her quite well as she described herself, a princess in a fabled country. But I could also picture her as a little girl with long golden braids, a basket in her hand, treading through the dark forest. A world full of Disney creatures and dancing toadstools and traps and enchantments. She knew about dark roads, this one, but she preferred the sunlight. The Persian leapt gracefully up on my lounge chair, startling me. The cat hadn't been my constant shadow lately, so that when it did appear, I became wary. Good chance I was about to make a spectacle of myself.

She reached for a handful of chips and leaned back again, her eyes closed and her voice dreamy. 'So don't you have a favorite fantasy?'

For a brief, heady instant I considered telling her that she was my fantasy, but I knew better. 'I've got this thing for fairy godmothers,' I said solemnly. 'Sooner or later I know that one of them is going to pop up and ask me what my three wishes are, and I want to be prepared.'

'I know what you'll say. You'll wish for a hundred more wishes with your first wish.'

'How crass. No, first I'll wish for world peace and an end to world hunger – and all the money in the world and immortality to spend it in.'

'That's four wishes.'

'So much for world hunger.'

175

'You'd want to live forever?'

'Sure,' I said, 'wouldn't you?'

'Only if I could stay young forever. It would be gross to be immortal if I couldn't stay the way I am now.'

A shadow fell over Sherry's head, and both of us looked up. Kim stood behind her chair, shading her eyes with her hand. 'How baroque,' she said. 'To believe that wherever you are is the best place to be. Don't you look forward to changing?'

'I'll never change,' Sherry said. 'I'll just become more myself.'

Kim hit the back of my chair with a friendly palm and sat down. 'Hey, Levine. Still hanging around?'

I was touched that she remembered my name. Maybe Sherry had mentioned it occasionally. 'Yeah. Somebody told me that the downtown bus comes through here at three. How've you been?'

'Okay. Cal is killing me, of course, but I'm making it. You two will have a big shock in store next year. Senior year is the easiest you'll ever have it. You better live it up.'

'Somebody's been telling me that ever since I was twelve,' Sherry said dryly, 'and it's usually been you, Kimmy.'

'Yeah, well, all I know is that I don't have time on a Saturday to lay out here and bask in the sun.' She crowded her sister over on the chaise longue.

'Then what are you doing?' Sherry protested, moving over grudgingly.

'If a person's going to be a martyr to learning, they might as well do it with a perfect tan.'

'Fry down,' I said solemnly. 'You deserve a break today.' I settled my sunglasses on my nose and my back down on the chaise. I peered surreptitiously at the two women, side by side, from behind the camouflage of lenses. I recalled reading somewhere about the Elizabethan concept that the eyes are windows to the soul. Sunglasses prove that we all have something to hide.

Sherry and Kim. An incredible expanse of territory to scan. Both had the same blond hair, though Kim's was slightly darker, as though she sat in shadow and Sherry sat in light. Both of them had the same perfect, even features, the identical tawny skin, the similar high rib cage and flat stomach. Sherry's breasts were smaller, but she was the more beautiful of the two. Kim's body suggested ripeness; Sherry's said all things might be possible.

I rolled over to conceal my growing erection and pillowed my cheek on my arms, watching them behind my glasses. A red ladybug, watching me from Sherry's leg, seemed to crack in half as it rose in flight. Between the dark hairs on my bicep I could see the small beads of sweat forming on Sherry's chest, tiny pearl-dew nestled in the dark space between her breasts. Down past the ribbon band of the pink bikini top, over the arch of her ribs, rising and falling slowly, to where her belly button hid in shadow. An innie, of course. The best kind. Around her belly button there was a light corona of blond hairs, which only added to her sheen. And then another bank of pink, a gentle mounding over her pubis –

I turned my head to the other side and muffled a groan.

'So, Levine,' Kim said drowsily, 'how's your senior year shaping up?'

I cleared my throat as though I came back from death. 'Okay, so far.' I willed myself to turn and look at her, but she still had her arm over her eyes. Sherry didn't stir. 'I'm working on a project in bio that keeps me busy and off the streets.'

'Cloning a new species?'

Sherry giggled. 'One that discos.'

The two girls laughed together, their eyes still closed.

'Actually, I'm working on an improvement of an old model. Females with zippable mouths.' The Persian's eyes went to tiny slits, and I could swear it heaved a weary sigh.

Kim turned to Sherry. 'That's the problem with these scientific types. Always the obvious solution. No subtlety.' And then to me: 'I thought maybe you wanted to be a philosopher.'

'What makes you say that?'

A slow smile. 'Nothing special. A few letters here and there.'

Sherry poked her hard in the ribs. 'Kimmy!'

'You read my letters?' I was amazed. A little abashed. 'Sherry, you let her read – '

'He *wanted* you to let us read them, silly,' Kim said casually to her sister. 'They weren't love letters, after all. Actually,' she said to me, 'I have to tell you I was impressed. We all were. I believe you just might make it in the real world, Levine.'

I flopped on my back, my eyes closed again. Try as I might, I couldn't keep the smile from my face. She had thought enough of the letters to share them with her parents and her sister, and they had judged them worthy. And me, in the process. All in all, not a major disaster. Even the Persian purred.

A clicking of heels came from upwind, and Sherry's mother hurried out to the patio. 'There you are, girls.' She smiled at me and waved gaily. 'Listen, I'm going into Encino to do some shopping, and I won't be home for dinner. Maggie'll fix something for you, and I'll be back before you go to bed.'

Sherry opened her eyes and shaded them against the sun, gazing at her mother. Mrs Gentry was dressed in a short denim skirt, a Navaho silver belt studded with

178

turquoise slung low on her hips. 'Dad won't be home for dinner?'

'Is he ever?' She sounded snappy. 'As usual, he calls an hour before he's supposed to be here to say he won't be.' She turned to me with a brittle grin. 'David, when you get married, tell your wife ahead of time if you never intend to be around, that way she can plan her own life, at least, and not spend it waiting for the Phantom.'

'Bye, Mom,' Kim said. 'Have a good shop.'

'Bye, chicks,' she called over her shoulder, her heels clicking away. 'Don't do anything I wouldn't do.'

'Well, *that* certainly gives us ample latitude,' Kim said quietly.

'That makes about the third time this week,' Sherry said. 'He's never home lately.'

'Do you blame him?' Kim got up and adjusted her bikini deftly. 'She's always at him.'

'Oh, they get along okay,' Sherry said. 'When they go off, just the two of them, they're better.'

'So she says. "Remember girls,"' Kim said with an evil imitation of her mother's voice, '"don't give it away. You'll learn that fast enough."'

Sherry giggled. '"Once he's got what he wants, he'll be gone. Or worse, you'll have him forever and something else besides that you can't get rid of."'

I was quietly appalled. This was obviously a game they'd played frequently; they were quite good at it.

'"Make him *pay*!"' Kim ended with a witch's cackle. '"He won't buy the cow if he gets the milk for free!"' They were laughing in unison now. 'Remember? God!' Kim patted her sister on the leg affectionately. 'Well, I've got to run, kiddo.' To me she added as she walked off: 'Stay cool, Levine. That bus should be along anytime now.'

I lay there in silence. The shadows were getting longer

179

and the air was growing cooler. It was time for me to go, but I hated to leave Sherry when she was down. She turned over, pulled her bikini bottom at the edges, and then curled her hands up by her chin. We were face-to-face now, sunglasses off.

'Is your dad home every night for dinner?' she asked wistfully.

'Yeah. Unless there's some kind of emergency. He's *always* there; his office is in the house.'

'That must be neat.'

'It ties up the phone a lot.'

'Do your folks get along?'

'Pretty well. No great passion, but they seem to like each other.'

She murmured, 'My folks started with a big passion, I think. And sometimes you can still see it. But it's like she's mad all the time at somebody.' She shrugged. 'Usually Kim. Sometimes me.'

'She didn't sound mad at you just now.'

'No. But she didn't want to stay around here, either.' She closed her eyes, her voice still drowsy. 'You know, I remember something that happened a long time ago. Or maybe it didn't really happen. Maybe I just dreamed it. Anyway, I remember finding these two old boxes of pictures of my father. Old photos taken when he was in the navy. He had on this sailor suit, and he looked so young! His ears looked bigger then, and he had this big Adam's apple on a skinny neck. I used to love to look at those old pictures by the hour. And I picked out one of them, my favorite, and I put it under my pillow.'

'How old were you?'

'Oh, I don't know. Eight, maybe. Ten. Anyway, I carried this picture around with me and looked at it all the time. And my mother saw me doing it and teased me to death about it. Finally, she told me I had to give it

180

back. I said why? because she had a lot of others just like it. But she said it was hers, not mine, and that I would wreck it. I said I was being real careful with it and showed her how I'd wrapped it in wax paper. But she got ticked off and wanted it back. I told her no.'

'Stubborn,' I said quietly.

'Yeah, I was then. Anyway, she grabbed for it, and it tore down the middle. See? she said. I *told* you you'd ruin it. Now, keep your hands off of my things! And she hid away the two boxes of pictures of my father, and I never could find them again.'

I scarcely knew what to say. I wanted to reach across and touch her, but I didn't want to break the spell. I was touched that she confided so easily in me. 'Did that really happen?'

'Maybe not,' she said. 'Lots of times I dream things, and then I don't remember later if they really happened or not.'

'Do you ever talk to anyone else about stuff like this?'

'To Kim sometimes. To my dad. Who do you talk to the most?'

I thought about it. At different stages in my life I'd been closer to one parent than the other. There was a time when my mother received all my secrets; now it seemed my dad and I had more to say to each other. No doubt, it would shift again in time. 'Both of them, really. It just depends who's handy.'

She smiled. 'That must be great. To have them both handy.'

All of a sudden I wanted to be home. To be back where the rhythms were comfortable. I glanced at my watch and said, 'Wow, I've got to go. You've got a date, and I've got stuff to do too.' I stood up and she rolled over, shading her eyes with her hand. 'Thanks for the hospitality. And let me know next time we're up for Religion of the Month, I'll be sure to save you a seat.'

She grinned. 'You got it.'

I never thought I'd be ready to leave her before she was ready to kick me out, but I couldn't wait to get back out to the street, grab the wheel of the Hog of Steel, and head for home.

Now that I look back on it, I spent a lot of time at Sherry's pool. Increasingly, if she had nothing much to do, she decided to do it with me. I didn't know then how tight and tidy the web strands were being woven.

I took inventory often in those days. I was presentable-looking, possessed of a spacious and sympathetic intelligence, a gift of the gab, as it were – but I knew I wasn't sexy. At least not to her. But I did make her laugh. My parents and teachers told me my mouth was the oldest organ on my body, but I was trying to learn how to listen as well. I became her best audience, sensitive to the most subtle gesture or encouragement she might offer, though we scarcely had done more than touch fingertips.

Her favorite game was to do water ballet in the pool. She pushed off from the bottom, her arms moving gracefully like swan wings, her eyes shut but her mouth smiling. She came into the shallow end, turning and twisting underwater, striking poses with her arms and her legs, and finally ending with a pirouette where she fell over backward in a long, floating swoon. She never looked back to see if I would be there to catch her. I always was.

I wasn't her lover, but neither was I just a pal. After a faltering try at asking her out again, a try that left us both embarrassed and edgy when she said no, I resolved not to push it. But we grew closer and closer. Clearly, I was more than just a casual friend.

You don't tell a casual friend all your hopes and dreams and fears, I thought, and you don't tell a casual friend the

182

problems you're having with other guys, either – which she did blithely, to my intense and camouflaged discomfort.

But I kept wanting some sort of definition. The best I could devise was a word Miriam had used once: *confidant*. It implied to me trust, secrets, and intimacy. I asked her if that was the way she saw us.

'*Confidant?* You mean, like a girlfriend?'

That threw me off completely. 'No, not like a *girl* friend, like a – more like a – blood brother. Or something like that, anyway.' I was suddenly, intensely, embarrassed and wished to God I had never asked.

She laughed delightedly. 'Why do you have to put a label on it, David? And besides, whatever we decide it is, it'll change tomorrow.'

'What's happening tomorrow?'

'Nothing, silly, but there's one thing you should have learned about me by now. I say a whole lot of things I mean at the time – '

'And don't mean them later?'

'Not exactly. It's just that . . . well, the time moves on, you know? Like a wheel that's moving over ground, only touching in one place at a time. It's always in the present.' And she smiled like she had just made me a gift of the secret of life.

One day, while we were in her kitchen piling plates with leftovers to take out by the pool, the doorbell rang. 'I'll get it!' she hollered out to Maggie. Sherry turned and disappeared into the living room.

I continued to stack peanut butter crackers on my plate, expecting her to return any moment. I found a wedge of Sara Lee chocolate cake shoved way back in the refrigerator, and I pulled that out for her to consider. Also, I noticed a row of eggs in the egg bin, each one marked with a penciled 'H'. Hard-boiled, I thought, plucking a few out and making a small pile of salt and pepper on the edge of my plate. Mustard. Must be in the pantry.

But what was taking her so long? I stuck my head around the kitchen door but couldn't see her. Voices from the living room, male voices, getting louder and inquisitional. I ventured out around the corner, gripping a napkin in one hand.

Sherry was seated on the long white sofa, clutching a green pillow to her stomach. Across from her, Rod and Don sat in two separate chairs. Both of their faces were set and angry. Rod leaned back, his arms crossed; Don sat forward, gesturing almost in Sherry's face.

'Then it's true, isn't it? Everything he said?'

She didn't reply. Her face was pale, her head dropped low.

Rod said, 'She's a lying little bitch, man. Pretends to be Miss Goody-Two-Shoes, all the time she's going down for whoever asks her.'

A small gasp from Sherry, but she didn't lift her head.

I shrank back along the entry wall so I couldn't be seen if they looked up. Don looked almost as upset as Sherry did. Rod's face, on the other hand, was contorted with disgust.

'Look at me, lady,' Don said quietly. 'Just tell us the truth.'

'For once,' Rod added.

Don glared at him, but Sherry didn't see it. 'You told me that you were a virgin. That you hadn't' – he faltered, and I could hear the pain in his voice – 'that you hadn't done stuff with guys before. That I was the only one.'

'She told me the same thing, man,' Rod sneered. 'Christ, she probably told a *hundred* guys the same thing!'

'Shut up,' Don said coldly. 'Sherry?'

She didn't raise her head.

'Did you let him feel you up?'

184

I winced. Sherry turned her head away.

Rod snapped, 'Ask her if she sucked me off, man. The Girl with the Golden Cunt.'

Don moved swift as a snake, and the loud wap of his clenched fist on Rod's jaw startled everyone in the room. Sherry raised her head now, her eyes wide, her mouth contorted. Both men were on their feet, fists balled, inches from each other's chest. I had a wild thought that the glass cocktail table would be the first to go; I was just coming from the entryway to stop them when Sherry rose, her voice trembling. 'You guys, please! Please stop.'

'Tell him to get out,' Don growled. His chest rose and fell as though he were sobbing.

'I think you both should leave,' I said quietly.

All eyes swiveled to me and then away, as though I were no more important than the wall.

'That's right,' Sherry said. 'Both of you, get out.'

Rod relaxed slightly, his fists lowering. He turned to Sherry, but his eyes stayed on Don. 'This is really low, Sherry. You lied to both of us. Probably to about fifty other guys too. When I think of all the times you put me off, made me beg for it – ' He shook his head, a twisted smile. 'Shit. You wouldn't fuck me, but you probably did everybody else.'

She blanched even paler, and I thought for an instant she might fall headfirst on the table.

'She didn't fuck you?' Don asked quietly.

'Everything but, man,' Rod said. 'You?'

Don shook his head, his fists down now.

'So I guess she's a technical virgin, for what it's worth.' He laughed, a bitter snort. 'When I think of all the times I worried about going too fast for her!'

It was as if she weren't in the room at all.

'That's enough, guys,' I said, moving closer. 'Give her a break.'

185

Don turned, as though suddenly aware of my presence. 'A break? Like she's had it so tough!' He turned back to Sherry, his voice low, intense. 'I *loved* you. I really cared about you. You were my – my golden princess.'

'Get in line, man,' Rod said gruffly.

Sherry lifted her head now, and her jaw was out like a plow. 'Both of you, go home. I don't want to see you anymore.'

Rod laughed, shaking his head. 'Hey, baby, don't worry! You ain't worth the fuckin' misery.' He stomped toward the door. 'Come on, man,' he called back to Don. 'She's already got a new sucker in tow,' glancing at me. 'But maybe we can spread the word and save a few others the trouble.' He opened the door and went out, leaving it agape.

Don said, 'Don't worry. He'll keep his mouth shut or I'll shut it for him. But Sherry' – he put one hand lightly on her shoulder – 'you better be careful. Some guys might not be so understanding.' He walked to the door and with one hand on it he turned and added, 'You're really special, girl. But nobody's *that* special.' He turned on his heel and shut the door quietly behind him.

Sherry looked up at me, her eyes wide and blank. She sank slowly back into the sofa, one hand plucking aimlessly at the pillow fringe.

I sat down at her side, setting the balled napkin on the table. 'I thought you weren't going out with Swenson anymore,' I said quietly. 'After that blanket bit you told me about on the beach.'

'I wasn't going to,' she said, 'but he kept coming around and coming around and finally, I just gave in.'

That much is evident, I wanted to say, but held my tongue.

'They'll tell everybody in the whole school,' she added, almost wistfully. 'Every guy on the team.'

'Don said they wouldn't,' I said, and I felt the weakness in my avowal even as she shrugged it away. There were a million questions in my mind. Was it true? It had to be, or they wouldn't have come. She didn't deny it, and God, what an ordeal for her, what she must have thought when she saw them both standing together on her step, must have wanted to slam the door and run out the back, screaming. But on the other hand, what are we really talking about here? Nothing but a lot of petting in backseats. She didn't actually go all the way, they said – at least not with them.

But then my mind floated up an unsavory vision of Sherry doing what Rod said she did, and I turned away from her momentarily so that she wouldn't see my eyes.

She read the gesture. 'Listen, Levine,' she said tiredly. 'You better go too.'

I felt instantly contrite, but I still couldn't bring myself to touch her. 'They didn't have any right to come here like that,' I said, reaching for some way to soothe her. 'I mean, who the hell do they think they are? It's a free country, right? You can do what you want to do with whoever you want, last I heard.' I tried for a smile. 'And they're way off base on one thing, for sure. You *are* worth it.'

She shook her head sadly. 'I am worth it, and they didn't have the right to say that to me, but it doesn't matter. It also doesn't matter if a hundred girls are doing it right now with their boyfriends, they all lie to one another and say they aren't.' A brittle smile, her eyes very bright. 'God, the lies! See, it doesn't matter if you do it with only one guy, that's okay, so long as he doesn't tell. But if you do it with *more* than one guy, you're easy. And if you do it with more than one guy at the same time, you're a slut for life.' She looked down at her hands. 'They always want something from you, and you have to

187

deliver or they find someone else who will. And then, when you do, they don't look at you the same way anymore. It's like you disappear.'

I didn't understand much of what she was saying then, but I sensed that it was far more important to her than it should have been. There have got to be more vital things to worry about, I thought dismally, but just then I couldn't think of one. I remembered Miriam's words about Critter's girl, Marsha. About how her life was ruined, at least the high school part. 'You couldn't be a slut if you sold it at window B in the lunch area, right along with the grilled cheese,' I said. 'And if anybody asks, I'll tell them you've been a regular ice maiden with me.'

'Thanks, David,' she said softly. 'You're a good friend. But right now, if you don't mind, I'd like to be by myself.'

I patted her hand, feeling feeble. When she didn't look up I let myself out the front door.

Part Three

Without the shedding of blood, there is no remission of sins.

— John Brown

She never spoke of it again. Which was odd, since Sherry had talked of nearly everything else with me that could matter. She had confided her feelings about her childhood, her parents, her sister. She had tallied up for me her various friends and their foibles, the guys she had known. She had even told me her basic philosophy of life.

But she never alluded to that scene in her living room. And somehow I couldn't bring myself to ask. I waited to hear the whispers in the locker room, wondering, when it came down to it, how many I'd kill for her. I saw Swenson a few times, but neither of us saw fit to acknowledge the other. Just a quick nod and then look away. The real source of danger to her reputation was Rod, of course; he was the most vindictive. But either he never said a word or the word never got as far as general fodder for the locker room, because I never heard Sherry's name mentioned with anything but the usual genuflection.

Would it have been different if she weren't so beautiful? Would she, like Critter's girl and so many others, have been trashed and left for dead if the word got around? Or was she somehow inviolable, shielded by her face and her hair as though she wore a golden halo?

If anything, despite her silence about that awful scene, I felt we were closer than before. New dates rushed in to fill the void left by Rod and Don, and Sherry seemed no more changed by that searing confrontation than a field is changed by summer.

Everybody was talking of college that spring. SAT scores, school apps and letters of recommendation, entrance quotas, the words rolled trippingly off our tongues as we jockeyed for position. I'd finally heard back from Columbia and NYU, who wanted me. Harvard and Cornell didn't, but I could live with that. I had two months to decide where I wanted to go, and it seemed that every other event of my life depended upon the rightness of my choice. But it was one more topic I couldn't share with Sherry.

'You know,' I told her, 'I really think you ought to give this more thought than you have.'

She rolled her eyes and shook her head gently.

'Don't look like I just asked you to run away to Tahiti or something. I mean, I honestly think you're short-changing yourself.' It was about the sixth time we'd talked about it, and she obviously wasn't any closer to a mind-change than she'd been two months ago, but I couldn't let it alone. 'It's not too late to send out apps for in-state schools, you know. And for state colleges, you can practically wait until August. UCLA, USC, maybe? Your grades are decent, and it's not as if your folks couldn't afford to send you. God, when I think of all the kids who would kill to be in your place, and you don't even want to go. How come?'

'You sound just like my mother.'

I hesitated. Not a good move, to come off parental. Last time I'd tried to advise her about anything cerebral, she almost didn't go out with me. I leaned down and turned up the stereo, a new blaster I'd added, and the Byrds were singing,

> To everything (*turn, turn, turn*)
> There is a season (*turn, turn, turn*)
> And a time to every purpose, under heaven . . .

sounding like warbling, soaring, slightly maddened larks.

We were on our way to Thirty-one Flavors for a set of double dippers.

'I don't know why people make such a big deal about college anyway,' she said thoughtfully. 'Like it's some sort of religious experience. I think it's probably quite overrated, like a lot of things. Besides, it would be a waste of time and money for me to go before I know what I want to do with my life. They want you to declare a major in your first quarter, right? Who can honestly say what they want to study for the next four years when they first get there? Except maybe you, Dobie, who's known you wanted to dissect bugs since you were five.'

'Not bugs. Rhinos.' She had taken to calling me Dobie or Maynard G. 'You could go and just take courses. Kind of sample things to see what you like. Your usual cafeteria approach to life. You don't have to declare that early.'

'You don't have to go at all, either.'

Actually, I respected her stance. Most kids in the Valley just automatically assumed they would go to college. They graduated, their dads wrote out the checks, and they shuffled off to school. The big thought process was where they would go – how impressive were their credentials – not whether or not they would go at all. At least, that's what the majority did. The fringe groups – the greasers and shop kids – well, it was a given they'd never darken the halls of Higher Education again, not unless they went through some sort of major sea-change in their senior year and then decided to grapple for a scholarship or something. Their destiny was set for the most part.

But Sherry's had been too. And here she was, shrugging it off her shoulders like a badly fitting coat.

'Are you afraid you can't do the work?' I asked it softly, half to myself, in case she wanted to ignore it.

She turned to me and smiled. 'I think we both know better than that. I'm not afraid; I'm just not all that interested.'

'What do you want to do instead?'

'Does there have to be a plan?'

That one stumped me. We'd talked a lot about what I was going to do. Dean's list at some East Coast biggie, whiz through graduate programs in biology, discover the secret to genetic life, achieve instant fame and garner the Nobel Prize at the end of a long and illustrious life of Dedicated Scientist. All sewn up. I could scarcely imagine not having a vision of it before me.

'Maybe being really mature is not needing to know what's going to happen next,' she said. 'Anyway, there's something about the freedom that appeals to me.'

'I don't know. I was raised to believe that if you had certain gifts and didn't use them, it was a sin. I mean, you've got the brains to go to college, you could really make a contribution, you know?' I was faltering. Sounding like a fat old uncle with a trust fund and a gold watch and chain.

'I was raised the same way,' she said calmly. 'But that doesn't mean you can't alter the brainwashing. It's my life, after all. I want to live my version of it, not someone else's.'

Of course, there's no way to argue with a statement like that. That's why people *make* statements like that. 'I'll bet you change your mind. When everybody goes off next fall, scattering like leaves to colleges all over the country, I'll bet you're sorry you didn't send off your apps earlier.'

'You sound like the ant talking to the grasshopper,' she moaned. 'Next, you'll be telling me how high the snow's going to be next winter.'

I grinned. 'Well, go ahead and fiddle then, Miss Smartpants. What are you going to do next year at this time after graduation? Just hang out by yourself at the mall?'

A scornful curl of her beautiful mouth. 'Right. Make a meal of some bright-eyed junior, maybe.' She leaned forward, counting off her fingers. 'There's the Peace Corps. There's traveling to Europe, for example, maybe stay in a youth hostel or climb the Alps or something. There's get a job and start my life instead of putting it on hold like you'll be doing, there's hitchhiking across the country and meeting some weird and dubious characters, there's signing up for the astronaut program, there's moving to Australia and learning to surf – ' She was running out of fingers. 'Did I leave anything out?'

I couldn't help but laugh, but the whole time I was horrified, picturing her doing any or all of it in a swift collage of electric movement across my mind. 'There's getting married. Having babies.'

'Now, *there's* an education. I think I'd rather be adopted by an Amazonian tribe.'

I shook my head. 'You're mad,' I said finally. 'They'll never let you get away with this.'

She smiled triumphantly. 'You just watch me, Dobie.'

We were coming to the end of our senior year. It seemed to me that everything I had worked to become, every scrap of specialness I had polished and buffed inside myself was now moving into place in some invisible but perfect machine. I felt an inner excitement, a certainty that anything I wanted, any challenge I wanted to conquer, was mine – or would be by, oh, say, June. Graduation loomed ahead like a fragrant secret garden, wafting promises of godlike invincibility before me.

Change seemed everywhere, but always far away. Stray issues of the new *Berkeley Barb* floated down from that enclave of radicalism up north, and I saw some article about Free Speech that had more 'fucks' in it than a blue movie. Another piece reported the antiwar rally on campus and Allen Ginsberg's idea that 'flower power' would change society as we knew it, but none of my friends were particularly impressed. The latest craze in the Valley was a TV show called *My Mother the Car*, starring Jerry Van Dyke. Kids up and down the halls could spout the best lines at lunch break, and any number of senior girls could be a hell of an Ann Sothern imitation.

As though from another planet, I heard the news that New York had been hit by a huge blackout, stalling elevators in mid-floor for hours, plunging most of Manhattan into darkness. When I turned on Huntley and Brinkley, they were sitting in candlelight, broadcasting from the East Coast with only emergency generators. I wondered what Ruth was doing that night, but I could scarcely picture her face anymore.

California seemed so far away from such realities. Shortages of any kind were impossible to conceive in a place where fruit hung from the tree in mid-December and you could go to the beach in February.

I began to make friends who surfed. At first, I just hung out at the pier, watching them take the waves. The rhythms were easeful down there, guys carrying surfboards, and girls, more girls at the beach than I'd ever seen in one place in my life, a blur of tanned legs and sun-streaked hair, sucking on Sno-Cones and Mr Softees, the chords from a hundred radios turned up loud.

> I'm in with the in crowd,
> I go where the in crowd goes,
> When you're in with the in crowd,
> You know what the in crowd knows . . .

The girls came at you like punches. One, two, to the stomach, three, four, to the head. They all took the same stance, one hip jutted out and angled away from the pelvis, the head half turned with the hair blowing and the tanned cheekbones like those of a cougar, speculative and feline.

196

The beach was a liberating force. In New York, everybody always wore clothes, even in a hundred-degree heat. But here, the girls walked around in bikinis, even in and out of the shopping centers and grocery stores, in an unselfconscious display which made embarrassment an impossibility.

Sometimes I felt like a ghost among these girls. And ghosts learn to watch things very carefully. I listened too. Caught the exotic rhythms of the speech down at the water, like the cries of the gulls. Surf's up: hot doggers and gremmies, hodads and wipeouts, grab a stick and make for the soup, good swells and knobbies – like a foreign language it was at first.

I watched them squat patiently out on their boards like a covey of hypnotized sea birds. Waiting for some form of liquid perfection. And finally, I got the nerve to think I might paddle out and join them.

The shops that lined the pier were crammed with boards of all shapes and sizes, like colored candy bars glinting inside plate glass wrappers. I picked a store and walked in. The walls were covered with surfing posters and debris: old wooden boards incredibly banged-up and pocked, trophies, photos of huge green tubes of water. There was a kid out front wiping down the new boards with a rag. Inside at the counter a couple of girls in crocheted bikinis perched up on the glass top. Two guys sat behind it. They all looked alike to me with their sunburned noses and blue eyes. One of the guys asked, 'Need a board, man?'

I was instantly pleased that I looked like a man about to surf. 'Yeah, for a novice,' I said, ignoring the girls.

The guy walked over and patted a yellow board tilted on one edge against the wall. 'I can make you a good deal on this one. It's a hot stick.' It was long and thin and pointed at both ends like a bullet. 'You like it?'

I ran my fingers along the side. It was obviously used,

197

the decal of a wave within a circle on one end was a little frayed but what the hell. 'How much?'

'Cash, thirty bucks. Credit, forty. No returns on this one, but for your size it should be good. Not too heavy in the water.'

Thirty bucks suddenly seemed like a pittance for the incredible world it opened, even though it was about all I had in my pocket until the end of the week. I stood by the cash register while the kid rang up the sale. I was very much aware of the girls watching me. The music from the stereo on the wall was loud, and the sun coming through the glass felt hot on my face. The other guy behind the counter pulled out a couple of colored cubes and pushed them at me.

'What are these?'

'Wax. Rub it on good, and it makes it easier to stand up, man.'

So there *was* a secret or two to this thing! I slipped the wax into the pocket of my jeans, feeling like Dumbo with his magic feather. As I picked up the board and walked out, one of the girls called, 'Ride 'em, cowboy!' and the other girl laughed. I flushed, smiled, and kept on walking. I got up the first time, I kept telling myself. Maybe it was just a fluke, but I did it anyway. And I can do it again.

I carried the board down to the water, amazed at how tired my shoulders got so fast. It was an incredible relief to finally lay the thing down in the foam. After I got my breath I walked the board out to knee-depth and got on, straddling it carefully. With just a few paddles I remembered instantly that the waves that looked small from the pier got a hell of a lot bigger when you were looking at them from underneath. Getting out was every bit as tough as before, and I kept sliding off the board when a wave knocked me sideways. The place where the waves made the smooth green hills seemed so far away, but I kept

198

digging away at the water, getting rolled in the white, until finally the ocean seemed to placid out and I was bobbing with the rest of them in a lineup.

A shout went up from the end of the line, and I looked back over my shoulder to see a large set of waves coming right for us. I'm not ready, I realized with a cold start of panic, too tired still, and I turned the board toward the open sea to push beyond them. Lots of guys were paddling around me, and the roar of the water seemed to go on forever, and then I was being lifted right to the top of a wave, somehow managed to get myself sideways and backward all at once, and right at me another board was coming fast as the hissing water, the guy yelling at me loudly. At the last instant we brushed, rolled, and submerged.

I came up gasping for air, reaching for my board. Miraculously, it was just a few yards away. As I swam for it, I saw the other surfer swimming toward me. I clung to my board, thinking maybe the guy was coming to see if I was all right. The surfer's board was just beyond me, and he reached it, swung it close to me, and with no warning punched me hard, right in the mouth.

'Stay the fuck out of the way, dickhead!' the guy screamed and paddled away.

I sat limply, letting the water carry me up and down, waiting for the pain in my jaw to cease. I glanced around, wondering how many others had witnessed my humiliation, or if they wanted to punch me too. Gradually, the sun warmed me again, and I was able to lift my head and feel alive. I just sat and studied the situation.

The waves out beyond the pier had a way of breaking far outside and rolling toward the beach in long, churning lines, obviously why so many guys picked this spot. There was a point, though, where the white water began to re-form, to swell up into a new smaller wave that would go

199

on to break only a few yards from shore. It was away from most of the traffic and unlikely to be a place where the big dogs pissed. I felt better now and began to paddle over to this second inside break to practice.

It was a long day. I spent hours paddling just beyond the shore break, letting the wall of white water catch my board, and then trying to stand up as the wave was building. A hundred times I wondered what I was doing wrong, that I had evidently done so right – and luckily – the first time out. Over and over again I fell off the board and it shot straight off to the side, or I tried to turn and slid off the front of it, and each time I caught it again and crawled on like a dead man. I knew if I gave up, I'd probably never come back again, and it killed me to waste the thirty bucks, not to mention the chance. And then, at the end of the afternoon, something different happened. I got into a wall of white water from a larger wave; it grabbed my board and sent it skimming along the surface of the water, and I stood up. The speed and power of the wave actually made it much easier to maneuver, and I leaned into it, swinging the board under me like it had wheels. It was smooth, it was fast. I was riding a wave. It slid me all the way to the beach, and I stepped off like Poseidon with a crown.

Now I knew what the hoots and hollers were all about. I felt like shouting, and I raised my arms over my head and shook my fists at the sea. I ran through the shallows, kicking up great arcs of spray, grinning like an idiot, and then sat down on my board in the wet sand. Staring out over the water, turning gold now in the setting sun, I tried to remember every detail of what I had done and how it had felt. Out there, the green walls were still forming, but I could see – could feel – the shadows in those walls as well, and knew how to deal with them.

Next time I heard a Beach Boys song, I knew they were singing to me.

On the way home that night, with my board strapped carefully to the Hog of Steel, I had the feeling that I could strike sparks anywhere. There was a fantastic universe out there, and I had been born at exactly the right time, thrust into exactly the right place.

Feeling as I did, it was pretty impossible to carry a grudge. My only real regret for my senior year was Miriam. I finally called her after over a month of silence. There were other, more attractive girls to date, but I couldn't quite get her out of my mind. And somehow I just couldn't walk away, leaving it as we had.

When she answered the phone I said, 'Please don't hang up! I'm in a phone booth, and I've just used my last dime, and yours was the only number I could remember to call.'

'David?'

'Miriam?'

'Are you all right?'

'No. Actually I'm not all right at all. I would *be* all right if you would talk to me, though.'

A frosty silence. 'I'm listening.'

'Well, that's a start,' I said. 'Though to be perfectly accurate, talking was what I asked for.'

'Don't push your luck.'

I smiled but didn't allow it to show in my voice. 'You know, I've given it a lot of thought, really. Played it over and over in my head, what you said, and I want you to know that you're probably right. I'm probably less than humble.'

More silence.

'In truth, I'm just a pissant. A complete geek, an adolescent fart, a lame-o.' A pause. 'An asshole.'

'It's getting deep.'

'It's a small phone booth. Listen, Miriam, I'm sorry. That's what I'm trying to say. I didn't handle it very well when you said what you said, and maybe I deserved it. I don't know. But anyway, I'd like to see you. I've missed you.'

'Oh, David,' she said, her voice suddenly small. 'I don't know.'

'Are you dating anyone else steady?'

'No one special. But I haven't been exactly sitting home.'

'I'm sure of it. Listen, I've learned to surf! Columbia took me! I want to tell you all about it and I want to hear what you've been doing too. Did you hear from Radcliffe?'

'I'm in.'

'That's terrific. Not that I ever doubted it. They ain't fools out there. So.'

Silence.

'Would you consider adding me to your dance card?'

I heard the smile begin in her voice. 'Are you still the Dip King?'

'Absolutely. Shall we put our cards on the table? Let bygones be bygones? See if the shoe fits, bury the hatchet, clean the slate?'

'How trite.'

'That's what I always liked so much about you, Miriam, you have such high standards. And you get it.'

'What?'

'Everything I say.'

'Well, it's not that tough, David. I am, as they say, almost a high school grad-u-ate.'

'So, what do you say? Will you go out with me again?'

She hesitated. 'I guess we could give it a try. Are you dating Sherry Gentry?'

'We're just friends. We were always just friends, that's

202

what I tried to tell you. But I swear, mad dogs will roam the streets of Woodland Hills barking perfect English before I mention her name to you again. Next Saturday?'

'I'm busy.'

'Of course. I knew that. How about the following Saturday?'

'No doubling?'

'Just the two of us. Okay? Seven o'clock?'

'It's hardly even dark then.'

'Well, whenever you say.'

'Seven-thirty. But you better call me the night before.'

Did they all read the same manuals on this, or what? 'I'll call you every night until Saturday if you want. Really, Miriam, I want us to start fresh if we can. I feel bad about what happened between us, and I really have missed – just talking to you, if nothing else. Did you miss me?'

'Sure,' she said pertly. 'Your name again?'

'Arrogant prick,' I said softly.

'Oh yes, I vaguely remember. Are you really in a phone booth?'

'Yeah, but I should be out by a week from Saturday.'

'Good.' A small but interesting giggle. 'I don't do my best work in tight places.'

Well, there was no way I was going to touch that; it was going too well. Wondering what strange and new paths Miriam had explored in the past weeks, I rang off, telling her I looked forward to seeing her again.

When I picked her up I was nervous. And surprised at myself. You had to be on your toes with this girl, I thought. She was a challenge, but definitely worth the trouble.

As if seeing Miriam weren't enough, Councilman Weld met me at the door.

'David,' he said formally, gesturing me inside, 'Miriam will be ready in a moment.'

Great, I thought mournfully, I should have known I wasn't going to be able to put this off. Naturally, he'd be here. With my luck her mother will be right behind him.

Not right behind, but sitting in the easy chair, waiting for me, with some sort of embroidery work in her lap like Madame Defarge. I had a fleeting moment of vigor that shot down my legs, almost moving me back out the door, down the steps, and all the way to the car. But then my knees sagged with resignation, and I took a seat on the sofa across from them both.

'Found the place all right?' Miriam's father asked dryly. 'I'm surprised to see you still know the way.'

Perspiration sprang instantly to my armpits, and I yearned to be fifty years old and way beyond this moment. But for all I knew, Miriam might be waiting, listening in the hallway. Nothing else to do but chew it down. 'I know it's been a long time,' I said as calmly as I could. 'I suppose you know that Miriam and I had a fight.'

'We heard a rumor to that effect,' Mrs Weld said quietly, her head down over her needle.

'What was it about?' Miriam's father asked, the question like a bullet in the air.

Frankly, I was amazed he asked. I kept expecting Mrs Weld to shush her husband, soften him, mothers often did that, but she just looked up expectantly. Christ, I thought, I should probably tell them that people know I'm here. The body would be missed. 'Well,' I began uneasily, 'I'm not really sure.' What did she tell them? 'You know how it is, somebody says something and somebody else misinterprets it, and then it just escalates –' I looked around for help, but the Persian cat was nowhere to be seen. 'Anyway, I called her up because I wanted to be friends again. I'm really sorry it happened.' I dropped my head, feeling my resentment start to rise.

'Friends?'

At Mr Weld's question I raised my head, and I saw in his face an apprehension that made me feel strong and slightly sad for him. He was afraid of the power that a young man had to come into his house, wheedle his daughter around, answer his questions or not as the whim might move him, and ultimately take her away. 'Yes,' I said with more confidence. 'Friends. I believe we have a lot in common. In spite of our problems.' I stood up. 'I expect she's told you most of this, though.' I remember thinking then how tough it must be to carry the yoke of father to a teenaged girl!

As though on cue, Miriam came into the room. She wore a light yellow dress, filmy at the shoulders and tight around the hips, and I wondered how – over such a short time – she had come to seem so sophisticated. 'You look terrific,' I said, and meant it. With my words a softening came over the room, and everybody smiled again.

She took my arm carefully, her body never grazing mine. 'We'll be home late,' she said to her parents. And we escaped into the night.

I had decided the minute I asked her that the thing to do was take Miriam someplace really special. No drive-ins, no Bob's Big Boys, but an event. Something to prove that I really did care about her, that I wasn't nearly as selfish and manipulative as she supposed: in short, a Date to Remember.

By an incredible stroke of luck the Rolling Stones were playing in Laguna and I had two tickets. In those days I considered access to the Stones concrete evidence that a benevolent God did exist and, further, was benignly tinkering with my destiny.

As we made our way to the middle of the bleacher seats, we could see that the auditorium was packed. I was focused, however, on Miriam. We sat down and I took her hand. Her large, capable-looking hand.

She didn't take it away. 'I thought you might call me pretty soon,' she said.

'You did?'

'I thought you'd take almost two months to think about it, and then you'd call. You didn't take quite two months.' She smiled. 'I was a little off.'

There was something about this that both intrigued and rankled me. 'Would you have called me?'

She squeezed my hand but shook her head. 'I wasn't exactly desperate.'

'Neither was I.'

'I didn't say you were.' A stiff pause. 'So,' she said, 'you've been doing a lot of surfing?'

It was a safe topic. 'Yeah, I've got a board now, trying to get better on it. I guess I go about twice a week or so.'

'Made some new friends?'

Back into choppy waters. 'Not really. Still hanging around with the same guys. Harvard turned me down.'

'Are you upset about it?'

I shook my head. 'I still haven't decided which one I want, though. I've got two months, they say. Then they want an answer.'

'I've always known what I wanted,' she said softly.

To my relief, the opening band came on, and Miriam bounced in her seat but didn't let go of my hand. The Dave Clark Five were singing 'Glad All Over', and I was impressed that the Stones would pick such a well-known band, one that had even been on *The Ed Sullivan Show*, where he'd called them 'nice, neat boys'. They warmed up the crowd with 'Catch Us If You Can' and 'Over and Over', plus a few new ones I hadn't heard before.

But the crowd was getting antsy. There was something so bland about the Five. Any other time, the audience would have been satisfied to hear them play, but now they'd come to see the Stones, and nothing else would do. When the announcer finally came out shouting, 'Here they are, ladies and gentlemen, all the way from London, the Rolling Stones!' the shrieks rose in an almost painful wail, something desperate and supplicative in the mass moaning, and Mick Jagger stepped from behind the curtain, all alone on the stage.

There was nothing clean-cut about him. Two years before I had seen the Stones on the *Hullabaloo* show. They looked like bargain-basement Beatles then, same short hair, modish suits. When Dean Martin introduced them on *The Hollywood Place*, he obviously wondered what all the fuss was about. Then, they toured with opening acts like Bobby Goldsboro, Bobby Vee, and the Chiffons.

Now Jagger looked like he just came off a three-day binge. His hair was longer, scruffier, and his jeans were skin tight. No suit jacket, just a T-shirt with spangles on the front. From behind the curtain came the leering tease of a fuzz-tone guitar and drums. He half sang, half chanted,

> I'm so glad to be here tonight, so glad to be home,
> And I got a message for every woman and man tonight
> That ever needed someone to love . . .

The guitar rose in a pulsing backbeat as Jagger mugged,

> Someone to love them really bad!

The curtain pulled back abruptly and the rest of the band came into view, Keith and Brian and Bill and Charlie, and they swung into, 'Ev-er-ybody, needs some-body, to love!' By now the whole audience was shouting the words along with Mick, but his whine rose above us, leading us like a maddened mosquito. *And I need you! You! You!* Contorting his body, gyrating about the stage, dancing steps that no one could follow or name, he exhorted and shouted and preened, jacking us higher and higher.

No one sat down; Miriam was up and clapping and swaying from side to side as though a string connected her body and Mick's. Even his pelvic thrusts were shivering through her, and I didn't know which one to watch. The Stones went through song after song with hardly a letup or a slowdown. Most bands sang one or two fast songs, then a slow ballad for a change of pace. Not Mick. Every song was driving, driving, a barrage of drums and thunder and pulsing rhythm with no pause for breath. They ripped through 'Down Home Girl' and 'Mona' with Mick vamping and stretching his lips around the words of 'Oh Baby' and 'Little Red Rooster', and when they hit the first chords of 'I Can't Get No Satisfaction', the place threatened to split down the middle from the screams.

After two hours of energy, too many songs to count, with a sense that the beat had taken up permanent residence in my backbone, Miriam and I finally staggered out to the parking lot, our arms wrapped around each other.

'God, it was fantastic!' she said breathlessly. 'They are absolutely incredible! Did you see the way Charlie Watts smiles? Like a devil or something. And Mick!' She squeezed me tight. 'It was just great. Where's the car?'

I was dazed. Completely out of touch with any sort of reality, much less the parking lot. Finally, I threaded my way up a familiar corridor and found the wagon. The minute we were in the car, Miriam scooted over next to me as though the last two months apart had never happened at all. She was chattering happily, flicking the radio dial around trying to find a Stones song and I thought, nothing's changed. What did I expect? Some sort of dramatic reconciliation, a passionate falling together as though we were soul-mates?

We stopped to eat and then drove toward Miriam's house. As we came up her hill, she snuggled close with her head on my shoulder. 'It was really nice tonight,' she said softly. 'I'm glad you finally called.'

'Me too.'

'David,' she said gently, 'why don't you turn down that street and go the back way?'

It was our old parking routine. This road led to a cul-de-sac shadowed by big pepper trees, the only private parking place within five miles of her house. Without a word I turned the wheel as she directed. When I had the car parked, she moved in my arms so that she was facing me, tucked behind the steering wheel and nestled against my chest.

'I missed you,' she said.

'Me too.'

'I've been doing a lot of thinking, David.'

Suddenly, the last thing I wanted was another long conversation with Miriam about life or love or philosophy or any other damn thing that might come up. I kissed her, my mouth covering hers completely, my hands on the back of her head. To my amazement, she kissed me back with an energy and a fever that I had never felt from her before. As though she had somehow started without me, she was yielding and warm, and again I had the strange sensation that I could sink into her mouth, right into her head, and never come out again.

We kissed over and over, my mouth moving sometimes down her throat, sometimes over her cheeks, her eyes, and she began to make small sounds of desire, whimpering moans that seemed half pain and half delight. I realized that if I wanted to, I could go further with her

209

than ever before. I began to fondle her breasts, and she took my hands and led them to her nipples, squeezing them herself with my fingers. Still kissing, kissing, until I felt that my mouth must be twice its size and smeared all over my face, but I couldn't stop myself. She didn't seem to want me to stop.

The windows were beginning to fog by the time I had eased her dress up around her hips and touched her, outside her underwear. In the dark I could see only this white startling patch against the darker lightness of her skin, could feel the slickness of the fabric catching on the prickly hairs beneath. Incredible heat came from her when I touched her, and when her hand went to my crotch, I took one hand away to swiftly undo my jeans, setting my erection free, and as she hesitantly touched me, I slipped one finger around the elastic of her underwear and deeply inside her.

She gasped, and her hand stopped moving immediately. I kissed her again, murmuring to her that it was going to be all right, even as I wondered, far away in some distant part of my mind, what in the world I was doing. Her hand began to stroke me again, and it was all I could do not to gnaw my way into her neck. I dropped my mouth to her breasts, and she gasped again when I tongued her nipples, still moving my finger inside her. She was wet and warm, so wet that I could sometimes hardly tell whether I was inside her or outside in a fold of skin, and I wished fervently I'd paid more attention to the anatomy part of biology. Somewhere there was supposed to be a button or something, that much I knew, but I couldn't find it and she wasn't directing me anyplace special. Her hips were moving under my hand, though, and either she was in pain or she was enjoying it, with all the moans she made.

My cock was out of whatever mind it had left. It jerked and twitched like it had electrodes attached to it, and I kept lifting off the car seat to try to get more room, more freedom.

She was over against the passenger window, and I was pressing against her, when suddenly she pulled back and looked at me intently. Her mouth was swollen and her eyes were almost closed. 'David,' she whispered, 'I want you.'

'You do?' I wondered what else I should be saying. Surely there's some sort of protocol for this, I thought desperately, something I'm supposed to be doing besides talking about it.

'I want you to do it tonight. I'm ready, I think.'

Jesus! I always thought that when I finally lost my virginity it would be something I planned for, something I looked forward to and knew would be coming up on a particular night with a certain girl I'd laid the groundwork with for weeks. Now here it was, the moment I thought I'd been waiting for, what *every* guy waited for, and it was with a girl I hadn't spoken to for months. Essentially, a first date! And of all things, with Miriam the Councilman's Daughter.

My finger was still inside her. 'Are you sure?' I whispered finally. 'Are you safe?'

For answer, she only kissed me, gripping my erection so fiercely with both hands that I winced and bobbed like a fish pole with a whopper at the end.

Well, of course things went very fast after that, so fast that today I can scarcely recall the details. Which is a major disappointment because even then I was completely aware that I would want to inscribe this night on my memory forever. I can remember my jeans down around my knees. I can recall vividly the smell and the feel of her as I put what seemed like half my hand inside her, can remember her lying down with her head behind the steering wheel, one leg up on the dash, but it was

211

impossible that way. I lowered myself onto her, but there wasn't enough room. I thought I would scream at one point from the frustration, and fell back from her in exhaustion. As I sat there, my knees spread and quivering, she knelt over me, one knee on either side, and straddled me, hovering just over my cock. I put it just inside her and she gasped and pulled up. I looked into her eyes and saw there a certainty, a pleading for something, I wasn't sure what. Without another thought I reached up and put my hands on her shoulders, pushing her hard down on me. She cried out, and I held her down, pressing her to my chest. A few seconds later, with perhaps only two or three thrusts, I cried out, too, as I felt myself flood into her.

We were very quiet after, I remember that much. I held her. She may have even cried a little. There was so much moisture between us, it was hard to tell. I had a sense that the car would forever smell like her – like us – and I was amazed that people ever went out and earned a living, ever went to movies and ball games, ever did *anything* but this.

'Are you sorry?' I asked her once just before I started up the car. Now I found it hard to meet her eyes.

'No,' she said softly. 'It was time. I wanted it to be you.'

I reached out and stroked the side of her face. 'So did I.'

'Was it your first time?'

I grinned. 'Couldn't you tell? I thought I set some sort of landspeed record.'

She didn't say anything.

I put an arm around her shoulders. 'Hey. Are you okay?'

She nodded.

'Are you on the pill?'

'No.'

I felt my stomach freeze.

'But I'm safe. Don't worry about it.'

God, I'd heard about this, but I never rehearsed the conversation and wasn't at all sure I wanted to know any more. Finally, I asked, 'Was it – was it any good for you at all?'

She turned and smiled at me and I felt a flood of relief. 'I have no regrets, David. Stop worrying.'

For the first time that evening she sounded like the old Miriam. I reached down and turned on the radio, keeping it low. We rode the rest of the way home in companionable, easy silence. I felt a strange combination of tenderness and triumph for this complex creature who I could not predict, could not quite love, and, evidently, could not leave alone. And when she turned to kiss me good night she said, 'I won't ever forget this. Neither will you.'

'I'll call you first thing tomorrow,' I said.

'Good.' She smiled and slipped away, tripping up to the light over the door.

So Miriam and I were a couple again. When I told Sherry, she put her lower lip out like the spout of a pitcher. 'Two-timer,' she said. 'You guys are all alike.'

'Hey,' I answered wryly, 'anytime you want to dump your latest tag team and go out with me, I'll seriously consider it. But in the meantime, I was growing moss. A guy can't sit home forever, you know.'

'Does she know you come to see me all the time?'

We were sprawled on the floor in her rec room, a stack of records splayed all around us. Sherry was leafing idly through a pile of old Peter, Paul, and Mary albums.

'She knows we're friends,' I said a little stiffly.

She grinned. 'Does she know you're here right now, David Levine?'

'It's not absolutely necessary for me to check in and out with her every time I leave the house.'

'She doesn't know. You fink. Keeping us both on the string.' She leaned a little closer, almost grazing my cheeks with her lips. 'Must be nice,' she whispered, 'to have such powerful sex appeal.'

'It is,' I said dryly. 'I bow to Mecca every morning. Now, can we drop it?'

'Yes, if you'll answer one question. Honestly and true-blue.'

That was our code word. When she wanted me to answer as a friend and not as a would-be lover, she asked me to tell her 'true-blue'.

'Why her?' she continued. 'You could have picked a new girl, without all the muddy water between you. After what she said to you, I'm surprised you even called her.'

I thought for a moment. She had, after all, asked for honesty. 'I like her. Also, she doesn't bore me. And she's not weird.'

'You think I am?'

'Alien, more like.'

She grinned. 'Well, it's not like you weren't warned.'

'Actually, *most* of the girls I know could qualify for strange on some level. From the planet Lulu. But Miriam's more sane than most. And just when I think I've got her figured out, she comes up with something new to say or think. I used to feel pretty comfortable with her too. That'll come back, I guess, in time.'

'It doesn't hurt that she's adequately pretty.'

'Not a bit.'

'I guess I should be chlorophyll with jealousy, then.'

'No doubt.'

A pause. 'Have you gone all the way with her?'

I was genuinely shocked into silence. Also a little disappointed that she had asked. 'Hey. If you and I had

214

done it and she asked me, I wouldn't tell *her*.' I smiled slightly. 'So much of sex appeal is mystery, my dear. Allow me to keep my mystery.'

'Then you have,' she said shortly. She dropped her head and rummaged about in the albums for a moment. 'Why did you stop writing me letters, by the way?'

That one took me off guard. 'You never answered them.'

'Was I supposed to?'

'Well, I guess I just figured since we were seeing each other regularly, you probably didn't care about them so much. You never mentioned them anymore.'

'I saved them. I read them all the time. You know,' she said suddenly, 'I've been writing some new poems. Want to see them?'

'I'd love to.'

'Does Miriam write poetry?' She glanced sideways at me.

'No, she just doesn't have your multifaceted gifts' – I shrugged – 'your genius for eloquence. Your delicate sensitivity.'

'Damn straight.' She got up and went out of the room.

I felt a division between us, and it made me sad. Just the simple act of sex – whether or not she actually knew about it or whether it had even happened – seemed to separate people as much as it brought them together. For example, I noticed that I felt different around my own mother now. I looked at her and caught myself wondering what she was like with my father. The idea was so foreign, so distasteful on some level, I didn't feel as comfortable around her. Also, I had this sense that she might be able to see inside my body and tell that I was irrevocably and forever changed. In some way, no longer her child. The same with my father. At once I felt closer to him as a man and farther away as a son. It was unsettling.

And now Sherry. If she were truly my friend, I'd love to ask her a hundred questions about sex and women and what it was like for her, assuming she had something close to the same experience. If she were my lover, of course, the questions could be answered by first-hand research. But since she was somehow both and neither, sex lay like a fissure between us.

'I've been working out some new ideas,' she was saying as she came back in with a small box. Of course she would keep her poems in a leather-stitched case. She casually tossed the box in my lap as though she were suddenly embarrassed. 'You can read them if you want to.'

'Why don't you read them to me,' I said, opening the box carefully. 'That way I can really hear them.'

She glowered. 'I don't know if I should let you read them at all, considering you're in love with somebody else.' She put her hand out and closed the lid down.

'I'm not in love with her,' I said quickly. 'I told you.'

'But you're sleeping with her.'

'I didn't say that.'

'Well. I don't know.' She folded her hands in her lap. 'Okay, promise me one thing, then, David. If you do fall in love with her, you'll tell me.'

That seemed simple enough. 'You mean right at the instant it happens I should call you up, or what? What if I fall in love with somebody else in the meantime, like the carhop at Bob's while I'm out with Miriam or something? Do I call you then?'

'I'm serious.'

'Okay, I promise. But the elves from the planet Lulu are going to take you away.'

'There aren't any elves on the planet Lulu. Only hair-spray factories and manicurists.'

I opened the box again. 'Which one do you want to read first?'

She smiled and took the box from me, searching through the top layer of papers. 'I'll just read one to you now. Maybe we'll do more later.'

The poems were all on light blue sheets, as though they had been copied over carefully so they'd match. Always thinking of the package.

'Here's one,' she said, and then she read:

> ' "Build me a castle and build it high
> With balconies that reach the white sky
> That I may watch all of life pass by."
> "No," he said, "castles block the view."
>
> "Then buy me a stallion, black and sleek,
> His speed will stream the wind to my cheek,
> And I'll feel the freedom that I seek."
> "No," he said, "speed is not for you."
>
> "Then will you bring me the flowers of spring?
> Since you have said no to everything,
> Just flowers will do, tied in a string."
> "No," said he, "the blooms are too few."
>
> "Then show me a sunset in the sky,
> There's nothing you'll build or bring or buy,
> Surely this boon, you'll not deny."
> "No," he said, "but here's what I'll do.
>
> "Can you not see what you need from me?
> Not your wants, they are only debris,
> But all of your needs, I'll guarantee,
> And I'll stay with you your whole life through."
>
> She thought of all she had left behind,
> Of all her wealth and her goods combined,
> "Thank you," she said, and she knew her mind,
> "That's all I wanted. I'm glad you knew." '

Sherry finished, folded the paper carefully, and sat looking at me.

I hardly knew what to say, 'Did you really write that?'

She ducked her head and grinned. 'Sure. A month or two ago, I think.'

'Well, it's incredible!' I felt like getting up and jumping around the room. 'It's really good, Sherry. Read it again.'

'Oh no, once is enough. It's not all that profound or anything – '

'I think it's fantastic. I'm really surprised.' I thought for a moment. Clearly, the poem was hers, even if it did sound rather familiar. Even if she took the idea from something else, I could think of no poem that I'd ever read that was like it, and there was something about her shy pride that convinced me it was mostly original. It was a little clumsy in places, but it would make a wonderful ballad, a song for somebody like Joni Mitchell or the Seekers to sing.

'Why surprised?'

'Well, because I just didn't know you were that good. It's really complex. Read me another one.'

She shrugged. 'Oh, David, let's not go overboard. We'll do some more another time.'

'I really felt I was looking into your soul as you were reading. It's very beautiful.'

'My poem or my soul?' She smiled impishly.

'All of the above. Read one more.'

She took a deep breath and shuffled through a few more blue pages. 'Okay. Just one more and then that's it. I don't want to expose myself all at once.'

Again, she read:

'I never cared for men; they cared for me.
And so I thought I surely owed them some fidelity.
But faithfulness was something that they little prized,
I learned.
And having pledged it,
Trust became a point of small concern.

218

It's the challenge of the chase they want,
No matter what they claim,
So women's hearts become the pawns
In love's most ill-played game.'

Her smile was gone by the time she finished reading. This time she put the paper away without meeting my eyes. 'Well, that's a fairly new one. Anyway, that's enough for today.'

'I am really impressed. And touched. That last one, especially.' I decided to take a chance. 'Did you write that one after that hassle with Don and Rod?'

'I guess. I don't really remember when I wrote it.'

'Do you really feel that way? I mean, the way the poem says it, that guys just want the thrill of the chase?'

'I must have. At least when I wrote it.'

'Sherry, I've always wanted to ask you something. Remember that time when I first talked to you? In the car, when you'd been crying? I always wondered, what got you so upset that day?'

She shrugged. 'Just some guy.'

'I can't imagine you crying like that over just some guy.'

She looked at me completely seriously. 'I can't imagine crying like that over hardly anything else.'

'Did you love him?'

She shook her head. 'Not really. Well, maybe a little. At the time.'

'Have you ever really loved anybody? Any guy, I mean?'

'Probably not.' She smiled. 'Anyway, not enough to let them read my poems.'

I grinned helplessly, once more happy on my way to being stupid. 'Could I read a few more? I mean, if you don't feel like reading them out loud. Really, hasn't anybody else read them?'

'My dad's read a few. My sister, maybe. But nobody's read them all.'

'What's your favorite one? The one that means the most to you.'

She pulled another sheet from the box. 'This one.' She began:

> 'Golden lads and girls all must
> As chimney sweepers, come to dust'

'That's Shakespeare!' I said. 'I recognize that one.'

She laughed. 'Very good. You pass the literacy test, anyway.'

I looked at her, suddenly serious. 'What are the other ones I'm flunking?'

She looked away, closing up her leather box. 'It's not you, David, it's me.'

I smirked. 'You're afraid you're not good enough for me, is that it? That you'll drag me down to your level?'

Her lips tightened. 'I told you from the beginning that I wanted to be friends.'

'And I think we've accomplished that handily. But I don't see why we can't deepen this relationship into something more.'

'You just started dating Miriam again!'

I felt a twinge of remorse. 'Because you won't go out with me.'

She hooted. 'She'd love to hear that!'

'She never will.' I put one hand over hers. She left it there. 'What's the deal here? I'm not good-looking enough for public consumption? Cool enough for small-time, but not for introduction to the big leagues?'

'Oh, you know what they say, Dobie. East is East and West is West and never the twain shall meet. We're just too different.'

'I used to think East is East and West is irrelevant. But I changed. Now you're saying I'm not California enough?'

She pulled her hand away. 'Why do you make me say this stuff to you? Why can't you just leave it the way it is? I like you a lot, I think you're really special, but I'm just not attracted to you in that way, okay? Will you just leave it alone? Besides, you'll be going away soon.'

'Maybe. Maybe not. Maybe I'll drop Columbia and go to UCLA instead. It's a good school. What would you think of that?'

She shrugged. 'Whatever makes you happy.'

'Okay,' I said calmly. 'Sometimes I think I'm too nice to you, that's the problem.'

'What do you mean?'

'I mean, you seem to like the ones who make you miserable. Maybe I should tie you up and drag you behind my car, and then you'd find me irresistible.'

Her voice stiffened. 'Very droll. I don't *like* guys who make me miserable.'

'But you're more attracted to them,' I said quietly.

'You don't know the first thing about it. You think you do. Guys always think they know all about me, but they never do. You're my friend, so I'm different with you than with the guys I date. Most girls are.'

'Well, *that's* certainly depressing.'

'But it's true.' Her tone softened. 'Besides. In a way, you know me too well to date me.' She leaned over and kissed me gently on the cheek. 'Maybe someday. But right now you're too old for me.'

'What!'

'You've got an old head on young shoulders.'

'I'd like to point out to you that we are almost exactly the same age, give or take a few months. If I'm looking older, I've got you to thank for it. Sexual frustration, I

221

hear, can turn a man's hair white overnight. I read that someplace.'

She giggled. 'Take it to Miriam.'

'Cute.' I sighed and stretched, wondering if I could possibly remember not to bring this subject up again anytime soon. 'Well, in the unlikely event that you ever do decide to grow up and become worthy of me, you think you'd ever like to do anything with your poems? Maybe get them published?'

She shook her head. 'I doubt it. I don't think they're that great.'

'I do. I think you could develop into a real poet someday. And just think, I could say, "I knew her when."'

'Yes.' She smiled. 'You certainly could.'

Change was percolating through the Valley that year, I remember. The Monkees were still big, a band who looked like the Beatles run through a Xerox machine, and the Beach Boys' twenty-third hit, 'Barbara-Ann', was flooding the airwaves. But up in Berkeley, the capital of what seemed to be another state altogether, they were playing 'Mr Tambourine Man' by the Byrds, and Ken Kesey and his Merry Pranksters hosted the first public Acid Test in Santa Cruz, a huge LSD party that the press ballyhooed up and down the coast.

Skirts were shooting up, and it wasn't at all unusual to see, even in class, minidresses that flaunted legs longer than God. It made it damn tough to concentrate on logarithms.

I noticed a decided and growing nervousness in my parents, like fenced sheep who sense a thunderstorm moving in over the mountains. One night at the table my father came to dinner in an unusually surly mood.

'I see where a shop has opened on the public streets of

San Francisco,' he said, glowering around at his sons, 'and it's devoted entirely to the sale of illegal drugs. The Psychedelic Shop, they call it. They should close it down and throw the owners in jail. Have you boys heard any of your friends talking about such a thing?'

Discussion was usual at the Levine table. My parents encouraged us to come to dinner prepared to talk as well as to eat. Usually, however, opinions weren't expressed quite so adamantly, at least not until everyone had been heard.

'I don't know, Dad,' I said as I reached for more potatoes. Concentrating on how much gravy was left to divide between Avrom and myself, I didn't notice the storm flags in my father's voice. 'I heard they don't really sell drugs. Just records and posters and papers and stuff.'

'And all the schlock needed to smoke marijuana. Hookahs, they sell, like the opium dens. Next they'll be peddling hypodermics for the heroin addicts!'

'I'm sure the police will close it down,' my mother said soothingly. 'Don't upset yourself, Daniel. See look I have the nice herring in cream sauce with the fresh dill.' My mother ladled the concoction on my father's plate.

'Those kids up there with nothing better to do than sit around and get in trouble, rotting their brains with this garbage,' my father went on, 'better they should be worrying about staying in school. Most of them would benefit from a year or two in the army. I imagine the Vietnamese boys don't waste their health and their time on this marijuana.'

'I hear it's no worse than cigarettes.' At the look on my father's face, I added quickly, 'Not that I'd smoke either one, of course, but lots of kids have tried it – '

'Yeah, even in my class,' Avrom piped up.

Both parents turned to him with horror. 'There is marijuana in Parkman?' my father asked chillingly. 'In

223

the ninth grade now we have to worry for our children's souls?'

'I hope your friends realize that this thing is robbing them of their youth,' my mother said. 'Such a hurry they are to be adults! Why, I don't know, it's not such a great thing to be grown-up, and those who rush it, well, it's the early dog who gets the worms.'

Avrom and I sat quietly, trying to digest this last.

'I know of no adults who use marijuana,' my father said, turning his frown to her. 'Why do you suggest such a thing?'

'Well, the children aren't growing it in their biology classes. Somewhere they are getting it from, and not just the idea, either. Where else but their parents?'

'From dealers, who sell it to them!'

'Of course, but who gave them the idea it would be good to buy it? And who gave them the money to buy? It didn't just come from thin air.' She shook her head sadly. 'Some people should never have children; they should give them away when they reach the age of talking. It's harder to raise them out here than back home, but if you can't stand the heat, get out of the oven, I always say.'

I didn't venture another opinion. When elephants fight, it's best for the gophers to stay underground. I could certainly understand my parents' fear. It was a tough time to be raising kids. I never thought I'd slide into sin myself, but I wasn't prepared for the singular moment when a joint was passed to me.

It happened at a party, a small gathering that was supposed to be a big one, but a lot of kids didn't show, so it was fizzling out toward ten o'clock. Normally, I'd have been with Miriam, but she had a cold and was housebound all weekend. Foote said, 'Hey, when was the last time we hung out, just a bunch of guys, and got crazy? No women tonight, man. Let's do it.'

224

I was sitting on the floor with Watts and Foote and a few others when some guy named Rice pulled out a thick white cigarette and lit up. I'd never seen one before, but I knew instantly that I was staring at the glowing end of my parents' most chilling nightmare. The group fell silent, watching Rice suck in the smoke like a pro, his eyes slitted and amused.

'Hey, man,' someone said, 'don't do that here.'

Rice laughed without making a sound, all the breath still held in his lungs. 'Somebody's got to liven up this party. Bunch of deadheads.' He passed the joint to the girl next to him, a beauty from Reseda with straight black hair. She held the thing in her slender fingers, tossed back her head, and took a long drag as he had. With a smile she turned to Foote and held it out to him.

'Want to try it?'

I held my breath. It was one thing to read about it in *Time* or hear about it on the six o'clock news, but it was an altogether arresting revelation to see my friend, Jim Foote, holding gingerly to the end of a burning marijuana cigarette. I had a quick desire to smash the thing out of Foote's mouth and crush it to the carpet, screaming like an Old Testament prophet, 'Sinners, beware!'

But she was so pretty. Foote hesitated, glancing around the circle and finally at me. I shrugged slightly. Foote put the thing to his lips and drew in, puffing out right away.

'Hold it in,' Rice said. 'You're just wasting it that way.' He slipped it from Jim's fingers, took another drag, and then passed it back, motioning Jim to do as he did. The guy looked like a reddening bullfrog, his chest and shoulders puffed out. Jim imitated him and coughed once, then recovered.

'Can I try it?' Watts suddenly asked.

I looked at him, startled.

'Well, I guess it's no big deal. Just to see what all the

225

screaming's about.' He grinned sheepishly and took a puff on the proffered joint, then passed it to me.

Out of the corner of my eye I could see Rice taking out another one of these things. The Reseda beauty leaned forward and said, 'Let me help you out.' The cigarette was now down to less than two inches, and she held the thing with two dainty fingernails, putting it to my mouth.

Closing my eyes and sending up a small prayer to what surely was an outraged God, I took in the smoke. It was harsh and it burned. My eyes watered, but I saw Foote watching me and I kept my breath still. Not a cough.

'Again,' she said softly. 'Finish it off.'

I let out what smoke was left – where did it go, was it, dear Lord, already absorbed in my bloodstream? – and took another drag. This time I nearly choked, and the burning at the back of my throat made me panic instantly. I could almost feel the cancer cells proliferating down there.

The second cigarette was circulating now, and a few more kids leaned forward to try it.

'It's no big deal,' Watts said. 'What's the big deal?'

Somebody got up, brought back a huge Coke, and passed it around. I took hold of the cold bottle gratefully and tipped it up, feeling the peppery burn soothe my throat. Somebody at the fringe of the circle fumbled the joint, and it fell to the carpet. A flurry of pattings and brushings and yelps to put it out, as though it left blood on the floor rather than ashes. I all but said, 'Did you see what God just did to us?' but restrained myself. Another joint came out and nervous giggles followed it around from one novice to the next.

'The third hit's the best,' Rice said confidentially. 'You don't feel it much before that.'

'I don't feel it at all,' Foote grinned.

For some reason I found that simple statement hilarious. I began to chuckle, was soon weeping with laughter, and all the while I had this sense that the Reseda girl was watching me and laughing, not with me but at me, and still I couldn't stop, didn't care, and yet felt this deep panic. The room smelled smoky-sweet. The lights had small and distinct halos around them. I had a fierce erection and at the same time wanted nothing more than to sleep and make it all go away. Some small part of my mind registered that perhaps an hour or so had passed, but my skin felt it had been only moments. The sensation was brief, actually. The euphoria lasted only a short time. And then I was leadened with sadness.

Later, as I drove home and tried to remember the details of my first drug experience – the very word 'drug' was a sword I deliberately impaled myself on, just as I deliberately conjured up my mother's *'feh!'* to exacerbate my shame – I was conscious most of all of the sense of lost time. Perhaps that's where the sadness came from. The realization that, after all, time was going by so quickly and that it was being wasted on nothing more than a few electrical numbings of the brain.

I wondered if I would never be able to switch off the watcher inside me. Was I the only one who sat in a circle of kids smoking dope (why do you think they call it dope?) and felt a part of myself floating above us, watching me as I lived my life? Would I ever just *live* it? Would any sensation I ever had be intense enough to turn off the commentator inside me?

I remember that I felt as alone as I ever had. And I was fervently grateful that Miriam hadn't seen me put that thing to my lips.

The smog was getting worse and worse that year. The heat hovered over the Valley like an upside-down iron kettle. You could scarcely see the golden hills for the brown haze, and tempers grew short in the fast lane. If you didn't keep it at nearly seventy, some frenzied commuter might just bump your rear fender and flip you the bird as he came roaring around on the right.

They called it 'atmospheric inversion', as though naming it might lend some comfort. Kids were kept in, and somebody on KMPC said you could develop film negatives just by hanging them out on the line. After Miriam came back from a particularly harrowing trip to the mall, where some old lady tried to punch her out for taking a parking space, she said, 'I don't know why they're trying so hard to get men to the moon. We've got the first experimental space colony right here in the Valley.'

'Either that,' I said, wiping my streaming eyes, 'or the world's largest barbecue. And we're the briquets.'

The papers were full of dramas that season about people who had succumbed to the smog. There was one family who had been an item just a few months before. They lived in their motor home full-time, the mother, the father, and two kids. At night they'd park in a public lot somewhere in the city. In the morning she got up and put on the coffee, changed the baby, and got breakfast while he drove up the freeway to his job. After she dropped him off she drove back over the hill to leave the babies with her mother and then get over to her part-time job. When she was through there, she picked up the kids and drove back over the hill to pick up her husband. While he drove back to their overnight lot, she cooked dinner on the move and readied the kids for bed. They used a drive-in cleaners, a drive-in bank, and went to a drive-in movie and a drive-in McDonald's for fun. Actually, the man said, it wasn't a bad life at all. He put 128 miles a day on the rig and used fourteen gallons of gas, but it beat a mortgage. The papers called them symbols of our new mobile culture. Sixties gypsies.

But that week they found the man and woman slumped over in the trailer, suffering from carbon monoxide poisoning. The combination of the freeway fumes and the unusually heavy smog finally got them.

Dusk became my favorite time of the day. When night came, the air seemed to simmer down to the ground, and it was actually balmy. As though the palm trees had swept out the sky of all the gray air, the normal Valley smells of hay, oranges, and gasoline percolated to the top.

But with the smog came an early crop of Santa Ana winds.

The Santa Anas. The very name made natives cast ominous glances at one another. The winds typically came up when there hadn't been any rain for six or seven months. Then the air masses shifted, and the winds swept in from distant deserts instead of from the ocean. They pushed up the barometer as they blew, gaining force with each mountain they roared past. Local flight patterns at the airport had to be reversed, the atmosphere cleared with dramatic suddenness, and the smog all vanished out to sea.

But nobody rejoiced. The heat rose even higher, shimmering over the concrete and the beaches like a quivering visible hand. The humidity dropped to zero. Forest fires started in the distant San Gabriels, and the sky took on a yellow cast.

I knew the scientific explanation for it. I read about it in my chemistry magazines. 'It jacks up the positive ions in the air, see, and so if you're the nervous type,' I told Foote, 'it just makes it worse. Like rubbing a cat the wrong way until you both get a little shock.'

'No one likes a smartass,' Foote said irritably, snapping his towel at me. We were in the locker room, a cooler refuge, thanks to all the concrete. 'Why don't you invent something to help, Einstein, instead of just adding to the hot air.'

I didn't have the energy to muster a decent retort. Besides, I knew that bar fights, suicides, and traffic wrecks had escalated as the winds rose. The day before, two guys on the freeway pulled over a third driver who had cut them both off. They dragged him out of the car, beat him up, and each then took turns trying to run him down in their cars. The papers said to report all crime and to try to be good to one another. And meanwhile, the Santa Anas rose to seventy-five miles an hour and blew for two solid weeks.

Inevitably, we got the word at school that a hillside fire had started in the Valley. Kids were loaded on the buses, and those who drove were given permission to head for home because there was some chance that the flames would inch over Chalk Hill and threaten the campus. But as I passed the Ventura offramp, I could see that the fire was a lot closer to my own neighborhood than to Taft.

I pulled into the driveway. My mother was out on the lawn staring up at the nearby hills, her hand shading her eyes. I followed her gaze and saw a line of dark billowing smoke at the crest of the hills behind us. I couldn't see the flames, but I could almost feel their heat coming closer. The winds were whipping, and in the distance I could hear the sirens of what seemed like a hundred fire trucks.

'Did you see your brother?' she asked when I came to her side. 'The school called and said they were sending him home too.'

'He's probably walking from the bus stop now.'

'Your father will be here soon. He just called and said to get all the hoses out, the rest of the men told him he

230

should water down the roof. Me on the roof, I should live so long!'

Avrom came up the drive then and she herded us around back to gather up every container we could find to fill with water. We covered the pool with tarps to keep the ashes out – already a fine film of soot lay on the water – and then I climbed up on the roof with all the hoses joined together, my mother down below hollering instructions.

From up there I could see all the way down the street in both directions and over the tops of the houses to the hills. The fire was closer now, the smoke darker and higher in the sky. My father's car pulled into the driveway just as I was wetting down the front of the roof.

He hurried up the drive, his hair standing on end. I unconsciously touched my own hair and felt it rise under my hand, the heat and the electricity in the air were so powerful.

My father shouted, 'I'm coming up! Keep the water on the front of the house!'

All over the neighborhood, people were clambering about on their roofs, dragging hoses behind them. Women stood on the lawns with dogs and children, their faces anxious, their hands gesturing this way and that. The fire crested the ridge of the hill now, and for the first time I could see flames. A dull orange-yellow line of color at the base of the gray smoke, crawling irregularly, deceptively slowly, down the face of the golden hill. A small plane droned overhead, dipping down into the smoke, dropping some sort of white material.

At one point I moved the hose to the side of the house, turning my back on the burning hills. There, behind us, the traffic moved on the freeway normally, the sky was blue, and life was completely undisturbed. I could see the parking lot at the mall, full as usual. But then I turned around once more and saw a building inferno. All according to which way you looked.

My father was climbing up on the edge of the roof, clinging precariously to the ladder. He pulled himself up and then crouched over, holding to one of the shingles. Slowly, he stood upright, and I was surprised to see how tired he looked. Shorter, somehow, too.

'My God,' he said quietly, 'it's moving fast. Isn't it? Hasn't it moved a lot closer since you got up here?' He stood and stared at the line of the fire. You could see the firefighters and their trucks on this side of the hill now; some of them out in the brush cutting swathes, others manning large hoses.

I took the smaller hose and my father took the larger one; we stood side by side soaking the roof, neither of us saying much. Down below, you could hear my mother hollering directions to Avrom. They were putting things in boxes.

I could see over the tops of the houses to Sherry's street. The fire line was closer to her house than to ours.

We kept the hoses on for a long while, and I stood thinking, mesmerized by the movement of the water, willing myself not to watch the flames. I wondered what I would remember of this later: my father and I fighting together to save our home? My mother's voice, with that high harsh sound of fright? Would a day come when I'd water my lawn, a time when I had a wife and kids of my own in some suburban two-car-garage fortress, and stand transfixed by this memory?

I know now that my memory is rigged with hundreds of tiny trip mines, waiting for me to stumble over the right trigger and blow myself from serenity into long-forgotten grief or terror or humiliation. But at seventeen I believed I'd remember it all as it was.

The fire began to slow, and it looked now as though the fighters had cut a complete circle around it.

'I guess they'll contain it,' my father said suddenly. 'And we'll probably have a leaky roof when the rains come. Or it'll rot next summer.' He stuck his head over the edge of the roof. 'Myra, don't do that!'

She stopped carrying a box to the car and looked up, surprised.

'It's never going to get this far. You're just going to have to put them all back again.'

She set the box down, wiping a strand of hair back from her face. At that instant she looked eighteen. She stared up at the burning ridge. 'So you just want to wait until it's at Murphy's mailbox?'

Murphy was the guy across the street.

'Trust me,' my father said. 'It's not going to even make it to the bottom of the hill.'

She was muttering to herself, picking up the box again and heading for the house. 'A person had to move out to the edge of the world. A person had to start life all over in paradise, complete with earthquakes and fires. Now a person's got to soak the roof and make leaks. Avrom, stop packing. We're staying put!'

I began to coil up the hose. 'Dad, if you don't need me anymore, I'd like to take off for a while. Just a half hour or so. You can save some boxes for me, and I'll do them later.'

My father turned and frowned. 'That little girlfriend of yours? The blond one?'

I felt myself redden, and I wondered what other secrets I had that my father had known all along. He didn't, for a moment, assume it was Miriam. I nodded. 'She lives just a few blocks over.'

'I know where she lives.'

'Well, I thought I'd just go check to see if she needs a

hand with anything. Probably she and her mother are there alone.'

My father busied himself with the hose, coiling it up. 'I suppose. But I wish you wouldn't make a habit of it, David.'

I stopped with one leg on the ladder. 'Well, I'm not. But how come you said that?'

'Simply because she wouldn't be our first choice for you. Now that you're seeing that nice Weld girl again, I don't see why you have to keep running over to Sherry Gentry's house.'

I thought for an instant. Didn't really want to stir it up but didn't want it to simmer unlidded either. 'You don't like her?'

'It isn't that.'

'Because she isn't Jewish?'

My father turned to face me. 'That's part of it, of course. But more important, she's not really right for you.'

'Well, I'm not planning to marry her or anything. You and Mom can stop worrying,' I said offhandedly as I started down. 'She's just a good friend.'

'You spend a lot of time with her for just friends. And you'd like it to be more than that.'

'Dad, I'm not in *love* with her.' I tried to put as much scorn as I could into the word.

'Perhaps not. But you are certainly bewitched.'

All of a sudden I felt like I was back in the Old Country. 'I am not!'

'Fascinated, then.'

I shrugged, unable to keep the smile from my face. 'Maybe. Maybe I'll give you "fascinated". What's wrong with that?'

'Nothing. I've been there. It's not so terrible, that

feeling. But I remember in my moments of "fascination", that I'd do just about anything the girl wanted me to do.'

'Well, give me a little more credit than that. She's not going to tell me to do anything, and if she did, I wouldn't do it if I didn't want to.'

Now my father smiled. Sadly. 'You'll want to. Because she asks.'

'You make it sound like she's some kind of dybbuk, Dad. She's only seventeen, just like me. She's not out to get me.'

'Of course not,' my father said mildly. 'Does the avalanche decide to bury the skier?'

'Don't worry so much. The one who gets me,' I added just before I stepped down, 'is going to have to be fast on her feet, right?'

My father shrugged and turned away. 'Right. Just keep dancing, son. But come back before dark.'

As I drove the short blocks to Sherry's house, I thought about my father's words. I was surprised to see how deep their disapproval went. But then, I supposed I could understand it. She was certainly different from any other girl I'd dated, like some sort of exotic bird, next to Miriam. But they always told me it was good to have a lot of different friends.

Maybe it was better for them not to know quite so much about my life, I thought. Where I come and go. They don't have to know every single time I visit her, after all. It's not a big deal. Besides, I've always done exactly as they wanted me to do, always been the perfect son. It wouldn't hurt them not to get their way every single time they asked for it.

As I pulled up into her driveway, I looked up and saw that Sherry was sitting on the roof. The ladder leaned against the side of the house by the cactus, and she was up there with binoculars to her eyes.

'Hey!' she shouted when she saw me. 'Come on up, you can see forever up here!'

I climbed up the ladder, grabbing the hand she extended to me. She had a blanket all spread out, as if she were going to a picnic. 'Aren't you afraid you'll catch your hair on fire or something?' I asked. 'I figured your mother would have invited the firemen in for beer and chips.'

'No, she saves that for high school guys. Dad came home and said it wasn't a big deal, that they were going to put it out soon. He went on back to work.'

'God, *my* mother's already got the baby pictures and the good silver packed. The roof's a sponge, we've poured so much water on it.'

'Well, we're used to it. This is the third time since we've lived here.'

'You're kidding.'

'Nope. Three times that hill's burned. Comes every few years or so, just like the earthquakes. And nothing ever happens. They always put it out before it reaches the bottom. See those planes over there?'

I put the binoculars to my eyes and saw two low-diving planes dropping more white powder on the flames. She was right; the line of fire was dwindling. The hill was being eaten at a much slower pace. 'It's really something. It must be like hell in the middle of that.'

'Yeah,' she said, throwing back her hair. 'At first, you could feel the heat from here.'

I handed her the binoculars and reached up to take a small bit of ash from her bangs.

'So, tell me,' she said all of a sudden, 'every time there's some sort of major disaster, I can count on you to come running up here to save me, right? This is twice now.'

'You've about filled your quota. Two per customer,

236

and then I leave the field open to the second team. The lesser heroes.'

'I doubt that, David Levine.' She smiled. 'I highly doubt that.'

On the way home I pictured her wrestling the ladder out of the garage, getting it up against the house, climbing up there all by herself with a blanket over one arm and the binoculars around her neck. How many other girls would do that? Miriam would have been down on the lawn, dragging out boxes full of valuables along with my mother. But Sherry Gentry sits on the roof, the better to see the whole show.

The fire was almost out. The scorched black hill looked like a deep wound in the earth. But in a few months I knew it would be green again, and by the following summer as gold and lush as though the fire had never happened. The hills never really changed unless man put houses on them. They just became more themselves.

My senior year was rolling by in a juggernaut fashion, flattening some and elevating others to new and heady heights. I could see definite patterns developing. Those who were out of it as freshmen never really quite escaped that slot, except for a few key girls who grew incredible bodies and so created new auras for themselves. Those who were popular early tended to remain popular, that is unless they began to date somebody who was out it, or unless – again, this applied only to the girls – they got bad reputations for running too fast.

Senior year. It was something I'd looked forward to for what seemed to be all of my life. I expected everyone to be different somehow. Older and taller certainly, but also layered with a discernible veneer of serene grace and certitude about them, a poise which went beyond mature and meant 'senior'.

And the women. They would all be beautiful, complex, and accessible. My friends who managed the key positions in Flaw Patrol would be out of jobs forever. Flaw Patrol was, of course, the responsibility of everyone, but especially if a buddy looked like he was getting too blinded by lust to make an intelligent judgment of a girl. You had to count on your friends to help you see the light.

'Hey, Watts, you taking Mary Bay to the prom?'

'Yeah, man. She's the best thing walking to my mind.'

'Well, you obviously have neglected to take a good look at her feet.'

'Her feet? What's the matter with her feet?'

'Nothing maimed, really. But aren't they just a little big?'

Watts would be able to see nothing else but Mary Bay's feet the next time he took her out, and if it was *real*, then he'd get over it. If not, he'd be on to the next ideal.

But I naturally assumed that the Flaw Patrol would be idle when we hit senior year, because, of course, all the girls were perfect. But only one could be the most perfect of all.

It was a given that Sherry Gentry would be May Queen her senior year. We went through the motions of voting, of course, just to keep the faculty happy, but no one ever doubted that when the crown settled on some shining head, it would be hers.

May Queen. Taft's most stellar height. I teased her, naturally. Called her 'shoe-in' and 'star' for weeks. 'So how does it feel,' I asked her, 'to have your fantasy come true at such an early age? You wanted to be royalty, you said. Now you've got it knocked.'

She smiled. 'So they say. But I could still blow it before the coronation dance.'

'Only by death or extensive maiming.'

238

'No, then they'd probably give it to me post mortem. I'd get the sympathy vote. But I'd lose it fast enough if some girls decided that I wasn't nice. Or enough guys decided that I was too easy, or some stupid lies circulated about me or something. It doesn't take much, really. Two years ago Marcy Weller almost lost it because a bunch of people saw her drunk at a party.'

'Everybody get drunk at a party once in a while.'

'Not the May Queen. And also, the May Queen doesn't go out to the car and not come back for two hours, and when she does, she shouldn't look like she's been doing it for a week. The only reason she got it at all was that it happened the weekend before, and there wasn't time for a lot of people to hear about it. Another day or two, and she'd never have been voted in.'

'So you have to be really careful for the next few weeks.'

I was only kidding, but her sigh held some true regret.

'I've had to be careful, *always*. You never know who might be watching. Or telling, after.' She smiled ruefully. 'You know, my mother was a real fox when she was young. She told me once that being pretty and popular was like living in a back leg of an all-glass piano. It's uncomfortable, it's noisy, everyone can watch what you do, and you can't do much.'

I gave that one a lot of thought. She sounded a little lonely when she said it. Maybe that was one of the prices of beauty, something like what my mother said. That a pretty face costs.

Now, I know that every woman who is pretty is also alone at some level. That solitude is a coefficient of beauty, a price women pay for their loveliness.

When I was seventeen I thought that only in high school was sex such a big deal. I couldn't imagine adults worrying

239

about reputation and popularity and beauty and loneliness. These things get sorted out properly, I thought, just like hormones. You just had to get through it. Adults didn't worry about that sort of thing.

The ceremony took place on a Saturday night, at the Spring Ball, the biggest night of the year. Bigger even than the Senior Prom, because the whole school was invited. Of course, the younger grades weren't as well represented, and even though we were all in the same auditorium, there were certain distinct social strata that had to be maintained. For example, no sophomore boy strayed too close to the Senior Wall, the side of the room where the older stag boys loitered. And teachers herded the juniors back into the room if they wandered out into the dark halls, but they ignored the disappearance of any number of senior couples.

The auditorium was done up in the colors of springtime, with pink and white clouds of the sort of flowers – like dogwood and cherry blossoms and tulips – you'd find only in a place that really had a spring. Although those flowers didn't thrive in the Valley, no one seemed to notice the discrepancy. On the stage in front of the Taft High School band two thrones sat in red velvet splendor, and over them spangled banners read TAFT MAY QUEEN AND KING.

I was dancing with Miriam, moving around the room with the general flow of traffic. Her shoulder ruffles kept getting in my mouth and tickling my upper lip. It was like dancing with a wedding cake.

Nonetheless, I said, 'This is nice. About two months ago I was wondering if we'd ever be doing this again together.'

'And now we're part of each other.'

Well. We had made love several times, and I wasn't going to quibble with her tonight, but her phrasing seemed a little drastic. I wasn't dating anyone else; neither

240

was she. Still, there seemed to be more unfathomable distance between us which I sometimes didn't try to breach.

'Tonight,' she said, 'is one of those times that try women's souls.'

'What do you mean?'

'I mean a whole evening devoted to acknowledging the queen bee syndrome. I can't wait to look back on all this.'

'Really?' I was genuinely surprised. 'I thought all you girls loved this sort of stuff.'

'*I* don't.'

I shrugged. 'The other girls look pretty happy.' The room was filled with smiling, whirling women in bright colors. I sang quietly under my breath, 'A pretty girl is like a mel-o-dy – '

'More like a malady.'

'Oooh. You're hot tonight.'

She smiled wryly. 'This sort of spectacle brings out the best in me.'

'Aw, come on,' I said as I twirled her gently under my arm. 'You don't have a thing to be jealous about, if that's what's eating you. It's all just a game.' I beamed my best sap-smile. 'And you've already won the prize.'

'Right. Why do I get the feeling that most of you guys would prefer a raving beauty even if she has a brain the size of a hummingbird?'

I grinned. 'You'd be surprised how effective the selection process is, actually. Sometimes you even get a girl whose tongue is long as her arm.'

She laughed. 'I'm sure.'

I twirled and dipped her into the final drop, thinking a little masterly control wouldn't hurt Miriam at all, it just might loosen her up a little –

'Don't squeeze me so tight,' she said calmly. 'I'm not such a lard-o that you need a death grip.'

The band ended the song with a flourish and the dean of women, Mrs Eisee, came to the microphone. She looked like Jackie Kennedy, only twenty years older. After some coaxing, shy Mr Fox, the dean of men, came to the stand beside her.

'I know you're all waiting for the big news,' she said cheerily. 'And we won't keep you waiting any longer!' She gestured behind her like Doc Severinsen, and the drummer obliged with a thunderous roll. 'It is my great personal pleasure to announce Taft High's new May Court for the 1966 year!'

The crowd gathered at her feet, grinning with one open mouth, and I looked around for Sherry but couldn't see her anywhere.

Mrs Eisee went on about the judging and the voting process, the proper criteria for the perfect couple, their future and the future of all excellent prospects from Taft, and just about the time that I could have sworn she was going to mention the securities firm of Price Waterhouse, a blushing freshman girl ran onstage with two large envelopes.

'You open the boys',' Mrs Eisee said, shoving one of them at Mr Fox.

The dean of men smiled and fumbled with the thing, amazingly ill at ease in the spotlight. No wonder, I thought, since he spent the bulk of his time skulking around corners and hiding in the bathrooms trying to catch cutters and smokers and other trash. Now he gets to announce the cream, and the man's all foolish. He finally got the card out and held it up in triumph. Some of the older boys snickered, but Fox was too excited to notice. 'The May King for 1966 is – '

For a swift instant I wanted it to be my own name so badly that I almost winced when it wasn't. Even though I *knew* it wouldn't be, couldn't be, never had been and never would be –

'Don Swenson!'

The crowd exploded in glee and Swenson came forward from the rear of the room, getting the slaps on the back and the attaboys, slumping his shoulders in a modest pose that they all just ate up. He stepped up on the stage and stood still, grinning, while Mrs Eisee reached up on tiptoe and gingerly settled the crown on his head, Mr Fox pumping away at his hand. The cheers and squeals from the girls in the front row were like the roar of the sea.

'I hope he passes bio,' Miriam said quietly. 'It's going to be pretty embarrassing if Taft's best flunks out, crown and all.'

I hoped just the opposite and hated myself. It was the same sort of evil that made me wish briefly that the motorcyclist who just shimmied and weaseled his way past me on the clogged freeway would die on the next turn in a fiery heap. I apologized quickly to God and my mother.

'And now,' Mrs Eisee was saying, 'every king needs a queen! The May Queen for 1966, the special girl you have selected to represent the very best Taft has to offer is' – another drum-roll-and-trumpet flourish – 'Miss Sherry Gentry!'

This time the cheers were deafening, and to my surprise the girls in the front row screamed just as hard for Sherry as they had for Don. She came from way back in the room, and rather than crowding forward to slap her back and pump her arm, the crowd fell away from her like the parting of the Red Sea.

She walked slowly, her hair shining around her like a nimbus of light, her head down and demure as befitted a virgin princess. Almost, you might have thought she was coming forward to be married; almost you could visualize

243

a veil over her face, protecting nature's most beautiful features from the coarse glances of the ordinary souls around her.

'That's a great dress,' Miriam said evenly.

I hadn't even noticed. I had, however, noticed the look on a few of the guys' faces as she passed, and I wondered if I ever looked so foolish and worshipful. No one touched her as she walked, but as she paused to step up to the stage, ten hands reached out quickly to help her, as though she carried a long, heavy train. She was now under the spotlight, dressed all in white, a gleaming silver taper of tan skin and flowing silk and hair. Her smile was serene, almost thoughtful.

Mr Fox made some sort of clumsy speech about grace and poise under pressure and then carefully went to put the crown on her head. Sherry delicately took the crown from his hands and settled it on her hair properly, so that it wouldn't be tangled. She turned to her costar and kissed him on the cheek, taking his hand like a scepter.

At this, the first-row girls collapsed into weeping fits, the band struck up the school anthem, and couples clasped each other as though they were watching their own children mated. Sherry led Don to the dance floor and they began their first official tour of the room as the May Queen and King.

'Very pretty,' Miriam said. 'I thought it would be sort of stupid, but it wasn't.'

'Didn't you go to any of the other balls?' I asked. 'Didn't you see Marcy Weller get it last year?'

'Oh, yeah, but I thought I'd feel different about it now that I'm a senior.' She pulled back and looked at me. 'Didn't you?'

I nodded. She was right. I expected to feel somehow above it all, but I didn't. Even though I could picture Don Swenson shivering with frustrated lust under a blanket in

244

his car, could hear him shouting at Sherry in her living room, could see her, so clearly, translucent with grief and fear as he confronted her, it didn't matter. They were still, in that moment, perfect. And judging from the way Mr Fox and Mrs Eisee and the other teachers were acting, they felt the same way. Lots of them were beaming at Sherry and Don as though they were church elders greeting new converts, even though I knew that not a few had cursed Don's laziness and Sherry's late reports in the past. It was rather a shock to realize that adults – thinking, mature, rational people in charge – could be just as seduced by glamour as anyone else.

Toward the end of the evening I finally claimed a single dance with Sherry. 'Well?' I asked when she was in my arms. 'How does it feel to be perfect?'

She laughed deliciously, hugging me around the neck. 'Don't you dare tease me, David. You're not allowed to tonight.'

'How will you know it's me, then?' I asked in mock bewilderment.

'By your Fred Astaire feet.' She was looking around her constantly as we danced.

The music was surprisingly good for the Taft dance band, and for long moments I was lulled into a perfect sense of contentment, as though in a dream. I believed, in that instant, that whatever I did, whatever we all did, would be right, somehow perfect and universally fitting, that we would conquer the old forces of evil and mediocrity, that we would prevail over the future, that we had the momentum and nothing could turn us aside from our glittering promise. Sherry's cheek was nestled on my shoulder, and she was humming softly to the music.

'You tired at all?' I asked.

'Not a speck. I wish it would go on forever.'

Out of the corner of my eye I saw Miriam waiting on

the edge of the dance floor, back from the powder room. She was talking to a few girlfriends. Her eyes met mine once, then swiveled away.

Almost without realizing it I whispered, 'I wish I could take you home.'

She didn't take her cheek off my shoulder. 'I do too, David Levine, but you're spoken for again.'

Long after the dance was over, long after I had taken Miriam out the door, parked with her, made love with her, and dropped her off at her house, I thought of Sherry's words over and over. 'I do too, David Levine.'

Grad Night was the highlight of senior year. The payoff for months of holding it together when you sometimes felt like you wanted to scream at all the parents, teachers, college applications and counselors, 'Get off my back!'

Grad Night was actually a full week ahead of graduation itself – had to be to accommodate all the California seniors. But we didn't mind its adjustment because we knew that no place else in the country celebrated graduation like Southern California because no place else in the country had Disneyland.

Disneyland, the Magic Kingdom. The place where Donald and Mickey and Tinker Bell were born. A paradise of seven realms of fantasy, acres of complete joyous abandon – and here was the kicker: Disneyland, for only a few nights a year, was open till dawn for all the graduating seniors in Southern California, with nobody else admitted. No parents, no teachers, no chaperons, no bus drivers. Like Pinocchio's Pleasure Island, where all the boys go to break windows and eat their weight in candy before they turn into donkeys, Disneyland beckoned before us as a shining symbol of the last of our childhood.

My only problem was that I really didn't want to take a

date. Watts and Critter started it, actually. Critter said to Foote and me one day at lunch, 'You know, Grad Night should be our last night to howl. Like men, without the women around.'

'Yeah!' Watts agreed emphatically. 'We should stag it.'

'You're kidding, I'm sure,' Foote said amiably. 'Sounds like a drag.'

'No, really,' Critter said. 'We can tear it up, get crazy, take over Tom Sawyer's Island or something. You know, take the girls out before we get there, but then cut loose and be free agents once we're inside the gates. Maybe meet them at the end for a dance or two or something. What do you say?'

'I say they'll kill us,' I answered quickly.

'Not if we all stick together,' Watts said. 'Hell, they may even like the idea. They can pal around together for a few hours and so can we, then we'll all meet up later. This'll probably be the last time we'll have the pack together. You guys'll be splitting over the summer, we'll all be heading off to different colleges, and that'll be it.' He burped gloriously, loud and long. 'I say we do it. Start a trend.'

Foote laughed. 'I think if we start out stag, we'll end up that way, but if you guys want to do it, I'm game. There's other things in life besides pussy.'

'Name one!' Watts said, slapping Critter on the back and making him spill his Dr Pepper all down the front of his jersey.

Well, I had to admit there was something about it that appealed to me. Disneyland after dark. Just a bunch of guys raising hell, and then back to the women when that got old. Critter was sort of immature, but once in a while he hit a nerve. It definitely had possibilities.

I gingerly opened the subject up for discussion when

247

Miriam and I had just finished making love one Saturday night. She was fixing her lipstick in the rearview mirror. 'A couple of the guys had kind of an interesting idea the other day.'

'What guys?'

'Watts, Critter, you know.'

'The Charm Brothers.'

I laughed politely. 'Yeah. Well, anyway, this one's not such a dumb idea. Foote thought it had possibilities.'

She turned to me, waiting calmly.

This was the part I hated. The Negotiation. Some piece of me wanted to just drop it on her, Hey, bitch, I'll catch you later. And don't wait up. 'Actually, it might be kind of fun,' I went on breezily. 'We have a pre-party before we get to Disneyland, see, everybody all together and everything, and then when we actually get inside the gates, off the bus and everything, then we split up and meet back later, toward the end of the evening.'

'And do what in between?'

I paused, as though in thought. 'Well, just run loose, I guess. The guys all together and the girls all together. Just for old time's sake.'

'Sounds groovy,' she said, the sarcasm lowering her voice. 'Spending my Grad Night with the girls.'

'It'll be the last time you see most of them, maybe.'

'If that was a major heartbreak for me, I'd organize a slumber party. Besides, it'll be a long summer. We'll all see each other, I'm sure.'

'I'm not so sure. Everybody'll be off their separate ways. It won't be the same.'

'Nothing ever is. That's why they call it graduation.'

I fell silent.

She turned back to the mirror and began to brush her hair. It crackled slightly and stood out from her head in flyaway wisps.

'It'd be for only a few hours, really,' I said finally.

She turned on me swiftly. 'Why don't you just come right out and say it, David? You're the one who thought of it. You don't want to be with me on Grad Night. Just say it.'

Why was she always so testy after we had sex? And why didn't I get better at remembering that? 'That's not true,' I said tiredly. 'I *do* want to be with you. I invited you, didn't I?'

'And now you're *un*inviting me.'

'I am not. I'm just wondering if we have to be together every single minute we're inside the park, that's all. I just thought it would be fun to go off with the guys and get crazy for a while. But never mind.' I leaned against the car door, my cheek pressed against the cool glass. 'Shit, it's not worth the uproar.' I watched her out of the corner of my eye.

Miriam's lower lip had this incredible ability to transmit emotion, to telegraph what she was feeling. I could have sworn it had actually gotten bigger in the last year, and now it protruded out in a major pout, like the curled arm of an overstuffed sofa. She was yanking her sweater on, her head down in the shadows.

Well, I wasn't going to say another thing. I wasn't going to beg her. Lately all we ever did was bicker anyway. I thought, she's lucky I just don't dump her the night before Grad Night or something, just leave her ass flat –

'So we'd go to a party before? All together?'

I didn't speak, just turned my head slightly away.

'I guess we could set up some kind of meeting place. When the dancing starts, anyway.'

I started up the car.

'Although it sounds so juvenile. What did the other girls say?'

'I told you,' I said finally, 'it was just an idea a few of

249

us had. It's no big deal. I don't even know if the other guys have talked to their dates yet. I wanted to talk to you first.'

Well, she liked that. I could see it in the leveling of her shoulders.

'If it's going to get you all mad, just forget it. It's not worth it.'

'I'm not all mad,' she said gently, scooting over closer to me. 'It just took me by surprise, is all. I guess if you really want to – '

'*I* don't give a damn actually,' I said vehemently. 'I told you. The other guys thought it would be kind of fun, and I said I'd have to run it by you first.'

'You did?'

'Of course. It's your Grad Night too.'

She smiled and put her head on my shoulder. 'I guess it wouldn't hurt. I mean, we'd be together before and after, when it really counts. Say you guys take off from one to four or something. And we'll do the same thing, and then we'll meet back together and pair up again.' She poked me playfully. 'Of course, if any of us gets a better offer in between, you guys might be out of luck.'

I pulled her closer and kissed her, my eyes open and on the road. 'Maybe this isn't such a good idea after all.'

'I think it's rather intriguing,' she said, her mouth moving under mine. 'Tell Critter he's not as dumb as he looks.'

By the time the buses pulled up in the Disneyland parking lot, by itself an acreage large enough to – if it were plowed – feed half the state, I was sure most of the kids were screamed hoarse. We'd gone through every Taft High fight song, every slightly bawdy or singularly filthy college song we'd ever heard, a few, I swore, somebody drunk in the back was making up as we went along, and nobody's

250

voice was normal. It took twenty buses to transport us all, and we were only one of more than a dozen high school senior classes attending that night. There had been six pre-parties from which to choose. Some of the girls were in prom formals, the guys in rented tuxes. Others had already changed into serious carousing clothes, just one step up from jeans, which weren't allowed. We ran a phalanx of parents and teachers just to climb aboard the buses, and they checked all large purses for contraband.

And then we were inside the gates, beyond the adult world together, within the walls of Disneyland. I took Miriam's hand and hurried out to Main Street. We stood, just staring up the avenue at the quaint Victorian shops and the trees all covered with a million tiny white lights. Beyond lay Fantasyland, Sleeping Beauty's Castle, Frontierland, Adventureland, Tomorrowland, and too many wonders to contemplate all at once.

It really was so magical that water came to my eyes. Miriam squeezed my hand in silence, and we walked down Main Street USA, stopping to peer into each storefront window. Each shop was different; each had its own personality. There was the soda fountain and the old movie theater, which had nickel egg creams and root beer floats and old black and white silent Charlie Chaplin films. In one of the arcades a mechanical Gypsy with a trailing silk scarf told fortunes for a dime. There was an ancient apothecary shop with glass jars filled with herbs and medicines, and in the back an old grocery store with cracker barrels and pickle barrels, a pot-belly stove, and penny candy in glass cabinets. Smoked hams hung from the ceiling, and you could almost imagine a cold winter's night in New Hampshire or the Appalachians, when Zeke and Zeb would swap bear-hunting stories over their pipes.

The Kodak store was next, and besides film and postcards, it also had a great display of all the old cameras of history, and a guy dressed up in an antique photographer's outfit with cape and glasses and handlebar mustache.

'The details are incredible,' Miriam said wonderingly.

I realized instantly that she had hit on the key to Disneyland's magic. The streets were cobblestone and immaculately clean, each pathway lined with flowers. Even the old streetlamps were authentic. The stores had the same tourist stuff to sell: the T-shirts, the coffee mugs, the place mats, the key chains and hats, but they were somehow better than usual, and more fitting. The hats weren't just hats, they were Mickey Mouse ears that you could have personally embroidered with your name. The mugs were extra wide and deep, and you had the choice of Pluto or Tinker Bell to stare at while you drank your coffee.

'He's my hero,' I said.

'Who?' Miriam was holding up a Goofy T-shirt to her chest; her breasts were going to do amazing things to his white-gloved hands.

'Walt Disney. What an incredible mind he must have to imagine all this. To make it all come true.'

'Yes, I know,' she said happily. 'You've never been here, right? I can't believe your parents never brought you. Mine did, almost the first week we moved here. I remember something that happened that sort of summed it all up for me. We were standing in line for the Jungle Boat Ride. You know that one? Well, anyway, the ticket taker was giving his spiel, about how dangerous it was, and how there were huge hippos which had eaten a few boats and crocodiles and head hunters, and, of course, I knew it was all just bull, but I couldn't help getting a little nervous, because you really *do* get in a boat, and it goes around the bend where you can't see it, and then you hear roars and gunshots and everything. So the guy was going on and on, and then he said everybody would have to line up for their tsetse-fly shots. Well, I freaked.'

'There aren't any tsetse flies in Orange County. Last I heard, anyway.'

'I *knew* that, but I still was all caught up in it and I began to get even more nervous because I hate shots. Sometimes I even faint when I have to get a tetanus shot every year. Anyway, this guy is going on and on and the crowd is laughing, but not me – I'm wondering how I can get out of line without making a fool of myself or maybe sneak on the boat without a shot.'

I shook my head, grinning.

'Don't laugh! You just wait until the Haunted House and then tell me about it! Anyway, you know what I did? I just kept telling myself, Walt Disney would never hurt me, Walt Disney would never hurt me. And so, sure enough, they really weren't handing out shots, and the crocodiles didn't get me, and to this day I sometimes find myself praying to Walt instead of to God.' She plunked a set of Mickey Mouse ears on her head and grinned defiantly.

'Hey, it's perfectly understandable. I prayed to Annette Funicello every night of my adolescence.'

'And still do, no doubt. So when and where do you want to meet?' She was looking around at the T-shirts and sweatshirts with a familiar gleam in her eye, and I knew she'd be there for another half hour, minimum.

'Three A.M., on the Sleeping Beauty bridge.'

I moved closer and put my arms around her. 'You sure this is okay with you?'

She smiled. 'Absolutely. But if I'm not there in fifteen minutes, don't wait for me. I might get a better offer from a sailor and take off for San Diego.'

'Just don't get a tattoo.' I kissed her quickly and went out before she could change her mind.

Once out in the street I looked up toward the castle, and all I could see were acres of lights and kids and hear only music and the throbbing of what seemed like a million happy hearts. A brief flit of sadness passed over me then, as though I stood for an instant on a high place and could see my childhood behind me, dropping away swiftly like a dream as I came awake. I sensed that no other time in all of my years left to me might be so free, so careless and easy, and I felt myself slipping – or, rather, settling – through some invisible ceiling or floor onto another level of my life. But then I shook it away and hurried across the flowered pathways to meet Watts, Foote, and Critter at the foot of the castle drawbridge.

They were already dazed with freedom, all three of them jittering and bouncing against one another like badly made toys, careening through crowds and dragging me with them. We headed immediately for Tom Sawyer's Island, which soon became a gravitational pull for every stag male in the park. Within an hour we'd taken possession of it, along with a dozen guys from Taft, running off all women and necking couples and parts of the Reseda swim team. As our commando group grew, we started a ferocious capture-the-flag game, shattering limbs and leaving each other bloodied and broken with imaginary machine guns, hauling off captives and screaming pirate threats at the huge paddle ship *Columbia*, which sailed up regularly, thronged with well-dressed couples.

The midnight hours went by swiftly. Occasionally, we made land forays in groups of twos and threes, stealthily sneaking into line at the Pirates of the Caribbean ride or the Haunted House, generally running amok from Frontierland to Adventureland. We finally found ourselves in the shadows in front of Mr Toad's Wild Ride.

'This one's supposed to be the only decent ride in Fantasyland,' Critter said as we piled, four of us, into two jammed cars. The attendants had long ago stopped trying for order and were now only doing their best to prevent actual maiming. One guy screamed at us to sit down as our cars jostled over the tracks and into the darkness of the tunnel ride.

While Sleeping Beauty and Peter Pan were familiar characters, I didn't know Mr Toad. I couldn't figure out what all these evil-looking rats and weasels were doing in a Disney ride – not to mention little red devils from hell! Of course, it was over too quickly, and then we were out again into the lights.

'Stay on, stay on!' Foote screamed, and since the line wasn't long, the attendants shrugged and pushed the buttons for our two packed cars to go through again.

'Get off, get off!' Watts yelled once we were inside the dark caverns of Mr Toad, and he jumped from the moving car. Foote was right behind him.

'You guys are nuts!' I screamed back over the music, but I jerked myself out of the car and watched it go past. Now all four of us were loose in Toad Hall. We ducked back behind some cardboard flames and watched two cars full of girls go by, screaming and laughing, reaching way out to touch the moving figures of Ratty and Mole.

It was dark in there, too dark to be able to tell the outlines of the cavern, and eyes gleamed in the gloom, just about ankle high. They're cardboard, too, I told myself, and moved closer to the others. Watts and Foote were hiding behind some fake barrels, waiting for the next car. The barrels began to twirl and twist and tip on cue, as though they were going to crash down on the approaching passengers. As the car came round the bend, the guys jumped out from behind the tipping barrels and screeched horribly into the faces of two strange girls.

Well, it was dark, but not so black that I couldn't see that one girl tried to climb her friend like a tree and left welts on her neck and cheek. The instant they saw that it was only a couple of guys and not all the demons of Disneyland come to get them, they hollered furiously and flipped us the finger.

'Poor sports,' Critter said mildly. 'Probably from Canoga.'

The ride stopped in moments, and no more cars were coming through.

'They're coming to get us!' I shouted, moving quickly for the small green exit sign I suddenly spied above me. We raced out right ahead of the attendants, jumped the guardrail, and sped away from Mr Toad's Wild Ride toward the spinning Mad Hatter Teacups.

'Let's hit Tomorrowland,' Foote said, veering off and moving quickly through the crowds. 'Do the Moon Ride. Critter should feel right at home with the rest of the aliens.'

We came around the corner of the Matterhorn and ran smack into the longest line we'd found all night. Kids were leaning up against the guardrail, couples wrapped around each other, Cokes passed up and down, and the high giggles of happy girls floated over it all like fireworks. I glanced over by the submarine ride, some sort of viewing rest stop for taking pictures, and I saw Sherry Gentry standing there with a guy I hadn't seen before.

He looked like a college jock, short but stocky with a neck like a wall. 'Let's do the Matterhorn while we're here,' I said to the guys, slowing down.

'The line's too long,' Watts said, barely glancing at it.

'It's not going to get any shorter,' I said, and stopped abruptly, easing myself behind the last kid in line. 'I'm going to take it now.'

The rest of them congealed around me, and while I was waiting, I watched Sherry with her date. He was embracing her; her back was against the guardrail, her eyes closed. I couldn't see her mouth; it was pressed against this guy's jacket. There seemed to be a little turbulence around them, as though they were slightly off balance, and all of a sudden she pulled away and put her elbows up between them, saying something I couldn't hear.

'This is the pits,' Watts said, 'we should get our asses over to the space stuff.'

'Do you know,' Critter replied rather dreamily, 'I was reading the other day that you can go to East Tennessee and for eight hundred and fifty bucks, you can buy a three-day supply of whiskey, a pickup truck, a forty-five, and a woman who doesn't know any better.'

'Better than what?' Foote asked.

'You know. That's what this article said in *Field and Stream*. Just think. Eight hundred and fifty bucks for all that. Here, you couldn't even buy a woman for that.'

'A whole pickup?' Watts snorted. 'Not just the parts?'

'Running.'

'So is the woman, probably,' Foote said dryly. 'From open sores.'

Sherry was pulling away from him now, and his voice rose, saying something angry that I couldn't quite catch.

'Your material's getting better,' Foote was saying to Critter, 'who's doing it now? The School for Nearly-Intelligent Life Forms?'

As fast as a breath, she yanked her hand away from him and slapped his face, he grabbed her shoulders, and I jumped out of line. I had my hand on the guy's jacket before I even knew I'd moved. Somewhere behind me I was vaguely aware that somebody, probably Foote, hollered out. Watts shouted, 'Whoa, boy!' but every ounce of blood in my body seemed concentrated in my face, my pounding heart, as the guy whirled to face me.

'What do *you* want, fuckface?'

257

'She's a friend of mine,' I said, amazed that my throat would work at all. 'Leave her alone.'

'Well, she's a *woman* of mine, so I guess this doesn't concern you, *friend*.' He moved menacingly closer.

I had a brief swift sense of wonderment that I was doing this, that the guy was so incredibly broad, that upper bodies seemed to look so much bigger when you got closer, and before I could think of all the reasons not to, my fist shot out and caught the guy on the upper cheek, jolting him backward.

A few squeals from the line behind me, female squeals of fright and excitement, and I felt the crowd moving closer, like they might be trying to push me into the guy. Sherry was saying something, calling me, crying out, but I could hear only a high hard buzz in my ears, the pumping and wheezing of blood, and then something solid caught me in the side of the jaw. The bright lights overhead all had halos for an instant, but I thought: I've been hit and it hardly hurt and I'm still standing, with half of Taft here to watch, and I could see Sherry's face looming closer, her mouth open in fear, and I swung again.

This time there was no pause between the pain in my hand and the answering pain in my jaw, and my head snapped around, wondering from which side the blow had come, and I slumped to the ground, dazed. I expected a kick next, but the guy glared angrily at everybody, cursed at Sherry, and strode away.

She floated down around me in a swirl of skirts, repeating my name. Her voice in my ear almost drowned out Foote and Watts in the background, saying, 'Jesus Christ, he's out cold! Did you see him take that punch?'

I'm not out, I thought, and forced my mouth to say words, but nothing much came out. My jaw wasn't working, and my face felt incredibly huge. I put one hand to my nose and brought it down bloody.

258

'David,' she was saying over and over, 'are you all right? Are you hurt?'

I was finally able to mumble, 'Nuh-uh-no.' I must have bit my tongue because it was swollen like a cucumber. So this, I thought, is what a fight with a big guy is like.

The crowd began to thin, except for my friends. 'He's a fucking Galahad!' Watts crowed happily.

I frowned, and the effort moved my nose to agony. Sherry was sitting down beside me now, mopping at my face with a damp Kleenex. 'He's a real creep,' she said, her voice low.

'I – noticed,' I finally got out. 'What was his problem?'

'His ego,' she started – and then began to weep. Her hands went over her face and her head bowed, and I could hear the sobs coming from deep down inside her. The rest of the world suddenly disappeared as I hoisted myself upright and held her tightly. Her face was now muffled on my shoulder as I'd seen her with other guys, her mouth moving against my jacket.

'What did he want?' I asked her.

'The usual,' she said with real bitterness in her voice. 'He wanted me to go with him to his car.'

I thought for a moment, holding her. It suddenly occurred to me that she cried a lot. I tried to count up the times she had cried in my arms or around me, and it seemed that her tears were beginning to be a major theme with us. For some insane reason, the face of Jimmy the Mouseketeer floated up again, but this time with my mother's voice, whispering, 'A pretty face costs.'

I was exhausted all in an instant. Watts and Foote and Critter had melted back into the Matterhorn line, but I could still feel eyes on me. Nothing really mattered but her despair.

'How come,' I finally asked as she began to quiet, 'how come they always get so mad when you turn them down?'

She pulled back her head and peered at me quizzically.

'I mean, *I* don't get mad when you reject me. How do you keep coming up with these jerks?' I was amazed at how much this small sentence tired me out. I felt suddenly as though I wanted to do nothing more than lie down somewhere and stop quivering. But I kept holding her.

'They're not all jerks.'

'Sherry,' I said gently, 'I haven't seen you with a real hero yet. I mean, maybe you're dating one on the side that I don't know about, but all the ones I see you with treat you like shit. Why is that?'

'I don't know,' she moaned miserably. 'You think I bring out the violence in men or something?'

'Not in me.'

'You think I *ask* for it?' She was starting to get angry.

'I didn't say that.' I pulled her down on the bench and waited until her breath came easier.

When she had finally stopped weeping, she asked, 'What were you doing before this happened?'

'Waiting in line.'

'Who with?'

'Just the guys.'

'Where's Miriam?'

I shrugged. 'We decided we didn't have to be joined at the hip for this thing. I'll see her later.'

'Her idea or yours?'

'Mutual.'

'That means it was yours.' She smiled now, softly. 'Always the gentleman, David Levine. So when do you have to meet her again?'

'I don't *have* to do anything.'

She cocked her head. 'Oh?'

'Oh.'

She made as if to rise, and I went to help her, only to

discover that I needed more help than she did just to get to my feet.

'Do you want to go and get a Coke or something?' she asked. 'Sit down for a while?'

We went off in the direction of the Space Shuttle Bar, right around the corner in Tomorrowland. Of course, it served only juice and soft drinks, but it was probably the most adult theme bar in the park, since it had rock and roll music blaring out of eight-foot speakers. By the time she got the drinks and threaded her way back to the tiny table I was holding down, my shakes had stopped. A feeling of euphoria had replaced them, and I felt suddenly that there was nothing I couldn't do and very little that I couldn't make my own if I wanted it. I had fought some ganef for Sherry Gentry's honor. She had stayed with me and was even now bringing me a Coke like we'd been going steady for years. If there was anything else at that moment I needed to be happy, except maybe a few aspirin, I didn't know what it was.

'You okay?' she said, sliding into her seat.

'Sure.'

'You look a little groggy still.'

'With worship.' I reached out and took her hand, emboldened by what had gone before.

And this time she actually leaned forward to me, put her other hand around mine, and smiled in a way I believed I'd never seen before. 'You really are pretty wonderful, you know that? You always seem to be there for me.'

'She noticed.' I took a long swig of my drink, watching her over the edge. She had never seemed more luminous, here in the neon from the Space Bar.

'Let's stay together tonight,' she said gently.

I kept my face fairly bland. 'You mean Grad Night?'

'I mean all night. Whatever's left of it.'

I put down my drink and took her hands again, this time in both of mine. I was supposed to meet Miriam in two hours. If I didn't, I might as well throw her number away, because I'd damn sure never need it. She wouldn't speak to me again if I spent the rest of the year on my knees.

'Are you in love with Miriam?'

I shook my head numbly.

'I'm not in love with anyone either,' she said, dropping her head, suddenly demure.

'Do you want to be?'

Her turn to nod.

'With me?'

She smiled and squeezed my hands. 'Maybe.'

Let's get this straight, part of my mind was groaning, once and for all. Is she serious? Are we talking going steady here or only for the moment? Is Sherry Gentry actually hinting that I should ask her out for real?

Without another word she lifted my hand to her lips and kissed my scraped knuckles gently. I didn't even wince.

'What are you doing next month?' I asked.

'What night?'

'All nights. I think we should go steady.'

She grimaced slightly. 'I hate that.'

'The words or the concept?'

'The words. Going steady. Like something from the fifties. Like an Archie and Veronica comic book.' She looked up. 'But we could see each other exclusively. Nobody else. And we could find out what comes of it.'

'Then you can call it anything you want,' I said, sliding close to her and kissing her for the first time with complete confidence that she would actually kiss me back, really wanted me to kiss her, and might even welcome it a second time.

There was a warning whisper in my head, of course, which hectored at me with pursed lips. Could I trust her? Did I realize what I was giving up? Was she worth it? Could any man ever totally trust a woman?

A sudden thought came, one I recognized even then as startling, that the gap between men and women might just stem from the fact that we are so biologically different. Like the game between the cat and the mouse. That simple. Maybe, to be a man and a woman together meant that you were always essentially and irrevocably adversaries on some level.

The whispers in my head could not drown out the thunders in my blood, however, and as her lips opened under mine, I found her soft tongue quickly and forgot everything but the feel of her, of Sherry Gentry, kissing me at last.

Of course, I was right. After Grad Night was over, Miriam looked right through me as though I no longer existed on any plane she inhabited at all. I tried to call her once. I didn't have any real explanation except the truth, but I felt it should be accompanied by an apology. She wouldn't take my call.

When I thought of it, I felt sharp remorse. I never even went back to meet Miriam at Sleeping Beauty Bridge. I spent the whole night with Sherry, could not bring myself to leave her side, even just to go tell Miriam not to wait. We sought out the darkest rides, the most shadowed corners, and we whispered softly, held each other, and kissed until I felt my mouth would never be the same again.

Fortunately, there were only five more days of classes, because I walked around in a haze of love. Jolted only vaguely by those times I had to pass a door that Miriam might exit, Sherry and I clung to each other like two

263

addled paramecia. I found it difficult to remember what my life had been like before we were together, and I felt both impatient with and sad for those who had not been so in love. As she walked down the street, ran sometimes to meet me with open arms, her tanned legs moving gracefully, men stopped to stare at her.

Graduation day came, and we sat together in a vast sea of black robes out on the football field. Up in the bleachers I could see my mother's red dress, an outfit she had selected so that I might pick her out of the crowd.

'We won't be able to see which one is you,' she had said, 'but at least you'll see where we are.'

'Why don't you sit with Sherry's parents?' I asked. My mother was standing before me, straightening my tie, something she hadn't done since I was fifteen.

She cocked her head like a robin considering a likely worm. 'Oh, we can meet them after. And then we'll come home and celebrate! Your father has the whole afternoon planned, and your aunts will be by at two with your presents – '

'But I thought I'd go out with my friends. Sherry and I were going to the beach.'

'You'll have the rest of the summer to be with your friends, David. This is one day that should be family.'

'Can I invite her to come?'

'Just family. You can see her tonight.'

I held Sherry's hand as the principal called out name after name. I sat up proudly as she went up to the podium before me, noting how small bursts of applause broke out in the senior ranks as she passed, and when I made the trek in my turn, I glanced back at her and grinned at her wave. Then I looked back at the bleachers and saw that my whole family – my father, my mother, and Avrom – were standing and waving and cheering as I took my diploma.

I was buoyed by love on all sides. And at that moment I felt that my life was actually beginning in earnest. I was two weeks from eighteen, I was graduating with honors, and I knew that I could make miracles happen for myself. My eyes watered with pride so that I had to reach up and adjust my glasses as I walked back to my row. I wanted to hug every member of the graduating class and fall to my knees, overwhelmed by faith in a God of wisdom and benevolent power who had a plan for us all.

That night we went to the boardwalk at Pacific Ocean Park. We were walking along sharing a cotton candy when I noticed that Sherry's mood had changed. She'd been wistful all evening, but I figured it was because of graduation. Now when she wasn't smiling, I tilted her chin to me and asked, 'You miss it already?'

She nodded. She was so quiet. I could hear the barks of the sea lions under the pier, and even those didn't make her smile.

I put my arm around her. 'Think of it as a beginning, not an ending.'

'David,' she said, her voice low and sober, 'I have to ask you something.'

'What?'

'And when I ask you, you have to promise not to say okay if you really think you can't handle it. You have to promise to tell the truth about how you feel.'

'I thought we were past that. We agreed to always tell the truth, no matter what.'

'Yes,' she said, 'I know.' She smiled absently, but I wasn't warmed. She flicked a bit of hair back from her eyes. 'I'm going to Mexico with my sister. She needs to get an abortion.' Her eyes watered but her mouth didn't change. 'I want you to go with me. If you think you can, I mean.'

I felt like a slow sore was opening in my stomach. 'An

abortion? You're kidding.' I knew she wasn't. I turned and dropped the cotton candy into a trash can.

'She's two months. My parents don't know, they'd kill her if they knew.'

'They would not,' I said quickly. 'Not as fast as a Mexican abortion might.' I turned away, shaking my head. 'This is *not* a good idea. Your parents would help her, they're rich enough, they could probably find somebody, some good doctor right here to do it for her.'

'She's going.'

'But it's dangerous! Doesn't she read the papers? Girls go down there and they never even find the bodies!'

She winced, as though I'd cuffed her shoulders. 'She won't tell them. She says she'd rather die than tell my mother.'

'Jesus,' I said softly.

'She's going, I know her. She says she is, and she is. She can't go alone, I won't let her go down there by herself.' She moved into my arms, which opened for her as automatically as though she had stepped on some secret foot pedal. Her shoulders were still; she wasn't crying. She had wept at so many other times when it wasn't necessary, didn't even seem important, and now of all times, when she was justified, there was no evidence of tears.

I thought of my own parents. Abortion wasn't the critical mass issue with Jews that it was with some religions. I could recall my father telling about how, in medieval times, the Jewish midwives were the ones who performed the abortions in the villages. Which is why the Catholic Church hated them and hounded them. Called them baby-killers and Christ-killers. The Talmud says that the mother comes first, over the life of the child. That there are sometimes good reasons to end the life of the unborn. It always made sense to me.

266

But no matter what the Talmud had to say about it, no matter what the history of theological thought on the issue, I could picture my mother's face when I told her, and it wasn't a happy one. They wouldn't even let me go to Catalina on the ferry by myself, much less to Tijuana to be an accomplice to a bloody and illegal act. My head went light. It was incredible. I couldn't even picture myself crossing the border.

I had a sudden thought. 'What about the guy? Won't he go with her?'

'She doesn't know for sure who it is.'

'Oh. Well. What about one of her girlfriends? Somebody older, maybe?'

She pulled away from me slightly. 'Look, don't come if you don't want to, I'll understand. But don't try to talk me out of it. She's my sister, and I'm going.'

I felt small and cowardly then. 'Well, does she know where to go? How much will it cost? I mean, this sort of thing can be pretty radical, can't it? Could she be arrested, or something?' I heard my voice go high and childlike, and I hated my fear.

'She says she knows where to go. A girlfriend told her, someone who did it last year. She was okay.'

'Okay? What does that mean?'

'It means she's alive, okay?' Now Sherry's voice was high and getting louder. 'Listen, David, I wondered if I should ask you or not. Maybe it's not such a good idea for you to come after all. I mean, we can handle it ourselves, I'm sure, and she'll just go down there, have it done, and I'll bring her back. I just thought you've always been there for me, and I figured you'd want to know.'

'Of course I want to know,' I said impatiently. 'Of course I'll go with you. There's no way I'd let you two go down there by yourselves.' An incredible sadness settled on my shoulders like a damp, musty blanket, and I felt forty or more. 'She's sure? She really wants to do this?'

'She doesn't have any choice.'

'My God, I'll bet a hundred thousand girls a day face this and feel they've got a hell of a lot more choices than to go to Mexico for an abortion!'

'They're not my sister.'

'And nobody knows anybody up here who'll do it? Look, maybe I can ask around, find out from some of the guys, somebody must know somebody safer who'll do it – '

She shook her head. 'She's got it worked out. She's going, I told you. And it's to be in the next week, she says, or it gets less safe.'

'Less safe! There's nothing safe about it, from what I've heard. I mean, she could get infected, she could get kidnapped, she could disappear down there into some sewer and never come out again.'

'Are you going or not?'

'I told you I would.'

She went back into my arms, and I held her tighter, smelling the salt in her hair. She was wearing high heels and a thin dress, and she was almost as tall as I was. I was still so aware of her body, no matter what my mind was doing. We hadn't actually made love yet, but we'd begun to neck with a savagery which I knew would take us in only one direction, and that was further into each other.

'Why do you wear those shoes?' I whispered into her hair. 'You can hardly walk in them.'

She was silently rocking back and forth in my arms, teetering on the heels.

'I think you wear them because you like almost falling,' I murmured gently, stroking her hair now, 'and then almost catching yourself.'

'No, that's not it,' she whispered back. 'I like being taller than you.'

'You're not.' I squeezed her tighter. 'You're thigmotropic.'

'What's that?'

'Something that likes to be in tight places. Like an eel.'

She rocked back and forth, less steadily. 'I feel,' she said plaintively, 'like a ghost of myself.'

Her face was remote, and for a moment I felt like she came only up to my knee. I held her tightly then so she couldn't rock at all.

Crossing the border wasn't really so bad, not as terrifying as I'd expected. I drove the Hog of Steel down the concrete ramps, past the Cyclone fences, and into the customs area. Streams of traffic everywhere, and all I could think of was whether or not my insurance was any good in Mexico. Sherry and Kim were very quiet. Sherry leaned over against the passenger side; Kim huddled in the corner of the backseat. All the way down we had the radio set on major decibels, as though to avoid the need for speech.

My parents thought I was on a two-day surfing trip to San Onofre, and my board clanked around in the back like a forgotten corpse. Neon lights were on all over the Mexican buildings, even though it was hot and bright. The customs officer waved us through.

'They don't even check?' I murmured wonderingly.

'They don't care what you take into Mexico,' Kim said. 'You could have the whole back end loaded with heroin, and they wouldn't blink. It's what you bring back.'

I glanced in the rearview mirror, alarmed. 'You don't have any grass on you, do you?'

'Just a little, but it'll be gone by the time we come back.'

269

We drove up the main street of Tijuana, me checking my mirrors constantly for drivers crazed with tequila.

'Let's park and walk,' Sherry said suddenly. 'We don't have to be there for a few hours.'

I felt myself moving as though in a dream. The two women seemed to have it all worked out. There was a clinic, of sorts, and Kim knew where it was by the map in her lap. There was a hotel close by. I imagined each room filled with moaning, bleeding, American teenage girls. There was an appointment to be kept, a parking place to be found, three hours to kill. It might have been a business trip to Philadelphia for all the tension showing on Kim's face.

We parked in a dirt lot behind the hotel and began to walk. It seemed ten degrees hotter on this side of the border. We rounded a building and three dogs ran past us, yelping and panting after a bitch who streaked by in a yellow blur.

'Maybe we should just go to the hotel now,' I said, glancing around at Kim. 'I don't know if you should be walking much.'

'She doesn't want to just sit around thinking about it,' Sherry said.

'Yeah, but all this heat and dust – '

A wry smile from Kim. 'You afraid I might lose the baby?'

I hated it when she used that word. It made the whole thing seem very real. When she referred to it as her problem, or the situation, or even the pregnancy, it was a condition. But a baby was something else again. The two women walked on ahead, shoulder to shoulder like a brace of horses in harness. I followed, wiping my upper lip of sweat.

We walked the streets of Tijuana, looking into the shop windows, grimacing at the fly-covered meat hanging in the butcher store, edging carefully around the sidewalk vendors. Kim bought two straw purses in what looked to be the K-Mart of the city, and Sherry bought a necklace which the little brown merchant swore was real jade. I kept my hands in my pockets. Nothing I saw seemed worth the effort to buy.

Twilight began to deepen between the buildings, and the dust made the shadows purple. The lights turned orange in the distance. As though by instinct, Kim brought us to the door of the little clinic. It was a bright pink stucco, and the yard in front was filled with bird of paradise flowers behind a rusting wrought-iron fence.

'You sure this is right?' I asked. 'Looks more like somebody's house.'

'This is it,' Kim said. 'A few more hours. The hotel is right around the corner, they said.'

'Anyway, now you'll know where we'll be,' Sherry said, 'just in case.'

'We?' I asked Sherry quietly, pulling her aside. 'Are you going in there with her?'

'Well, I wouldn't have come all this way if I weren't.' She pulled her arm away gently and smiled at Kim. 'It looks clean, anyway.'

I felt I should say this somehow, though I had no idea what I would do. 'If you're not back at the hotel when you're supposed to be, I'll come for you.' I never felt so impotent in my life. 'It's not too late to change your mind.'

'Yes it is,' Kim said. 'Let's go rest until it's time.'

As we walked into the hotel, I had this crazy thought that my parents would be waiting in the lobby. They would have somehow found out where I was, came down here, and were waiting to see me check into a Mexican hotel with my girlfriend. Avrom would be sitting in the wicker chair, his glasses shining and his mouth turned down in disgust. And the big problem, of course, would be to keep them from also finding out the reason we were here.

I felt that somehow I had missed a chapter or two in the instruction manual for growing up. Somewhere there was advice about this sort of thing, and I hadn't read it: that life was racing by me and I wasn't up on the owner's guide at all.

But in the lobby nobody waited. Nobody cared at all that we went upstairs to two small rooms with windows overlooking a little courtyard with a rusted washing machine lying on its side in one corner. A pomegranate bush dominated the yard, heavily laden with dusty red fruit.

Sherry and I went to one room; Kim to the other. Sherry sat down on the bed, brushing at the spread. It was a worn Indian madras that looked like the kind you saw at Pier One Imports. 'Did you give them your real name?'

'Yeah. I thought they might ask me for ID.'

She lay down on the bed and moved over to one side. 'Did you lock the door?'

I stepped to it and turned the small lock, tested it, then went to her. She took my hand, smiling faintly up at a point past my shoulder. 'You think she'll be okay?'

I lay down beside her, taking her in my arms. I was instantly aware that it was the first time her whole body had been next to mine, curve to curve on a bed.

'I feel so sad,' she said softly.

I did too, of course, but increasingly, no matter how I tried to feel with her, sigh with her, hold her with nothing more than tender concern and protectiveness, my cock was stirring, rising to life like an insistent arrow, pointing the way to other distractions. I began to kiss her, at first gently, moving my mouth down her throat, across her

272

eyes, her cheeks, her brow, and she returned my kisses, each for each, like a woman seeking a compass point by which she might steer. I felt almost drunk with sensation as I began to realize that the impossible might be about to occur. Her hand floated down to my zipper and tugged at it ineffectually, then floated away.

It was all I needed. I slid myself out of my pants with a sense of dumb wonder that she would want to make love at such a moment, that my cock could be so ready, conscienceless, and stubbornly rigid. Once, briefly, a swift succession of pictures flashed through my mind: Miriam in the backseat of the car under me, her white face open and staring and then sitting up, straightening her clothes, combing her hair; Kim on a table, her heels tied apart, her face twisted in agony; my mother standing behind her looking appalled – and then I shoved it all away once and for all, took Sherry's now-naked breast in my mouth, and clamped my eyes shut against all but her body, her beautiful face beneath me. I covered her mouth with my own, kissing her as though I were trying to drive her into me, passing silent vows of love to her with my tongue. I didn't know a human mouth could taste as sweet as hers. I hadn't realized a body could feel so perfectly molded to my own. I felt I was in the midst of a noisy storm, and my blindness was almost complete. For the last time in my life I regretted that I was not handsome enough to be loved forever by Sherry Gentry.

And then she put her hand back again on my cock and held it tightly, and my hand went to her open legs, to that warm place of darkness and moss that I could smell from way above her neck. I felt the exquisite pressure of her hand, the delicate way her fingers folded around the length and width of me, and I almost moaned aloud from the pleasure, the intense need to be inside her. She drew me to her slowly, and only for an instant did I wonder

273

where and with whom she had learned such touching, and then I was feeling her warm-wetness on me, around me, sliding effortlessly into her with more heat than I ever dreamed possible. It was a revelation. Nothing had ever felt so right. I fell in alignment with all the forces of nature and knew I would never be the same. Sometime, in the next moments, I heard her cry out against my neck, sometime I felt myself spurt in her, painfully letting go all hope of control, but I couldn't have said which came first or cared.

When it was all over and she lay in my arms, I knew that no other woman would ever claim me as she had. There was a long moment of silken silence, and I became aware of the pigeons cooing outside the window. They sounded just like American pigeons.

'I love you,' I said, gazing down at her. 'I think I always have.'

She smiled blissfully, rubbing her cheek against mine.

'I want to marry you. After I get out of college or in five years or two years or now. Marry me.'

'You're the first who's ever asked me.'

'Really? I thought I'd be about tenth in line.'

She closed her eyes and nestled closer. 'I always thought it would be in a restaurant someplace or maybe in a park, with him on his knees.'

'Would you say yes if I got on my knees?' I made as though to vault out of bed, tangling myself in the sheets.

She pulled me back gently. 'We're too young to even talk about it.'

'Eighteen's not too young. I love you. And you love me, I know you do.'

'We haven't been together long enough for you to love me,' she said languorously. 'You don't hardly know me, really.'

'Bullshit. No one knows you better.'

She smiled. 'Well, then I don't know *you* well enough.'

274

'You know me well enough to know I won't go off and leave you flat at the mercy of a million Mexican T-shirt salesmen.'

She chuckled. 'No, you wouldn't do that, no matter how many times I turn you down.'

'*Are* you turning me down?'

'Not exactly.' She turned her face away.

I took her chin and turned it gently back to face me. 'Well, what then, exactly? It's really simple, Sherry. I love you. I believe you love me. We're good together.' I leaned closer and whispered in her ear. 'This is called real life, lady. People fall in love and they get married. It's not exactly the impossible dream, happens every day. I'm young, but I'm old enough to know what I want, and it's you. I can go to UCLA instead of back East. We can be together. We can make a life together. If not right away, then when you're ready. Don't you love me?'

'I don't know.'

I said it quickly, to hide the hurt. 'That's fair. I can accept that. Maybe you need a little more time.'

There was a small silence. She said, 'I want to remember this always. And I want you to remember it too.'

'In every cell.'

'I want you to remember how you love me right now. You probably won't always love me like this, but I wish you'd remember that someplace inside me, no matter what we do or where we go, there'll be this girl you love as you do now.'

'I told you, in every cell.' I thought about what she said. 'Sherry, how many guys have told you that they loved you before? I mean, really *loved* you.' A dozen, maybe. Two dozen, she'll say –

'Two or three,' she said. 'Maybe four.'

'You don't remember exactly?'

She gazed at me calmly. 'No. Not really.'

That fazed me. That she could not even remember how many had declared their love for her. 'Except for family, nobody's ever told me that at all,' I said quietly, 'and I've never said it to anyone else before.'

'Well, I've never told that to anyone either,' she said almost proudly.

I couldn't muster up much glee.

'Let's not talk anymore,' she said, moving her mouth to mine. 'Every time you talk, you spoil it.'

Her lips were so soft, insistent, and my body began to stir to life again as though she held some sort of invisible cord on me. I put my fingers deep inside her, and it was sweet and warm and alive. It was like the shock of touching a wild animal – a shock of delight and almost-fear. I was humming with pain and pleasure, feeling as if my entire life up to now had been only preamble. I was not going somewhere; I was there. I was not waiting for something to happen; it was happening. For the first time – maybe the last – I felt I wasn't outside myself with a woman, wasn't watching, had shed the observer in my soul. There was no voice in my head as there is so often now, saying, There, honey, do you like that? Does that feel good? No, I was with her totally, lost in her, and when I slipped myself inside her again, began to move with her, finally shuddered to completion, I felt we had somehow sliced ourselves open inside and had merged bloodstreams forever.

It was dark when a knock at the door woke me. 'It's time,' Kim said softly. Sherry was already dressed and sitting on the side of the bed. I wondered how long she'd been watching me sleep. She bent and squeezed my shoulder and brushed past me. 'Wish us luck,' she murmured, with her hand on the knob.

'I wish you'd change your mind,' I said.

'I can't,' she said, and opened the door. I caught a

quick glimpse of Kim in the hallway, her hair haloed by the dingy wrought-iron lantern on the wall, and then they were gone.

I wanted to stay awake. I felt that was the least I could do. I thought about the difference between the two sisters, how Sherry looked so much fresher – not just younger – but somehow less used up than Kim. There was a basic unfairness about sex, it seemed to me then. The more girls a boy has, the better. He gets a brighter look to him, looks well fed and full of juice. The guys I knew who had a list of women in their lives strode around full-shouldered and confident. You got the feeling they had more to them, were fuller, fatter, and had better stories to tell.

But the girls didn't reap the same harvest. For a girl, with each guy she had, it was like she lost something. One more petal plucked. The essence of that freshness got diluted, like a watered-down sauce. Like the difference between Kim and Sherry.

Finally I fell asleep in the darkened room, and I woke only when Kim and Sherry came back in. I pulled the sheets around me and sat up, embarrassed by the room as I knew it must look in Kim's eyes: cheap and tawdry, smelling of sex and sleep and cowardice.

'Are you all right?' I asked Kim. 'It didn't take as long as I thought.'

She was pale, leaning up against the doorjamb. 'They knew what they were doing,' she murmured. 'It wasn't as bad as I expected.'

Sherry sank down wearily on the bed. 'I want to go home,' she said.

I frowned at Kim worriedly. 'Can you travel already? We've got the room for the whole night; maybe you should rest.'

'I can rest at home,' she said. Her voice was whispery

and dry. 'Besides, if anything happens, I'd rather be at home to deal with it. They said they got it all.'

I looked at Sherry. She looked almost as dazed as her sister. I didn't want to know what she had witnessed in the past two hours.

'Let's go,' Kim said. 'We can be home by midnight.'

'He proposed tonight,' Sherry said suddenly.

Kim looked back in bewilderment. 'He did? What did you tell him?'

'I told him no, of course,' Sherry said. Her voice was sullen.

Something flared in me, a quick violence that made me want to shake her. 'No, you didn't,' I said. 'You didn't say no!'

She whirled on me, her face almost obscured for an instant by her tangled hair. 'Well, I should have. I'm only eighteen. I don't want to get married, I don't want to have babies, and I don't want to love you!' She followed Kim out to the hall and slammed the door.

Part Four

At first, man's passions are like a cobweb's threads; at last, they become like thickest cords.

Talmud, Sukkah, 52a

I was a fool to ask her, of course. Light in the head and weak in the knees, I ignored all reason and proposed marriage at one of the worst possible times. And I shouldn't have been dismayed at rejection.

But I was. And the tone of her rejection seemed to close all doors between us. No matter what else I might remember of that sultry afternoon, the twilight and evening shadows we ushered in with our lovemaking, I could never forget, have never forgotten, the way she said no.

I drove the two sisters home, and I made no effort at small talk. I could tell by the set of Sherry's jaw, by the gentle way she took my hand but averted her eyes, that it had changed. That I had traded Miriam's milk cow for three magic beans which likely grew a vine to nowhere.

For a week I called her three times a day. She was never home . . . at least not to me.

My parents did their best to cheer me up. Without ever mentioning Sherry's name or Miriam's, they organized a family party for my eighteenth birthday, celebrated my graduation, and honored me as only a Jewish family can honor an eldest son, first to have crossed the bar of high school. Surrounded by aunts, uncles, and treacly hugs, I couldn't have felt more bereft.

'So!' Uncle Simon said, patting me on the back and steering me into the kitchen alcove, lowering his voice as though he intended to share the Secrets of Men. 'Columbia is a fine school, a fine school. So is New York University. Which one you going to choose, eh? With your grades – '

'Uncle Simon, a three-point-two is hardly Einstein category.'

'But straight As in science, right? Straight As! Don't tell me that don't count on their cockamamie scorecards. You should be going to Harvard, no?' – he nudged me amiably – 'rub shoulders with the *balbatim*.'

Balbatim was Yiddish for those of high standing in the community. The opposite of the Great Unwashed. My father liked to tell a joke about how young Rabbi Shulman finally summoned up enough courage to say to Mr Benenson, one of the *balbatim* of the temple, 'I trust you won't mind my mentioning it, but I can't help noticing that you always fall asleep when I'm preaching.'

'Why not?' replied Benenson. 'Would I sleep if I didn't trust you?' At that, my father always smiled wryly and added, 'I hope they never trust me *that* much.'

'Harvard didn't take me.' I took a deep breath. Now was as good a time as any to make the announcement. 'Actually, I don't think I'll be going to either Columbia or NYC, Uncle. I'm going to UCLA.'

'UCLA? In Los Angeles, this is?'

'It's a good school. Top-notch in science, Uncle Simon. It's cheaper, closer to home, and I won't have to wear long underwear to class.'

'Cheaper, smeaper, you should have the very best, money is no object!'

'It *is* the very best. You don't have to go across country to find good schools, you know. UCLA. I've decided.'

'You've decided! And does your father know of this decision?' He dropped his voice to a whisper. 'You haven't told him!'

I shook my head.

'*Gevalt.*' Uncle Simon closed his eyes in pain. 'A state college, when your father can afford to send you, money-is-no-object.'

My mother came into the kitchen, picked up a tray of kishke and bustled out, throwing over her shoulder, 'That's easy for *you* to say, you want to put the second son through college, it's all right by me.'

Uncle Simon waited until the swinging door closed behind her and whispered confidentially, 'You çan tell me, Davy. Is your heart broken? You picked that UCLA because your little blond shiksa goes there, right?'

I shook my head firmly. 'She's not going to college. I picked UCLA because *I* want to go there.'

Uncle Simon drew back, appalled. 'She's not going to college? She's going to be a dropout?'

'You gotta drop *in* before you can drop *out*. She wants to start living her life, she said.'

'Oy, her poor parents!' Uncle Simon mourned, his mouth pulled down. 'Better you should find this out now, David, than later. That one will come to nothing but trouble. Live her life! What sort of life can she live without an education!'

I refrained from pointing out to him that Aunt Sophie, his wife, had managed just fine without the benefits of a college degree, as had the majority of relatives in the next room. My mother stuck her head back in the kitchen and said, 'Stop filling the scholar's head with mishmash, Simon. He's missing his own party out here.'

She withdrew, and my uncle nodded earnestly and dug in his coat pocket for an envelope which looked fat with bills. 'For the scholar, then. To be spent on frivolous fun. Or' – he poked me playfully in the ribs – 'on the *new* heartbreak, right?'

As I reached for it, my thanks already in my mouth, he snatched it away, attempting to hold it over my head. The fact that Uncle Simon was nearly a foot shorter than me didn't dampen his enthusiasm. 'But first! But first, the scholar must answer a riddle!'

'Simon!' Sophie's voice came from the dining room. 'Let the boy go!'

He ignored her. 'So what is green, wet, hangs on the wall, and whistles?'

Oh Christ. I hesitated just long enough to make it believable. 'I give up.'

'A herring!' Uncle Simon shouted with a whoop.

'A herring?' I repeated by rote. 'A herring doesn't hang on the wall.'

'So hang it there.'

'But a herring isn't green.'

'So paint it.'

'But a herring isn't wet.'

'If it's just painted, it's wet.'

'But,' I said, summoning up my dignity and pretended outrage, '*a herring doesn't whistle!*'

'Right, scholar,' my Uncle Simon smiled. 'I just put that in to make it hard.' And then he laughed and laughed at that oldest of jokes, one which every Jewish child surely learns in the womb and which I had repeated for him almost every birthday of my life. He slapped me on the back and handed me the envelope. '*Now* you're ready for this UCLA.'

He tucked his hand under my arm. 'And we go to tell them of your decision together.'

We pushed the swinging kitchen doors open and Uncle Simon said calmly, 'I want to propose a toast to the rising star of this family, yes?' He took up a glass from the table and raised it above my head. 'His little brother will follow him soon, and between colleges and weddings and babies, we'll all wear out our arms with their *mazel*!' My mother and father smiled at me, at Avrom, and raised their glasses as well. 'To David. Who has brought pride to our table today. Who goes on to manhood with the courage of his convictions. Who has the brains to be accepted by some of the finest schools in this country. He had made a decision, and we should all join in congratulating him on his decision. Tell them, David. Tell them where you go.'

I cleared my throat and looked right at my father. 'I've decided to go to UCLA.'

'A fine school,' Uncle Simon added quickly. 'Tops in science, I heard. The best.'

My mother's mouth dropped, and my father's eyes widened. 'UCLA?' my father said slowly. 'This is your choice?'

'You didn't even apply there!' my mother added.

'I did. A month ago.'

Silence wreathed the table, and the aunts set down their glasses one by one.

'And you've been accepted?' my father asked.

'I will be.'

'They'll take anyone at this UCLA?' Aunt Sophie murmured, grabbing hold of Uncle Simon's coat. He pulled gently away from her. 'Shah, shah, of course not. But him they'll take.'

'But you've been planning for years. Columbia. NYU. Harvard, even.' My mother glanced anxiously at my father. 'A state college. In California!'

'A university, Ma. And Harvard didn't take me,' I said patiently. 'And plans change. I don't want to go all the way back east. I don't feel like that's home anymore. I don't need to go clear across the country and buy three overcoats to get a good education.'

'It's because of this girl,' my mother began, her eyes narrowing –

'She's not going there,' Uncle Simon chimed in. 'He told me.'

'David, we can talk of this later,' my father said gently. 'You have many choices, many things to weigh in this decision – '

285

'I've already decided, Dad.' I raised my glass to eye level and looked at my family through the sparkling crystal. 'It's an excellent school, it's at the top in science, it's one third the cost for the same education. What I'd spend in phone calls and airfare, I can put into books and tutoring, if I need it. It's the most practical choice and it's the school I want. Now, will you toast my future?'

My father looked at my mother. They exchanged a gaze, one I could not translate but understood in my heart. He took her hand and pulled her up so they stood together, shoulder to shoulder, and linked his wrist around hers. 'To your future, my son,' he said softly, and the two drank from their glasses simultaneously.

'To David's future!' Uncle Simon called out again.

The aunts and uncles chorused the toast. I caught Avrom's grin over the edge of my glass. He rolled his eyes at me, shaking his head in disbelief.

Of course, it wasn't the last conversation on the subject. But over the next week I convinced my parents that UCLA was the appropriate choice, and that Sherry Gentry had nothing to do with my decision.

'Well,' my mother finally said, 'if this is what you want, then you will have it. But don't think you can just come home anytime you want to just because you're only an hour away.'

'What do you mean?' I asked.

'I mean, you go to this UCLA like you would go to any school back east. You don't come running home every weekend, anytime you have a problem or dirty laundry to do. You go, you work, you grow up. That's what college is for. That's what you'll do.'

'You planning to rent out my room?'

'Just your place at the table.'

'Ah, Ma – ' I groaned.

'I mean it. You go, you work, you grow. You meet new

friends. You don't come back every Friday night to call up a certain girlie to see if she's free. You made your decision, yes? So now you sleep in it.'

We were standing in the kitchen, my mother at the sink peeling carrots, my father silently listening at the refrigerator. I put my arm around her. 'You mean to tell me I won't be welcome home on Shabbes for your *knaydiach* soup? You'll turn me away at the door?'

She leaned into me, frowning. 'You're welcome, already. But you've had the limelight long enough now. It's your brother's turn, I think. You go to this UCLA. And you come home at holidays and exam breaks, like all the other college students do. You don't hang around the neighborhood, looking for trouble.' She looked at my father and found in his eyes the support she needed. She pulled away from me gently. 'You made your decision. So you live by it now.'

I thought their assent would make me happy. Make me feel more committed to my choice. But I couldn't seem to care about much of anything, even my own future. I spent the summer floating from the beach to the Strip, waiting to feel connected with someone or something. Watts and Foote were accepted at Stanford and UC Santa Barbara, and Critter – to our quiet amazement – was going back to MIT. We hung out together about once a week, but it was harder and harder to make everybody's schedules mesh. Two of them were working; Foote was at the library every day as though classes had already started, and when we got together, it wasn't the same. In our minds we'd already donned our new uniforms, and we didn't seem to belong to the same band anymore.

By August I was relieved that UCLA was on the quarter system, shortening my summer by three weeks. I began to drive to Westwood regularly, just to familiarize myself with the route and the campus. The week before

287

classes started my mother took me aside for a heart-to-heart.

'I want you to remember what your job is at UCLA,' she said earnestly. 'Lots of boys will be working part-time to help pay for their education. We don't ask you to do this, so far there's enough to pay the bills, *halevai*, so long as your father doesn't drop dead of a heart attack next week, but we expect you to study hard, to learn, to make something of your time there. The Sotolov boy, you remember Bobby Sotolov? Went up to Berkeley last year, against his father's wishes.'

'I didn't know him,' I said, hoping to deflect her.

'It's just as well. Anyway, his parents were willing to send him to USC, to Stanford, to anyplace he wanted to go and where did he choose? That hotbed of revolution they have growing up there. And now, after two semesters and almost four thousand dollars of aggravation, he is dropping out to go and live on a commune in Mendocino! His mother's heart is broken – a fire should burn in his heart, God forbid – and all because he forgot his obligations.'

'Well, UCLA isn't exactly a hotbed.'

'Any bed can be hot if you want it to. Do you hear what I'm saying to you, David?'

'Yes,' I nodded dutifully. Please God, don't let her get more explicit. 'And I promise I'll do my best.'

She beamed. 'I know you will. We're so proud of you, your father and I. Despite some – little ups and downs – you did a good job in high school. We know you're going to do wonderful things with your life. But then, that Sotolov boy never had your IQ, either. Out of snow you can't make cheesecake.'

By the time classes started, I knew my way around. I'd discovered the closest parking structure to my last class of the day – even that choice implied, I felt, a superior strategy. I figured I'd have more books to carry to the car at the end of the day than I'd have at the beginning, what with trips to the library and the student union bookstore, so I had it planned to save myself the least tonnage per mile. I'd picked three different places to eat lunch midway between my third class and my fourth class, so if two were crowded, I'd have an optional refuge. And I got one of the few carrels at the library assigned to freshmen. In a pinch, I'd even have someplace to sleep.

My comfort level soared by the hour. In fact, the campus at UCLA had the same feel to it as Columbia: Some of the buildings were just as ivy-covered, others were shining new examples of the latest in architectural design. I could, with very little self-delusion, convince my wary soul that UCLA had been here, encrusted with pedants, for just as long as Columbia, racking up just as many scholarly honors. I also told myself that Sherry Gentry had little if nothing to do with my choice. I wanted to stay in California, and that was that.

On my first day of college I owned the place. I knew what was around every corner; I was as essential to its aura as the brick rotundas and the fountains, and I stopped often to give directions to other freshmen huddled over centerfold maps of the campus, sending them off with a benign and fraternal smile.

My confidence lasted through English, wavered slightly during the last half of French, and melted away the instant I stepped into the chemistry auditorium.

Instead of the cozy lab I'd known at Taft, with the sinks and spigots, the nose-prickling smells, the colorful charts of elements and internal organs, the skeleton named Clancy hanging in the corner, I now stood in a vast arena of seats. I had entered a frightening funnel ringed with row after row of chair/desk combos, all tilted down to the fulcrum of learning, a podium with a microphone. Two side doors were at the bottom. I wouldn't have been surprised to see lions or gladiators come out of them. No question who were the Christians.

I took a seat in the middle, scared to go too close, jostled and bumped by what seemed to be a thousand freshmen selecting their perches, and watched in awe as the instructor entered a side door, slammed a huge briefcase on a table, and strode to the podium.

'This,' he intoned with a voice like God, 'is freshman chemistry.' He resettled his dark glasses on his nose, mirrors you couldn't see through, like he was a crazed biker in a business suit. 'Half of you will never get out of here alive, somebody tell me why.'

Not a soul whimpered; not a hand rose.

'Because half of you will fail this course, that's why. It happens every quarter, and I anticipate no sudden surge of brilliance in this class versus the twenty which came before it, and so I can say to you without fear of repudiation that half of you will drop or be failing freshman chemistry inside of three months. Somebody tell me why.'

Frozen silence.

'Because this department cannot conceivably handle eight hundred and forty-three incoming freshmen, cannot possibly expect to find sufficient seats for your withered little souls much less enough TAs to grade your wretched little tests, and so we must winnow! That is our *job*, people. Yours is to be the winnow-ees. Half of you can expect to be changing your life plans inside of sixty days, to be deeply committed to another major in ninety, and to be well on your way to wiping out any memory of chemistry from your brain pans by Christmas. Half of you will be *elsewhere* before I've even had to read your midterms. Somebody tell me where.'

One hand slowly rose in the front. The entire auditorium leaned forward on tilt to see who could be so stupendously idiotic –

'You!' the professor barked out with a pointed finger.

A young male voice quavered, 'Limbo?'

The auditorium convulsed in terrified laughter.

The instructor grinned. 'Ah. A future English major in our midst. Yes! A goodly half will be winnowed to things like Kiddie Lit, Miltonic Poetry, and Education classes. And may God have pity on your souls.'

He picked up a flap of papers from his briefcase, slapped them on the table and added, 'Pick up your syllabus, read the first assignment, see you back here on Wednesday.' He reached for a cord above him, drew down a floating blackboard, and scrawled a name across it quickly. I swear to God, the man's name was Ted Bellial.

'Hey.' In shock, I murmured to the guy next to me, 'That's not the professor.'

'I guess it's the TA,' he said dazedly. 'I wonder if it's too late to change sections?'

'Or majors,' the girl on the other side of me said weakly.

'Or schools,' someone behind us added.

I inched down the line to the syllabus table, feeling like a first-grader in the assembly hall waiting to see if I'd been promoted. Sure enough, the syllabus was every bit as appalling as Mr Bellial promised. No less than three chapters and sixty pages to be digested by day after tomorrow.

I passed out no more directions that day, cut back on my benign smiles to fellow inmates, and scuttled off to my carrel to recoup. It took an hour of internal dialogue before I was ready for European History I.

But inside of a week or two I began to hit my rhythm.

291

The classes were intimidating but not impossible. With careful planning and diligence I was able to see that mine would not be one of the four hundred and twenty-one names erased by Ted Bellial and his ilk, nor did I see myself trundling off to the med center for Valium regularly like about a third of my dorm floor. I thought often of Sherry, of course, but I tried to ration myself to minor nostalgia. I kept remembering what she had said about the absurdity of the freshman commitment, but it was hard not to believe that what I was doing was Real Life.

I lived at Weyburn Hall, one of the coed housing units on campus. Twelve skyscraping floors of pandemonium. That was one major mistake my parents made, an error I would never admit to them, that they forced me to live on campus my first year. We'd agreed that the commute would cut back on my study time and that part of the collegiate experience was moving away from home and growing up. But let me say that when my daughter is of age, I can guarantee she'll spend her freshman year in her own pink room down the hall from mine if she chooses a college within one hundred miles.

At Weyburn the first six floors were for guys, the next six for women. If you got drunk and punched seven, you reeled out of the elevator into a hall filled with squealing, towel-wrapped girls and came back down smelling temporarily of My Sin and perm solution.

I shared a room with the Invisible Man. Larry Furuno was a math major, member of the Nisei Bruins, already pinned to a black-haired nymph, Dorie Iwata, and never available for bullshit sessions into the night. He came back to pick up clothes, shower, and change sets of books. Sometimes the only phantom contact I'd have with him for two or three days running occurred as his Code-A-Phone beeped on and off with his messages. When the machine's green light blinked and then stopped, I knew he'd picked up his calls by remote. Believe me, when the Japanese took over California twenty years later, I for one was not surprised, thanks to the early example set by Larry Furuno.

After the compression of Taft and my family, it was easy to be lonely at UCLA. Parts of the campus looked like factory warehouses, others like cloistered ivy towers. UCLA didn't have the feeling of being a little medieval township in and unto itself like an East Coast college. It was a city within a city, and Los Angeles didn't respect its edges, but spilled over into campus life invasively. We were all so serious then, and it was hard to find time for, as Uncle Simon put it, frivolous fun. Toward the end of my freshman year I began to think that I might have enough spare energy and hours for an expanded social life – in other words, I hadn't been laid in six months.

The Greek fires beckoned. At about the moment that I realized my whole collegiate world was comprised of a dorm, several library rooms, and classes, fraternities on campus were throwing their spring rush parties. It seemed like a good idea at the time. Within a week I'd pledged the Lambda Chi house. Pledged to what, it took me a bit longer to discover.

The Lambda Chi house looked solid enough on the outside: substantial brick building, regular guys, lots of promises in the brochure about building men with 'fairness, decency, and good manners'. In asides, the Brothers promised, as well, that a guy could find all the action he wanted in such company.

But on Hell Night, the ordeal of initiation which I'd heard other pledges describing in horrified whispers, I discovered that 'fairness' meant letting the Brothers scream obscenities in my face, blow cigar smoke in my eyes, and ask me a thousand times an hour to recite 'The True Gentleman' in fourteen seconds flat:

293

'The True Gentleman is the man whose conduct proceeds from good will and an acute sense of propriety, and whose self-control is equal to all emergencies; who does not make the poor man conscious of his poverty, the obscure man of his obscurity, or any man of his inferiority or deformity; who is himself humbled if necessity compels him to humble another; who does not flatter wealth, cringe before power, or boast of his own possessions or achievements; who speaks with frankness but always with sincerity and sympathy; whose deed follows his word; who thinks of the rights and feelings of others rather than his own; and who appears well in any company, a man with whom honor is sacred and virtue is safe, *sir*!'

'Decency' means I was required by those same Brothers to bray like a donkey, bleat like a goat, and sit on the edge of a cold bathtub, naked, waiting to be covered with ice, while somebody played Ravel's *Bolero* fortissimo, right in my shivering ears. And 'good manners' was translated into my ability to pick an olive off the chapter-room floor, using nothing but my naked ass-cheeks, and deliver it to a waiting martini glass, while the Actives cheered my performance.

But once I was in, there was a whole new world of men. Yes, they still got drunk and dropped their trousers in public. They still lighted their farts and put people's heads in toilets, but they also wore coats and ties and hosted cocktail parties for alumns and beautiful sorority girls; they served on boards and tutored one another for exams, and they defined themselves as civilized comrades in a barbarian world. All in all, it beat parading up and down the quad with a sign displaying a grim death's head, picketing the Dow Chemical Company and protesting the war.

From my Brothers I learned that you could still be an individual – in fact, we all were. We might each use the same handshake, keep the same secrets, and share the same women, but we were men and we knew where to draw the bottom line. I drew the line at the Winstons the other guys smoked and took up the habit of a meerschaum pipe.

So, ignoring my parents' inquisitive phone calls, I moved into the Lambda Chi house, falling in with the resident intellectuals. My roommate was pledged as a social asset he'd bring to sorority mixers. A face man whose father had been Lambda Chi at Boston U., Paul was actually rather shy, tall with sloped shoulders, puppy-brown curls, and just a trace of East Coast aristocracy in his speech.

When I asked him why UCLA, he said, 'I got tired of baked beans and ivy.'

'Be serious.'

'Be serious? I got tired of that too. Weary of guys who stayed up all night debating Kant and Proust and who carried copies of the *Partisan Review* in their briefcases.'

'You knew guys like that in *high* school?'

He nodded soberly. 'They were practicing for Harvard by the time they were off training wheels. I decided I wanted to come to paradise. Where people had never heard of Allen Ginsberg, didn't know the words to "We Shall Overcome", and didn't read *The Village Voice*.'

My grin was twisted. 'Yeah, they're not big on politics out here.'

'Or on history. Most guys in this house don't know where the Pilgrims landed, much less who got off the boat. And that's fine with me.'

'What did your folks say?'

He picked up a large book and sailed it across the room, chuckling. 'They keep sending me tomes of Henry James to read, filled with perfect smooth green lawns, old houses, and formal tea settings.' He opened up a tattered copy of *Rolling Stone*. 'I think I've found my niche.'

Our more enlightened pals in the house included Mike,

a gung-ho ROTC cadet who looked like he sprang from his mother's womb a full-fledged marine. The guy clipped his hair so short that you could see the wrinkles in his scalp. But Mike had a very unmilitary imagination. He believed that a giant Sock Monster lived in the fraternity laundry room.

Mike said he was down there looking for his lost socks when something dark and furry scuttled out of sight behind the dryer. He probed deeply into the cobwebs, escaped buttons, and old undershorts, and then he heard it growl. He said he would never forget that noise: like two static shirts being pulled apart.

Mike, being trained for battle, attempted to subdue the beast, but it was too fast for him. He caught only a fleeting glimpse of it, with one old crew sock hanging from its horrid mouth, as the creature slithered up the washer drainpipe.

Mike also discovered the infamous Rack Bird, and he was in charge of indoctrinating new pledges against its evil powers.

'You're sitting at your desk cramming for a midterm, right?' he'd say with all those young eyes on him, 'and you can feel the molten red eyes of this feathered behemoth right on your neck. He's perched on your headboard, pretending to look out the window every time you glance his way. You try to concentrate, but little weasel words keep creeping into your brain. Maybe the prof will be sick tomorrow. Maybe it'll be open book. Maybe you could change majors.'

The pledges would glance at one another with small, worried grins.

'That's right,' Mike'd say, 'and then you get your only really brilliant idea of the night. Maybe you could concentrate better in bed. Now if you'd look, ladies, you'd see the Rack Bird slowly start to smile. But you're relieved.

You've hit on the obvious solution. So you gather up all your books, your Magic Markers, you even stop to sharpen your pencil for good luck. And you climb onto your bed. On top of the covers, just to show how disciplined you are. Now, ladies, the Rack Bird quietly giggles.'

Usually at this point some pledge would giggle, too, but Mike would stop him short with a fierce scowl.

'Oh, yes, fool, laugh on! You think you're really rolling now, you're reading and taking notes, eating up those pages, but pretty soon you realize that you're getting relaxed. Maybe even *too* relaxed. Your eyes are getting heavy and gritty. You roll over to let gravity move them a little easier. Still, your eyes refuse to move back and forth like you want them to. You're disgusted with these weak-pussy eyes, but you decide to give them five minutes, *just five minutes*, of rest. Facedown on your book. As you close your eyes, the Rack Bird floats over gently and settles on your head. And the next sound you'll hear, ladies, the *only* applause you'll get the next morning, is the cry of the infamous Rack Bird – *ra-aa-aak!* – claiming another victim.'

Mike ran the pledges like the best drill sergeant, but he was, in turn, ruled by a shrill-voiced harpy, a lovely Kappa wanton, who came over to study in his room, got regularly offended by his conduct, and then threw him out and turned the key. Almost nightly Mike would be outside in the hall, pounding on his own door and hollering, 'Honey! Goddammit, honey, let me in!'

It was Paul who introduced me to the strange and wonderful liaison between Tom and Terry, two crew jocks who shared a bunk bed in a room off the main hall, more tree house, actually, than room, which was regularly flooded in the spring rains.

'You've got to see this,' Paul told me one night and led me to their door to watch and listen.

Terry slept on the top bunk; Tom on the bottom. Because they rowed crew practice four hours a day after classes, they hit their bunks with the ardor of collapsing buffalo. But that night it began to drizzle.

'Terry,' Tom said sleepily, 'you left the door open.'

Paul and I smirked and drew back against the wall.

'Terry,' Tom added, 'it's raining. Get up and close the door.'

'I don't care if it's open,' Terry replied with a yawn, 'you close it if you want it closed.'

Silence.

'You also left the light on.'

'I'm not getting up. I *like* the light on.'

'Oh yeah?'

'Yeah.'

'Well, so do I.' Tom paused. 'In fact, I like it so much, I think I'll sleep with my eyes open all night just so I don't miss any of it.'

'So will I,' Terry agreed.

'Yeah?'

'Yeah.'

Another pause. 'Terry, you forgot to close the window too.'

'No, I didn't. I like the rain.'

By now it's really coming down hard and there's a puddle forming in the middle of the room.

Tom put one hand out to catch a few drops and sprinkled his eyes. 'Rain. Oh, yes. Oh, so do I.'

'Yeah?'

'Yeah. In fact, I like it so much, I'm going to kick off the covers and drag one foot in the water here around the bed.'

'Me too.'

'You're not so fortunate as to be able to reach the water with your foot,' Tom said smugly.

'That's right, but there's a pool right here at the end of the mattress I can make do with,' Terry replied.

So the two of them lay there, eyes wide open and covers off, door and window pouring in rain, until Paul and I finally gave up and, laughing fit to die, turned off the lights, closed the window, and covered them both.

'Aren't pledges wonderful?' Tom said to Terry wistfully and turned over and burrowed into his mattress.

'A regular band of angels,' Terry sighed as he snored off.

Lance Carlson was a pal with a purpose. He was a professional at the college sport of Excuses. We'd be at the breakfast table, reading the funnies by the light of a beautiful California morning, when Lance would look out the window and say, 'Looks like rain.'

I'd glance up, surprised.

'Well, that tears it,' Lance would groan. 'I can't go to class.'

'Why not?' Paul and I would ask in chorus.

'Because I forgot my umbrella.'

'I'll loan you mine,' Paul offered.

'Then what'll *you* do?'

'It's okay,' I added quickly, 'I heard they were going to erect a dome over campus today so we can go to class and not get wet.'

'I still can't go.'

'Why not?'

'Because I forgot my dome pass.'

'Oh. Well, then in that case you'll need an Excuse.' Paul grinned.

And Lance would ceremoniously pull out a piece of paper to pen, 'To Whom It May Concern: Lance Carlson has been incarcerated with a severe infection of his –'

He'd look up and sigh. 'What haven't I used?'

'Medulla?' Paul had a brother who was pre-med at Duke.

A satisfied smile. 'Medulla. He will be in recumbency for an unspecified period of time.' Signed, Lancelot Carlson the Third, MD, DDS, PhD, THUD.

The Lambda Chi house in that first year filled a lot of my needs. Friends, a semblance of family, and a covey of lovelies who regularly flushed through the fraternity for rush parties, keggers, and formal white-gloved alumn receptions. I didn't go home for three months, and it was April before I allowed myself to fall in love again.

Actually, it was less the season than the fact that I had received my first and last letter from Sherry Gentry. A small yellow envelope was forwarded to me by my mother without comment. I inspected it carefully before I opened it. No sign of tampering. A stray trace of a hauntingly familiar perfume.

And then her own handwriting, the same I had seen on so many blue pages of poetry. I closed my eyes with an almost physical pain, then blinked and scanned the letter quickly. She was fine, still living at home, had found a job in a Valley real estate office, working on her license at night. Business was incredible, she wrote, and it was easy to make a lot of money just helping land change hands.

'You know the fruit orchard across from the Alpha Beta? It's going to be a shopping center. And they're putting up an athletic club by where you used to wait for the bus. With just a few thousand dollars to invest, you can make a fortune,' she wrote. I read the lines again, searching for something more personal. Finally, the last paragraph:

'Miss you, Dobie. Sorry we ended like we did. But I always told you that we'd be better friends than lovers. Come by and see me when you come home for vacation.'

300

As it happened, her letter came four days before Easter Break, so it wasn't out of my way to take her up on her offer.

I went home for Easter break. Avrom was on a camping trip with some friends in Death Valley, so *Pesach* was just the three of us. When my father closed the seder with the prayer, 'Now we are slaves; in the year ahead may we be free men,' I said a silent and hearty amen.

After dinner I drove up her street slowly. Her house looked the same. Perhaps a little smaller, as everything in the neighborhood did, but otherwise the white fairy-frosting that I remembered so well. Mr Gentry answered the bell.

'Well, college boy!' he said, reaching out and shaking my hand heartily. 'You look older already.'

I didn't know whether to say thanks for such an observation or not, but at least it was clear she'd mentioned my name in the past year. We talked for a moment about school, the state of the freeways, the weather, and then her father said, 'Well, it's a shame you missed her. She's in Hawaii for ten days with some friends.'

It took a heartbeat for me to get it. 'Hawaii?'

'Yeah, do you believe it? Rather an exercise in redundancy, if you ask me. I guess the beaches over there are somehow superior to the ones in her own backyard, I don't know. Maybe the sun tans faster or something. Anyway, she took off a few days ago with some girls. They've rented a condo in Lahaina. She didn't write and tell you?'

I shook my head reluctantly. 'Actually, I haven't heard much from her. Just one letter recently.'

Mr Gentry crossed his arms and leaned back against the door. 'I'm sorry to hear that,' he said gently. So gently that I looked up quickly, surprised. 'Well, she's a big girl these days. No telling what she might do in time. The choices she might make.'

I put out my hand. 'That's for sure.' We shook on her inscrutability. 'Tell her I came by. Kim doing all right?' I watched him carefully on that one.

'Just great, just great.'

Not a trace of a frown. She must have pulled Mexico off without them ever knowing.

'She graduates this year, thinking about going on for her master's.'

'Great. Well' – I backed off the porch – 'tell Sherry she's allowed to write me more than once a year.' I smiled, to make it less pitiful.

'I'll do that, David,' the man said, softly closing the door.

I went back to my car and took Sherry's letter out of my pocket. 'Tepid' was the first word that came up for me as I reread it. The words, her mood, even my response. Maybe I was over her at last, I thought. Time to turn my attention to the birds at hand.

I met Callan Banner at a cocktail reception given for a brace of southern alumns up from Texas. Paul introduced me to her, saying, 'Here's another East Coast refugee, David. A Tri Delt with a brain. And if you muck up her first impression with your usual tawdry maneuvers, Callan Banner isn't the type to give you a second chance.' With that he walked away and left us gazing at each other.

'Nice to meet you,' I said.

'Thank you,' she murmured. 'You're Paul's room-mate?'

'Yes, but he really doesn't know me very well.'

A bemused lifting of one perfect brow.

'My maneuvers are perfectly acceptable.'

She smiled. 'I'm happy to hear that.'

'So, where do you know Paul from?'

'We all but grew up together.' Now I could hear the Boston in her speech. She had a regal air about her, unusual for a college girl. I instantly suspected her family must be one of the Boston Brahmins, part of the established Yankee aristocracy used to the brick-lined elegance of Beacon Hill. She certainly looked the part. Black-haired, tall, and willowy, with a solemn and studious demeanor.

The music began to filter from the rec room, which had been transformed for the occasion. A three-piece ensemble played elevator music and Frank Sinatra.

'Want to dance?'

She went into my arms gracefully, averting her chin slightly in what I assumed to be the proper Boston Brahmin position. 'What's your major?' I asked. The obligatory question.

'I don't have one,' she said, smiling softly, her gray eyes level with my own.

I was instantly assailed by memory. Sherry saying how stupid it was for freshmen to attempt to narrow their choices so early in life . . .

'That's smart,' I said quickly. 'It's ridiculous to sign up for four years of some course of study the minute you get here. I wish I'd had the courage to go undeclared. That's what college should be anyway, an exploration of self.' I maneuvered her around the room in an intricate fox-trot which she had no trouble following at all.

'You're quite deft,' she said a little breathlessly.

'Well, you're very easy to have in my arms,' I returned.

That night I probed Paul about his childhood chum. He answered all my questions, verifying most of my assumptions about her, and then asked, 'So. Are you in love or in lust?'

I grinned slowly down at him from the dark of the top

bunk, upside down like the Cheshire cat. 'Let's just say I've got that old black magic feeling.'

'Praise the Lord,' he said dryly. 'Eliza has been saved from the ice.'

'What do you mean?'

He rolled over and punched up his pillow as though he intended to talk till dawn. 'Well, you've been mooning around here for two quarters, and I think it's about time you gave her up as a lost cause.'

I was genuinely shocked. 'I have not!'

'I don't think you realize how many times Ms Gentry's fair charms have come up in conversation, bubba. I'm just glad to see you're still capable of a normal red-blooded response to a warm female body.'

I had talked about Sherry, sure, but I was certain I hadn't displayed such an obsession as he claimed. Anyway, it sure wasn't something I was going to admit. 'Hey, she's past history.'

'Glad to hear it,' he said softly. 'Another wandering sinner refuged from the storm.' Paul sometimes sounded more Southern Baptist than the Yankee Calvinist that he was. 'So if you need a place to explore Ms Banner's – possibilities – I could vacate the premises for a night.'

'Right. And have six perverts pounding on the door and screaming, "Fuck her, Davy!" right when I'm making my move. No thanks, brother. I can't quite picture me slipping Callan Banner up the backstairs.'

Neither could I imagine her relishing sex in the back of the Hog of Steel. Truth be known, I couldn't imagine her relishing sex at all. She didn't ooze juiciness like a lot of women did. In fact, in my imagination she was part of a tradition that included James's Isabel Archer, Whistler's 'White Girl', and Katharine Hepburn. I knew she could be depended upon to do and say the right thing at the right time, which relieved me of much of the obligation to protect her, somehow. She was obviously perfectly capable of protecting herself.

After a month of dating I was still waiting to fall in love with her as I'd expected. As I wanted. We'd progressed to entangled kisses, a skill which Callan had perfected, and were moving rapidly to, as Lance called it, Intensified Fondling II. She had a way of gazing at me steadily when I spoke; it was exciting and unnerving to have her complete attention. I never knew what she was thinking completely, but I sensed that she was usually way ahead of me in her understanding of the more subtle layers of men and women together. I was looking forward to peeling off Callan's outer layer and discovering what moved her.

But I was distracted from that exploration by exams. They loomed over us all, a frightening miasma that proved we were moving through another one of the great divisions of life and time: the end of our freshman year. The end of another plateau of innocence. I had the sense, as I did after graduation from high school, that life would never again be so sweet, seamless, and golden. But since I'd felt this way before, I recognized the mood more quickly. I came to believe that I would always go through these periods of exhilaration and loss, quivering like a violin tuned to infinity.

After agonizing over freshman finals, I was eager to go home and do nothing but bake at the edge of the pool. Driving up the Ventura Freeway, blondes were everywhere, in a larger proportion than on campus. I saw them on the streets, in passing cars, all of them slender and tan and moving quickly with a swirl of sun-hair, a slash of bare arms and legs, a glint of white teeth in wide, easy smiles, as though they had proliferated in the Valley since my absence. You could go snow-blind from all the white teeth and hair and shining skin. It suddenly seemed to me as if the continent had tilted long ago, and all the color had drained into Southern California, leaving the rest of the country – particularly Boston – emptied and gray and dim. Callan began to look like an altogether different female species.

First night home I noticed the subtle differences only a year could make. While my attention had been consummately diverted elsewhere, Avrom had grown up. He was now a full-fledged teenager, and it gave me a pang of pride and bewildering sadness to think my brother was as I used to be – but taller.

And my father. As the conversation at dinner flowed over and around me, I observed Rabbi Levine with what seemed to be new insight. The man was aging, no doubt about it. When he stood by the table, he seemed smaller in all dimensions, as though he were a balloon with a slow leak. And yet his eyes were just as piercing, just as alert. His mouth a little softer perhaps around the edges, but no less alive. If anything, he was even more attentive to my mother, nodding slowly when she spoke, cocking his head toward her with what appeared to be genuine interest.

I hoped fervently that I could feel that way after twenty-two years of marriage. We cleared off the tacos, shrimp enchiladas, and fruit salad, my favorite meal, and drew forward around the pitcher of sangria, a small maternal salute to my new adulthood. As I took out my pipe, I caught the swift glance of indulgent pride that passed between my parents. Like two halves of the same whole, they spoke without speaking, touched without touching. I took my time with the loading and the lighting just to give them something else to talk about in bed that night. I answered all the questions about classes, my friends, the fraternity, acquitting myself well, I thought, and striking just the right balance between College Man and Good Son.

Later out by the pool, I had a chance to catch up with Avrom in private.

'So school's good?' I asked. 'Any changes at Taft?'

'It's still standing.' My brother shrugged. 'But I don't know if you'd recognize it.'

'Really? In one year?'

'Yeah, you've been gone only one year, but the three years between us makes a big difference. It's been three years since you were where I am now. And that's almost like a generation. Did kids do a lot of drugs when you were my age?'

I shook my head slowly. 'Just drinking. Maybe a little grass when we were seniors, but nothing heavy.'

'Well, it's heavy now. Grass and acid and hash, everybody's into it now, even freshmen.'

'Everybody?' I gazed at him pointedly.

He looked away. 'I've tried my share. But I'm not really into it much.'

I felt a genuine sorrow sweep me, close my heart like a fist. 'What else?'

Avrom laughed mirthlessly. 'Well, let's just say you don't have to be a virgin to be May Queen anymore. In fact, if they took a poll, I don't know if anybody'd stand in line for the honor.'

'It was such a big deal when I was a senior!'

'Yeah, a lot's changed. It isn't cool to be so rah-rah anymore.'

Honor Roll, Girls' League, Boys' League, team sports, French Club, racking up activities to put on your college apps so you'd look well-rounded, cheerleaders, student body government, it was all important. It mattered. And now, three years later – from freshman class to freshman class, same school, same family – it wasn't worth the effort. It was enough to make you wonder if it ever was. 'So,' I asked finally, 'how's your love life?'

I expected a brush-off, the victory sign, a grin, the usual bullshit routine guys gave one another. Instead, Avrom looked sober. 'Not too good, actually. I was in love with this girl – well, I guess I still am, in fact. But she dumped me.'

'Is that right?'

'You probably don't know her. Missy Bowen? Short little blonde in my class?'

I shook my head.

'Well, we got pretty close this last year. But then she started running with the jock crowd, and I lost her.' His eyes got glassy and I looked down to give him time to recover. 'Anyway, it's taken me longer than I thought to get over it.'

I was quietly amazed. My little brother was in love. He was suffering, grappling with larger emotions than I'd thought him capable of feeling. I'd seen him briefly at Hanukkah, missed him at Passover, and all the while I was off at college, I pictured the guy still in knee pants. Now I couldn't think of anything to say that would be helpful. I patted him awkwardly. 'Man, I know how you feel. I've been there.'

'Sherry Gentry?'

'Miss Heartbreak of 1966.'

'Well, mine's this year's runner-up. And she's only a freshman.'

'These California women'll kill you.'

'Blind you first.'

We began to laugh ruefully, and I pushed him away, clapping him to me with the same gesture. From across the yard my parents walked toward us. I noted with pleasure that they were holding hands.

'It's so good to see my boys together,' my mother said.

'Well, you've got a whole summer of it to look forward to,' Avrom said, 'but right now I've got to run.'

He was dating so young! 'Yeah, me too,' I added quickly.

'Tonight? You're going out your first night back?'

'Mom,' Avrom sighed, 'I told you last week I had plans for tonight – '

'And I've got plans too,' I said. I grinned at my father. 'So many women; so little time.'

My mother smiled reluctantly. 'You should live so long, Mr Big Talker.'

'See you tomorrow,' Avrom called over his shoulder to me. 'We'll hit the beach or something.'

'So you are going to see whom?' my father asked, turning back to me.

'Just drive around, catch up with some old friends. It'll be light for another hour.'

'You're planning to see Sherry Gentry again.' My mother could scarcely say the name without a frown.

I stiffened slightly. 'I might. Among others.'

'I wish you would leave that girl alone,' my mother said calmly. 'You know how your father and I feel about her. You have a nice girl now, lots of others to choose from, why give yourself this heartache? Enough is enough already. The girl doesn't want you, right? So there are plenty of other clams in the chowder.'

I felt a growing sense of indignation, but I didn't let it show in my voice. 'I don't know where you got the idea she doesn't want me,' I said reasonably. 'She happened to invite me to come by. But anyway, she's not the only one I want to see.' I began to walk away. 'Just don't worry about it, okay? I think I can manage my social life just fine without supervision.'

That sounded definitive enough, I thought. I left my parents standing together shoulder to shoulder in the shadows. They were still holding hands.

This time she was home. I knew because the blue MG

was parked on the street, as though she had just pulled in for a moment, to change clothes or something, and was on her way out again. I rang the bell as I always did, long/short, short/long, feeling like I'd come home once more. The old song, 'The Name Game', the one Sherry had taught me, rolled through my mind. 'Sherry, Sherry, Bo Berry, Banana-Fana Fo Ferry, Fe-Fi-Mo-Merry. Sherry.' It'll work with everything but Chuck, she told me. I grinned and buzzed again.

She pulled open the door, and for an instant I couldn't speak. I had forgotten how very lovely she was. Before she even said hello I reached out and touched her shining blond mane. 'Enough hair for two people,' I said. 'Just like I remember.'

'David!' she shrieked happily, hugging me quickly. 'When did you get home?'

'A few days ago. Did your dad tell you I came by over spring break?'

'Yeah; I was *so* sorry I missed you – ' She was dragging me inside, linking her arm through mine. 'Did you get my letter? Hawaii was a blast, have you ever been there? You'd love it, really a kick.'

While she was chattering and pulling me out to the pool, I glanced around swiftly. Dusk just made everything more dramatic. Nothing looked different, but nothing looked the same either. As in my own home, the walls themselves seemed closer together. The only fixture that still was larger than life was Sherry herself. We sprawled on the lounge chairs, facing each other.

'So, have you gone all cerebal on me now?' she teased, throwing one hand over her head in a gesture of abandon. 'All Greek Intellectual? I bet you even wear jackets and ties to dinner these days.'

'Yup,' I admitted, 'I wear patches on the elbows of my

310

tweed pajamas too. How about you? *Playboy* called you up yet?'

'Yeah, but I told them I was saving myself for marriage.' She smirked. 'Are you?'

'You know sorority girls don't do it until they've got their china patterns registered. Even in California, I think it's some sort of house ordinance or something – '

'Right.' She winced. 'I'll just bet. I can tell by looking that you've hardly been starving yourself.'

'Where does it show?' I asked in mock alarm, glancing down at everywhere but my crotch.

'Your eyebrows are bushier. That's the first indication of a basically bestial nature.'

I grinned and closed my eyes, my face to the setting sun. She'd been reading more books with big words. I could tell. 'So how about you?' I finally asked casually. 'Are you in love at the moment?'

She smiled softly. I suddenly hated that smile. 'There's a vicious rumor to that effect.'

'Who?'

'Nobody you know, Davy. A guy I met in Hawaii.'

'He moved here for you?'

She reached over and tapped me lightly on the head. 'Silly. He's from Canoga. You'd like him.'

'No doubt. Is he one of your usual pussycats?'

She stiffened slightly. 'What do you mean?'

'I mean,' I continued, keeping my voice level, 'does he get pissed off when you won't put out, and slap you around? Kick you out of moving vehicles? Call you names in public and, in short, respect and worship you as you obviously deserve – and never get?'

Her voice turned instantly cold. 'What's your problem, Levine?'

'No problem at all,' I said evenly. 'Strictly curiosity. I mean, I'm slightly out of practice. Haven't had to fight for your honor in almost a year now. They don't go in for that much in college. If I need to beef up, be sure and tell me in advance.'

She sat up abruptly and glared at me. 'Thanks for coming to see me, David. It was a real treat.' As she walked toward the house, she threw back over her shoulder, 'I know you can find your way out. And next time you feel like being a shit, why not give another one of your old girlfriends first dibs, huh? Like Miriam. I'm sure she'd be thrilled.'

I lay back down on the lounger, my eyes closed against the final red of the sunset. Now, why the hell did I do that, I asked myself calmly. How did it happen? She greeted you, she teased with you, everything was fine. You asked if she was in love. She sort of said she was, some guy from Canoga, and it went downhill from there. Or rather, I jacked it up, greased the skids, and *pushed* it downhill as hard as I could.

A part of me was wailing in despair, running after her and groveling at her slender ankles for forgiveness. A part of me was standing up and walking out, almost relieved that I was leaving. I felt, mainly, only a sort of detached scientific interest, as though I had dropped a beaker, hadn't tried hard enough to catch it, and it had shattered, cutting me and burning my feet and hands with invisible acid in the process. And I just stood and watched the blood well up slowly. Numb. Incredulous and passive and suddenly so very weary of it all.

I got up and left. At the front door I stopped for an instant with my hand on the knob. Last chance, Levine. Either you beg for forgiveness now, or you forget it. At least for a long time. I glanced around the pristine and silent living room, brilliant in its whiteness, wondering if I would ever stand in this house again. Quietly, I turned the knob and went out.

* * *

Most summers of my life had gone by too quickly. I was amazed to discover that this one was an exception. After the first few weeks of gratitude that I didn't have to wake up at a certain time, study all night, or wonder what I had forgotten to do, the days droned on as though they had their bellies full of summer honey. And my boredom was complicated by the fact that I had to disguise it. If even once my parents got the impression that I had no plans, they were quick to provide suggestions how I might remedy my sloth. Like take up rabbinical study.

How could that have even been a consideration? How can parents live in the same house with a child for nearly twenty years and know so little about his perversions? Couldn't they sense, even on some subliminal level, how drawn I was to debauch? How easily seduced by temptation?

Yet, they persevered.

'A wonderful opportunity is available for you, David, if you move quickly.' My father folded his breakfast paper and peered at me amiably over the top of it.

'Oh?' I asked warily, recapping the jam. 'What's that?'

'A once-in-a-lifetime opportunity!' my mother began.

'Well, maybe not once-in-a-lifetime, but certainly once-in-a-summer,' my father cut in with a chuckle. 'It's the rabbinical version of summer camp, I guess you'd call it. Two weeks of study and meditation, talking with young men like yourself and rabbis of commitment, learning about what it is to be a Jew. What it is, also, to be a leader in our faith.'

'I think I've had enough study for a while,' I said quickly.

'It's not all work, David. There'll be plenty of time for outdoor activities. Relaxation. I should think this seminar offered by the Reform Council would be just the thing for a young man after his first year of college, especially if he's at all interested in rabbinical work.'

I took a deep breath. 'But I'm not.'

My father sagged slightly, the paper crinkling all the way to the table. 'Not at all?'

It took me all of my strength to shake my head.

'Then what *do* you plan to do all summer?' my mother asked. 'You can't just loiter around, mooning after the girls.'

'I don't intend to moon, Mother. And loitering wasn't in my plans, either,' I said dryly.

'Then what? Maybe you should be studying ahead for next year – '

'Do I have to have a plan? Right this instant?'

My father put his hand out and touched my arm, instantly calming me down. 'No, no, of course not, son. I'm disappointed though that you don't want to take advantage of this opportunity. But you don't have to decide right now. Perhaps later on you may think better of it. After you've had a chance to relax.'

'Yes, and get bored,' my mother added. 'It's going to be a long summer.'

'Not nearly long enough,' I said under my breath as I pushed myself away from the table.

But I was wrong. Within a few weeks I was bored with relaxing and ripe for seduction again. San Francisco beckoned. It was the Summer of Love in Haight-Ashbury, and word trickled – no, *poured* – down into Southern California that the biggest party of the century was taking place just a few hours north. Half-naked women dancing on park lawns; beaded, bearded, leather-vested and long-haired freaks sharing pipes and singing of peace; girls going braless, bottomless, boyless everywhere; rock bands playing for free at the Fillmore; people painting themselves with psychedelic flowers and Indian mantras; and

Free Love on every corner: it was billed as the Magical Mystery Tour of Life.

The San Francisco Chronicle, the most straitlaced of the four papers we took, began a week-long investigation series called 'I Was a Hippie'. Written by a reporter who went undercover on assignment to live as a hippie for a month, the series revealed the spiciest details of life in a crash pad, how marijuana was bought and sold, and the intricate, orgiastic sexual acrobatics practiced by those who advocated 'free love'.

I half expected the *Chronicle* to be suddenly squirreled away wherever my parents hid the *Playboys*.

But they must have shrugged their collective shoulders in resignation, because madness was all around us then and inescapable. Just for that summer in California, nobody cared that Israeli jets had wiped out most of the air forces of the Arab countries in a six-day war. Nobody noticed that despite President Johnson's upbeat assessment of Vietnam, casualties were up to 14,000 dead and 86,000 wounded, with more coming in every day. It was far more fascinating that a dozen Yippies, led by Jerry Rubin, threw dollar bills from the visitor's gallery of the New York Stock Exchange, bringing the business nerve-center of the nation to a grinding halt.

I turned the Hog of Steel north and headed for the City by the Bay. Feeling like I could almost follow the spore of marijuana on the wind, I parked the car by the Golden Gate Park and walked down the lawn, merging with the crowds.

A girl spun past me, her arms out in the air, a blissful smile on her face, eyes closed, chanting, 'the colors, the colors, the colors,' and then she spiraled away among the flowers.

A huge banner was stretched across the stage up ahead, scrawled in happy-child crayon colors, SUMMER OF LOVE!

and music seemed to come from all corners of the sky. Scott McKenzie was onstage singing, 'If you're going to San Fran-cisco, be sure to wear some flowers in your hair – '

I leaned down without a thought and plucked a rose from a bush, stripped the thorns, and stuck it behind my ear. On any normal Sunday I wouldn't have pillaged public flora, but that day that rose belonged to all of us.

Along the left of the field, a line of uniformed cops stood, calmly facing the crowd. A few of the hippies were teasing them, offering them flowers, a toke off a joint, a swig from a Southern Comfort bottle, but the cops continued to smile. A few took the flowers and put them under their helmet straps.

'This is far out,' a guy next to me said dreamily, holding out his hand. 'Take one, man, it's free.'

He held a tiny blue pill in his palm. It looked impossibly small.

'Is this acid?' I asked, clearing my throat. Could I absorb it through my skin if I merely held it?

The guy giggled happily. 'Righteous shit, man. Wow.'

I grinned. 'I think I'll pass, thanks. I don't like to fuck with something that's too small to hold or too big to hold down.' As I walked away, the guy was balancing the pill on his nose like Flipper.

I remember the one time I tried LSD. It was years later, when I was no longer so frightened of things I couldn't control. I took one small pill and was up all weekend, never went to bed, called everybody I knew long distance at three A.M., and can recall vague snatches of being in a bathtub for hours, playing with the washcloth underwater. That was before we knew anything about serial hallucinations and chromosome damage. Now I'm grateful that my innate cowardice kept me from inevitable mutation. I mean, can Timothy Leary even balance a checkbook these days?

I'd like to be able to tell you that the Summer of Love was, for David Levine at eighteen, a blissful, bacchic romp through fields of Orgy and Abandon, but I've come too far to lie. I spent a week up there in San Francisco, sleeping out in the park, hanging around at bookstores and head shops, trying to feel like a player. But the watcher in me was vigilant, and I finally went home, dirty and depressed. I couldn't seem to feel a part of anything, even my own generation. Couldn't catch the rhythm of all that giddy joy. But I gave it a second chance with the Monterey Pop Festival.

For three days in June I sat on a wide meadow at the county fairgrounds, surrounded by electricity. Kids came from all over to hear Simon and Garfunkel, the Steve Miller Band, Buffalo Springfield, the Who, the Grateful Dead, the Mamas and the Papas, Otis Redding, the Jefferson Airplane, the Byrds, Jimi Hendrix, and a lot more bands I've never even heard of, in five concerts of incredible power. The banner across the stage proclaimed, MUSIC, LOVE, AND FLOWERS, and girls danced nearly naked in the sunlight. Medical trailers for bad trips were set up at the fringes of the crowd, and all roads in and out of Monterey were blocked completely for seventy-two hours.

I wandered up the road midway along the stage, where hundreds of kids sold incense, hash pipes, beads, tie-dyed T-shirts, god's eyes, psychedelic posters, buttons, paper dresses, and drugs.

I found a place on the grass and watched Janis Joplin singing with Big Brother and the Holding Company, screaming until her voice was like a buzzsaw, holding on to a Southern Comfort bottle for luck. The Who came

317

onstage and, after a blistering set, smashed their equipment at the end of 'My Generation', deafening those in the front rows with the moans and shrieks of the microphones and amps as they died. Jimi Hendrix fingered his guitar like a demon, humped his amplifiers, and then sprayed lighter fluid on his Stratocaster and set it ablaze.

I remember feeling alarmed at the eager violence in the acts, the frenzy of destruction and noise and bedlam. But I was also fascinated and angry at the same time, wrung out at the end of Hendrix's set as though I'd been in a street brawl.

It was a welcome relief when Ravi Shankar came on for his meditative guitar solo, and attendants filled the stage with orchids and incense. Like a humming Monet painting, the stage seemed to shimmer with color and summer heat. People were passing joints, and I took one as it floated by. The guy next to me, with a beaded ankus headband, smiled and nodded at me in brotherly acceptance. I took a few token puffs and closed my eyes, absorbing the serenity. That was a rare moment, one which is etched in my memory, when I almost slipped away from myself into the experience, and was able to beam and bounce to the music like those on either side of me, blissed out as a single cell in a complex and harmonious organism.

Remember the song by the Who, 'I Can See for Miles'? That lyric summed up for me the whole texture of Monterey, the sense of being part of a generation that really did have a new vision of the world. A vision that somehow made the world larger, yet small enough to hold in your hand.

Well, the Summer of Love spread all over the country that season, and we heard reports that in Greenwich Village students gathered with tambourines and guitars to protest the dog-leash law. They chanted 'What is *dog* spelled backward?' and 'LBJ, pull out like your father should have!' In Dallas they danced in the shopping malls; in DC they had a 'smoke-in' in Lafayette Park, right across the street from the White House, to lobby for marijuana legalization.

You could hear the amused condescension in the voices of the Los Angeles newscasters. Anything that was happening in the rest of the country was obviously reactive, imitative, and too little, too late. Like a big brother watching his little brother play dress-up in his old tux, Californians already felt they were onto something new.

So the summer of 1967 faded into the dry palomino grasses of September, and it was time to go back to the factory of learning. My mother picked my last night at home to say her piece.

'Your father and I are very proud of you, you know that, don't you?'

We were sitting on the sofa, in the more formal area of the house. I almost felt like I was on a job interview. I should have been suspicious when my father took Avrom away from the table, out by the pool. 'Sure, Mom. And I really appreciate all you guys are doing for me. Someday I hope to pay you back.'

She shook her head impatiently. 'We don't look for that, David, although next summer I think you should definitely get a job. But you got good grades this year – Bs in college are nothing to sneeze at, we know, and you'll pull up that C in French – just keep doing your best. That's the only reward we want.'

I noticed that she had subtly altered her usual Yiddish-Mama pose, and I became more wary.

'You've been calling this Callan girl regularly?'

'Yup,' I said breezily. 'We agreed we'd sort of take it easy this summer, what with her back at Boston and all.

But I call her once a week. She's doing fine. Looking forward to seeing me this fall. No problem.'

'That's good, that's good. No problem. A boy should have no problems with his love life. Plenty of time for that later when he becomes a man. But you do *have* a love life, right?'

That one confused me. 'Sure, Mom.' What was she getting at? Not, ohgod, a lecture on sex. 'Dad and I have talked about it plenty – '

'I know, I know, your father and you have joked about your little girlfriends, David, but it's nothing to joke about at your age.'

'Well,' I tried with a grin, 'it's nothing to cry about either.'

She patted my hand. 'There was a time when your father had to point out to you that what you did in your schoolwork counted. That you were at a stage when it went on your record forever, and you couldn't fool around anymore. Now it's time for your mother to tell you the same thing about your love life.'

'I wish you wouldn't call it that,' I mumbled.

'What? Love life? It's not a good way?'

'It's so old-fashioned.'

She snorted. 'You think you kids invented this man-and-woman thing? It *is* old-fashioned, nothing older than God.'

'Well, you make it sound like such a big deal. I date a girl, she's back east for the summer, it's nothing serious.'

'But you've told us about this Callan girl, and she doesn't sound' – she hesitated for the first time and glanced around the room, as though looking for signposts – 'quite right for you, David.' She settled on that with a nod. 'A nice girl, but not good potential.'

Now, that got me. 'Not good potential? She's smart, she's pretty, she comes from a good family, she's got a hell of a lot more class than *I've* got, that's for sure. If that's not potential, I don't know what is. I suppose you'd like me to date Bess Myerson, Ma, but so far as I know, she's not free next Saturday.'

She brushed my diversion aside. 'You know what I mean.'

'You mean she's not Jewish.'

She smiled.

'Well, don't worry so much. It's no big deal, like I said. Maybe we'll stay together next year, maybe not, but it's nothing serious.'

Her smile widened. 'That's okay by me. But maybe *she* thinks it's something serious, right? And maybe she wants it to be. And maybe, just maybe, you are not the only one to have control over whether or not it is. So listen to me now, David – '

'Do I have a choice?'

'Yes, you do and that's what we're talking about here. Your choices. You don't make them so good.'

'What do you mean?'

'I mean, you make friends with a nice girl, Miriam, and then you drop her like a hot knish for that Sherry Gentry dolly. That's such a good choice? Then, when you go off to college, you take up with a girl who lives at the other end of the country and might as well live in another universe, that much you have in common. Smart choice number two. And when you come home for the summer, a time when you could be making new friends, you run off to Sherry Gentry's house and call this Boston *bubke* and moon around like I don't know what, strike three and you're out on good choices.'

'Mom!'

She held up her hand for silence. 'This is your mother talking now, not one of your little fruitcakes. It's time, David, for you to take an accounting, I think.' She leaned forward, her hand on my knee, and looked gently into my eyes. 'You want to have fun, don't I know that? But it's time to be thinking of your future. You're not a *boychik* anymore. Your father and I, we said, okay, let the boy have his fun, let him get his milk teeth on other eggs, because he's young. But now you're past nineteen, it matters, and you don't seem to be making better choices. You should be flocking with birds of your own feather.'

'You mean Jewish girls,' I said sullenly.

'And also' – she nodded – 'the *right* kind of girl. Not a flighty blond hoyden or a ritzy-titzy *allrightnikeh* either like that Boston Banner girl – oh, don't look so shocked, don't I know what's going on with my only firstborn? – but a girl who will make you happy. A girl you have more in common with than you both like the same songs on the radio.'

'You mean a girl who will make *you* happy.'

She threw up her hands. 'Of course! Of course I mean exactly that. I make no bones about it, David, your father and I would have sour stomachs for the rest of our natural days if you brought home the kind of girl you usually hang over with.'

'Hang out with.'

'Whatever. Do you see what I mean?'

'You want me to marry a girl like Miriam Weld.'

She smiled. 'That would be lovely. Or like Ruth, you remember Ruth from the old neighborhood? She doesn't have to be gorgeous, God knows, but she should have that inner shine to her soul. You'll know it when you see it. She should be a good person. A nice girl. Somebody with some sense to them. Somebody like *you* are.'

'What makes you think *I'm* so serious?'

She shook her head wistfully. 'You don't know yourself, David, you're too young for that. Sometimes I think the old ways were better. The father and mother picked out a suitable wife for their son; he was happy, she was happy, and they had happy grandchildren. But you, your head is turned by pretty smiles that won't last. Listen to your mother if you want to know yourself. It's not for nothing that your father had you read the classics when you were so small you could barely lift the books; it's not for nothing you can recite poetry like a cantor. You think most boys your age have such sensitivities? Their mothers should be so lucky. But you, *you* have a philosopher in your soul, and you won't be happy with a *goldeneh medina*.'

A fool's paradise. A place paved with gold – or a person who was more sizzle than steak.

I pulled up stiffly with all the dignity I could muster. 'I really think I can handle what you so quaintly call my love life by myself. I'm doing just fine. I don't think I need any more advice on the subject.'

'Oh, really, Mr I-Can-Have-Any-Girl-I-Want. Well, it seems to your father and myself that you aren't exactly hitting home runs on this one. And if you keep doing as well as you have been, all the good ones will be taken by the time you wake up and get serious about it. Three girls in two years, and none of them are coming to dinner tonight at the home of Mr Romeo Levine.'

I pulled away, stung.

Her tone gentled instantly. 'I'm only saying, darling, if you go barking up the right tree, you'll catch a better bird. Now, when you go back to campus, I want you to look into the local Jewish clubs and organizations available. They must have social groups for the young people, right? So find out where they go and go there. Meet some young women who are more likely to appreciate who you are and what you have to offer.' She smiled. 'Save yourself a little heartache, is all I'm saying. Don't go chasing after trouble, David, life will bring plenty to your plate without planting it in your own backyard. Like should marry like. Is that so bad for a mother to say?'

I couldn't help smiling. 'I guess not.'

She hugged me quickly. 'He guesses not, he guesses not, of *course* not. After all, you're not the only one who has to live with her, you know. You take a woman to wife and you take her into our life, too, and you might as well ask a goat to live with a tiger as ask me to live with – well, with *some* of these California girls I've seen around here. This Sherry person – '

'Mom,' I said firmly, my jaw tight again, 'she's a nice girl. If you knew her, you'd like her.'

She appraised me carefully. After a moment of silence: 'Okay. If you say so. I'm not going to make a big brouhaha if you see her, David, but I'm not going to be happy about it, either. Don't I remember what it's like to be young? That nothing is more seductive than the forbidden? So I won't forbid her. But I will say, you'll find out soon enough that you're too smart for her. Maybe even, God willing, she'll find it out too.'

'Like I said,' I sighed wearily, 'she won't even speak to me anymore.'

Her face softened with love. She patted my cheek lightly. 'That's just today's news. But you're a good son; I knew you'd be receptive. At first I was going to tell you, find yourself a nice girl by next year or we'll start making your choices for you – '

'What do you mean?'

'I mean, there'd be no more fraternities, no more sorority girls with big smiles and empty hearts, no more money to do these things, but *lots* of invitations to dances and meetings where the girls of best potential would likely be.'

'Like Hadassah teas.'

'You got it. But I can see these sort of drastic measures

324

won't be necessary. I told your father so. Just remember that we love you and we want only the best for you.' She beamed. 'Now, go back to school and hang over with the best.'

When I saw Callan my first night back, she told me gently that she was 'involved' with someone new. An old boyfriend she had seen over the summer. When I thought back, I realized that her calls had been more friendly, less intimate with each week that passed. Next time, I vowed, I'd see the signals before it was too late.

I sat in my room for three days playing the Who song, 'I Can See for Miles' and 'Windy', by the Association, and I thought about what my mother had said.

The dance was getting more complicated. And what made it even more confusing is that nobody I knew, not a single guy, really talked about it much. I knew men who idealized women, who feared them, who used them, who were used by them, who loved them but didn't like them, who liked them well enough but couldn't love them, all sorts of folly and delusion. And what was the truth about women?

Well, one thing I'd learned for sure by nineteen is that they were different from one another. I no longer thought that all I had to do was get a grip on one of them to know everything about the rest of them. I suspected that some of them didn't know any more about being a woman than I did.

But I'd learned another thing as well. Without a woman in my life, I felt incomplete. Cosmically alone. And deadly numb in any number of crucial extremities.

'Paul-boy,' I mourned to my roommate, 'I want this all to be over.'

'What?'

'This. College. Youth. The part I'm supposed to be

325

having such a blast during. I want to hurry up and be rich and famous so that Callan Banner will eat her pillow every night for having missed out on me.'

'I expect she will soon enough,' Paul said kindly.

'Right. Ah, mother of raving God,' I moaned, 'will we ever get to the point where we just don't give a damn whether or not *they* give a damn? I mean, what do women *want*?'

'Whatever it is, one thing's for sure.'

'What?'

'The minute we figure it out, they're going to change the rules. They'll make up a new game plan,' Paul said softly, almost like a chant, 'while we're asleep. In the middle of the night. Then we'll cry out again, with great exasperation and for the millionth time, "What do you *want*?" and they'll just look cute and smile and shake their pretty heads. But they won't tell us. Not ever. And then it will start up all over again.'

When I look back on it, my college years are the ones I remember with least clarity. The quarters flowed by in a rush as the months built to periodic climaxes of exams, meandering when vacations and breaks slowed the momentum. But certain key times stand out in my memory.

I remember Callan's solemn dignity when we argued – 'discussed', as she would have it – the political implications of Dow Chemical recruiting on campus. I remember another girl I dated for a while, Susan Anders, and her bright laugh when I finally slipped her up to my room while a party was going on downstairs. When we left, she tripped over a guy out cold on the hall stairs, shrieked, and the whole house rushed to the bottom of the banister to see us descend.

I can completely recall my rush of triumph and pride

when the miracle of DNA was decoded by a UCLA biology professor, though I can't now remember his name. And I remember walking along the paths to school with Paul, falling in love momentarily with one cute coed face after another as they went past.

Memories: girls I dated, some of them closer to what my parents wanted, others as far away as alien races, the laughs I shared with friends, the blaze of green the campus was in spring, the moments of pride when I made a grade, wrote up a good lab experiment, felt at least at that instant that I was doing something worthwhile. These things all have lasted.

Also, the moments when I reached despair and loneliness and bottomed-out exhaustion, when I wondered if I'd ever graduate, ever see the outside world again. When I pictured days at Taft, my senior year in the Valley, those times seemed sealed in amber, hemmed in by the ocean, the mountains, the desert, as strange and perfect as a new planet.

Now I look back on my college years in vaguely pastel shades, and the linear definitions between one thing and the next are wavered and indistinct. Old songs bring back old moments. The score from *Hair*, particularly the song by the Fifth Dimension, 'Aquarius/Let the Sunshine In', always makes me feel wistful. 'Sitting on the Dock of the Bay' by Otis can always make me feel a sense of loss; sometimes it seems like R & B died along with the man in that plane crash in a cold Wisconsin lake. But with the old songs you never really have to say good-bye.

Do our parents think of music in the same way? What do they mean, all these songs, so connected with my past and my hormones? All these melodies and lyrics that tell of mating and breaking up, of love and its losses, of the anticipation of that first encounter, and each time I hear the special ones, I shut my eyes, touch my past and

327

become the song. Perhaps the real difference between our generation and theirs is the car radio – nothing more.

And so today I sometimes find myself blinking back tears over the endless chorus of 'Hey Jude', in which the Beatles could be heard disappearing and dissolving forever. Sing a sad song to make it better. And then 'Clouds' by Joni Mitchell makes me feel serene again, no matter where I hear it.

When I look back on it, of course, I realize that historically, those years were far from serene. Like the slow-motion shoot-up in *Bonnie and Clyde*, there was a sense that things were out of control and spiraling down toward dark places at last. That perhaps the bad guys might win this one after all. *The Graduate* proved that grown-ups didn't know how to fix it, either.

Over the next twenty-four months, women trashed an American institution in Atlantic City crowning a live sheep 'Miss America' before forty rolling cameras. Richard Nixon came on *Laugh-In* to say 'Sock it to me!' Dennis Hopper and Peter Fonda were blown away by rednecks in *Easy Rider*. It was as if nothing made much sense anymore.

Tommie Smith and John Carlos stood on the center stage at the Mexico City Olympics, wearing black sweatsuits, black socks, and single black gloves. As the world watched, they raised their fists in a black power salute for the 'Star-Spangled Banner'. Harvard and Berkeley were taken over by SDS members who manhandled the deans, locked the doors with bicycle chains, and demanded ROTC be kicked off campus. The Indians captured Alcatraz, Hershey's put an end to the five-cent chocolate bar, and the Democratic Convention exploded in Chicago. It was as though nobody was in charge anymore.

Ted Kennedy drove off a bridge in Chappaquiddick, taking ten hours to call somebody to help him find Mary

Jo Kopechne's body. Charles Manson and his crazies murdered Sharon Tate and her friends in Malibu. Dr Martin Luther King was assassinated in Memphis, and Bobby Kennedy was shot down in LA. It was as though nothing would ever be the same again.

I clearly remember the Elvis special I saw on TV that winter of 1969 with the cameras focused tight on the King's smoldering glare. Elvis Aaron Presley, with his immaculate pompadour, his black-leather snake hips, and his famous sneer, sang 'You lookin' for trouble? You come to the right place, lookin' for trouble, then look right in my face.' The innocence of sanitized pop records, B-movie kisses, and army uniforms was over. He was back, straining at the leash, and flaunting it. And he brought the women in the audience to their knees, screaming with delight.

In those years, everything became personal. My memories of 1968 and 1969 are irrevocably woven with what was happening outside myself. I know exactly where I was and what I was thinking when I first heard of Dr King's assassination, and that knowledge grew from a personal and visceral response as though, somehow, I had been there and seen the blood on the balcony.

My last two years of college were no longer a refuge. Kids were losing their student deferments if they didn't keep their grades up. The Viet Cong had launched the Tet offensive, and Westmoreland was sending in another 206,000 American troops. Rumors circulated on campus that President Johnson thought most of the student subversives were on the West Coast and, grades or no grades, if your name appeared on somebody's secret list of troublemakers, you were headed for 'Nam in a hurry. But nobody knew who made the lists, and nobody knew what might constitute trouble. Were you safe if you were on the ROTC roster? If you were a Young Republican? If you dated pretty sorority girls whose fathers lived in Brentwood?

The Lambda Chi house was evenly divided between cowards and killers. Guys you thought you knew suddenly began to talk about running to Canada or joining the Green Berets. An occasional fistfight broke out, with ugly names shouted in the halls like 'Commie Creep! Peace Freak!' alternating with 'War Monger! Baby-Killer!'

And then, in December of 1969, my worst nightmare jelled to a more finite possibility. Nixon started up the first draft since 1942, and they were calling up 850,000 boys between the ages of nineteen and twenty-six.

I realized with a quiet horror that they could take me, sooner or later. I lay awake at night, talking with Paul, thinking of all the reasons why they might not.

Paul was more willing to go, if called, but he didn't exactly hunger for an M-16 in his arms. I could no more imagine myself in a Vietnamese rice field than I could picture myself in bed with my mother. Some things, I told Paul solemnly, are just too obscene to contemplate. But I carried a wad of guilt in my gut because I knew, no matter how many intellectual arguments about the war I might muster, my real reason was that I was afraid. No one else seemed to speak it aloud.

Some guys had maps of the war zone on their walls, marking wins and losses with colored pins. They watched the six o'clock news with the same bright avidity with which the jocks viewed Saturday morning cartoons. But for me the whole thing was macabre. To actually watch on the news as boy-soldiers hacked through the jungle, called for medics, hissed frantically into radios, dragged off their wounded, zoomed low over thatched villages dropping off black smoke clouds and deafening explosions – on one hand, it was too real to watch. On the other, it seemed callous to turn away. I felt like a junkie with a rising tolerance to shock.

All I knew for sure was that I was deeply frightened. If I screwed up, they'd get me. They'd get us all.

But there were diversions. In July, Armstrong and Aldrin bounced on the moon, raising little clouds of stellar dust. They came in peace for all mankind – a commodity we seemed to need more of on our own planet. And the following month, news of Woodstock floated west.

It was the first summer I'd stayed on campus. Almost a senior, I'd finally begun a demanding series of experiments and papers in biopolymers, and I had an opportunity to do an early tutorial on ligand binding, helping out Professor Litman in the lab. I was excited to get my hands on the absorption spectroscope – but you don't want to hear about that.

One part of me didn't either. Part of me yearned to be in an old Volkswagen bus, headed for an alfalfa field in Bethel, New York, for two days in August called Woodstock. A couple of the guys from the house went – fellow rock-and-roll freaks with Commie pacifist tendencies – and they came back with tales of screaming decibels, sexual excess, and pig-wallow fun. They danced, they smoked, they drank out of strange bottles. They carried women around on their shoulders and never even asked their names, and they slept leaning up against an abandoned food tent in the rain and mud, their jackets wadded under their heads.

But my draft number was 108, and I was twenty years old. I didn't dare play hooky from real life.

I went home for a week before fall quarter started. Almost hated to, since I didn't have anything to show for the whole summer but a head full of biochemistry. I'd dated a few women, but no one I knew would meet the induction criteria into the Levine Hall of Fame, so far as my parents were concerned.

We couldn't even get through the first evening without the subject rearing its head.

'I don't suppose too many girls take classes in this biopolyester field,' my mother said brightly, pouring iced tea in my glass.

She knew it was biopolymers. She hoped to soften the inquisition with a laugh. But I didn't acknowledge her effort. 'Not many,' I said, busily rearranging my plate.

'You probably haven't had much time for socializing anyway,' she added.

'Not much.' I glanced up at my father. He smiled, rolled his eyes ever so slightly, and turned his attention to his brisket. I was on my own.

'But this next quarter will be a little easier? After all, it's your senior year – '

I laughed mirthlessly. 'That's high school, Ma. It just gets tougher and tougher. No letup just because it's my last year. If anything, now's the time I've got to prove myself even more if I'm going to get good sponsors for grad school. It's not automatic, you know, that I'll get in.'

Her face was still bland. 'So, you won't have much more time this next year than you had last year to meet new people?'

'Less.'

She took a deep swig of her tea and sighed.

As irritated as she made me, I still felt a twinge of guilt. I knew she only wanted my happiness, bottomline. It was true, I'd picked a field with few females. Didn't look like those odds would pick up in grad school, either. 'Look,' I said, 'try not to worry about it. When it's time, it'll happen.'

'You don't give it a chance to happen,' she said softly.

'I do. I went to two dances, I told you, one at that

332

Jewish sorority and the other at the B'nai B'rith. Real memorable evenings.'

'And you didn't see a single girl at either place that you liked?'

I shrugged. 'A few. I told you, I dated two of them a couple of times, but it didn't go anywhere.'

'You didn't let it – '

'Myra,' my father said quietly, 'perhaps we should save this for another time.'

'When, Daniel?' She turned to him, and I could hear sadness and silver in her voice. 'When he's twenty-five? Thirty? And still chasing after rainbows or hiding away in labs if he can't have exactly the perfect woman? Who doesn't exist anyway and wouldn't have him even he *did* come down from his ivory tower because by then, he doesn't even remember how to talk to a girl.'

'Oh, for God's sake,' I said wearily, 'you're not even rational on the subject anymore. A subject, by the way, which isn't any of your business.'

Her eyebrows rose but her voice calmed. 'Not my business? Well, excuse me. When did my son's happiness become none of my business?'

'When you decided that he had to be happy *your* way, or not at all,' I said firmly, setting down my fork. 'And if we're going to keep harping on this, I'll just go back to school. I've got too much to do to waste time being nagged about a problem that isn't a problem.' For the first time in my life, I met her gaze and didn't flinch. Dammit, I loved her and I felt sorry for her, but this was getting old.

There was a long moment of silence. My father looked the least comfortable. He kept clearing his throat, but he couldn't seem to find the words to oil the waters.

Finally, my mother said gently, 'Well, I don't want to impose myself into my son's life where I'm not wanted. I was going to offer a suggestion, but I guess I'll just let you handle it your own way.'

'Good,' I said promptly.

'I suppose you wouldn't be interested in seeing her again, anyway.'

'Probably not.' I was *not* going to take out some daughter of a cousin, some niece of a friend, some fix-up from my mother whose sole redeeming feature would be but she's such a *nice* girl.

'Of course, she's changed a lot. You probably wouldn't even recognize her.'

I closed my eyes and shook my head resignedly. This was going to keep up until I asked. 'Okay, Mother. Get it off your chest. Who is it?'

She smiled. 'Do you really want to know?'

'No,' I chuckled dryly. 'Maybe you better keep it a secret until the holidays. Give me my presents all at once. Of course, I won't be able to sleep all the rest of the year, for the anticipatory excitement – '

'Okay, Mr Wise-College-Mouth, I won't tell you. She probably wouldn't want to see you anyway.'

My father was now smiling broadly.

Now it was my turn to sigh. 'Mom. Just tell me.'

'Miriam Weld lives just a few blocks from your fraternity house. She transferred from Radcliffe this summer.'

I must admit, that one silenced me.

'Although, as I said,' she added innocently, finishing off her tea, 'I doubt she'd want to see you.'

I glanced at her sharply. 'I don't know why you'd say that.'

'Neither do I. Except that generally, when a boy stands a girl up and ruins her graduation night, he's not high on her list of heroes.' She didn't even look at me but continued to drink with casual unconcern.

Christ. She must know the whole story, I thought. Of

334

course, Miriam was the type to confide in her parents, and certainly my mother wouldn't have been too shy to ask them why we weren't seeing each other anymore – no doubt, the entire temple knew that I was perfectly capable of being a total asshole. Had known it, in fact, for the whole last four years I thought I was being so collegiate-impressive. 'Well. Why UCLA?'

She shrugged. 'Some hotshot professor she wants to work with is here. She always did want the best.'

I didn't know what else to say. 'Well, I guess you're right anyway. She probably wouldn't want to see me. Even if I did want to see her.'

'Why wouldn't you want to see her?' my father asked.

I shrugged, again trying for casual. 'Lots of muddy water between us.'

'At least there *is* water between you,' my mother said wryly. 'Better you should have a drought like everyplace else?'

My father folded his napkin and stood up. 'Well, I think this subject has just about exhausted itself,' he said amiably. 'I'm sure if David is interested, he will do what he thinks best.'

'So where exactly does she live?'

My mother stood up, too, following my father out of the dining room. 'You're right, dear,' she said to him, ignoring me. 'It's really none of our business.'

I want you to know that I thought about it for a solid week before I even tried to find her. I mean, there *was* a good chance she'd spit in my eye. There was also a good chance that she would want to see me again, but we'd get back into the same routines, and I didn't need that. On the other hand, I had to admit that I was lonely. And Miriam was always someone I could talk to easily. I guess, too, I was more than a little curious to see what she looked like after nearly four years.

I found her apartment by going to the registrar's office, read her name on the mailbox – her small, precise handwriting gave me a jar of recognition – and then sat vigil in Paul's car across the street. I knew she'd recognize the Hog of Steel, and I wanted to have the chance to abort the encounter if I changed my mind.

It was a smallish apartment complex. Nine mailboxes, a total of twenty-four names. After sitting there for two hours in the sun, it occurred to me that I might not even know her if I saw her. I was just about to give up and consider leaving a note on her door when I glimpsed a woman coming down the street toward the car, not from the apartment and not from the direction of campus.

My mother was wrong. I recognized her immediately. She had her hair shorter, but her walk gave her away: confident, determined, with that individual swing to her step that I knew the moment I saw it again. Whatever plans I had to be circumspect flew right out of my head, and I leapt out of the car, slammed the door, and hollered, 'Miriam!'

She turned and put her hand to her eyes, shading them against the sun.

I walked quickly to her, and I saw the expression on her face change from puzzlement, to dawning knowledge, to wry amusement in an instant. She waited calmly, and my steps slowed significantly the closer I got.

'Hi,' I said a little breathlessly, 'remember me?'

'David,' she said amiably with no trace of surprise, 'how nice to see you.'

'Well, I just wanted to welcome you to UCLA, see how you were. You transferred from Boston?'

She nodded. 'I'm finishing up in international relations

336

and going on to do grad work in political conflict management. There's a professor here I want to work with who's offered me a TA position. UCLA's got a good department, better than Harvard's.'

'Well. That's great.' Political conflict management! Sounded intimidating – also left me a lead-in for a joke, if I dared . . .

'You're going on to graduate school too?' She reshuffled the books in her arms as though they were heavy, leaving one hand free.

'Yup, going to try, anyway. Can't do much with a BA in biochemistry.'

She suddenly grazed my arm with her hand, and I felt it all the way down to my feet. 'That's great, David. I wish you all the best, you deserve it.' She began to turn away, adding, 'It was really good to run into you again, but I've got a ton of things to do – '

'I've been waiting for about half a day, hoping to catch you,' I said.

She turned back. 'Really? It's a hot day for that. Why didn't you just call me?'

'Well' – I hesitated – 'I wasn't sure you'd take my call. I thought if I came in person, it might go better.'

She crossed her arms over her books and smiled. 'What might go better?'

All of a sudden I felt exhausted by it all, the wait, the heat, so I slumped to the ground and sat right down on the sidewalk at her feet. 'Look, I know you might not want to ever speak to me again. I'm not expecting any miracles or anything, but when my mother told me you'd transferred, I just couldn't *not* come and see you, you know? I always cared about you, Miriam, always liked you a lot, no matter what you might think.'

She looked down at me, cocking her head. 'I know that, David,' she said gently.

'And there really hasn't been anybody in my life for almost four years. So I thought, what the hell, I'd come see you, apologize for my past lives, and maybe we could be friends again. Anyway, I thought it was worth a try.' Her face had changed very little, really. If anything, she had grown into her features more, becoming even more attractive. Still the same wide, calm brow, the same gray eyes which gazed down at mine appraisingly.

'We can be friends,' she said.

'Have you got time to go for coffee or something?'

'Not really – '

'Well, how about tomorrow? Maybe after class I could pick you up.'

'Is that your car?'

I flushed. 'No, that's my roommate's car. I'm still driving the Hog of Steel.'

She chuckled. 'But you didn't want me to recognize you before you had a chance to check me out, so you sat there incognito, just in case. You haven't changed a bit, David.'

'You have. You're more beautiful than you were in high school.'

She looked down, silent.

'How about dinner tomorrow night?'

She lifted her chin and said briskly, 'Well, actually, I'm involved with someone right now. I don't think dinner will work out for me.'

'Oh. Involved. Does that mean engaged?'

She shook her head.

'Living together?'

She smiled. 'Are you kidding? With *my* parents? Almost twenty-one, and they're still upset that I pierced my ears.' She tossed her head, and I saw the tiny pearls nestled in between the dark strands of hair.

This was going nowhere. How involved could she be,

she only just transferred? I stood up and put my hands on her shoulders. 'Then tell him you're going to see a long-lost friend for the evening. No big deal. He can surely let you loose for one night.' She didn't shrug my hands away, but neither did she lean toward me at all. I dropped my hands. 'Just one dinner. For old times' sake.'

'I would think,' she said throatily, 'that you wouldn't really want to remind me of old times.'

'I recall a lot of old times that are well worth remembering. Don't you?' At that instant I wanted to touch her more than I'd wanted anything in a long time. But I didn't, of course.

Finally, she said, 'It'll have to be an early dinner. I need to be home by ten or so.'

'How about five?'

She smiled then. 'Six. It's not even dark by five.'

'Shall I call you the night before?'

She laughed softly and turned to cross the street. 'That won't be necessary, David. We're grown-ups now.'

The next night, we sat in a private booth at one of Westwood's finest, L'Auberge, contemplating baby lamb chops and each other. Despite the shadowy glimmers of crystal, the candles, and the prices, I didn't feel so grown-up after all. She'd asked of my parents; I'd asked of hers. I drew her out about her studies; she listened to tales of lab experiments and politely laughed at my fraternity stories. By eight o'clock we had carefully avoided any subject that was too intimate or which drew us into 'remember whens', and I was getting impatient with the courtesies.

'So tell me about this guy,' I finally said over the edge of my wineglass. 'The one who holds the key to your heart and your apartment.'

She glanced at me through lowered lashes, licked the raspberry glacé off her spoon, and set the spoon down very deliberately. 'His name is Stan, and he's a grad student in Latin American studies.'

She didn't deny he had claims. 'Where'd you meet?'

'Through friends. We dated when he was at BU.'

'So you've known each other awhile? Did you follow him out here?'

She smiled. 'If you're asking if we're serious, the answer is not yet. But he's a good man, and I think a lot of him. You'd probably approve if you met him. My parents do.'

I toyed with my glass, rubbing my finger over the rim. 'Do you love him?'

She dropped her eyes. 'Like I said. Not yet.' She looked up, scowling. 'He loves me, though.'

'That's not hard to understand.'

She leaned closer to me and touched my hand briefly, then pulled away. 'Don't do this to me again, David. Say what you mean and mean what you say for once. Are we here just so you can feel better about yourself? So that my mother and your mother can let it go and so can we?'

'What do you mean?'

'I mean, you knew I was here for a week before you came to look for me, right? Your mother told my mother. So what made you finally find me?' She put her face next to mine and murmured intensely, 'What do you want? Absolution? Okay, I absolve you. Go and tell your mother and let's get on with our lives.'

A thrill of recognition went through me, as though I'd just touched her naked flesh. Talking to her was like coming home. I remembered the cadence, the rhythm of thrust-and-parry, the sharp alertness to nuance she brought to every word – and my grin was irrepressible.

'What's so funny?'

I shook my head and took her hand. She let me. 'You don't love him. That's all I'm hearing.'

340

She laughed and squeezed my fingers. 'You are such a fool, Levine. You haven't changed a bit.'

'I have. Really. Let me show you.'

'Not a chance.'

But I was still holding her hand. 'I'll tell your mother.'

'She'll applaud.'

'Like hell. They want us to be together. Maybe they know something we don't.' My grin widened. 'What have you got to lose?'

'A decent man. Possibly my standing in the department. Certainly my sanity and self-respect.'

'Next to unbridled lust, a few feathers on the scales.'

'Oh, is that what we're talking about here? Lust? Well, thanks loads, but I can get that elsewhere. And a lot cheaper too.'

With that, I couldn't bandy with her anymore, I wanted only to hold her, to win both the argument and the woman at once. I put both arms around her and pulled her to me, kissing her with a yearning and power to make the past real again and then to make it dissolve. Her lips under mine were instantly familiar and simultaneously exotic, and I was aroused in a way I hadn't felt in years, despite the fact that we were in public. She kissed me, holding nothing back, but when she pulled away she said, 'It's not going to be that easy, David.'

'I know.'

'I don't trust you anymore. I don't even know if I like you.'

'Trust me,' I said huskily, 'you like me.'

She chuckled wryly. 'Okay, I like you. But that's not enough.'

'It's a start. I'll settle for that for now.'

She was silent for a moment, and when she looked up at me again, her eyes were defiant. There would be no more kisses this night, I could tell. 'Look, you've only

341

just seen me after almost four years. I'm way past the stage when I used to think a man was the singular of amen and the answer to every maiden's prayers.'

'I didn't know you ever were in that stage.'

'I hid it better than most. We barely know each other anymore, and I'm not sure I *want* to get to know you again. I don't think you really know what you want, and I certainly don't know what *I* want. But if you think you want to continue this relationship, or whatever in God's name this is supposed to be, then here are the ground rules. I'll see you once a week for lunch and once a week for dinner. That's all I can offer for now. And I think,' she added, her tone softening, 'that under the circumstances, that's quite a bit.'

'Okay,' I said slowly, 'I guess I can live with that. For now. But I want you to know, Miriam, that there's nobody else in my life. If I'm going to get to see you only one night a week, that's the only night a week I'll be doing anything at all.'

'I know that.'

'You do? How do you know that?'

She smiled. 'If I hadn't known that, I wouldn't have agreed to go out with you at all.'

I sighed. 'Am I allowed to have the lunch and dinner in the same day?'

She laughed delightedly. 'You really *haven't* changed a bit. You'll still take a feast every time, even if it means a famine to follow.'

I lifted my wineglass. '*L'chayim*.'

She lifted hers and clinked mine gently. '*Mazel tov*, Levine.'

There were two considerations which gave me hope, despite her ground rules. First, she had definitely kissed me back. Second, she hadn't said a word about no sex.

Frankly, I'd have expected a ban on anything physical for as long as it took her to begin to trust me. My hope was that she wanted me on some level, however subterranean and repressed it might be.

Now that I look back on it, it amazes me that I gave so little thought to our reunion. The moment I saw her, it was as if the years were erased. I never paused to consider that, in fact, we'd had some problems even at our best. That somehow I'd never been able to commit to her with the passion both of us wanted. I saw her, I wanted her, and I went after her with a deliberateness that I'd never shown when it might have made a difference.

I put it down to synchronicity. If you look that up, you won't find it in Webster's, but there isn't a man or woman who doesn't know its power. That sense of being in the right place at the right time, of being ready for a certain phase in life, looking around, and picking the best person available to phase-in with. I was ready to get serious. Miriam was not only the best person available, I could argue that she was the best person, period. With my head leading my heart for the first time in my life, I decided that nothing was more important than convincing Miriam to love me back.

For several weeks I kept to her rules. I called her as often as she'd let me; I saw her each time she allowed it. Lunches and movies and dance dates were getting more like preludes to long make-out sessions, and she was beginning to turn up in my fantasies on a regular basis. We gradually eased back into familiar and comfortable patterns of conversation and silence as though we hadn't been apart for years. But one topic was never explored. She never brought up Sherry Gentry once. Neither did she ever mention my abandonment of her on our graduation night. Also, she never let me get inside her physically any further than she had emotionally, as though one invasion had to run alongside the other in tandem.

But one night I brought her back home and I sensed an immediate difference in her apartment. Usually, if she invited me in, her roommate was home, a poly sci major with a minor in awkward. She'd gangle around the living room until I'd had my coffee, making small talk about grad school politics, and no matter how energized I had been when I came in, I left feeling exhausted.

That night no one was home. I felt it the instant we walked in the door. Moreover, I knew that Miriam had expected the privacy. My nerves hummed with new alertness, and suddenly the last thing I wanted was coffee. She brought me a beer, but I barely sipped it, walking around the living room as if seeing it for the first time. I scanned the rack of albums braced by two huge polished geodes. 'Let's dance,' I said, sliding a Johnny Mathis record on her turntable, and took her into my arms.

The music was slow and warm, full of liquid yearning and romance. It was that time of night when it was easy to imagine that no world at all existed beyond the door and windows. We said nothing. After two songs we were scarcely moving at all, simply holding and swaying.

I moved my mouth to that hollow space behind her ear, kissing her, slowly trailing her neck, her cheek, to her lips, and clung there, tasting her deeply. My hands moved down to her waist, her hips, rocking her back and forth against me, and I knew she had to feel my erection.

'David,' she murmured under my mouth, 'don't move so fast.'

I slid my hands down to her buttocks, pulling her still closer, and my mouth was now on her neck, bending her back. 'So fast? We've been at this for years,' I whispered. 'You know we have.'

'I'm not the same as I was four years ago.' Her words fluttered up between us like sensuous doves.

'Who is? But some things don't change.'

She moved her hands to my chest, less to push away than to cling to me, her fingers grasping small folds of my shirt. 'What do you want?' she moaned.

'You.' I kissed her again, and the wild lathering sweetness of her mouth pulled up dark memories of old pleasures; I felt myself sinking into her as I recalled doing so many years earlier.

'What else?' Her hands had drifted down now to my waist, to my hips, pulling me as close as I was pulling her.

'That's all,' I murmured. 'That's enough, I swear.'

We eased down to the sofa, one body with four legs, and I melted to the floor, my head in her lap, her hands in my hair, my arms wrapped tightly around her hips. I lifted my head as she moved her hands to her breasts, began to unbutton her blouse. She wore a white shirt, almost like a man's, and there, in the shadows from the light in the kitchen, I thought that no black lace, no glamorous gown, could ever be as heady as that simple white linen against her skin, her dark hair. Her hands slowly pulled off her shirt, her breasts fell out of the white cloth, and I was beside her then, my fingers on her nipples, my mouth again on hers. I eased her down on her back, her legs up around me, her loose flowered skirt up over her hips, and my hand found her quickly, cupped the hot moist V of her legs, and I rubbed my palm over her, one hand yanking at my own pants.

Her hand floated down and pulled one side, and we were both free then, naked together from the waist down, her breasts spilling to the side under that white shirt, all softness under the starched edges and buttons. My hand was still moving on her, I kissed her neck, took first one, then the other nipple into my mouth and tugged gently,

345

yearning to be rougher with her, to claim her somehow. A sheen of sweat came to her skin, and our hands slid faster and easier, up my arms, my back, pressing on the back of my spine, up her breasts, roaming over her face, her hair, still moving between her thighs. Her face was flushed now, her eyes shut tightly, her mouth in a moan almost like mourning.

My mouth was moving now, out of control, kissing and tonguing and sucking her breasts, her nipples, even her underarms, her sweat, the taste of her body, and I was rubbing my cock on her belly, so close, so close, I thought I'd go crazy, but then I stopped moving and realized that I wanted something even more than I wanted to be inside her. I wanted to have her. To claim her in a way no one else had, in a way I never had loved a woman before. I wanted her open, not clenched.

I gripped her hips and slid lower, moving my head under her skirt, my mouth over that red slit, parting the hair with my tongue and lips, and slipped my tongue inside her before either of us could think about it. She moaned loudly, a distant sound that seemed almost to come from another room, so muffled was I in skirts and heat. Inside the tent I moved my hands up and down her inner thighs and drew back for an instant to discover that she was quivering, open before me and trembling, wet, waiting. She was open. Mine. Back again to her, my mouth sucking at her, a flavor of bread and salt, not nearly so foreign as I had imagined, no crow or snakes or black bats, and the heat and wet made me ache to come.

I found her hard clit with my tongue, circled it and sucked it, feeling her stiffen, her hands now on my head, her hips moving, and I wanted to be inside her, body and soul, wanted to reach deeply into her with everything I had. I was astonished, she was so open to me, I was almost frightened at her lack of resistance, as if every

346

wish I wanted had come true and gravity had suddenly turned upside down. And then she suddenly came with my mouth on her, shook and arched and quivered, crying out, 'Mygod, mygod, mygod,' and I could hold her down, hold her to earth with only my mouth. But then I could wait no longer, moved up out of her skirts, over her, and slid my cock into her, moving with her now, sinking into such a degree of wanting that we both cried out again as waves traveled up and down us both, and then the heat of that final explosion, and the heaviness, the scent of both of us, the slow loosening and melting down again as if still another layer of clothing, of flesh, had been removed.

In those moments after, I felt a tenderness, a coming-home rightness that I had never known before. Before when we made love, Miriam and I were using each other, and we knew it, it was good, and it was all I asked. Now it seemed that something was using us, coming through us, and when it lifted off us, I was left feeling not worshipful, not wary but only happy. Simply and profoundly at peace. I took one finger and smoothed the hair back behind her ear, gazing into her eyes. 'Will it last?' I asked her.

'It will last,' she whispered.

And then her hands began to move on me again, and mine on her, and I was talking to her skin once more, then to the bones beneath the flesh, and to her blood, then our bloods were racing and pulsing together until I didn't know whose flowed in which body.

I wish I could tell you that everything instantly changed with that one act of love. That Stan the Man disappeared, that all her cautiousness, our history, merged into one flowing stream of happily-ever-after. None of the above. But we did somehow ease the edges between us, and with each time together, our bodies were building bridges that our hearts hadn't yet crossed.

One pivotal event for us was my decision to go to the Stones concert at Altamont and take Miriam along. It was no small part of my decision that the first time we ever had sex, it had been after a Stones concert four years before.

They were playing at the Altamont Raceway in San Francisco that December. The Stones hadn't even toured since 1967, the year the Big Three – Dylan, the Beatles, and Jagger & Co. – had all stopped the concert circuit. Now they were back. And they were, for one night, free. We were home for the holidays, so we drove up the coast, while KABL played 'Shangri-La' on the radio.

The clouds were low, and the San Rafael bridge seemed to climb straight into the sky and disappear. We couldn't park the car close enough, so we hiked to the gates. We laid our sleeping bags down by a chain-link barrier in the yellow grass, and Miriam busied herself making a tidy area around us while I started a fire. By nightfall bonfires glowed all over the fields around the raceway and somewhere somebody kept playing 'Things We Said Today' all night.

> Someday when we're dreaming, deep in love,
> Not a lot to say, then we will remember,
> Things we said today.

Paul McCartney's voice was like a gift that night in the field, a ticket to a time machine back to when things seemed to promise to stay the same forever. We zipped together the bags and held each other all night, and I felt like primeval man protecting his mate from the wilderness beyond the fringe of our lights.

At seven A.M. the gates opened and people poured past us, around us, over us, down to the stage. In minutes we could scarcely move for the crowd. Hell's Angels, who had been hired to guard the stage, gunned their bikes through the throngs, and people couldn't even get out of their way.

For a few hours it was tolerable, and we settled down to have a good time. We couldn't sit, we were too close to the stage, but Miriam leaned back against me, and the pressure of the shoulders kept us upright.

'This is one of those things,' she said, 'that we'll be amazed we did when we look back on it.'

'I wouldn't do it for anybody but the Stones,' I grumbled wearily, edging into a space that seemed to have more breathing area. 'Sit down here, and we'll take turns.' I took off my jacket and made a pallet for her.

By eleven, temperatures were rising, and the crowd was getting restless. In the front, things were getting ugly, where, shoved together like lemmings, people couldn't even sit at all. Pills and joints were being passed around, and a contingent of assholes to one side was throwing half-full beer cans at perceived adversaries on the other side.

The guy next to me said, 'They say we're up over three hundred thousand. That's bigger than Woodstock.'

'That's bigger than Chile,' Miriam countered.

'They say,' he added, 'that we're the biggest crowd ever to congregate in California's history.'

A girl on the other side of him, with long frizzy hair and a flower painted on her forehead, said, 'If this is a congregation, then the minister's the devil.'

When Santana started playing, the crowd surged forward like flames, pushing those in front up into the stage. The Angels were pulling girls up who were smothered and screaming and dumping them off the back of the platform. I began to think this wasn't such a good idea.

But we'd come this far and stood for so long, we hated to leave.

By nightfall the Stones opened the set with 'Midnight Rambler', and the crowd was out of control. Music that once seemed sexy and playful and irreverent now had the distinct and nasty throb of menace. It was a killer sound, and Mick the Ripper was dancing above our heads. Keith Richard and Mick Taylor were turning guitar licks into hellhound wails. Angels were diving into the front of the mass, shoving and pushing people off the stage.

'We've got to get out of here!' Miriam shouted to me, her face pale and frightened.

'How?' I hollered back. It was too late to make a move to the rear, people were pushing forward irresistibly, and I had the sense that I could do nothing but swell with the force. Jagger looked smaller onstage, suddenly thin and scared. Despite his dramatic costume – he wore black pants with silver studs, a devil's cape, and an Uncle Sam hat – he kept stopping the music to plead with the crowd, 'Brothers and sisters, why are we fighting?'

The only direction to go was to the side, and I grabbed Miriam's shoulders, hooked her behind me, and began to fight my way to the fringe away from the stage. By turning sideways and shoving, I managed to make my way, dragging her along behind, foot by foot, and when the driving beat for 'Under My Thumb' revved up, people began to jiggle and move, making it easier to slip through. Finally, sweating and exhausted, we were in an area where the stage was barely visible and the crowds were thinner. There was a sudden commotion at the front of the mass, screams and a surging backward, and the music stopped abruptly. Shouts of 'What happened? What is it?' all around us, then word filtered back quickly that somebody had been stabbed.

'Oh my God,' Miriam said, 'I want *out* of here.'

I took her hand without looking back, and we struggled to the car. We wrenched open the doors, threw ourselves in, and just sat there, shivering.

The familiar smells and relative quiet of the car calmed me, and the crowds streaming past began to seem more like a television screen than real life. 'Never again,' I said quietly.

'Too much drugs, too much noise, too much violence, too much everything,' Miriam said weakly.

Helicopters were clapping overhead now, and we could clearly hear the blare of commands to the crowd to 'Disperse quietly! The concert is over!'

As we drove home we heard on the radio that an eighteen-year-old had been killed, maybe by one of the Hell's Angels, maybe just by accident in the frenzy. I began to weep and had to pull over. 'I'm so sorry I took you,' I said painfully.

She moved over and cradled my head on her breast. I was not ashamed of my weeping at that moment, but gave in to the relief and the release. Her eyes were filled with tears as well. 'My sweet, sweet man. How good that we can care. It was awful, just awful,' she murmured, 'but I'm glad I was there with you.' Her voice thickened. 'God, I feel so sad. Like my family just died or something.'

I squeezed her tightly, and we held to each other as though we were all we could depend on in a shifting, dangerous world. Something was ending, not ebbing, as was the natural order of things, but was being eaten away from the inside, like cancer.

I guess the final blow to our generation's sense of invulnerability happened in May of the next year, one month from graduation, when the news flashed over campus that National Guardsmen at Kent State had opened fire on student demonstrators. Miriam and I sat watching the television in horror as four were killed and eleven were wounded. Even after all these years I am occasionally haunted in dreams by the vision of a young woman, on one bended knee, her hands open in supplication and stark despair, while a boy bleeds to death at her feet.

'You don't even have to go to Vietnam,' Miriam said quietly. 'Just stay on campus and take a bullet at home.'

Two hundred schools erupted in rage, many of them closed down by angry riots. Kids milled around the student union, looking for a fight. Just let me out, I prayed privately. It seemed like everywhere, from Czechoslovakia to Northern Ireland to Berkeley, all you could hear was the sound of marching, charging feet.

Miriam and I graduated together in June, with little of the festive joy we deserved after four years of effort. I felt like Chet Huntley when he signed off for the last time on NBC news. 'There will be better and happier news one day, if we work at it. Good night, David.'

The sixties were over. So was my youth.

That summer, Miriam and I were inseparable. We knew that the rigors of graduate school lay ahead, and this might be the last season of relative calm in our lives. We were twenty-one, and for me the only thing that was firm and rooted and dependable in my future seemed to be Miriam. One night in August we were up in my room reading. We were lying on my bed, she with her head on my belly, me deeply into a Heinlein novel, she reading *The Sound and the Fury* for the sixth time. The California night outside was alive with birdsong and insect buzz, as if the darkness signified nothing, only a temporary slowdown in the factory of summer that hummed twenty-four hours a day. I was very aware that my parents were downstairs, but it didn't matter. We had such couple-credibility in their eyes that we could have, I think, stayed up in my room for three days, sending out for meals, and they wouldn't have knocked on the door.

'Have you decided where you want to live next quarter?' I asked drowsily. Heinlein was going off on an abstract tangent and was losing me.

'Not yet.' She turned a page, and with her free hand lazily stroked my stomach.

'I think we should consider getting a place together,' I said, closing my book. 'It'd be great.'

'Really?' She put her book down on her chest and gazed up at me.

'Absolutely.'

'Are you ready for that?'

I thought about it. We'd been together now for almost a year. Any rivals had long since slipped out of the picture, the conversation was terrific, so was the sex, there wasn't anybody else I wanted –

'It's a pretty big commitment,' she added. 'My parents would have a fit.'

'Well, so would mine.' But it suddenly seemed like the most natural thing in the world. 'Maybe we should get married instead.'

Now she hoisted herself up on one elbow and stared at me. 'You're kidding.'

I felt myself internally to see if I was injured anywhere. I'd actually said it. The 'M' word. No contusions. No hidden hemorrhages. I seemed to have survived it. 'No,' I said slowly, 'I don't think I am.'

'Really? Married, as in real life? As in forever-and-ever, standing under the marriage canopy, picking out china patterns, having-babies married?'

'Could we not say the word "baby" right now? Let me just deal with one mind-expansion at a time.' This was my last chance to back out and still keep her. My last time to consider waiting for something better. I certainly hadn't figured on getting married so soon, but suddenly it seemed the most obvious, inevitable, and comfortable idea I could imagine. I reached down and pulled her up to me so that she was on my chest. 'Do you love me?'

'I always have,' she said softly. 'I think you know that.'

'And I love you,' I said in a state of wonder. 'I think that means only one thing in our neck of the woods. We get married.'

'So this is a proposal?'

One last moment of savoring my freedom, of waving good-bye to it as it disappeared over the next horizon, just to be sure. I couldn't help remembering the only other time I'd proposed and measuring the differences in my feelings. With Sherry I'd been in a state of ecstasy; with Miriam, one of serenity. Finally, I said, smiling, 'Yes. A proposal. I believe it is.'

She scowled daintily. 'Well then, will you say it right, at least?'

I held her face close to mine. 'Will you marry me, Miriam Weld?'

'I'll have to give it some thought,' she said promptly.

'Imagine how thrilled at least two sets of parents are going to be when they hear this.'

'But that's not the reason we're doing this,' she said quickly, '*if* we do.'

I kissed her. 'We're doing this because we love each other, we want to be together, and it's time to start our lives.'

'How will we support ourselves?'

'We'll both get part-time jobs, we'll live on campus and save money that way. I've got enough saved to get us through the first two years, and then when you get your MA, you'll be able to work full-time while I go on for my doctorate. Or maybe I won't go on for my doctorate, and we'll both be done in two years. Whatever. We'll make it just fine. And we'll be together.'

'Well,' she said slowly, 'I'm still thinking about it.' She frowned soberly. 'Okay. I've thought about it.' She grinned.

'Oooh. When you smile like that, I could eat your lips.'

'Yes.'

'Yes?'

'I will marry you, David Levine.'

I whooped and hugged her, rolling her over and over on the bed. Finally, I stopped and gazed into her lovely gray eyes. 'Are we really going to do this?'

She smiled. 'We really are.'

'And we're going to live happily ever after?'

'Or a fair facsimile thereof.'

'Wow,' I said softly.

'Yes,' she murmured in my neck. 'Wow.'

Part Five

It is difficult to return to the places of one's early happiness. The young girls in the flower of their youth still laugh and chatter on the seashore, but he who watches them gradually loses his right to love them, just as those he has loved lose the power to be loved.

— Albert Camus

You know, it's funny how intense our memories are of a single segment of our lives, and how vague other long stretches can be. I recall the smallest details of my senior year in high school, yet my college years go by in a blur. I can remember the early years of my marriage more clearly, some days, than I can recall the last ten.

I know I finished grad school; I've got the degree to show for it on my office wall. But if you asked me to detail a typical day I spent at UCLA during those last few years, I couldn't even remember the name of the coffee shop I frequented most. We married (I have the pictures to prove that too) in a huge ceremony, largely orchestrated by my mother and Miriam's, and I can remember the exact feel of that glass smashing under my foot more than I can the specific details of our wedding night.

How selective our memories are, and how telling. Yet, I want to give you a portrait of our marriage, as true as I can make it, so that you'll understand the final wrenching decision I made and the impact it has made on my life. So that you'll know, too, how I ultimately saved my soul.

I have this theory that the number three is magic in our culture. It's obvious, if you think about it. The Three Faces of Eve; Three Coins in the Fountain; Wynken, Blynken, and Nod; the Red, White, and Blue; Of the People, by the People, for the People; the Three Little Pigs – I could go on and on. The number three in western culture sets up certain psychological and chemical expectations in our collective mind. If the hero's facing a dragon, he'll kill him not on the first try, not on the second, but on the third swipe of his mighty sword. If he's trying for the beautiful maiden, he'll win her heart not on the second or the fourth try, but on the third. Or he won't. Three strikes and you're out.

So I'll pick three perfect memories of the last two decades to show you, if I can, how our marriage was: the way we were.

Scene number one. It's appropriate to start with this one, because it comes first in line. We'd been married two years, both of us struggling through graduate school. I had a TA post that paid me enough to feed us; she had a part-time stint at the registrar's office that paid her enough to house us. Together, we made up what we lacked in material comfort with an abundance of love. In other words, we were already a cliché. I came home one day to find, center stage in our tiny kitchen, an old-fashioned Victorian perambulator filled with tiny stuffed animals.

'My mother's been here, right?' I said, eyeing it warily and tossing my books on the table. 'Well, I guess we can use it to carry laundry for a few years.'

'Actually,' Miriam said, coming from the stove and wiping her hands, 'I bought it myself. It was a wonderful buy, do you know how much these things normally cost? Guess.' I was struck dumb, so she went on. 'At least three hundred dollars. If you can find one. But the guy really wanted to sell it, so I got it for under half. A hundred and twenty dollars, isn't that a steal? Isn't it gorgeous?' She rocked it with one hand, wrapping her other arm around my shoulder.

I hesitantly picked up one of the stuffed toys, a small pink bear. 'And these are for if we get lonely?'

She laughed and picked up another one. 'The guy was so thrilled to get rid of the stroller, he threw these in. A pink one for a baby girl, a blue one for a baby boy.'

A chill frisson went up the back of my neck. 'But we don't have one. Of either.'

She turned and put both arms around my neck. 'Not yet, we don't.'

I slid down to a chair, feeling for it with my hand. 'Oh my God.'

She peered into my face. 'You don't sound very happy.'

'Oh my God.'

'Look,' she said gently, 'sometimes things happen in life no matter how careful we are. We can do everything right, and still things happen out of our control. You can't plan everything. You shouldn't even *try* to plan everything. The real test of character is not did you have everything under control, but when it went out of control, did you stay in.'

'Oh my God. A baby?'

'That's right.' She beamed. 'Just like you and me, only smaller.'

I sunk my head on my arms, trying to figure out how a baby was going to fit into a bedroom that didn't have enough room to change a shirt and the sheets at the same time.

'You look upset,' she said, running a hand over my hair.

'Not upset. Upside down.' And then I thought of what might happen if everything didn't turn out normal, what if she got sick, what if the *baby* got sick – 'Oh my *God*!'

She sighed. 'I wish you'd say something besides "omigod".'

I put up my hand and caught her wrist, pulling her down into my lap. 'I'm going to have a baby?'

She nodded and smiled.

'I'm going to have a baby.' Finally, I was able to smile as well.

'I know.'

'I'm going to have a baby.' I couldn't stop saying it.

She hugged me. 'So am I.'

And we did. Seven months later, Christina was born, a replica of her maternal grandmother, down to her cleft chin and worry lines. My mother brought her a full complement of the essential texts: *The Joys of Yiddish*, *A Treasury of the Midrash*, and *Cooking Kosher*, which nestled between the blue bear and the pink bear on her shelf for the next fifteen years.

She has been the only marathon miracle in our lives.

Scene number two. It's only fair to tell you that we fought. If there was one thing, you recall, that I pegged Miriam on from jump street, it was that she was a worthy adversary, even then. She certainly didn't diminish that capacity over time.

Perhaps the most memorable clash we ever survived occurred after about eight years of marriage over, of all things, a eucalyptus tree. Isn't that always the way it is? It's never over the ecology, national debt, or political positions, it's always over who drank the last of the milk, who didn't put a stamp on the mortgage payment, and eucalyptus trees.

We had moved north to San Jose so that I could take an offer from Genentech to head their biochemistry R & D efforts. It was a good promotion, and the extra money eased our climb into a strapping mortgage for a great house which we could almost afford. You know how it is: house-rich and cash-poor. Since Miriam quit her editorial job five years before to raise Christina full-time, we'd had to watch the budget. The extra cash she brought in for part-time work at home helped, but it didn't leave much extra for frivolities. So we were always cutting corners where we could.

The setup goes like this: we need the trees trimmed around the house and pool. It's Labor Day weekend. A

362

guy comes to the door with a chain saw, looking for work. He looks eager and energetic, he'll work cheap, so I hire him for a day's cutting and clearing.

First of many mistakes. You see, hiring and overseeing of labor is her job. She always takes the bids, juggles the schedules, supervises those improvements that are part of the joys of home ownership. Therefore, by telling this guy he could do the work, I'd pissed in her corner of the yard. Also, I didn't follow her usual procedure of checking references, taking bids for any job over a few hundred bucks, and arranging a time when she could be there to oversee the job. I hired him, then I said we were going out for the day. She said this was *not* the way to do these things, and I told her she made too big a deal out of small details. We drove off with her upper lip already stiff.

We came back at the end of the afternoon to find the driveway so full of limbs and debris that we couldn't pull the car in. She hopped out and ran around to the corner of the house to see how the worker was doing, and I could hear her shriek all the way out to the curb.

The guy had cut down a thirty-foot eucalyptus tree, the only shade and privacy on the east side of the house, the single set of branches, which shielded the pool from street-eyes, right down to the ground. As well as two full-bearing peach trees which, he had decided, looked a little straggly. Clearly a matter of bad communication.

Well, Miriam communicated with him at the level of planets colliding for about ten minutes until, out of sympathy for the cringing moron (and with an eye to the chain saw he still held in his hands), I dragged her off of him. Then she turned on me.

'I begged you to get references, to at *least* hang around and watch the guy, but you wouldn't listen! You had to do it your way, as usual, you had to take charge of something you know absolutely *nothing* about, of all the

363

stupid, senseless wastes of perfectly good trees! We're going to sue that idiot! Sue his ass! Go out there and tell him he better figure out how he's going to replace a fifty-year-old eucalyptus and two peach trees by the end of the weekend, or I'll kill him! *And* you! I can't *believe* you did this!'

It went downhill from there. When the man heard her screaming about lawsuits and homicide, he packed his chain saw and left, leaving the debris where it fell. We couldn't even walk through the driveway, much less liberate the other car – and this, on the first day of a three-day weekend. His flight moved me from humility to anger, since if she hadn't screeched at him like a harpy, we might have been able to work out a deal.

'Work out a deal! That's how this whole damn mess got started! You *had* to work out a deal! That's what this whole thing is about – ego! It's *always* ego with you. Like the day you were born, you heard this secret voice whispering, "You are one of the chosen, you are one of the chosen," and you've taken it as the law of the land ever since! Your goddamned mother ruined you for real life!'

'That's funny. You sound just like *yours* right now, Miriam. Same understanding and nurturing support. Same honeyed disposition.'

'*Schmuck!*'

'*BITCH!*'

After an hour of shouting back and forth, I finally took the car keys off the dresser and said, 'One more word, Miriam. One more, and I'm out of here, I swear to God.'

Her eyes almost popped out of her head with the effort to muzzle her mouth, and she rushed at me, wrestling with me, half hitting, half grabbing at me in fury and frustration, sobbing and flinging us both on the bed.

Something snapped then, and we both began to weep, holding each other.

'I'm sorry,' I said when I could.

'I'm an asshole,' she said as her breathing calmed. 'What will we do?'

'I'll take care of it,' I said.

To her credit, she didn't speak the words that surely must have been hovering on her lips. It took me all of two days, but I finally got a guy to come with a truck and clear away all the debris off the yard, the pool decking, and the driveway. A few days later we planted saplings where once-tall monarchs stood. And we've talked about that worst of all wars many times since.

'I think it was really over power,' she said.

'That, and control,' I agreed.

'It frightened me,' she whispered, 'to see how angry we could get with each other over something like that.'

'Me too.'

'How close to throwing it all away.'

'I had the keys in my hand.'

'You almost hit me that day, didn't you?'

'You *did* hit me. I had the bruises on my arms for a week.'

'We have to promise ourselves we won't let things get out of control like that again,' she said.

'You're right,' I replied. But we both knew that wondering if we'd fight again was like wondering if gravity would work tomorrow morning. We were married; we fought. It was one of life's corollaries. But we did try, after that one, to be a little more gentle with each other. At least for a while.

Scene number three. You know, this is tough? To select out of the thousands of moments, three singular dramas that somehow tell an entire story? But I've thought of one. Subtle but telling. It was the day my daughter became a woman. She was only twelve and a half, a colty, angular girl with her mother's black hair, frizzed out and uncontrolled as her laugh. On a perfectly normal day, with no warning, she started her menses. To my great surprise, Miriam found this the one climacteric in Christina's life that she couldn't handle.

'Go and talk to her, David,' she said, coming at me when I walked in the door that evening. 'She needs you to tell her what to do.'

'What do you mean? Haven't you already talked to her?'

'Well, of course' – she gestured impatiently – 'I've already shown her what to do with the mechanics and all, but you need to tell her about sex.'

'Me? You mean she doesn't already know?'

'How should she know?'

'Well, I just assumed you'd told her – '

'This should come from her father.'

'It should?'

'Absolutely. Not from me, not from her girlfriends, not from books, but from her father.'

I set down my briefcase and loosened my tie. It was a warm June evening, the pool beckoned, and I wanted a beer and a swim, not a long conversation with my daughter about penises and herpes. 'Christ,' I said wearily, 'I thought mothers were supposed to do this gig.'

'That's old-fashioned,' she said, hanging up my coat. 'The current research shows that daughters who hear about sex from their fathers are more apt to have good attitudes about men and to trust them in later life.' She handed me my swim trunks and leaned against the closet door, watching me change. 'Mothers are more apt to pass along their own prejudices and poison their daughters' minds. What are you going to say?'

'That birds do it, bees do it, even educated fleas do it.'

She grinned. 'You'll be great. I can't wait to hear all about it.' She kissed me in passing. 'She's out by the pool, waiting. I told her you'd be having a father-to-daughter talk with her, and she's all excited.'

I groaned. 'You mean she can go in the pool?'

She snorted. 'You *are* out of it, aren't you? Of course she can, girls can do anything they want these days. And for your further edification, Victoria's no longer on the throne of England, either.' She patted my arm. 'Try to be hip, dear,' and walked out, leaving me to face the sliding glass doors to the pool all alone.

I put on an eager-salesman's smile and strode manfully out to the pair of chaises longues that Christina had arranged by the shallow end.

'Hi, Dad,' she beamed brightly. 'Did you hear the news? I'm official jailbait now.'

My face fell slightly. My lovely daughter, long-limbed, sharp little narrow shoulders, barely mounded chest, carrying the wide-brow and strong-jaw badges of every Levine woman since the leaving of Egypt, was sitting there speaking of carnal and illicit advances as if she'd just told me she got a new pair of Reeboks. But I could tell she was nervous. She kept her thighs together as though she were trying to hide a loaf of Wonder bread in there.

'Yes, I heard,' I said gently. 'Congratulations. How do you feel?'

'A little achy, but okay, I guess. Mom says all the women in our family have backaches.' She grinned. 'Mine's killing me right now.'

'Well, you pay a price for everything in life,' I said, bemused. 'They've got pills for that now, right?'

'Right. They've got pills for *everything*.'

Ahem. Right on target. 'So. It's a special day. You think you might want to be bas mitzvahed? If you were a boy, we'd be doing it.'

She wrinkled her nose. 'I don't think so, Dad. I mean, it's not like I have to wear a sign or something.'

'No, that's true. In the days of child marriages, it mattered, but I guess we can forgo that particular custom. How about a present? Just to sort of mark the occasion?'

'Well,' she smiled slowly, 'I guess that would be okay.'

'What would you like?'

The answer was swift and sure. 'My own phone.'

'You mean, your own extension?' I teased.

'*No*, Dad, my own *line*. So I won't tie up yours all the time.'

'To talk to boys.'

The smile widened. 'And other people too.'

I shook my head in mock dismay. 'Teeny, Teeny, Teeny. Boys? Haven't you heard how much trouble they can be?'

'A little,' she said shyly.

'More than a little. Do you have any questions about them? Boys, I mean?'

It was as if she mentally reached into her jeans pocket and pulled out a list she'd been carrying around for a year. Methodically, she ticked off, one after the other, queries about the masculine sex, and as she spoke I could tell she knew all she needed to about the actual biology of the species: it was the emotional makeup of the male that confounded her, and I could suddenly understand why her mother was so eager to hear the outcome of this little heart-to-heart.

Why, she asked, are they so stupid about perfectly obvious things like manners and priorities and the simple basics of adult conversation? Why do they never talk to you when their buddies are hanging around? Why do they act silly and flail around on the dance floor? And why, oh why, do they never tell you what they're feeling even if they're about to burst with it?

368

I answered her questions as best I could, posed a few of my own, and in no time I could tell that my daughter had been quietly having her own triumphs and heart-breaks in what passed for love at twelve. I ached for her – and for all the future triumphs and heartbreaks ahead. In a spontaneous gesture I reached out and hugged her, but the sudden touching of all that unclothed skin made her slide away from me, embarrassed.

That, I thought, is the major difference now. When she was ten, I could cuddle her to me with only swimsuits between us, and she scarcely noticed. Now the flesh, however familiar, is a fence between us, because it is now and forevermore, Male and Female, as well as Daddy and Daughter. My sadness lent a gentle benediction to my tone, and I said, 'Honey, it will all be clearer to you as you get older. But some things will never be easy to understand. And maybe that's the way it should be. You wouldn't want your best friend to also be your husband.'

'Why not?'

'Because it would take away some of the magic. Some of the passion.'

'Yeah, but it would make it so much easier to talk. To do things together. Everybody would get along so much better.'

'Sure, he'd be familiar as an old shoe. He'd never pinch your foot and you could walk for miles together, but it wouldn't be very exciting to put him on each day.'

'I don't get it.' She frowned. 'Who wants exciting in a shoe?'

I shook my head. 'I guess I'm not explaining it very well. But believe me, someday you'll fall in love and then you'll understand. You'll be with a man whose very differences are exciting, a challenge, and you'll come together in a way that seems to you to be the most beautiful, most powerful thing you've ever known. Then you'll grow together and build a life together and get closer, but you'll always remember that you are not the same, but different. And from that difference comes the magic. You won't be best pals, but you will be mates. And each time he touches you, you'll know the difference.' I was so intent on what I was saying, on hearing my own words, that I didn't notice when the tears first started inching down my daughter's cheeks.

'Teeny,' I said, touching her hand, 'why are you crying?'

'Oh, Daddy,' she whispered, squeezing my fingers as she did when she was little, 'you make it sound so beautiful.'

This time when I hugged her, she didn't flinch. 'It is, honey. And you should wait until you feel like that. Because you deserve it to be that beautiful. You'll have a lot of opportunities to settle for second-best in your life, but you should never settle for second-best in love.' I tilted her face up to mine and kissed her cheek. 'Okay?'

She nodded and wiped her palm across her wet nose, the gesture of a child.

'Any more questions?'

'You mean about intercourse and condoms and all that stuff?'

I inwardly flinched to even hear the words from her lips. The miracles of modern education. 'Yup,' I managed. 'All that stuff.'

She smiled quaveringly and shook her head. 'I know all that.'

'Okay,' I said softly, 'but if the time ever comes when you *don't* know all that. Or anything else you wonder about, will you do me the great honor and privilege of letting me be first in line?'

'To what?'

'To give you my opinion. That's all I've got, you know,'

I added. 'Just a lot of opinions to give you. But if I don't get to unload them on you, I'll get old and cranky before my time. So will you give me a break and let me bore you?'

She wrapped her arms around my neck. 'You're the best bore I know,' she said. 'And, Dad?'

'I'm still here.'

'Could you not call me Teeny anymore?'

The sadness suffused into a small balloon of pride so that I could no longer tell whether I would laugh or cry. 'What then?'

'Teena. With two Es. Okay?'

I looked at her closely and saw that, in fact, she was my Teeny no longer. When had it happened? How did it come to be that I could no longer hold her two hands in one of mine?

I kissed her other cheek. 'I christen thee Teena forevermore.'

'Well,' she smiled, 'just this year. Till I see if I like it.' Then she scampered off, her hips swishing just slightly in a new rhythm.

God, what a wonder. That was the day I knew that she might have her grandmother's jaw, but she was every inch her mother's daughter.

In short, our marriage was solid. Our high expectations, our hopes, whatever passion we once shared, were all scaled down after a decade and a half of living together, of course, compromised or given up in the day-to-day juggles of who would do the dishes and who would change the baby. What was left was much less than what seemed so possible when we began but much more than so many other couples seemed to have.

I still couldn't keep my eye from darting to strange women on the street, though I'd learned an incredible finesse of camouflage. The old predation was impossible to repress. Women in cars, on the street, in shops and offices: seconds from my day which amounted to years of fantasy. I look, she looks, an electric current surges around us, she passes on. So simple. But I run the movies of those seconds over and over, blowing up the film until her gesture is clear, her smile piercing and private, and it never loosens its grip. I saw faces daily that could launch a thousand ships apiece, and I was constantly racked by expeditions to Troy I did not, could not, make.

It's the old conundrum. If we don't want it, we can have it, like the air we breathe, married love. But passion – that yearning – if we desire it deeply, we never find it. It's an ancient whip, a biological trick. In my DNA there's a gene for hunting, for predation so endless and insatiable that it sends me careening after female phantoms, twisting my head to follow the click of high heels, the sway of the skirt and the fluid roll of hips, the sweep of blond hair, the eyes that beckon and betray.

One day I'll plow into the car ahead of me for turning to stare at a passing figment, and the final dying image on my snuffed retina will be, fittingly, the one that has haunted me all my life.

Not that married love isn't good, of course. But it's a lie to say it's all. It isn't and can't ever be transcendent passion. When a man owns the key to what once was a secret mansion, when he walks the same halls each day, sits in the same chair, looks out the windows and sees the same views, it's his daily bread. Security and affection and a 'good relationship'. Which is very good indeed, may even be the best he could hope for, but it's not passion. It's not mystery. He knows it, and no matter how comfortable the mansion, he feels its walls. He feels a loss because he's not nearly so wise or strong as he pretends. And so sometimes he can scarcely bear his normal, fortunate life, and he drives himself into a frenzy of quiet longing.

In his state of longing it often feels that God has turned

away from him. Not that He has died, but that He's no longer interested. He is too busy to care about the personal destiny of a man who has wasted his finest potential on yearning, fantasies, and dreams.

It was an omen, I think, that the invitation to our twentieth high-school reunion arrived on the day of our fifteenth wedding anniversary. I found it in a stack of mail that Miriam dropped on my desk as she whisked past with the laundry basket. 'You better hurry if we're going to make that reservation,' she said. 'I don't think they hold it past fifteen minutes.'

We were driving to Tahoe for the weekend, booked into Caesars, and holding a much-coveted reservation for a corner booth at the Lakefront, out favorite special-occasion restaurant.

'Hey!' I called out as I passed her on the way to the shower. 'Did you see that our reunion is coming up?'

'What reunion?'

'Taft's, of course.' I stopped and added, 'This one, I really want to make.'

She followed me into the bathroom, holding folded towels. 'Why? You didn't care about the tenth.'

'I did so, *you* were the one who didn't want to go.'

'I would have gone if you'd pushed it. I wasn't particularly thrilled at the prospect of spending an evening with people I wouldn't recognize if I met them on the street, most of whom I didn't like that much when I knew them at their best, no, but if *you* had wanted to go, I would have.' She was hanging up towels so that the labels were to the wall, something I always neglected to do exactly the way she wanted them done.

'Well, I really want to go to this one.'

'Why?'

'Because this one really matters, don't you see? Every-

373

body's finally grown-up. There's not that much difference between eighteen and twenty-eight – '

'You thought there was at the time!'

'Yeah, but not compared with eighteen and thirty-eight. It should be really interesting.' I reached out and yanked off one of her towels. 'Besides,' I grinned, 'I've got a BMW now. So I can go and hold my head up.'

'Oh, for God's sake,' she said, rolling her eyes. 'Is that what this is all about? Who's got the most toys?'

'You don't have to go if you don't want to. I can fly down, do a little business in the LA office, catch the reunion, and be back by Sunday brunch.'

I thought she'd rally a magnificent defense at that suggestion, but instead she just shrugged. 'That's fine with me. I'm not excited about it. You can go and tell me what everybody looked like.'

I pulled the towel down from my face. 'Really? You don't want to come?'

'It seems pretty irrelevant. Like trying to recapture the past.'

'And you don't mind if I go alone?'

She hesitated. 'Will you promise to miss me?'

'I'll take pictures of you and Christina and bore everyone to tears.' I wrapped the towel around my waist and drew her to me. 'Why don't you want to go? Really.'

She frowned. 'Because it'll make me crazy. I'll have to go on a diet, go shopping for some amazing dress, have my hair done, have fake nails put on, the works. If I'm going, I have to do it right.' She nuzzled up to my neck. 'Frankly, my dear, I don't give a damn.'

'Okay, then. What'll I tell people?'

'Tell them I'm climbing Annapurna. When the invitation came, I was at twenty-thousand feet, building an ice cave, and couldn't be reached for comment.' She suddenly dropped her arms and withdrew.

'What?'

'Nothing. Except do be sure to take a picture of me that shows my best side.'

Sherry Gentry. That was the one name she wouldn't mention, the only reason she'd have said that. I embraced her again. 'You don't have a bad side,' I murmured into her hair.

'Neither do you,' she said firmly. 'Just be sure you remember that.'

Since I knew I'd be asked, I thought about my answer on the flight down south. What was I doing these days? I could sum up my career in a sentence or two: Director of Research and Development in biochemistry for a major biotech company in Silicon Valley. Sounded intense. My marriage: married for fifteen years (yes, fifteen years, same woman!), content, one perfect woman-child.

Content. Did that catch the gist of it? Yes, I thought, almost with a tinge of regret, it did. No great passion, no drama, no flights to the moon on gossamer wings, but we got along well. Knew each other's curves and curve balls.

And my family? Foote and Critter might ask. Folks doing well, settled into old age comfortably, no major aches or pains. Avrom was set. Graduated from UCLA, snagged a berth with a good accounting firm, married to a beauty from Brentwood. Good Jewish girls for both of us, our parents were serene.

The memories from that senior year flooded back to me, high over the California coastline. Was it possible that the finest, free-est time of my life was in high school? Only in that one year did everything seem not just possible, but likely.

So much had washed out to sea since then. Last time I went back to the Valley, I took Teena to Griffith Park, only to discover there weren't any more pony rides. I drove by the old Bob's Big Boy drive-in, but it had evolved into a car wash. Up in San Francisco, where I'd found the Summer of Love with kids in orange robes and ankle bells, shaved heads shouting 'Have a really good day!' it was all business suits and briefcases today. Free Huey, Shambala, brown rice, and bare feet. Stepping over smoke bombs on the way to the People's Park in Berkeley. Hey, Jude. Blown away on the wind. The memories made me feel cold.

But through the window of the plane I could feel the rich warm sunlight of approaching Southern California, and I missed it at that moment like a drug.

I went right from the plane to my parents' home, where my mother was serving Shabbes supper. Like every Friday night I can remember, she put out the same plates of *kreplach*, brisket, and chicken, the same goblet of wine. I realized that my love of dreaming was born from my father, but from my mother I got my high sense of order, my need for the folded napkin, the pressed pant leg, the ironed hour, and the tucked-in afternoon. Now, like a haunting melody in a minor key, my father sang the same Shabbes song to his wife.

> Strength and honor are her clothing . . .
> She opened her mouth with wisdom . . .
> Her children arise up and call her blessed,
> Her husband also, and he praiseth her . . .

And I sat and watched the dust motes in the dining room turning orange in the dimming afternoon light, shared laughs with them over Christina's latest adolescent dramas, and filled my mouth with memory.

After dinner I picked up the Valley phone book and began to find numbers. First call had to be to Jim Foote's old house. To my delight, he answered the phone, and I was instantly seventeen again.

'Hey, I'm glad you called!' he said. 'I didn't particularly want to go to this gig alone.'

'What about your wife?'

'She split. We got divorced three years ago. Has Miriam kicked you out?'

'Not yet. But she wasn't keen to come, so I'm batching it.'

'Just like old times.'

'Not quite!' I could picture the guy sprawled across his corduroy bedspread. Wondered if he still had the Taft football pennants on the walls.

We exchanged the usual catch-up conversation, both of us apologizing for not keeping in touch for a decade. Then he said, 'So great, we'll go together. Can you borrow your dad's car?'

'Some things never change. You never *did* drive when we doubled. If we had any class at all, we'd rent a limo.'

'If we had any class at all, we probably wouldn't *go*.'

'Hell, I wouldn't miss it,' I chuckled. 'I want to see how many of those ex-jocks are going bald.'

'Hey.'

'Don't tell me.'

Jim sighed. 'It's so humiliating. I've got more hair on my ass these days than on my head. But they say premature hair loss is a sign of virility.'

'We'll have that printed up on small engraved cards, and you can pass them out at the door.'

'Eat me, Levine.'

'Just like old times.'

The gym was gaily decorated with ribbons and balloons, a table was laden with punch and food, and a bar set up in the back corner. A huge sign was draped across the stage: WELCOME BACK CLASS OF 1966! We signed in at the table up front, collected a badge with our name and graduation photo on it, and got our picture taken for the scrapbook. Women were leaping into one another's arms, shrieking and jumping up and down, while husbands stood back, looking bemused. Guys were huddled in tight clumps, shaking hands and pounding on one another's backs, and the minute Jim and I walked in the door, Watts spied us.

'Hey!' he hollered, rushing toward us. 'I knew you guys'd make it. And together, no less, without women, just like the old days.'

I hardly recognized Watts. He had a bigger belly, his face was sort of florid, and he'd grown a mustache that handled down toward his chin. 'Pancho Villa, I presume?' I said, shaking his hand. 'You look like shit, man. I'm amazed you had the balls to show up.'

Watts guffawed and pounded us both happily. 'Yeah, I've been putting it away this spring. Hurt my leg skiing at Tahoe and couldn't work out for a few months. But I'll be back on track by summer. You two look dippy as ever. Where are your wives?'

'Mine's rafting the Amazon,' I said. 'Took our daughter on a pleasure cruise.'

'Mine's dead,' Jim said calmly.

'No shit!' Watts said, suddenly hushed. 'Christ, I'm really sorry, man.'

Jim laughed and clapped him on the shoulder. 'I'm just kidding, fool. We're divorced. I'm on the prowl.'

'Well, great,' Watts said, relieved. 'So am I, like always. Never could find one that was worth giving up all the others for. And there's a right-smart mess of 'em here tonight to choose from.' He stopped abruptly. 'Is your wife dead too, Levine?'

'Miriam's fine. So's Christina, our daughter. Remind me to plague you with pictures later.'

'How old is she now?'

'Fourteen.'

'Oh, God,' Watts moaned, 'it's not possible we're that old!' He peered at us both closely. 'You two don't look

378

different. Still geeks. But I guess by now you're at least getting laid. I think you were the last of us, weren't you, Levine? Even Critter got his first.'

'Is Critter here?' Jim asked quickly, looking around. 'This is going to be great.'

Watts steered us over to one side of the room, through a hundred people who stopped us, stared at our faces, at our name tags, and screamed our names. It made for slow going across the floor, but we finally reached a sandy-haired bespectacled guy next to a little plump wren in pink taffeta.

'Critter?' I said, reaching out to shake his hand. 'Man, you don't look a day over thirty-seven.'

'Levine! Foote! Hey, you guys, I want you to meet my wife, Melanie. We've been married for seventeen years now, right out of college. Mel, show them the pictures.'

Melanie's arms bulged when she moved, like a boa constrictor eating rabbits. She smiled indulgently at Critter and pulled a folder of photos out of her huge black purse, handing them over. I examined them politely, then handed them over to Jim.

'Two boys and two girls, do you believe it?' Critter laughed. 'We were going for a full team of something, weren't we, honey? She just kept pumping them out!' He grinned and wrapped his arm around pink Melanie.

We started to circulate around the room and somewhere I lost Jim while I was talking to a few of the guys from the wrestling team. About an hour into the evening there was a slight ripple, a new rhythm in the noise closest to the door, and I looked around, figuring it was the band coming in.

Sherry Gentry walked into the room all alone, and my heart turned like a gaffed fish in my chest. She was immediately surrounded, and I could barely see her through the people, but I heard girls squealing to one another in her direction, and the excitement waved over me.

I was talking to somebody's wife. 'Who's that?' she asked.

'Ex-May Queen,' her husband walked up and said. 'I'm surprised she's alone.'

'The infamous Sherry Gentry I've heard so much about?'

The guy all but blushed.

'Well, she probably came by herself so that she wouldn't feel tied down all night,' his wife went on. Laughing wryly, she added, 'Any bets she'll go home alone?'

I excused myself and moved closer, then stood aside and watched her for a moment. From a distance she looked exactly the same. The identical white-blond hair, still long and cascading over her shoulders, curlier at the ends, but no real difference there. Still looked tanned, slender, and full of life, her eyes moving everywhere at once, her hands gesturing as she spoke. She moved from person to person fluidly, touching this one on the arm, that one on the cheek. Some of the men she touched on the chest, leaning into them in a more intimate manner. That's why she got Class Flirt, I thought swiftly, and she doesn't even know she does it. She just likes to touch people.

The band was beginning to set up now, and people were already crowding around the stage, asking for songs from the sixties. I moved a little closer. She was wearing a white dress with gold sequins sprinkled over the shoulders and hips. Almost like a bride, she eased through the crowd, still the center of attention in every group. Everyone made a point to speak to her, as though their own evening wouldn't be complete without making contact.

I felt pride warm me. She was mine, once. In more

ways than one. Perhaps more mine than she was for any other man in this room. Because we were friends as well as lovers.

The bands began the quick pulse of 'California Girls', and even though the Beach Boys' harmonies were missing, couples surged out to dance, singing along as though it were a personal anthem. I walked over to Sherry and stood just behind her, tapping her lightly on the shoulder.

She turned and gasped, 'David Levine!' and threw herself into my arms.

That staggered me. I realized that I had rehearsed about a dozen different opening lines, but I hadn't imagined she would make all of them unnecessary. I held her tightly. She even smelled the same.

She pulled back her head and gazed up at me, smiling. 'You don't look a bit different. Your glasses are gone!'

'Contacts.'

'Well, I'd have recognized you anywhere.'

'You look different, I think.'

'I do?'

'Yes' – I pretended to inspect her hair and face carefully – 'right around here, maybe,' I added, tracing a light finger down her jaw. 'You're more beautiful there than you used to be.'

She beamed. 'Oh, you. Blind as ever.'

I could see over her shoulder that about a dozen people were swarming toward us, and I took her arm. 'Want to dance?' I called, leading her out to the floor.

'Do you still dip?' she asked, falling quickly into the old rhythms.

I twirled her once toward me and then away. 'Yeah, I've kept up my license. Didn't want to get busted for expired dips.'

Corny, but she laughed. The same tinkling laugh that always made me think of backyard pools and wind chimes.

We danced song after song together, and I relinquished her only when she pulled away, insisting that she had to go see someone she just recognized. But she kept coming back to me, as though it was understood that we were together.

Up close I could see that the years had changed her, of course. She was still beautiful; in some ways, even more lovely than before. Her face was a little looser, a bit more blurred around the edges. She'd lost her juicy-fruit look, and her voice was a little lower, but she still had that incredible animation and fever to her. Still the most desirable woman in the room.

Once, when she walked away, I was standing with a drink in my hand when a woman came to me, took the drink away and set it down on a table.

'David Levine. Do you remember me?'

I peered at her badge. 'Linda. Linda Markover. Right! I remember you. Homeroom, right?'

She smiled. 'Right. Want to dance?'

I really didn't want to give up my post, but she looked so hopeful, I couldn't say no. 'Why not,' I said, taking her into my arms.

'You look like Mr Successful,' Linda said softly.

'Do I?' I asked, surprised. 'I thought I looked like Mr Working-at-It.'

'Never,' she said gently. 'David Levine never had to work at it, as I recall.'

'Your memory dims.'

'Not a bit, I remember everything. Don't you?' She looked at me intently for an instant, then away. 'I remember you in homeroom, that's for sure. I can't believe how it all comes flooding back.'

She was a nice woman, plain but sturdy in my arms. Not wearing a wedding ring, either. 'I remember you too,' I said.

382

'What do you remember about me?'

I twirled her once, slowly. 'That you were a good dancer.'

'I could never keep up with you,' she replied, her eyes down. 'Though I tried to.'

'Well, you're doing great now, Linda,' I said.

After a moment's pause she asked, 'Has your life been everything you want? I picture you often, and when I do, you're always happy.'

I finally turned my attention completely to her and realized what she'd been saying. 'Nobody's life is exactly what they want,' I said hesitantly, 'but I guess mine is about what I deserve.'

'You deserve the best.' She gripped my arm a little tighter; I would have bet she didn't realize how tightly. 'But then, I guess you know that I always thought you were pretty special.'

'No, actually, I didn't know that.'

'I did, David.' She met my eyes unflinchingly. 'I swore that if I didn't do another thing tonight, I'd finally tell you that. I've been in love with you forever.'

I didn't know what to say. And when I did finally find a word, she shushed me.

'You don't have to say a thing. I know you're married, have a family, settled down and content. But I didn't want another year to go by without you knowing that I loved you.' She laughed weakly. 'Still do, I guess. Isn't that ridiculous, to carry a crush for twenty years?'

'No,' I said, moved by her courage, 'not ridiculous at all. But why didn't you tell me back then?'

'Are you kidding? Just waltz up to a guy and tell him you love him? Did that sort of thing happen to you very often?'

'Not once.'

'I imagine not. I could no more have told you how I

felt than I could have stopped feeling it. But anyway, I've told you now.' She laughed again, shaking her head as if warding off a blow.

'Well,' I said, 'I'm really glad you told me.'

'You are?'

The dance was ending, and I felt inexplicably sad. 'Yes, I really am. I hope you love a lot of other people, too, in your life. And I hope that you get to tell them about it a little sooner than you told me.'

She stopped moving, one hand still on my shoulder. 'Would it have made a difference?' she asked intensely.

I knew what she wanted me to say. But it wouldn't have been true. Or fair. 'Maybe,' I said softly, the best I could do. 'Maybe it would have. I know for sure it would have made a difference to you.'

'Well,' she smiled sadly, 'thanks for listening, anyway.'

'Hey. You made my evening.' I leaned down and kissed her on the cheek, startled and alarmed to see tears well in her eyes.

'That seems only fair,' she said ruefully, 'since you made my last twenty years.' And with that she walked away.

I picked up my drink again and retreated to a quieter corner. This was, I realized, exactly the sort of revelation I had looked for when I decided to come. I wondered how many guys were confessing long-held lusts for somebody else's wife; which women were maneuvering to whisper long-dead fantasies for somebody else's husband. Opportunities long gone, but alive for one night.

Sometimes, and this was one of those times, I had the appalling suspicion that our lives were nothing more meaningful than a series of alliances that we got into for a time, maybe just because we wanted the same things temporarily, and then abandoned them and each other. Without hostility, if we could manage it. Without dirtying the sheets and emptying the bank accounts. But few did manage so cleanly. Women thought that so long as you could talk about a relationship, it couldn't get into trouble. Men thought if you had to talk about a relationship, it already was *in* trouble.

It all seemed so wearisome at that moment. Learning to balance the space and the freedoms that you had to allow so as not to kill off the attraction in the first place, training each other past the frantic demands for proof and declarations of fidelity, sensing the waxing and waning of passion, the heaving, shifting, settling in, the endless dreary discussions and dissection, and then you come to a night when a total stranger says she's loved you forever. And wonders if you're happy, or if you'd like to dump it all and walk away into a new sunset.

Love was such an exercise in tidal patience. And here's someone who's been beached for years, still watching for that rescue ship on the horizon.

Then, Sherry found me in my corner, just as the band started 'I Heard It Through the Grapevine'.

'Come on!' she laughed, pulling me onto the floor. 'You can't sit this one out.'

And so the evening went by in a swirl of color and noise and giddy discoveries. I felt completely comfortable with Sherry, as though the years had never happened. We didn't talk much of the past, only the present. She told me she'd married once, but it didn't work out, no kids, no rancor. She was doing well in real estate, had her own beach house in Trancas, still saw some of the old crowd, traveled a lot, and never had gone back to school, except for some night classes.

'So give me some solid real estate advice,' I said. 'What's your theory for making the first million?'

'Remember it's all a game,' she grinned, 'and don't finance your dreams with a variable rate mortgage.' She swept her hair back from her neck as though to feel a breeze. 'My folks split up, did you know that?' she added. 'My mother finally pulled out, after threatening to do it for about a hundred years. She's still living in the house; Dad's moved to Westwood. Kim's got three kids!'

'Are you two still close?'

'Not as much as before, but we talk on the phone often. She's been after me to settle down, and I think I'm finally ready.'

'Really?'

'Well, after one bad marriage, it takes a while. I was in analysis for about a year. Also, I did Est. Did you?'

'No, I never quite got into that.'

She laughed. 'I can still read you like a book, David. You're thinking "California flake", right?'

'No, no, not at all. In fact, I plan to get Rolfed as soon as I leave here.'

'Great,' she said, smiling benignly, 'it'll do you a world of good.'

I stopped dancing suddenly and kissed her full on the mouth, holding it as long as I dared. A few couples around us began to clap and cheer. Finally, she feigned collapse in my arms, blushing and laughing.

'Actually,' I said, '*that* did me a world of good.'

She went back into my arms, but only for a moment. 'Let's get some air,' she said, leading me out the door to the old lunchroom quad. We wandered out in the night and found a bench on the senior lawn.

'This is so fantastic,' she said softly. 'I knew it would be.'

'Were you looking forward to it?'

'For months. I knew you'd be here.' She smiled at me in the darkness. 'David Levine never missed a Taft dance yet. I'm really glad you didn't bring Miriam.'

A quick stab of guilt. I was glad too.

'I've actually been dreaming about it for weeks,' she went on, 'but then, I dream about high school fairly regularly.'

'Really? I don't think of it much.'

'I do. I dream about this guy I used to see between classes, John Cassidy, do you remember him? He's not here tonight, but I didn't think he would be. He was sort of cute, but I didn't date him. About three years ago I started dreaming of him all the time. I finally called him up, and do you know what he said? That he was fat, that he sold insurance for a living, and that he never got married. I couldn't believe it, I mean, he used to be a jock. Used to surf. He told me he never even goes to the beach anymore.'

'Neither do I.'

'Really? You don't surf at all?'

I was surprised she was surprised. 'Nope. Not for years. I can't seem to squeeze it on my Day-Timer.'

'Well, at least you're in great shape, still. You don't look much past thirty, I swear.' She touched my temple gently. 'That little bit of gray just makes you look more dangerous.'

'Did you tell this guy you'd been dreaming about him?'

She nodded. 'And he told me that now that I know the truth, I wouldn't dream about him anymore.' She smiled wistfully. 'But I do still once in a while. And always in my dreams, he's still seventeen, he's still cute, and we're in love.'

'But you didn't even know him then.'

'Right. Isn't that odd?' She reached down and took my hand. 'Actually, you're the one I dream of most, if you want to know the truth.'

I covered her hand with my own, and I felt a quick shock of recognition when I touched her, the smallest of tingles, and then it was gone. I said, 'I've never forgotten you either.'

'But you did forget a promise you made.'

'I did?'

'You promised you would tell me, remember? If you fell in love with someone else.'

I smiled ruefully. 'You're right.'

'So,' she murmured, 'are you? Are you in love? Are you happy, David Levine?'

I put an arm around her and drew her close. 'More or less, I guess. I'm content. We fight, but we've been together for so long that we know each other's buttons. I can't really imagine life without her, though sometimes I dream about being free. She probably does too.'

'Do you ever dream about me?'

Her face was luminous, open, and perfect. 'Yes,' I confessed. 'I guess I'd have to say you're one of my favorite fantasies.'

'We could have been happy, you and I,' she said wistfully. 'I think we could have been incredible together if it weren't for Mexico.'

At that instant I remembered every detail of how we had been that night, together in bed. 'Mexico,' I said, my voice thickening, 'is also one of my favorite fantasies.'

'But that's where we ended.'

'I never knew why.'

'I couldn't face you after I had that abortion. You were a reminder of everything ugly that happened to me.'

I almost rocked back with the shock. 'What?'

'You didn't guess? After all this time?'

I shook my head dumbly.

'I thought you guessed. I thought that's why you were so hard on me sometimes. That was *my* abortion we went down there for, not Kim's. I couldn't bear to tell you, but I also couldn't bear to go there without you. And after,' she said softly, 'I couldn't forget it. Neither could my body, evidently. I've never been able to get pregnant again.'

I held her tightly. 'You should have told me. Whose was it?'

'I never knew. That much of what I told you was the truth.'

'God, why didn't you tell me then? I'd have loved you anyway.'

'I couldn't tell anybody. Still, nobody knows but Kim.'

'Not even your ex?'

She shook her head. 'I was never close enough to him. Not like I was to you. Remember when I used to read you my poems? He never even knew I wrote them.' She gazed up at me. 'In some way, I believe I loved you more than anyone. And I still do.'

Our lips were so close that I could feel her breath on mine, her body supple and alive in my arms, at once completely new and the most wonderful hidden secret I'd carried in my soul. She grazed my mouth hesitantly, then I kissed her, yearning toward her as though she held the key to all that was young, changeless, mine.

'David,' she whispered, 'I swore that if you came tonight alone, I'd make my fantasy come true. Of one complete night of passion with a man who has known me better than anyone, of a set of dreams I've carried around with me for twenty years. I want, just one more time, to feel what we felt together. I won't ask you to give up a thing, just to take something with you into the rest of your life. This one memory of the most intense desire either of us has ever known.'

She seemed almost rehearsed, her voice strong and sure, and in that moment I knew I was holding a woman, not a girl. Her pupils were very wide and dark in the moonlight. I inhaled deeply, wanting to take in everything about her. 'Sherry,' I moaned, kissing her again, 'God, I've always wanted you – '

'Then have me. Just once, and then we'll remember it forever. No one will ever know, we'll never speak of it again, but we'll have the pleasure of the memory when we're old and nobody loves us anymore, we'll know that just once we had every passion two people can share. You love me, I know you do – '

'I do,' I said longingly.

'Then nothing else matters for this night.'

I closed my eyes and kissed her brow, her cheeks, her neck, and my body began to ache to pull her down on the bench right there, to rush her into the car, to make it come true as quickly as I could, as though she were a carrier of divine fire and I a priest at her altar. Pure sensations dove and shrieked at me like bats. I wanted to enter her deeply, know her, stir her composure, her self-possession to tumult, wave upon crashing wave, until finally we were spent and beached on some private shore far away. But I knew that even that distant place, so far beyond where I could ever hope to go with her, wouldn't be far enough from our lives. So I stopped, my mouth still hovering over hers.

'I can't.'

'You can, you can,' she moved under my hands, 'we both can.'

'No, this can't happen now.'

She pulled back and gazed at me. 'Why not?'

'Because.' I pulled her hands from around my neck and held them tightly to my chest. 'Because now there are other people that I love too.'

'And you'll still love them after tonight.'

'Not in the same way, I won't.'

She took my face in her hands and pulled my nose to hers, my lips touching hers again. 'I'm offering you complete passion, my darling, with no strings attached. Safe desire, with no aftereffects, no responsibility, only to pleasure each other with a love we've stored for too many years. A love we deserve. Remember how you felt in Mexico? I asked you then to remember how you loved me at that moment. Imagine how it will be now, with both of us knowing how to make it even more incredible. Imagine how it will warm you when you're sixty, to think back on this one night. We'll look back on this like we look back on our youth. Remember? When everything was beautiful and uncomplicated.'

'It was never uncomplicated.'

'But it was beautiful. Wasn't it?' She had never seemed more powerful to me, more persuasive.

'Yes,' I said, 'it was beautiful.' I could vividly imagine us together; my whole body leaned into her desperately. But I also could imagine Miriam's face. Christina's smile. And at that instant I think I understood about marriage at last. The part that made us stay together, that was worthwhile, that kept us warming each other's feet for the last fifteen years and would, please God, keep us doing it until we died. These were the people who held the key to my past and my future. The one woman in the world who remembers the boy I used to be and who also cares about the old man I will be in all the years to come.

Miriam. My family. A word, a need as primeval as sex. Wife. Someone to come back to, a source of renewal, security, retreat. She holds my history. She remembers that kid I was, and though my youth is gone forever, it lives somehow in her memory, is kept alive so long as we stay together. Just as the last of the California girls has been kept alive in mine.

I squeezed Sherry's hands hard, picturing Miriam's in my head. When you've been married for a long time, there's a part of your wife's body which is even more

391

beautiful to you than her breasts, her legs, or her hair. Her hands. Her hands, which have touched you most, done most with you and for you. Her hands look a few years older than any other part of her because of all they've done to make a life for you and your child.

I knew then that no matter how Miriam changed, aged, dissolved, hardened, or rotted, there was no plastic surgeon so effective as loving memory. You love some people simply because they belong to you and you to them. Sherry Gentry never belonged to me, could never belong to anyone. We make the choice to belong, to attach, bind, and commit, and that's why people stay married, even when the Grand Passion dies away.

Sherry kissed me again, her soft and open lips moving back and forth, round and round, increasing pressure, her tongue slipping into my mouth tenderly, teasingly, promising, advancing and then flying away again. This passion was not an illusion, it was as real as life itself, but at that moment I knew that it was possible only at beginnings. And endings. And I also knew that the best I could hope for was regret. 'I can't,' I said painfully. 'Jesus Christ, I wish I could.'

'Well,' she said, pulling away slightly and gripping her hands together. 'You'll wish it even more as the years go on, believe me.' She stood up and put her hands on my shoulders. I gripped her hips, and it was all I could do not to bury my face in her skirt. Her expression was quizzical, enigmatic, and sad. 'I want to thank you for loving me the way you did. I've never forgotten it.' She leaned down and kissed me one last time, softly. 'I hope you have a happy life, David,' she added. 'I'll send you a Christmas card once a year.'

She turned and walked back toward the light of the auditorium, leaving me there in the shadows. As she walked away, the light shone around her hair like a halo, her dress glimmered, and I remembered so vividly the way she looked the first time I took her to her door after our first date. At that instant, if she had turned to me again with another kiss, I wouldn't have been surprised if we had been seventeen again, somehow magically transported back in time. I'd have been hers. The distance between us grew unbearably.

But someone, a man's voice, called to her from the auditorium door as she approached, 'Hey, there she is! They want you onstage for the "Least Changed" award, beauty. Come and give them a thrill.'

And the moment dissolved instantly. I knew I was free at last. As much as I ached for her, I finally understood that I was probably fortunate to have escaped Sherry Gentry intact. I knew then that she had never really been happy, in all the time I knew her, unless someone was in love with her. Unless some guy was helping her to explain herself, ratify her, giving her the only power she ever had and was willing to give up everything just for her smile.

Certainly, I never could have held her. Maybe no one could. She offered a vision of frozen-in-time beauty, a life of privilege and carefree pleasure, fun, fast cars, and parties. Beach Boys, frozen yogurt, and surfing and sex till you're sixty-five. Sno-Cones, Mr Softees, and Acapulco gold. A smile that sparkled like sun on the water and eyes you could dance to.

Passion. Passion is havoc. Primeval chaos. It burns and scars and makes every previous relationship seem tepid and outdated. It's fissionable. Its flash will melt your soul and its fireworks can gut your home. Passion. By its very definition, impossible to hold. And it had taken me twenty years of yearning to figure it out. For a man who put a hell of a lot of time and energy into understanding women, you'd think I'd have seen the light sooner. But few men do. We need them so much, it's all distorted. We project our dreams onto women, and they're so

393

damned good at letting us believe they're those dreams come to life.

A pretty face costs. Now I understand why. It costs the man who chases it, but it costs the woman who maintains it even more, living her life as a symbol. Well, there's more than one way for the scales to fall from a guy's eyes, I realized, and maybe the fastest is to love a California girl.

I looked up at the dark hills around me, starred with houselights like dust. California's web of dreams. Where nothing is within walking distance, and everybody's so plugged into the moment that nothing they do or say can be counted on to last. The end of the rainbow and the end of the line. The beautiful land of Mu by the sea, where the natives come to dance on the brink of the world.

From the auditorium came the sounds of 'Bye, Bye, Miss American Pie.' Finally, finally, I knew that what I had pursued was not out there, but in me. What I desired so desperately, I already had: my passion was in me, my very own, to fan wherever I chose to build the fire. If it was gone now, so evanescent as when it came, then I could have it again. Passion didn't come from women, it wasn't of their making, it was mine. Of my creation and control. And lovers don't finally find each other. They are in each other all along.

At that moment I knew that God had not abandoned me after all. Nothing had really changed since I was seventeen and I believed that He or She or whatever Natural Magnificence was out there, in here, had a benevolent plan for me. Maybe He was out creating more perfect worlds elsewhere, but He still took time to come back to provide a cosmic joke for David Levine. To reveal for me, with a laugh in the wrong place at the wrong time, a completely unexpected liberation. He wasn't gone, He was just behind the curtain, arranging in a gesture of divine playfulness, our pratfalls and stupendous recoveries.

I felt lighter, unburdened, and full of joy and peace. Something had ended, but the chorus went on. The music was timeless, pulling my past into my present, and there in the darkness I held out my arms and danced on the lawn alone, whirling a long-haired beauty around and around, a phantom, laughing lady who, for the first time in my fantasy life, had dark hair, not blond. Who looked, remarkably, like my wife. In the sound of her laughter I could have sworn I heard a purr as well.

I looked over her shoulder and saw a tiny white Persian looking up at me from the bench, shrunken and serene, as if it had been there all along.